TEMPESTS
and
SLAUGHTER

PRAISE FOR TAMORA PIERCE

'Tamora Pierce didn't just blaze a trail. Her heroines cut a swathe through the fantasy world with wit, strength, and savvy. Pierce is the real lioness, and we're all just running to keep pace.'
LEIGH BARDUGO, No.1 *New York Times* bestselling author

'Tamora Pierce creates epic worlds populated by girls and women of bravery, heart, and strength. Her work inspired a generation of writers and continues to inspire us.'
HOLLY BLACK, No.1 *New York Times* bestselling author

'Tamora Pierce's books shaped me not only as a young writer but also as a young woman. Her complex, unforgettable heroines and vibrant, intricate worlds blazed a trail for young adult fantasy – and I get to write what I love today because of the path she forged throughout her career. She is a pillar, an icon, and an inspiration.'
SARAH J. MAAS, No.1 *New York Times* bestselling author

'I take more comfort from and as great pleasure in Tamora Pierce's Tortall novels as I do from Game of Thrones.'
Washington Post

'Tamora Pierce and her brilliant heroines didn't just break down barriers; they smashed them with magical fire.'
KATHERINE ARDEN, author of *The Bear and the Nightingale*

TAMORA PIERCE

TEMPESTS
and
SLAUGHTER

HARPER
Voyager

HarperCollins*Publishers*
1 London Bridge Street
London SE1 9GF

www.harpervoyagerbooks.co.uk

Published by Harper*Voyager*
An imprint of HarperCollins*Publishers* 2018
1

A catalogue record for this book
is available from the British Library

ISBN 978-0-00-830431-7 (HB)
ISBN 978-0-00-830432-4 (TPB)

Typeset in Meridian by
Palimpsest Book Production Ltd, Falkirk, Stirlingshire

Printed and bound in Great Britain by
CPI Group (UK) Ltd, Croydon CR0 4YY

MIX
Paper from
responsible sources
FSC **FSC C007454**
www.fsc.org

To ladies of great generosity to stray and homeless cats:
Aurora Celeste (and her small future readers),
Jennifer Margaret Grosse,
Jonie,
Kat,
and Kate Kelley
with heartfelt thanks from my caretaking family and me

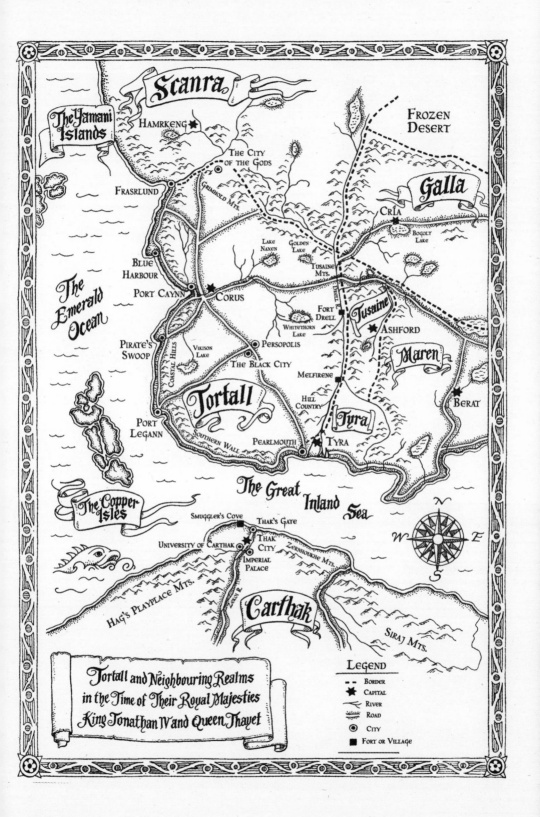

THE IMPERIAL UNIVERSITY OF CARTHAK

The School for Mages

The Lower Academy for Youthful Mages
SCHEDULE OF STUDY, AUTUMN TERM, 435 H.E.

Student: Arram Draper
Learning Level: 10

Breakfast – Third Morning Bell
Morning Classes

History of the Carthaki Empire
Essentials of Water Magic, beginning studies
Language: Old Thak

Lunch – Noon Bell
Afternoon Classes

Mathematics
Essential Earth Magic: Seed and Harvest (First Half Autumn Term);
   Stone and Earth (Spring)
Reading and Writing
The Tools of Magic: Bowls, Mortar and Pestle, Salt, Water, Vials

Supper – Seventh Afternoon Bell
Extra Study at Need

CHAPTER 1

August 30–September 1, 435

THE IMPERIAL COLISEUM, THAK CITY, THE CARTHAKI EMPIRE

Arram Draper hung on the rail of the great arena, hoisting himself until his belly was bent over the polished stone. It was the only way he could get between the two bulky men who blocked his view. He knew it was risky, but he couldn't waste his first chance to see the gladiators when they marched into the huge stadium. His father and grandfather were back at their seats, arguing about new business ventures. They weren't paying attention, waving him off when he asked to visit the privies and never realizing he'd squirmed his way down to the rail instead.

Apart from them, he was alone. There were no friends from school for company. They all said he was too young. He was eleven – well, ten, in truth, but he *told* them he was eleven. Even that didn't earn him friends among his older schoolfellows. Still, he wasn't a baby! If he didn't see the games with his family today, he might never get the chance, and he'd learned only last night he might not see Papa again for two years, even three. Carthak was a costly voyage for Yusaf Draper, and his new venture would take him away for a long time. But in the morning, Arram would be able to tell the older students that *he* had watched the games right from the arena wall!

Already he'd heard the trumpets and drums announcing the

arrival of the emperor and his heirs. He couldn't see their faces, but surely all the sparkling gold, silver, and gems meant the wearers were part of the imperial family. He could see the Grand Crier, who stood on a platform halfway between him and the royals. More important, he could plainly hear the man's booming voice as he announced the emperor's many titles and those of his heirs.

'Lookit!' The bruiser on Arram's left bumped him as he pointed north, to the emperor's dais. Arram wobbled and might have pitched headfirst onto the sands twenty feet below if the man on his other side hadn't caught him by the belt and hauled him inside the rail. Without appearing to notice Arram's near fall, the man on the left went on to say, 'There's the widow, and her son! She never comes to games!'

'Who's the widow?' Arram asked. 'Who's the son?'

The big men grinned at each other over his head. 'For all you're a brown boy, you don't know your imperials,' said the one who had bumped him. 'The widow is Princess Mahira, that was married to Prince Apodan.'

'He was killed fightin' rebels two year back,' the other man said. 'An' the boy is Prince Ozorne.'

Now Arram remembered. Ozorne was a year or two ahead of him in the Lower Academy.

From the podium, the crier bellowed that the emperor would bless the games. Everyone thundered to their feet and then hushed. His voice amplified, most likely by a mage, the emperor prayed to the gods for an excellent round of games. When he finished, everyone sat.

For a very long moment the arena was still. Then the boy felt a slow, regular thudding rise through the stone and up his legs. His body shuddered against the railing. Nearby, in the wall that took up a third of the southern end of the arena, huge barred gates swung inward.

Here came drummers and trumpeters, clad only in gold-trimmed scarlet loincloths. Their oiled bodies gleamed as brightly as the polished metal of their instruments. The brawny men represented every race of the empire in the colours of their skin and hair and the tattoos on their faces and bodies. One thing they had in common: iron slave rings around their throats.

Arram rubbed his own throat uneasily. His original home, Tyra, was not a slave country. Three years in Carthak had not made him comfortable with the practice, not when there were no slaves at his school. He saw them only when he was outside, and the sight of them made him edgy.

The leader of the musicians raised his staff. The trumpeters let loose a blare that made Arram jump, almost tipping him over the rail. The men caught him again.

'You're best off at your seat,' the friendly one advised. 'Ain't your mamma callin' yeh?'

'I'm *eleven*,' Arram lied. 'I don't need a mother – I'm a student at the School for Mages!'

The men's laughter was drowned out by a thunder of drum-rolls. Arram gave the sands what he called his special, *magical* squint. Now he saw waves of spells all over the arena floor. They sent ripples through the air, carrying the arena's noise even to the people in the seats high above.

'Why do they allow spells on the arena sand?' he shouted at the friendlier of the two men. As far as he knew, magic was forbidden here. Perhaps they allowed only their own magic, just as they allowed the emperor's magic.

'What spells?' the man bellowed. He reached over Arram's head and tapped his friend as the musicians marched past. 'The lad thinks there's magic on the sands!'

The other roughneck looked down his flattened nose at Arram. A couple of scars on his face told the boy he may have come by that nose in fighting. 'What're you, upstart?' he growled. 'Some kind of mage?'

'Of course I am!' Arram retorted. 'Didn't you hear me say I'm in the School for Mages?'

'He's simple,' the friendlier man said. 'Leave 'im be. Who're you bettin' on?'

The other man seized Arram by the collar and lifted him into the air. 'If you're a mage, spell me, then,' he growled. 'Turn me into somethin', before I break yer skinny neck for botherin' us.'

'Don't be stupid!' Arram cried. His mind, as always, had fixed on the question of magic. 'Only a great mage can turn a person into something else! Even—'

His foe choked off Arram's next comment – that he might never be a great mage – by turning his fist to cut off the boy's voice entirely. '*Stupid*, am I?' he shouted, his eyes bulging. 'You moneyed little piece of tripe—'

Arram might have corrected him concerning the state of his purse, but he couldn't breathe and had finally remembered a teacher's advice: 'You don't make friends when you tell someone you think he is stupid.' He was seeing light bursts against a darkening world. He called up the first bit of magic he'd ever created, after a walk on a silk carpet brought flame to his fingers. He drew that magic from the sands and seized the fist on his collar.

The tough yelped and released Arram instantly. 'You! What did you do to me?'

Arram couldn't answer. He hit the rail and went over backwards, arms flailing.

He was trying to think of lifesaving magic when a pair of strong, dark brown arms caught him just before he struck the ground. He looked into a man's face: eyes so brown they seemed black in the bright sun, a flattened nose, a grinning mouth, and holes in both earlobes. His head was shaved.

'You don't want to join us, lad, trust me, you don't,' he told Arram, already walking back against the line of marching gladiators. The ones closest to them were laughing and slapping or punching the big man on the shoulder. Like him, they wore leather armour. Like him, they were oiled all over. Some were missing ears or eyes. These were the beginners, the midlevel fighters, and the old-timers, not the heroes of the arena. Some didn't look at Arram; they were murmuring to themselves or fondling tiny god-images that hung on cords around their necks.

'Hurry, boy,' an older gladiator muttered to Arram's rescuer. 'Guards comin'.'

'You don't want the guards catching you,' the big man explained to Arram as he quickened his pace. 'They'll whip you before they cut you loose. Is your family here?'

'Sitting in the copper section,' Arram said miserably. He had no idea how he'd get back to Papa and Grandda.

'Don't fuss,' the big man told him. 'We'll fix it.'

Arram smelled something odd, like a barnyard thick with hay and dung. The ground under his rescuer shook. The boy looked up and cringed. Massive grey shapes approached, swaying as the sands thundered beneath their broad, flat feet. They waved huge, snake-like trunks painted in brightly coloured stripes, circles, and dots.

He had never been so close to an elephant! One halted in front of them as the others followed the parade of gladiators. As the gladiator lowered Arram to the ground, the gigantic creature knelt before them.

This elephant was decorated all over in red and bronze designs, even down to its toenails. It eyed Arram with one tiny eye and then the other before it stuck out its immense trunk and snuffled the boy. Despite his lingering fear, Arram grinned – the trunk's light touch on his face and neck tickled. Carefully he reached out and stroked it.

'This is Ua,' the big man told Arram. 'Her name means "flower".' He pointed to the rider, seated behind the creature's large, knobbed head. 'My friend's name is—' The name he pronounced sounded to Arram like 'Kipaeyoh.' 'It means "butterfly" in Old Thak. Kipepeo,' he called up to the armoured woman, 'this lad must return to the bleachers – Where?' He looked at Arram, who pointed. By now his father and grandfather had shoved up to the rail, next to the kinder burly man.

The one who had dumped Arram over the wall was nowhere to be seen.

'He must be placed there,' the big man told Kipepeo. 'Can you do it? Quickly?'

'For you, Musenda, my love, anything,' the woman called. She blew the man a kiss, then sounded a series of whistles.

'Ua will get us all out of trouble,' the man called Musenda told Arram. 'No yelping. Ua's as gentle as a kitten. For now.' The elephant twined her trunk around the boy's waist and lifted him. Arram yelped as his feet left the ground.

'Thank you – I think!' Arram called as Musenda trotted off to his place in line. The passing gladiators and elephant riders waved to Arram as they spread out in their ranks. Arram realized they were blocking the imperial soldiers who were trying to catch him. He clapped his hands over his face.

'Don't panic,' Ua's rider ordered. 'She won't let you come to harm.'

Arram lowered his hands and realized the elephant was too short to reach the top of the wall. 'Her trunk isn't long enough!' he cried.

Kipepeo laughed. Tapping the great animal with a long rod, she guided Ua to the wall just beneath Arram's relatives. Frightened and excited at the same time, the boy grabbed some of the coarse hairs on Ua's crown for balance, trying not to yank them. Then he prayed to the Graveyard Hag, Carthak's patron goddess and, he hoped, someone who might look after elephants and boys.

Kipepeo gave three sharp whistles.

Slowly, groaning in elephant, Ua straightened and stood on her back feet. Arram gasped as she lifted him high with her trunk. Now he was within easy reach of his father and grandfather. He raised his hands. They bent down, gripped him, and hauled him up and over the arena's rail.

On solid stone once more, Arram turned and shouted, 'Thank you, Ua! Thank you, Kipepeo!'

His two adults scolded him loud and long as they dragged him up the steps to the copper seating, but they also bought him a lemon ice and grilled lamb on skewers once they got the tale of his short adventure out of him. They even helped him to stand on the seat between them as the lengthy line of warriors, animals, and chariots finished their parade around the arena.

The gladiators bowed to the emperor, thrust out their fists, and shouted, 'Glory to the emperor! Glory to the empire!' The moment they finished, the elephants reared on their hind legs and trumpeted, the sound blasting against the arena walls. The crowd cheered, Arram and his family cheering with them.

Now the parade returned to the gate at the rear of the coliseum, with the exception of two groups of fighters.

'It's a scrimmage,' Yusaf explained.

'It's a fight between lesser fighters, like a small war,' Metan added. He was Arram's grandfather, owner of their cloth-selling business. 'The ones that need more experience. One team wears green armbands, and the other wears orange.'

'Have you a favourite?' Yusaf bellowed. The noise of the crowd was rising as people bet on Greens or Oranges.

Arram shook his head shyly. This fight was taking place right in front of the emperor's part of the stands: he could not see much detail.

'Here,' Yusaf said, pressing a spyglass into Arram's hand. 'You ought to have a really close look at your first fight!'

Arram smiled at his father and raised the glass to his eye. Yusaf showed him how to twist the parts until he could see the emperor as if he stood only a foot or two away. Arram gasped at the flash of jewels on the great man's robes, then swung the spyglass until he found the teams of fighters. Musenda was not among these gladiators.

A slave struck the great gong at the foot of the imperial dais, and the opposing forces charged with a roar of fury. They smashed one another without mercy, kicking and tripping when they were too close to swing their weapons. Arram stared, gape-mouthed.

This was *nothing* like the self-defence lessons taught in the Lower Academy! One fighter, a tall, glossy-skinned black woman, was glorious, her spear darting at her enemies like lightning as she held off two attackers at once.

The crowd gasped. A gladiator wearing a green armband sprawled in the sands. A long cut stretched from the downed man's left eyebrow across his nose; it bled freely. A pair of slaves raced forward to drag the fallen man from the arena as his opponent turned to fight someone else. The crowd booed their disapproval.

'Why are they angry?' Arram shouted in his father's ear.

'They prefer more serious injuries,' Yusaf replied.

'But he couldn't see!' Arram protested. 'How can he fight if he can't—'

Metan patted his arm, a signal for him to be quiet. Arram sighed. He was glad the slaves had taken the man away.

He looked for the woman and saw her knock a man down. She was raising her spear for a killing stab when one of his comrades swung at her, knocking her weapon from her grip. She lunged forward and grabbed his spear.

Suddenly a fellow Green stumbled into her, shoving her forward. Down onto her knees she went, clinging to her opponent's weapon. The crowd was on its feet, screaming.

The female gladiator still gripped the spear, but one of the two men fighting her had cut her deeply from her ribs to her hip bones. She knelt in the sand, fumbling with crimson-black ropes that spilled over her loincloth. Arram opened his mouth and swiftly clapped his hands over it: the gladiator was clutching her intestines. He shoved the spyglass into his grandfather's hold and forced his way through the crowd, praying that he would make it to the privies.

He didn't. Arram threw up in the tunnel, in the gutter off to the side. Even when he was being sick, he wondered if the trench was there to carry away vomit or water from the winter storms. He was able to save the rest of his stomach's contents for the privy. The immense stone room with its long line of stalls was empty, for which he was deeply grateful. He spewed everything in his belly. Finally he was able to rinse his face at one of the privy's fountains. Weak and disgusted with himself, he staggered outside to rest on a convenient bench. His father found him there.

'I thought you would like the games,' Yusaf said, beckoning to a water seller. He purchased two bamboo cups full and handed one to Arram. The boy drank slowly; his stomach heaved a little, then settled. 'Haven't you gone with your school friends?' His father sat next to him.

Arram shook his head. 'I don't have any friends,' he admitted softly. Would his father be ashamed of him? Quickly, he added, 'Well, I have some to talk to, but they're two or three years older than me. And my old friends say I'm too good for them now that I'm two terms ahead. But everyone talks about the games. I was *sure* I'd like them.' He hung his head. 'You should go back. I'm ruining this for you and Grandda.'

Yusaf rubbed his shoulder. 'Don't be foolish. We see you once a year, if we're lucky. It will be even longer if I get this new contract. Today we would far rather spend time with you. Wait here, and I'll get him.'

Arram sat in the shade and gazed at the buzzards overhead. He had spotted a golden hawk when he heard his grandfather's voice.

Metan purchased his own throwaway cup of water and came over to stand next to the bench. Arram put the spyglass in his lap and stared nervously at the old man. Metan's bite was worse than his bark, but even his bark drew blood sometimes.

Finally the old man said, 'What will you do when you must learn healing? Didn't you say you'll be cutting entire bodies open?'

Arram gulped. 'Maybe I'll get used to it,' he said. 'They have us doing worms and fishes now. It'll be years before I must work on big animals, or people. If I even get to do people. I'll be taught to make medicines first – herbalists are well paid, too,' he pointed out. He didn't tell them of the time he had been told to add a herb to repel snakes to a teacher's potion and, thinking of something else, had brought the man a herb that would attract poisonous spiders instead.

Yusaf nudged him. 'Arram!'

The boy twitched. 'Oh – I'm sorry, Father, Grandfather. I was thinking.'

'You are always thinking, youngster,' Metan said. 'Come – let's rent one of these carts. If your belly's up to it, we'll take an early supper in Thak City.' He walked towards the lines of carts for rent, calling back to Arram, 'You can tell me what you mean to study this year.' He chuckled. 'I daresay I will like that as much as you enjoyed the games.'

Two days later Arram stood at one of the many docks in Thak's Gate, watching his father and grandfather board the small shipping vessel that would take them across the Inland Sea to Tyra. He barely remembered the place: Carthak was his home now. He never said so, of course. His family would be hurt. But the truth was, they hardly seemed like family. The things they liked to talk or write to him about held little interest: shipping, cloth, cloth markets. The only thing about their way of life that fascinated Arram was the magic that could be worked with weaving and thread. His family scorned it – there was no status in such spells. Thread magic was the work of hedgewitches and goody-wives, not worth their attention. If Arram became a mage, then all the money they'd put into his education would be worth something, but only in terms of battle or healing magic. Those would bring the family status and fortune.

Arram sighed. They loved him. He knew that, from the gifts they sent – sweets, warm blankets and coats, coin for shoes – and their letters. He loved them, for their kindness, their letters, and their visits. But he didn't understand them, or they him. The games were just the most recent example.

He saw them waving and waved back. The ship was easing from the dock as sailors rushed up the masts and about the deck. A crowd gathered around Arram, waving and shouting to those who were sailing away.

Someone shoved him. Arram scowled at her, but she didn't even look down. He was insignificant. His temper roiled inside him. He was always too small, too young, always being put aside. His mood was strange today, prickly and restless. He was itchy inside his skin.

'Safe journey!' people shouted, and 'Swift journey!'

The thought sprouted up like it had been waiting. There was a way he could do something significant. They wouldn't know it, but *he* would. It wasn't much, but he'd feel better for it. He looked hurriedly at the inside of the hem of his tunic, searching for a loose thread. Only a couple of months ago, he had begun reading about weather magic. He had memorized a few spells from it to try when he had some time alone, out in the fields beyond the university, but surely this spell was safe enough. It was for hedgewitches, after all, a blessing for ships and voyages. It was a small thing.

He found a loose thread and tugged it free. It was red, even better! Red was for luck, hope, and strength. Holding it down in front of his belly so the people around him wouldn't see, he wove the two scarlet ends of the thread in and out of one another, murmuring the words of the old spell. His fingers and the back of his neck were tingling. Small breezes played with his heavy black curls. Sweat trickled down his temples as he finished with the traditional blessing for his relatives and the ship. The breeze tugged at the thread. The nervous energy that had plagued his insides all morning surged and tore the thread from his fingers. He could *swear* it was strange, strong power from inside him that did it, and not the gusting air. Whichever it was, his spell-thread yanked from his fingers to fly high over the harbour.

Right in front of everyone, the vessel that bore Arram's father and grandfather leaped into the air like an exuberant zebra, dropped lightly into the water, and zipped between the two lighthouses that guarded the opening to the Inland Sea.

For a moment there was only the slap of waves on the pilings. Then, nearby, someone who sounded very official yelled, 'Who cast that spell? I want him caught and held for breaking harbour law! Find him *right now*!'

Correctly guessing that no one would be looking for a ten-year-old boy, or even an eleven-year-old one, Arram squirmed his way out of the crowd. Once clear, Arram trotted to the spot where a cart regularly waited to take passengers along the eastern side of the city wall, paid his fare, and took a seat. He had a great deal to think about.

CHAPTER 2

September 2–October 14, 435

The day after Arram waved goodbye to his father and grand-father, the autumn term classes began. At first everything was exciting. Arram sometimes complained about the amount of work that he faced, but the truth was that he learned quickly and well. Now he dug into the new classes with enthusiasm. Soon enough, however, he discovered that the intense work of the previous two terms, and the sessions with tutors to help him catch up and keep up as he moved ahead, was over. He was moving at the same pace as his fellow mage students, with empty hours to fill. His new fellows were at least two or three years older than he was; it was beneath their dignity to spend their spare time with a younger boy. Worse, he was getting curious about what lay ahead, until his curiosity overcame him. He began to turn over new and different magic in his head. And since he hadn't had any fresh surges of oddness, he began to relax.

One place where he could not relax was Master Girisunika's Essentials of Water Magic class.

Master Girisunika, who frequently stressed that she would teach Lower Academy classes until there was an opening in the Upper Academy, did not care if her students were bored. She spent the month of September making them recite what they knew of water and its magical properties as they learned it from the text. Next she taught them to stop water in midair as they poured it from a pitcher into a dish. Next they caused water to form small waves in a dish, then made it swirl widdershins in it. Now, in the second week of October, they were to use the latest spell they had memorized to draw water up from the centre of the dish, then let it fall and rise like a fountain.

On that hot day, Arram was bored. He had taken his turn at the table in front of the class. There he was the first to be successful in raising a five-inch-tall spout of water from the broad, shallow dish. He also raised scowls from his older class-mates. Carefully ignoring them, he lowered the spout into the remaining water. Master Girisunika nodded, marked her slate, and beckoned to the next student without so much as a word of congratulations.

Arram watched the others work the same spell, except that it *wasn't* the same. So far they had all made mistakes or failed completely. Finally he gazed at a nearby window. Its sturdy wooden shutters were closed, the spells on it shimmering in his gaze. They were there to keep any accidental magics from escaping the room. Still, Arram didn't need to see outside to let his imagination go free.

He wished he'd had more time to fiddle with this spell. It wasn't hard, no matter how much his classmates struggled with it. They only had to lift out a touch of their magical Gifts, a fingertip's worth, set it on the water's centre, then lift it up. Imagining it, his eyes half closed, Arram saw how he could raise the water into the air, higher even than Girisunika had done. With three finger-touches, he could create a pretty three-armed fountain. He had an image in his head of a dish ringed by spouts of water when Girisunika tapped his shoulder with her long pointer.

'Do we bore you' – she consulted her list of students – 'Arram Draper? I know that you did the problem already, but it *is* possible to learn from others.'

Arram stared up at her, begging her silently to leave him alone. He was getting that panicky knot in his throat. He had tried not to get her attention this term. She didn't know his unhappy way of getting into trouble, particularly when he was rattled.

'Answer me, boy.'

Mithros help him, he had forgotten her question in his distress. 'Excuse me?'

'I was told you need *special* handling, but I had no idea it meant you were deficient in mind,' she snapped. 'Who helped you to do this spell before? Speak up!'

'N-nobody, Master. Lady. Instructor,' he stammered.

None of the titles he'd tried made her happy. 'I am a *master*,' she snapped. 'Not a master of water, but sufficiently educated in it to teach *this* class.'

They were surrounded by giggles now. Master Girisunika jerked from side to side, trying to spot the offenders, but the students wouldn't let her catch them. They'd had plenty of practice since Arram entered their lives.

Thwarted, she turned back to him. 'We'll see,' she said, and tapped the worktable with her pointer. 'Do it again.' As the students murmured, Girisunika swung around to glare at them. 'If you helped him before, you will not help him now,' she told them. Once Arram stood behind the table, she took a place at his shoulder. 'All of you, hands on desks. Should anyone move a finger, they will get punishment work for the rest of the term.'

He was as nervous as he'd ever been in a class, but he had to defend himself. 'No one aided me.'

She slapped his head with her palm. 'I did not ask for a debate, boy. I gave you an order. Now do the spell.'

He raised his hands. They shook. 'I can't concentrate,' he said hopelessly.

'A mage in the field must concentrate at all times,' she snapped. 'Report to me after your other lessons for three weeks. *Do the spell!*'

The giggles that filled the air stopped when she glared at his classmates.

With her attention locked on the others, Arram closed his eyes, sucked in a deep breath, and held it. Sometimes that helped. His magical Gift boiled in his chest, like the River Zekoi in flood season. He called the sparkling black magical fire up and let some of it stream through one shaking finger. Over the wide dish on the table, he wrote the spell-signs, using his power for ink.

It worked just as it did the first time. A vine of liquid rose into the air. This time he let it stretch as high as the master's nose instead of the five inches she had required. His fellow students hissed; they always did when he succeeded where they failed.

Arram glared at the water as it dropped into the bowl. It wasn't fair. Just because they couldn't work a bit of magic, they expected him to drag his feet.

He faced the master. 'I did it all alone,' he insisted. 'I could do more.'

She folded her arms over her chest, looking as if she'd gulped sour milk. 'Oh, truly? What more could you do, pray?'

He turned back to the dish. Placing drops of his Gift on his forefingers, he touched each to a different spot on his slender column of water. It split. Now three ropes of water flowed up and over, then back into the dish, like his favourite garden fountain. Feeling bolder, he turned his hand and called the spouts. They went two feet higher. At that height, the water splashed onto the dish, the table, Arram, Girisunika, and the students in the first two rows.

'Too messy,' he said, frowning in concentration. All of his focus and power were locked on his creation. It was a bad habit of his, paying attention only to his spell.

Carefully he reached into the dish and spun the water sunwise once. It twirled, winding the three spouts like thread on a spindle until they shaped a twist in the centre. The twist became a miniature cyclone, swaying to and fro.

Arram frowned. There wasn't enough water for people to see the glass-like swirls in his miniature cyclone. The bowl was nearly dry. He sent his Gift into the jar by the table, only to find less than a palmful of water inside.

He yanked it up and threw it into the bowl. Some of the students in the front began to snicker. Girisunika took a deep breath and announced with heavy meaning, '*If* you are finished, Draper . . .'

He was *not* finished. He could make it even more interesting. He scowled at the bowl and the cyclone, clenching his unsteady hand. Strength ran through him, coming from the floor – no, from beneath the floor. It soared up through his Gift almost as it had at the harbour six weeks ago. The feel of it was different, heavier.

It lanced through his hand and into the thin water cyclone. Without warning, the liquid shot into the air and sprayed throughout the room. Arram yelped and his fellow students howled as everyone was drenched.

'Calm yourselves!' Girisunika shouted. Raising a hand that shone with orange-red fire, she drew the water away from the students and back to the front of the room. It climbed until it formed a foot-deep pool-like block that enclosed Arram, the master, and the worktable. On the table, in the dish and above it, water continued to spout.

'Draper,' the master said, 'where is the water coming from?'

Arram glanced at her face. She was sweating. 'Where?' he asked blankly.

'Yes, dolt,' she snapped. 'Where did you get the water? There is far more here than before. Stop it at once!'

He had no more idea of the water's source than he did of the wind that thrust his relatives' ship out of the harbour. He scratched his head. He'd used no water signs other than those he'd placed at the spell's start. The strength of it must have come from that strange shove of power that had gripped him.

His imagination built a picture of his cyclone's thin tail passing through the dish, the table, and down through the marble floor. He bent and squinted at the table. The deepening pond of water had sprouted a rope of itself. Somehow it passed through the wood to feed his creation above.

Arram ducked underwater to find the source. A moment later a rough hand grabbed his collar and dragged him into the air. He struggled and spat. One of the bigger students had a strong grip on him.

'What are you *doing*?' Master Girisunika roared. 'Do you want to drown? No one else can undo your mess!' She motioned for his captor to release Arram. The youth obeyed.

'Draper, what have you created?' she demanded.

Arram held his head in his hands, but it was useless. Another surge ran through him, through his Gift. He lost control.

The spout exploded against the ceiling. The entire workroom was waist-high in water. The students were pounding on the doors. As was the rule when magic was being worked in class, the doors were closed and sealed to prevent outsiders from entering and causing just the kind of mess they presently had.

'Undo this gods-cursed spell, boy!' Girisunika yelled.

Arram shook from top to toe. They would send him home; he would never learn proper magic. Worse, they would lock him in one of those special cells the other boys talked about once the candles were doused. The cells where no one could use their Gift. He would be cut off forever from the thing he loved most, all because this instructor wouldn't leave him alone!

One of the doors slammed open, knocking aside the students standing there. Water flooded into the hall. An elderly black woman and a snowy-haired white man, both in the red robes of master mages, stepped into the classroom once the depth was down to ankle level.

Flood or no, the drenched students knew that everyone was supposed to keep their heads and follow the rules in any emergency. They hurried to stand beside their desks as required when masters entered the room. They did not know the old woman, but Arram recognized the man. He was Cosmas Sunyat, head of the School for Mages.

Master Cosmas made glowing signs with his hands; the old woman made different ones with hers. Slowly every trace of water, even of dampness, vanished. The dish where Arram's troubles had begun was empty even of a drop. It fell to the worktable with a clatter.

Arram picked it up and turned it over in his hands. Despite the bother, he was sad that his spell was gone. The surge of excitement had faded, too, leaving him no idea of how to call it back.

Girisunika was furious. 'Who helped him?' she demanded, glaring at Arram's classmates. She was so angry she ignored the newly arrived masters. 'He's a child – he couldn't do it himself! Which of you vile parasites connived at this?'

Master Cosmas thumped his ebony walking stick on the floor. 'Master Girisunika, control yourself!' he commanded. He surveyed the room. 'Youngsters, report to Hulak in the kitchen gardens. Let us see if you remember the difference between coriander and weeds.' As Arram's fellows gathered their things and filed out of the classroom, Master Cosmas added, 'Girisunika, Arram Draper, come with us.'

Masters Cosmas and Girisunika drew ahead as they walked through the marble halls. Arram, who had been raised to be polite, kept pace with the slower old woman. They had not gone far before she asked, 'Did you have help from the others?'

Arram looked at her. 'No, Master,' he said. 'They couldn't have done it anyway. They aren't very good.'

The woman snorted. 'They are perfectly suited to those studies for their age, young man – as you should be. I am Master Sebo Orimiri. Who are you?'

Arram bowed as he'd been taught. 'I'm Arram Draper.'

'So you are the Draper lad. That explains a great deal.' She walked on, making him trot to catch up.

'It explains something?' It was accepted in the Lower Academy that nothing explained the strange events that happened around Arram. 'Whatever it explains, I probably didn't do it on purpose,' the boy added.

'Tell me, what is your favourite place in the university?'

Arram looked at the master, sensing a trap but unable to figure out what manner of danger it could possibly hold. In the end he decided honesty would probably get him in the least amount of trouble. 'The river. Or – or the gardens. But usually the library, Master Sebo.'

'Only the Lower Academy library?' She glanced at him and smiled. 'The truth, lad. I'll know if you lie.'

Something about her convinced him that she meant what she said. 'No, Master. The mages' library for the Upper Academy.'

'Indeed!' He seemed to have surprised her. 'Not the Upper Academy? Aren't the mages' books too difficult?'

'Most of them,' he admitted. 'Usually I read encyclopedias and books like that. They aren't too hard, and I can look up the parts I don't understand.'

'I see. And how do you get past the librarians?'

'There is this one book . . . The spells make me seem like part of the background.' Arram smiled.

'But surely, when you move, they notice.'

'There was a note that you shouldn't move when people look at you,' Arram said.

'Very practical. And this spell is useful, I take it? Not just for reading?' Master Sebo asked drily.

He liked the look in her old, watery eyes very much. 'I'm tired of doing the same things over and over,' he explained. 'With the not-seeing spell I can watch the masters and seniors experiment after the library is . . .' He realized that he watched them when he was supposed to be in bed, after the masters and seniors had locked the doors. He sighed and dug his hands into his breeches pockets. Now he was truly in deep muck.

'Don't the masters inspect the library to ensure they have no witnesses?' If Master Sebo was angry, her voice did not give it away. 'I would like to think they are properly cautious.'

'The, um, the spell I used works on masters as well as seniors,' Arram mumbled.

Sebo halted, forcing Arram to do the same. 'Where did you get it?'

Arram looked at her crinkled face. Could he get in any more trouble? 'I found a little book on the upper level, mashed between . . . *Bladwyn's Book.* It's called *Bladwyn's Book.* It has all kinds of spells for fighting and concealment. I learned that spell from it. Most of the rest only made my head hurt.'

'I should think so,' the old woman replied. 'Bladwyn was a black robe mage who lived in the early three hundreds.' She tugged on one of the ropes of beads that hung around her neck. '*You* were trying to work a black robe's spells, Arram Draper. And here you are, alive and in trouble. How old are you?'

His breath hitched in his throat, but he managed to say, 'Eleven, Master.'

'Liar,' she told him cheerfully. She didn't seem to take offence.

The four of them entered the receiving room to the head-master's offices. The youth who sat reading there put aside his book and jumped to his feet. Cosmas beckoned to him and murmured instructions in his ear. The young man nodded and trotted out of the chamber. Cosmas ushered Master Girisunika and Master Sebo through the door to the inner office. Then the older man looked at Arram.

'Remain here until you are summoned, young Arram,' he said. 'I suggest you work on a ten-page essay for me. It will be upon the virtues of maintaining one's concentration, no matter what distractions may present themselves. In a while we shall summon you, understand?'

Arram understood. He understood that he was about to be very bored. He bowed to the head of the School for Mages. 'Yes, Master Cosmas.'

'Very good.' The older man walked into his office and closed the door.

Arram hated boredom. That was the source of many of his problems. Bored, he might tinker with the spells he was taught – just tinker, not actually cast the whole thing! Then came visits to the healer, unhappy interviews with instructors, and labour or essays after that.

The head of the academy had told him to think about an essay on concentration, he reminded himself. But how could a fellow concentrate when he was so easily *bored*? Boredom had set his grandmother to teaching him to read when he was three. The first teacher for his Gift had come soon after, when he accidentally burned a month's supply of firewood. He was six when his teachers gathered to tell his parents that the best – the only – place for him was the Imperial University of Carthak. No one in Tyra could teach a child whose Gift was so strong so young.

Yusaf hadn't wanted to send him away, but Mother, Metan, and Grandmother had overruled him. Farm children apprenticed in the weaving houses at Arram's age, they said. Embroiderers began their apprenticeships even younger. Besides, did Yusaf want to wait until Arram's Gift burned the house down?

With soot on his hands from fighting Arram's most recent workroom fire, Yusaf agreed. He brought Arram to Carthak himself and sat through his son's entrance examinations. Arram was the youngest student by far. He performed a number of written and spoken tests, then demonstrated the magic he had been taught. When he and Yusaf returned in the morning, a master was there to admit Arram to the Lower Academy. Arram had cheered, and hugged his father, and danced around the room. He had thought he would never be bored again.

Now he had truly made a mess of things. Surely Master Girisunika worked out that Arram's magic had somehow fetched water through the earth, and the tiles themselves, and the table, and the dish, without leaving a mark. He wondered if that had ever happened to Master Bladwyn, back in the old days. If it had, it wasn't in the little book. Bladwyn never made mistakes.

While he'd been thinking these gloomy thoughts, his instructors and other masters he did not know passed through the waiting room. They entered Master Cosmas's inner office, all demanding to know why they had been summoned. Arram put his face in his hands and wished he were on that ship with his father, bound for some far place beyond Carthak and Tyra.

He didn't know how long he'd been sitting there, listening to muffled voices and wishing more than anything he could eavesdrop, when the most beautiful girl he had ever seen walked into the room. She wore her bright golden hair in a long braid down her back. When she smiled at him, her blue eyes shone like gems. Her light blue gown was in the Northern style – coming from a family that dealt in cloth, Arram still looked at what people wore. And her smile was very, very sweet.

'Hello, there!' she said, her voice as sweet as her smile. 'Is Master Cosmas in?'

Reminded of his fate, Arram fell back into the glooms. He nodded. 'But he's having a meeting with other masters.'

The beautiful girl sighed. 'Well, I'll just have to wait. The master cook told me to hand this directly to Master Cosmas.' She raised the small package she held, then flopped into the chair next to Arram, her legs splayed before her. 'Cook believes that every message she sends is of *utmost* importance. Cook is *very* serious.' She pulled an overly serious face, startling a laugh out of Arram. 'I'm Varice Kingsford. What dreadful crime did you commit?'

'I'm Arram Draper.' He smiled despite his gloom. 'I lost control of my Gift.'

To his surprise, she laughed. 'I'm sorry, you look so glum, like they're going to take you out and shoot you at dawn. With poisoned arrows, no less. *Everyone* loses control around here. That's why all the workrooms are magicked to the rafters! That's why we're in the Lower Academy!'

'*You* lose control?' He couldn't believe it.

'Two months ago I knotted everyone's hair in the room, including the master's. They had to get three other masters in to figure out what I'd done,' she confided. 'I was just trying to make a net to catch stray magics, but . . .'

'It went awry,' Arram said. He was all too familiar with that problem.

'They expect our Gifts to tangle early on,' Varice told him. 'How will we learn to manage them if they don't?' She looked him over. 'Oh, come on. You look like you murdered someone. What happened?'

It took a little more encouragement and teasing from her, but soon he was telling the story of his morning. Instead of shocking her with his tale of runaway fountains, he saw her collapse into giggles. 'Oh, I wish I could have seen it!' she cried.

Then and there Arram promised himself that he would marry her one day.

The door opened and Master Cosmas looked out. 'Ah, Varice, I thought I heard your laughter. Another package from Master Cook?'

The girl sprang to her feet and bowed like a proper student, then presented Master Cosmas with the parcel. 'I was not permitted to return unless I had given it into your hands, Headmaster,' she said with a smile.

Cosmas chuckled. 'Thank you, my dear. You had best go before she thinks it went astray.'

She gave him a pretty curtsy and looked at Arram. 'I'll see you soon, Arram Draper!' Then she trotted off, her skirts flying out behind her.

Arram hung his head. Not if they send me home, he thought, glum again.

Cosmas put his arm around Arram's shoulders. 'It's not so bad as all that, my boy. Trust me.' They stood aside as the instructors and a couple of the masters left the office. This time they looked at Arram. One or two of the instructors smiled, though not Master Girisunika. She frowned and hustled away, clearly unhappy.

Cosmas frowned. 'Where are those runners of mine?'

As if they'd been summoned, a boy and a girl in Upper Academy robes came trotting into the room from outside. 'It's taken care of, Master,' the boy said, puffing.

'They're bringing the books, Master Cosmas,' the girl announced.

'Very good, both of you,' Master Cosmas said, beaming at them. 'Now, would you run down to the kitchens and ask them to send up lunch for, oh, ten masters and one very hungry boy? We shall dine here. No, Lyssy, not in my office,' he said. The girl had gone white. 'In my dining room.'

She hesitated. 'I should clear away the books and papers in there.'

Master Cosmas nodded. 'Very good. Nangla, if you will go to the kitchens? Tell them I will need lunch to be served at the hour past noon.' He smiled at Arram. 'That should give us suffi-cient time to have a good talk.'

The boy left; Master Cosmas led Arram into his personal dining room, where Lyssy had already gone to work. Arram looked around as Lyssy removed piles of books from the long table. There were a number of different chairs: the room was built for large gatherings. Now only seven places were filled, one by Master Sebo. Master Cosmas pointed Arram to the place next to her, then took a big cushioned chair across from them. He did not introduce the other masters seated there, but left it to them to introduce themselves. Yadeen, Chioké, Lindhall – even Arram lost track of them after a short time, because each mage had plenty of questions to throw at him in addition to a name.

Arram thought he had been tested when he first came to the university, but it was nothing compared to what these eight masters subjected him to over the next three hours. They threw questions at his head like his fellows threw balls at him during play hours. Many of them covered material he had studied in the past three years, but others did not. There was plenty he had never encountered, even in his secret explorations. They knew about those, somehow – had Sebo told them? They wanted the tiniest of details about what he had studied – magical and ordinary – at home, and even about things that weren't studies at all. They asked if he had tried drawing on his own, or building things, or handling animals. They asked if he sang, danced, or did gymnastics.

And then, with Sebo's eye on him, Arram finally confessed to reading what he could of *Bladwyn's Book*.

'*Bladwyn's Book*?' That was the master who frightened him the most, a tall, muscular black man whose heavy lower lids made his dark eyes seem huge. He leaned forward, scowling. Like the other masters, he wore a scarlet outer robe. Under it he wore a simple white cotton shirt and breeches, and plain leather sandals. If he did well as a mage, his clothes didn't show it, though Arram had been at the university long enough to learn that the best mages weren't always finely dressed. '*Bladwyn's Book*?' the big man repeated when Arram didn't reply immediately. 'You were actually able to work spells from it?'

'One spell,' Arram admitted. 'A hiding spell.'

The big mage flipped a large hand at him. 'Show.'

Arram looked at the floor. 'Do I have to?' he asked Master Cosmas.

'If you please,' the head of the school replied. 'Then we'll feed you, I promise.'

Arram sighed. In truth, he didn't see how doing it would get him into any worse trouble. He drew in his breath and let it out, then shaped the signs in his head. It wasn't the kind of spell that could be worked with smelly oils or signs written on the floor, not if a fellow wanted to go unnoticed, anyway.

At first nothing happened. He was too nervous. Had he used everything up with the water spells? He glanced at Cosmas, who nodded at him in a comforting way.

He drew in a breath, bringing his Gift up from his belly, and released the air. He imagined himself drawing the signs on a great chalkboard inside his head. His hand quivered, or his imagination did. When he looked down, half of him was invisible, and half of him was not.

'Relax, lad,' Master Sebo told him. 'That's good enough for now. Release it.'

Arram looked at her. 'I can do it right,' he protested. 'I work it all the time.'

'We know you can,' she said, glaring at the big mage in the chair across from them. 'And if Master Yadeen weren't so busy glaring at you, I imagine you would have done it properly.'

'I wasn't glaring,' retorted the big man. 'My face is always like this!'

Arram saw what Yadeen meant. He had the kind of eyes that looked as if they were set in an intimidating stare. 'It's just hard to concentrate,' the boy explained. 'Not because of Master Yadeen, though. I'm tired from the mess I made in class.' A couple of them smiled at that.

'By his account, he doesn't use the spells we teach the older students,' said a very beautiful master with glossy black hair and big brown eyes. She had introduced herself as Dagani. Arram was fascinated to see that she wore brown paint around her eyelids and crimson paint on her mouth. If he hadn't met Varice, he would have thought this woman, in a stomach-baring gold silk top and skirt under her robe, was the most beautiful female he had ever seen. The woman continued, 'Indeed, I have seen no masters use such a spell.'

Chioké sniffed. 'The structure is archaic.'

This time Yadeen *did* scowl. 'What is archaic is new to those who have never seen it, Chioké. Most defences against such spells would not be able to counter it.'

Master Cosmas stood and rubbed his hands together. 'I think it's time we had lunch. Arram, you may drop the spell and join us.' He opened the door. Kitchen servants trooped in with all manner of plates and pitchers, setting everything that was needed on a long side table.

Watching the adults, Arram saw he was to take an empty plate and choose whatever appealed to him, then carry it to the main table.

Sebo and the beautiful mage, Dagani, added their own selections to Arram's plate. He also found himself sitting between the two women at the table. They made certain he ate the greens and the fish they had given him, as well as hummus dip with bread. During the meal, Dagani got him to talk about his family and his normal day. She and Sebo exchanged looks when he admitted that mostly he read or walked in the gardens by himself.

He finally got the courage to ask, 'What is this about? Will I be dismissed?'

'Cosmas!' Dagani called, rapping her spoon on her plate. 'My dear sir! This poor lad thinks you mean to send him away!'

Arram sank into his chair.

Dagani tugged on his arm. 'Up,' she ordered, smiling. 'You look like a turtle.'

'Young man, I am sorry,' Cosmas said when Arram stuck his head over the table. 'I thought you knew what we were about. I will not send you home – that's the last place a lad of your talents should be. When you came to us, your Gift was sufficient for the basics, but – for the most part – dormant. Sleeping. Now, however, your body has begun to change. With it, your Gift will unfold. You should have been reexamined before, frankly. We questioned you so thoroughly to see where to place you next.'

Arram groaned. They were going to shift him *again*? 'Sir, that's the third time in three terms!'

'Speak to the master with respect,' Chioké told him severely.

'Don't be hard on the boy,' Dagani chided, her eyes flashing. 'He has not been taught to expect the extraordinary, as has Ozorne. He doesn't understand.' She turned to Arram. 'Did they tell you, when they moved you ahead these last two terms, that no two young mages grow at the same rate? Just as no two young bodies grow at the same rate—'

Arram nodded. He had noticed it among the older students.

'It is the same with their Gifts. And Gifts continue to change for years.'

'As will your mind,' commented a heavyset, broad-shouldered man with grey-brown eyes and short, tight-curled light brown hair. Unlike the other masters, he had said nothing during the meal, but scribbled in a notebook as he ate. He'd been introduced as Ramasu the healer. 'Surely you knew you were exceeding the reach of your fellows when you crept into libraries to read books that were not for you.'

Arram gulped. Those eyes were unnerving. 'But there were parts that I understood, sir.'

'We shall bring you to the level of those parts that you could not comprehend,' Master Cosmas said. 'And there are other students in your position. You will share classes with them. It will be some time before you are ready for the Upper Academy, but with these courses you will feel your curiosity properly challenged.'

'Out of the new mage classes,' Sebo began, 'are your students all to have masters as instructors? That will be a pretty bit of schedule adjustment.'

'You did load us up royally this term, Cosmas.' Arram sat upright. Master Lindhall Reed was going to take part in his education? He had seen him before on visits to the menagerie, wandering in and out of the enclosures. Lindhall was a tall, lanky Northerner with reddish-tanned skin, blond hair bleached nearly white by the Carthaki sun, and long, ropy muscles. His blue eyes were large and pale, his mouth wide and expressive. Another student had told Arram the foreigner was brought specially from the North and paid extravagantly by the emperor to oversee menageries in both school and palace.

Now Master Lindhall tucked fresh fruit and vegetables into his robe's pockets as he continued, 'I can't take another student this term. His Imperial Majesty requires that I overhaul the animal enclosures at the arena, gods help me.' He looked at Arram. 'And this lad is too young. You know I don't use anyone younger than seventeen.'

Arram slumped in his chair as Master Cosmas said, 'Then consider who can instruct him in animal life next term.' To the others he said, 'If you have a promising student, see if they can instruct Arram singly or with the others after Midwinter.'

He looked at Arram and smiled. 'We will sort matters out so you have a more engaging schedule. In the meantime, you must be shifted to quarters better suited to your current status. They'll be quieter, for one thing.'

Arram looked down to hide a grin. He'd often thought that studying in his dormitory was like studying in a barn, particularly when he was trying to read the more advanced books he slipped out of the library. This was a good thing!

'Off you go,' Cosmas said. 'The servants will come to move your belongings. I should have a new schedule on your door before you leave for supper.'

Arram scrambled to his feet. Not knowing what else to do, he bowed. 'Yessir, thank you, sir,' he babbled. 'Thank you, all of you! I'll do my very best!'

Sebo caught him at the door. Arram skidded to a stop in front of her. 'If you please, Arram Draper,' she said, looking up at him steadily. 'I believe you have something that belongs to the university.'

'I would *never*—' he began to protest. Then the copy of *Bladwyn's Book* began to jiggle inside his shirt. He had forgotten it was there. He always kept it with him in case his roommate searched his things. 'Oh.'

'Indeed,' she said, her wrinkled face grave. 'Oh.'

'I was going to take it back,' he said hotly.

'I will relieve you of the chore,' she replied.

Her full, dark eyes were as ungiving as stones. He sighed and wriggled until he could reach under his undershirt. The book practically leaped into his fingers.

'I didn't even get to the best parts,' he grumbled as he passed it over.

Sebo patted him on the chest. 'You will one day. Now scat.'

He scatted. He didn't tell her about the little copybook in his carrybag – the one in which he'd written down several of Bladwyn's most interesting spells.

CHAPTER 3

October 14-16, 435

By midafternoon, servants had moved Arram's trunks and books to his new home in the next wing to the north, closer to the library and classroom wings. Even on the ground floor, students slept only four to a room, not twenty-six. Most of the residents were teenagers hoping to move to the Upper Academy within the next year.

For now, Arram's room was shared by only one other person. His roommate plainly came from moneyed people; that much was visible in the fine wood and lacquered finish of the bow and quiver that hung by his window, accompanied by a good sword in a sheath studded with topazes. The boots tucked under his bed were nearly new, well-stitched leather with a glossy polish. Not only did this fellow possess a trunk made of fine teak, but beside the window was a matching cabinet. Arram dared a peek behind the wall that separated their cubicles – the desk matched the trunk and the cabinet, as did the chair. All four pieces had been carved by a master's hand. His envy over the furniture vanished when he saw the contents of the three shelves over the desk. This boy left his schoolbooks there. The books on the shelves were very different, showing none of the battering and spots on the school volumes. Arram spotted

Si-Cham's *Principles of Consistency* and Edo Clopein's *Quick Defence*, bound in fine leather with gold trim. Other classics, nearly as fresh as the day they'd been printed, occupied the shelves. His fingers twitched with greed; he actually whimpered.

Someone tapped on the outer door, and he jerked back into his own cubicle. He didn't want his new roommate to think he was a snoop. 'It's open,' he called, his voice squeaking.

'I can see it's open,' Sebo called. 'Come out here and meet someone.'

Her purpose, Arram quickly learned, was to introduce the floor's housekeeper to her newest charge. 'This is Irafa,' Sebo informed him with considerable pleasure. 'You are to do precisely as she says, understand?'

Arram looked up at the housekeeper and gulped. Irafa was tall and imperious, dressed in the red-on-red headcloth and wrapped dress of the northwestern Oda tribe. She smiled at him with satisfaction. 'Say thank you to Master Sebo,' she said. 'And be sure you do your bed up properly every morning, because I *will* check it.'

Arram bowed to Irafa and to Sebo, then retreated to his cubicle. He would have to wait to see how far he could open his window. In the meantime, he began to make up his bed. All was not yet lost. Tucked among his belongings was another small volume he had bought on a rare visit to the city's markets, one titled *On Coming and Going* by Rosto Cooper the Younger. He had already successfully worked two of the spells for walking around the campus without being seen. He slid it under his mattress as he made his bed, reminding himself to find a better place before the housekeeper's morning inspection.

He was pleased with his situation. His window commanded a view of a broad kitchen garden, and the ledge was low enough that hopping out would be easy. The scent of new herbs freshened the room when he left the shutters open.

He was arranging his books when someone else knocked politely on the open door.

Not only did the lovely Varice stand on his threshold, but she had a friend with her. The friend looked to be as old and as pale as the girl, and he was a couple of inches taller. Like most Carthakis, he wore a calf-length tunic, though he had skipped the shoulder drape due to the heat. The white cotton was embroidered at the hem, collar, and sleeves with green signs for health, protection, and wisdom. For adornment he had gold studs on his sandals, three gold rings on his fingers, and gold and gem earrings. His glossy brown hair was tied back in a horsetail. Just as Arram looked him over, he did the same, inspecting the younger, shorter boy from top to toe. His eyes were clear, straightforward, and curious.

Varice elbowed her companion. 'I told you it was him.' She smiled at Arram. 'When they said a boy was being advanced, I told Ozorne, "Depend on it. That's the one I met." This is your new roommate, by the way. Ozorne Tasikhe, this is Arram Draper. Arram, this is my best friend, Ozorne.'

Ozorne offered his hand with a crooked smile. 'How do you like the place? Unless Cosmas produces another child wonder, we should be safe with the whole thing to ourselves.'

'I'm not a child wonder,' Arram retorted, stung. 'I'm eleven!' Then he gulped, recognizing the name. This was the member of the imperial family called the leftover prince. He had just snapped at the emperor's nephew!

Ozorne's crooked smile changed into a real one. 'Are you? And I am thirteen, and Varice is twelve and a half. We shall take the world by storm, see if we don't.'

Varice sat cross-legged on one of the empty beds across from Arram's, while Ozorne dragged his desk chair over and slouched in it, smiling. 'You'll get used to her,' he told Arram, who sat gingerly on his own bed. 'Once she's decided you'll be her friend, she assumes command.'

Varice sniffed at him. '*You've* never complained.' To Arram she said, 'Ozorne and I are in the same classes most of the time. We've been friends for two years, I think.'

'So, what horrible thing did you do to end up in classes with us?' Ozorne asked. 'Varice said I had to hear it straight from you.'

Arram gulped. 'I flooded my classroom.' He got to his feet and looked out the window. 'I didn't do it on purpose! It just happened . . .' He faced the two older students again. 'I still don't understand why Master Cosmas is promoting me instead of sending me home.'

Ozorne smiled. 'What was my misdeed, Varice?'

The girl tapped her forefinger against her chin. 'We were in one master's gardens, stealing cherries, and you saw a bird you didn't recognize. You called to it, and called, and – well, I saw a great flood of your Gift roll from your hand, and the next thing I knew, the garden and every tree and plant in it was *covered* in birds! And then the master came, the one who managed the garden. He wanted us thrown out of the school for its ruin, because the birds refused to leave. I was laughing so hard I was crying by then, and Ozorne wasn't even listening because he was able to hold any bird he wanted . . .'

'All I had to do was point and call, and the bird would come to sit on my hand,' Ozorne said, dreamy-eyed. 'Even the hawks!'

Arram sat back down on his bed, fascinated. 'I've never heard of such a thing. In *The Magic of Birds* by Ayna Wingheart, she writes that the magical nature of birds is such that only the most powerful mages can control more than ten or so, and that even she could handle no more than twenty-three or twenty-four at a time.'

Ozorne smiled at him. 'What's this? A fellow bird scholar?'

Arram chuckled and drew a pattern on the coverlet. 'Oh, no, it's just for fun. I can't say I've *studied*.'

Ozorne got to his feet. 'Well, study or no, let's have a look at the bird enclosures in the menagerie! Varice?'

She stood and shook out her skirts. 'I never turn down a visit to the menagerie.'

The two older students were at the door when they stopped to look back. 'Aren't you coming?' Ozorne asked.

'I wasn't sure you meant it,' Arram explained.

'Anyone Varice likes is fine with me,' Ozorne said. 'And you still didn't tell me how you flooded your class, the Gift of it. We've both done that stupid spell, but we didn't get *those* results!'

When she saw Arram had a tendency to lag behind, Varice tucked her arm in his and forced him to keep up. To his delight, Arram discovered that the students who cared for the menagerie animals were well acquainted with his companions. Ozorne in particular was a favourite in the areas set aside for the birds. Once he had vouched for Arram – which Arram thought was taking a great deal on trust – the three young people were admitted to the big enclosure that housed the birds who could get along. When the students handed each of the young people a cloth bag, birds flew down from their perches to land on their arms, shoulders, and heads, just as the pigeons did in the city squares.

The bags contained the food specially made up for the birds: small bits of vegetables, fruit, and fat, as well as seeds of all kinds. Arram ended up scattering his to the birds that swarmed around his feet while he watched Ozorne and Varice. They knew the animals so well that they could get them to do tricks for a bite of something.

One large golden peacock strutted over to Arram. To the boy's surprise, the other birds backed away from him. A student attendant who had been keeping an eye on them all hurried over. She passed Arram another bag of feed. 'This is his,' she said, nodding to the bird. 'His lordship doesn't like to share with the others.'

Arram poured the bag's contents into his hand to find it was mostly brightly coloured food: melon, squash, orange, and bits of small golden fish. 'He's very particular, isn't he?' he asked.

Ozorne wandered over. 'One day I'll have a menagerie of my own, and I'll have all of them,' he announced. 'They're called goldwings. They come from all the way across the Emerald Ocean.'

'I only see this one,' Arram said, looking around.

'We have two here, and the emperor has the other four. Now, come, have you seen ordinary peacocks before? I'm sorry, your lordship,' added the prince, bowing to the goldwing, 'but you have to admit they're pretty, too. Or at least the males are.' Ozorne hooked Arram's arm and dragged him off to view birds with more colours in them than he'd ever seen in his life.

They barely made it to supper on time. Varice had refused to go until she'd changed her gown. *Boys* might be happy enough simply to dust themselves after birds had shed all over them, she informed her two friends, but *she* was not. They made it to the dining hall just before the monitors closed the doors.

'Close one,' a monitor chided as they skidded into the huge, noisy room.

Ozorne grinned at the older boy. 'Close still counts!'

Arram had thought they might have trouble finding a table, particularly with him in tow, but it seemed that Varice was as confident in the dining hall as Ozorne was in the menagerie. She swept through the lines of serving plates and dishes, not only making sure of her own choices, but seeing to it that the boys took proper foods as well. Then she led the way to a small, shockingly empty table near one of the doors that led to the outdoor tables and a garden. The door was open, but no one took advantage of the tables outside: the air was cooling off. Instead Varice and Ozorne sat at that empty little table and pointed Arram's new seat out to him. Only when everyone had eaten at least half of their dinners did Varice allow Ozorne to open the subject of water magic.

It was the best evening Arram had enjoyed at the university. Ozorne had some clever ideas on how to harness the power that had gone wrong that morning. Varice gave Arram some spells and charms for the manipulation of water she had learned from cooks and cook mages. If he worked hard he'd have them memorized by the end of the week. The water spells wouldn't get away from him any more!

They chattered outside one of the school's many libraries until the end-of-study bells told them it was time to get back to their rooms. The boys escorted Varice to her building, where she was housed with older girls, then ran for their dormitory. Ozorne showed Arram a shortcut by way of the gardens behind the buildings. They were approaching their own place when Ozorne held out his arm to stop Arram. They halted in a grove of lemon trees planted in the edges of the garden. Two figures in the brown shirts and breeches of the university stable and field staff were standing at Ozorne's window. The shutters were open; Ozorne had told Arram he always left them that way.

'I'll get the guards,' Arram whispered.

Ozorne put a hand on his arm. To Arram's shock, the older boy was chuckling softly. 'Just wait,' he murmured.

One of the would-be thieves boosted himself up and over the ledge. The second followed. There was a yelp.

'Come on!' Ozorne said. He raced for the door to the building; Arram followed, wondering if he knew any battle spells. He'd learned Ozorne had fighting lessons after university classes four days a week, but he'd had nothing of the kind.

When they entered their room, Ozorne produced a ball of light, one of the few magics they were allowed to do outside class. Arram gasped. Two ragged men lay on the floor. They looked as if they'd fallen into bronze spiderwebs and been rolled up in them.

Curious, Arram went over and poked at the substance. The man inside it spat at him. The webbing itself was far thicker than spiderweb and not sticky, but these men would not be going anywhere until they were freed by a mage. He looked at his new friend.

'I thought we weren't allowed to cast anything but tiny spells in our rooms, and only with permission,' he said, curious and awed.

Ozorne chuckled. 'Silly lad, I know that. But the university understands I might be a particular temptation to those who don't value their positions here.' He walked over to the other bundled thief. 'Master Chioké cast this trapping spell for me. Would you let the housekeeper know we've caught fish in our net?' he asked Arram. He nudged the man with a toe.

Arram was at the door when he heard his new friend ask softly, 'Are you Sirajit? I'll know if you lie.'

That's right, Arram thought as he knocked on the housekeeper's door. Ozorne's father was killed fighting Sirajit rebels. Arram had only been in Carthak for a year then, but he remembered the student in black, and the memorial celebrations for the hero father. Even though Siraj had been part of the empire for years, its mountain people still resisted imperial rule and frequently tried to fight it off.

When he returned with watchmen, Arram found Ozorne still questioning his captives. As far as Arram could tell, the men were unharmed.

Feeling himself to be in the way, he retreated to his own part of the room as the guards chained the would-be robbers and took them out. Ozorne followed them to the door and slipped a few coins into one guard's hand. 'For your trouble,' he told the man.

After closing the door, Ozorne flung himself into Arram's chair. 'Gods save us, why are you reading that dusty old thing?' the prince demanded, looking at a book on Arram's desk. 'You don't even have any class studies – you could read whatever you want. You could read something fun!'

Arram grinned at his new friend. 'But this *is* my idea of fun. Is trapping robbers yours?'

'I don't like strangers handling my things,' Ozorne said with a shrug. 'And now you needn't worry about more thieves. Once word gets around that our place is trapped, they'll think the better of it.'

'Were they actually servants here?' Arram asked, concerned. 'I wouldn't have thought it.'

'More like family of servants, or acquaintances who overheard who the servants wait on. Word will get around. And I can tell

Master Chioké the traps didn't even leave a mark.' Ozorne grinned. 'You now live in the safest room in the dormitories!'

The next morning was their day of worship, for those who chose to do so, and a day of rest for those who chose to relax. Arram heard Ozorne rise early and dress, but he went back to sleep. He had given up religious services not long after his arrival at the university, preferring to take one morning to loll in bed.

It wasn't long before someone tapped on the door. Ozorne, who had returned, opened it and spoke softly to his guest: Arram recognized Varice's reply. She asked him something, and Arram heard Ozorne walk closer. He turned over towards the wall and made a grumbling sound, as if he were still asleep. If they were going somewhere, he didn't want them to feel obligated to ask him along simply because he was Ozorne's roommate.

Ozorne hesitated, then left, closing the door quietly behind him.

Arram flipped on his back and sighed. He would have liked to go somewhere with them, but his pride got in his way. Pride was a horrible thing, and he wished he didn't have any, but it was his family's pride, so he was stuck with it. He didn't even want to sleep any more.

He had just got dressed when the door swung open.

'Oh, good,' Ozorne said. 'I'm on a mission. I'm not allowed to return to the Northern Gate without you. Varice says you no doubt pretended to be asleep because you thought we were going to invite you because we felt sorry for you, and you are supposed to stop being silly and come along.'

'But . . .' Arram said, knowing he ought to protest.

'Come *on*,' Ozorne insisted. 'We're going to lunch in town – my treat – and then there's a play in the Imperial Theatre. My treat also. She's right – you *are* being silly. We wouldn't invite you if we didn't like you. I'm much too selfish to do otherwise. You'll need better shoes than those sandals if you have them.'

Dazed by this whirlwind of information, Arram donned his holiday shoes.

Varice shook a finger at Arram when they joined her. 'Wicked boy!' she cried. 'Never do that again! You're *always* invited, until you're not! That's our rule! Now, let's go and have *fun.*'

Arram did, more than he ever had with his father and grandfather. He made the three-lined Sign against evil when he thought it, and left a copper in a corner shrine to Lady Wavewalker, goddess of the sea and those who sailed on it, but it was still true. It was one thing to walk along the stalls with someone who took interest only in cloth and clothing, being told no every time he asked for something unusual (though they were kind – to a limit – about books and maps). It was another to go with people who looked at the same things he looked at and discussed them; stopped to watch jugglers, fire eaters, acrobats, people who walked rings and balls along their arms and backs, and musicians; pondered over the second- and third-hand volumes at the booksellers; and looked at the animals for sale – only to be forced to leave when Ozorne began to shout at a seller who didn't clean the dung from the animals' cages.

'If I had the power, there would be a law that they would *have* to keep the animals clean and properly fed,' Ozorne said, fuming, as Varice and Arram dragged their friend away from the seller. The man shouted obscenities and threats as their party mocked him.

'Maybe when your cousin is emperor you could ask him for the law,' Varice suggested.

'Ha! If he even remembers my name,' Ozorne retorted. Varice's face turned sad, and he quickly put a hand on her shoulder. 'Oh, don't. I'll ask, when the day comes. I will.'

They moved on to the theatre and enjoyed themselves thoroughly. That night, when Arram flung himself onto his bed, he was too happy to sleep. They had eaten their supper from the market vendors' carts, sampling one another's dishes. He now had a list of new favourites to try in the dining hall. They had watched a puppet show that made them laugh themselves silly, just as they had at the short comedy before the play. The play itself was a heroic one, full of winged horses, a dragon, and a valiant hero. It was thoroughly satisfying, even from the high, cheap seats. Arram was surprised at how carefully his new friend paid out his coin, until Ozorne explained his mother said he must learn to manage his purse.

Arram thought of all of this as he lay in bed and grinned. What a fine day! He had friends!

At breakfast the next morning Varice looked at their bleary eyes and pale faces and smirked.

'Did you get any sleep?' she asked as they entered the dining hall.

'A little,' Ozorne mumbled. 'Then he woke me up by scribbling and muttering about immortals. I asked what fascinated him so, and the next we knew it was daybreak.'

'It was wonderful,' Arram said. 'Usually I talk to people about things and they just say "Huh?" or "Don't ask stupid questions."'

'But you're at the university now,' Varice protested.

'We were talking about the banishment of the immortals,' Ozorne explained.

Varice's face lit. 'I don't suppose *you* know if they used kitchen witches or hedgewitches, people like that to help, do you?' she asked Arram. 'I don't see how they could have kept the little creatures from escaping without mages to work the smaller magics.'

'I told you she ought to have been there,' Ozorne said as he disentangled himself to gather a tray, bowl, and spoon.

Arram did the same, frowning in preoccupation. 'I think I saw a book somewhere on how regular mages worked against the magics of the small immortals. It was very old but interesting, and it's written in Common.' He looked at Varice, who was putting melon and a roll on her tray. Embarrassed, he said, 'I'm sorry – you've probably read it.'

'No, I haven't!' she cried. 'And I'll die without it! Would you find it for me?'

Arram grinned at her. He really had found two actual friends, who talked about book things, watched exciting theatre shows, and enjoyed their food!

He took a chance with a personal question. 'You remember we told you about the robbers, don't you?'

She halted and cast a look at Ozorne. While they chose their meals, he was settling in at an empty table, out of hearing. 'Of course I do. It's just like Ozorne to have a trap laid.'

'Well, he asked one of the thieves if he was from Siraj. Why would he do that? Because of his father?'

Varice nodded. 'He took his father's passing very hard. So did his mother. His sisters are a little better. . . . I suppose it's different when you're a boy. You get ideas, like you should have been there, and you could have saved him. Don't ask him about it, though.'

'I won't – it's why I came to you,' Arram assured her.

She handed him an orange, then said quietly, 'Sometimes he . . . gets angry if he tangles with someone he believes is from Siraj. His friends – his *real* friends – do their best to keep him out of that kind of trouble.'

'Of course,' Arram said, looking at Ozorne. Their day at the market had been tremendously fun, due to him and to Varice. He'd do anything for them. 'You can count on me,' he told her.

THE IMPERIAL UNIVERSITY OF CARTHAK

The School for Mages

The Lower Academy for Youthful Mages
SCHEDULE OF STUDY, AUTUMN TERM, SECOND HALF,
435 H.E.–SPRING TERM, 436 H.E.

Student: Arram Draper
Learning Level: Semi-Independent

Breakfast – Third Morning Bell
Morning Classes

History of the Carthaki Empire
Birds and Lizards: Anatomy
Language: Old Thak

Lunch – Noon Bell
Afternoon Classes

Mathematics
Recognition of Sigils – Second Half Autumn Term
Fish and Shellfish: Anatomy – Spring Term
Analysis of the Written Word: The Technique of Common Writing
  – Second Half Autumn Term
Analysis of the Written Word: The Technique of Writing: Sigils
  – Spring Term
Meditation

Supper – Seventh Afternoon Bell
Extra Study at Need

CHAPTER 4

October 16, 435–March 436

They were finishing their supper when Ozorne nudged Varice. 'I think someone is hunting us.' Both Varice and Arram looked where Ozorne did: a proctor was pointing to their table.

An older student trotted over to them, waving a length of parchment. 'Arram Draper?' he asked when he was close enough to be heard. Ozorne and Varice pointed to Arram. 'With Headmaster Cosmas's regards,' the messenger said, handing his parchment to Arram. 'You poor young cluck.'

'If you peeked at that you'd know he's no cluck!' Varice shouted after him as the messenger hurried off. She took the parchment from Arram, who did not protest. He would never snatch anything away from her. Only when she and Ozorne had got a thorough look at it did they hand it to Arram: it was his new schedule for the remainder of the term.

He winced. The masters had not been jesting when they had said they were going to make him work. Looking at his afternoon's studies, he squeaked, 'I'll be bored to death!'

'Not unless the masters say you can die,' Ozorne replied with a chuckle. 'Cheer up, my lad. Varice and I have this class with you, and this one. I have this one, and I took these two last term, so you can use my notes.'

'You can use my notes for this one,' Varice added, pointing. 'And I have these two with you. It'll be all right. You'll see.'

'And we can study together,' Ozorne said cheerfully.

Ozorne also introduced him to the back halls and hidden shortcuts that got them places faster. He showed Arram the university's many hidden shrines to varied gods, where the friends left small gifts in thanks to the Great Mother; to Mithros, the god of men, boys, and scholars; and to the Black God, who oversaw not only death but also the arts of the mage. In his previous three years Arram had not learned as much about the university as he did with Ozorne and Varice.

One early November night he flung himself onto his bed and went to sleep, leaving the shutters wide open for any bit of cool air that might happen by. As a result, he was roused from his dreams when something dropped onto his face.

His teachers in animal studies all said that animals acted in two ways: fight or flight. Most of the boys boldly proclaimed *they* were fighters, while they sat at their desks on a bright day. Arram discovered that night that he did neither. Instead he froze as the small creature slapped him repeatedly with a leathery wing.

Slowly, with shaking hands and the greatest of care, he lifted it from his face. It scolded in the softest of squeaks. That and the wings told him that his visitor was a bat. Gently he rose and placed it on his bed, leaving it to flutter there. He'd already noticed that one of the wings wasn't working. Groping in the dim light of the half moon, he found his candle and flint. Within seconds, he had light enough to see clearly.

His two-inch visitor had broken a wing. This was beyond his skills. He found a basket and placed an old shirt in the bottom, then eased the bat inside as it continued to scold him. It settled somewhat after he took his hands away, quivering as it glared up at him.

'You'll be all right,' Arram assured it as he covered the basket with the shirtsleeves. 'I'm sure there's someone who can patch you up. Just be patient.' Arram dressed quickly and pulled on his sandals.

'What are you doing over there?' Ozorne complained sleepily. 'Don't tell me you talk in your sleep now.'

'Oh, good, you're awake,' Arram replied. He carried the basket over to Ozorne's cubicle, nearly tripping on a stack of books. He yelped. 'Someday you're going to break a bone this way.'

'Why? I know where I left them.' In the dim light from Ozorne's open window, Arram saw his friend make a twisted hand gesture. The candles on his desk lit.

'We're not allowed to do that,' Arram said wistfully. He in particular was forbidden to do anything of the kind without supervision.

'Why? Do you think you'll make your room explode?' Ozorne looked at Arram, who was tidying the cloth on top of the bat. 'Mithros save us, you *do* think you'll destroy your room.'

'It was a shed,' Arram mumbled. 'And then a pile of old crates. And then they wouldn't let me work any basic fire spells without a certified mage being present.' He gulped. 'They say I'll grow out of it.'

'Horse eggs,' Ozorne retorted. 'You just need the right teacher.'

'They say I need to meditate more and control my Gift,' Arram explained. 'But never mind me. This little thing is hurt. Can you help?'

'"Little thing"? What have you got? It had better not be a snake.' Ozorne carefully raised the shirtsleeves covering Arram's discovery. 'A bat!' He lifted the small animal and inspected her belly. 'A girl bat, see? You really ought to release her.'

'No, look – her left wing is broken. It has to be splinted, and she has to be kept quiet. Put her back, please? I'll get in trouble if she's in our room—'

Ozorne raised a finger. At last he said, 'Shoo for a moment. Let me get dressed. We'll take her to Master Lindhall.'

Arram returned to his mattress, murmuring reassurances to

his bat. She had a long muzzle tipped with a pair of nostrils that pointed in different directions. Before he covered her again, he saw that her fur was a dark cinnamon in colour. Her long ears pointed straight up.

She was the first animal who had come his way in a long time. He wanted so badly to keep her! In his first year he had smuggled in a tortoise and several lizards to live under his bed, only to get caught by the proctors. Away went his pets, and he was assigned extra schoolwork for punishment.

'Won't we get in trouble?' he asked his friend softly.

'Nonsense,' Ozorne said cheerfully. 'We're doing a merciful deed. No one can fault us for rescuing a wounded creature. How did she come to you?'

'She landed on my face.'

Ozorne was grinning when he joined Arram. 'I don't know if your luck is good or bad,' he whispered as he opened the door. 'It's certainly interesting.' He gestured for quiet, and they tiptoed out of the building.

He led Arram past the dormitories used by the Upper Academy students, who were studying for their mages' certificates, and the mastery students, who had certificates and now worked on specializations. Torches lit the way. There were always people in the libraries and workrooms, whatever the hour.

Beyond the student dormitories lay buildings for instructors and those masters who were teachers. One of these lay on the southernmost road within university property. Ozorne led him inside, up to the top floor, and down a softly lit hall.

Arram sniffed. The corridor smelled like . . . plants. And animals. Like the aviary, or an enclosed wing at the menagerie.

Ozorne knocked on a door. 'I hope I can wake him,' he told Arram over his shoulder. 'If he's been away he's hard to rouse. Otherwise we'll have to try his student, and *he's* a pain. . . .'

The door opened abruptly; Ozorne nearly fell in. A light, breathy voice said, 'It's the young fellow who's good with birds. What is so urgent that you must deny me my sleep, Prince Ozorne?'

Ozorne waved Arram forward. 'My friend has a hurt bat, Master Lindhall.'

'A bat, is it?'

Arram looked up at Master Lindhall. He'd really thought they'd find one of the master's student helpers, not the man himself – the man who had said Arram was much too young to study with him. Lindhall inspected him with bright blue eyes. 'Come in, come in. Quietly – my assistant is asleep.' He took Arram's basket and retreated into his rooms.

'Come along,' Ozorne whispered when Arram hesitated. 'Don't you want to see where he lives?'

They followed the master through a sitting room that doubled as a library. Shelves heavy with books seemed to lean from the walls, ready to collapse on the thick carpets and cushions at any moment. Arram craned to look at the titles, until Ozorne grabbed his arm and towed him down a corridor, passing closed doors. The scent of animal droppings and urine thickened.

The tall man entered a room and left the door open. He set the basket on a long counter and snapped his fingers. Light filled the lamps hanging overhead. When he lowered his hand they dimmed. Arram guessed that this was so they would be easier on the bat's eyes. He sighed with envy. Would he ever be as effortless in working magic as Ozorne and Master Lindhall?

Lindhall uncovered the bat. 'Hello, sweetheart,' he murmured. 'You've had a bad night. You were lucky to find someone kind . . . Don't mind my big old hands.' Gently he lifted the bat from the basket. 'You, my love, are a common pippistrelle. Your kindred are found along Carthak's northern shores, along the Inland Sea, on Tortall's shores, and inland as far north as the Great Road East. You *should* be thinking about hibernation, but it's been a warm autumn.' He carefully placed the bat on her back on Arram's cloth, spreading the left wing wide. 'Lovely, my dear. A perfect wing. You tried to feed as often as you could before the rains. It's worth the risk of a wetting, isn't it?'

The pippistrelle, who had struggled at first, calmed and

watched Master Lindhall with her large dark eyes as if she understood every word. Arram and Ozorne were quiet as well, observing as those big fingers handled the tiny creature.

'You broke your left wing, and the strongest part, the radius bone. Now, I have small bamboo splints around here somewhere, in a red clay cup . . .'

Arram saw a number of such cups on a shelf in front of him. They were different sizes, with bamboo and wooden splints of corresponding lengths, from a foot to three inches. He took down the cup of three-inch splints and showed it to Lindhall, who nodded. Ozorne offered a roll of loosely woven cotton to the master, who said, 'Would you be so good as to cut eight inches of that off for me?'

The boys watched as the man gently splinted the broken bone. He then bound the folded wing to the bat's side to keep it from moving. Whether it was due to fright, magic, or fascination with Lindhall's soft commentary, the bat remained still, her eyes fixed on her caretaker.

Finally Lindhall gathered her up and led the boys to a second room. Here a number of recovering animals, including two other bats, were housed in wood or metal cages. Lindhall placed the pippistrelle in one and filled its water dish. 'My student will feed you later,' he assured the bat. He ushered the boys into the hall as he cut off the light and closed the door.

Back in his sitting room, he looked at his guests. 'Still here?' he asked, shaking his head. 'You'll be useless in class in the morning. Off with you! Oh!' he added as they turned. 'You did right bringing her to me.'

They ran to their dormitory. They were settling in their beds when Arram said, 'Thank you for helping. I didn't know what else to do.'

Ozorne chuckled. 'Are you joking? I jump at any excuse to visit Master Lindhall! Go to sleep!'

Grinning, Arram turned over and slept.

* * *

The term passed so quickly that Arram hardly noticed when the cold weather set in and the rains followed. He did realize that for the first Midwinter festivities since his arrival at the university, he had friends to share the holiday and gifts with him. Instead of spending long days and nights reading on his cot, he was welcomed to parties by Varice and those who wanted to stay friends with her and Ozorne. The prince even got to join them on the fourth day of the holiday, the longest night of the year. In his honour the emperor presented the Lower Academy with a fabulous breakfast of fruits, eggs, meat, fresh breads, and cheeses to mark the return of the sun. Afterwards, everyone waddled to their beds for a long sleep before the evening's parties.

'This is far better,' Ozorne told Arram between yawns as they staggered into their cubicles. 'Mother didn't like me spending so much time only with a girl the last couple of years, so she'd drag me to the palace *every night* of the holiday. I'd have to be polite to every stiff statue in court, even though they can't be bothered to remember my name. Now that *we're* friends, though, Mother isn't clutching me so tightly.' He cleared his throat. 'I may have mentioned that you like Varice.'

'Well, of course I do!' Arram replied, startled. 'You two are the best friends . . .' He looked at Ozorne's grin and realized his friend meant a different kind of liking. That wouldn't do – Ozorne would tease him mercilessly if he believed Arram had feelings for their friend. 'Ozorne! I don't think of her like that!' he lied. 'She doesn't think of *me* like that!'

Ozorne wandered into his cubicle, shedding his long tunic. The beads rattled in his hair as he pulled on his nightshirt. '*So* sensitive,' he joked.

Arram made a rude noise and retired to his own cubicle to change into his night gear. He was drifting off when he said, 'I thought *you* liked Varice.'

Ozorne responded with a yawn, then said, 'We already have it worked out. It will be years and years before any of us have learned enough magic to make us happy. By then I will have the emperor's permission to set up as a mage on my own, perhaps in the central mountains. I could represent him there. Varice has agreed to be my housekeeper and hostess, and if you like, you can work with me as well. We'll keep the emperor's peace, study new plants, volcanoes, and waterfalls the size of entire towns, and no one will bother us. What do you say?'

'Sounds glorious,' Arram mumbled, then slept.

He was riding a log like a horse, bouncing along huge, roaring waves. Ahead of him the river thundered like the god's greatest wrath. It was exciting; it felt strange; he was scared to tumble into what had to be waterfalls ahead. One more bounce as the log dropped off the top of a wave—

He woke on his belly. Outside his shuttered window he could hear the roar of pouring rain. 'So that's what it is,' he muttered, and dropped his face into his pillow.

His male organ was pinching him somehow. He turned to the side. That at least took his weight off of it, but it still didn't feel quite right. He squirmed, but the feeling remained.

He touched his organ and flinched. It was not its usual relaxed and floppy self. 'Stop it!' he ordered softly, wondering if someone had bespelled him, or if he was going to die. There was no change in his body's new state.

He tried to hear if Ozorne was awake, but the rain drowned out his roommate's light snore. Arram clutched his covers around himself and addressed prayers to a number of gods. At last his midsection began to feel as it usually did. When he took another peek, the member was back to normal. He silently thanked whichever god had intervened.

He heard a thump on the other side of the wall. Ozorne was up.

'You'd best not be lolling about in bed,' his friend called. 'It's the first day of the new term. The sun returns, or at least Great Mithros is planning to, and the Crone also considers loosening her grip. We can hope for warmth instead of freezing in class.'

Through all this Arram could hear his friend clothing himself. He cautiously rose and did the same, checking his member repeatedly. It remained in its proper position, as still as a post. Perhaps 'post' was not the way to think of it, he realized, considering its earlier behaviour.

For a moment he considered asking Ozorne about it, then rejected the idea in panic. He knew of older boys and men who were considered to be *zoeg* in Thak, or a couple in Common, but he also knew plenty of boys who turned nasty when they thought another boy might be interested in them physically. More than once he'd seen one boy viciously attack another when it was suggested. He didn't want to risk it, and he didn't want to risk the friendship. Better to find a book about it, perhaps in the Library of Medicine, or suck up his courage and see a healer. And perhaps it would never happen again.

The term rushed along. For a time his member behaved itself, enough that Arram forgot its unusual act. He had other things on his mind. At lunch on the first day of the spring term Master Cosmas called Arram out of the room and gave him a square of parchment. 'Arram, I've made a bit of a change to your schedule. One of Master Lindhall's assistants will instruct you in fish and shellfish anatomy during the time when you formerly learned sigils. This is where you will find the workroom.'

'Yes, Master,' Arram murmured, reading the paper.

'You'll continue your study of sigils in your class on the written word and writing technique in the afternoon. Both your masters feel that you have made enough progress to manage the combination.'

Arram nodded, fingering the paper. Fish and shellfish meant more cutting dead animals up, as he did with birds and lizards, and drawing their insides. It was interesting in a peculiar way.

'Is something wrong?' Master Cosmas asked, his bright blue

eyes worried. 'Have I loaded you with too much? Several of your masters say you are outpacing what they planned for you this term.'

Arram smiled at the kind older man. Cosmas often checked to see how he was doing, slipping Arram a handful of sweets or an interesting book in addition. 'No, sir, I'll be fine. I'm twelve now, you know.'

Cosmas's eyes danced. As head of the school, he had access to Arram's records. He knew Arram's true age, but he never let on that he did. 'I believe I gave you a birthday present at the time,' he replied seriously. 'But you appear concerned.'

'Oh, I was only thinking that Varice will fuss over me working with fish and shellfish. She'll make me change clothes before supper, probably.'

Cosmas chuckled and looked up as the university's bells chimed. 'There's the hour – I'll walk you to mathematics. I have no doubt that she will do exactly that,' he said, continuing their earlier discussion. 'She is very precise. Did you expect her to make a fuss over your cutting up animals?'

'I did a bit when I started with birds and reptiles,' Arram confessed. 'But she was assigned to teach me how to do it. She's very good at it.'

Cosmas nodded. 'It's her experience as a cook,' he murmured. 'It makes her the most nimble-fingered student in this academy.' He looked at a group of rushing young students and called, 'You will get there in time. Proceed at a normal pace.'

One of them squeaked at the sight of the headmaster. They promptly obeyed, swerving to the opposite side of the corridor from Arram and his intimidating companion.

'Truthfully, I was never so happy as when Varice and Ozorne took you up,' Cosmas went on. 'Varice has been a wonderful friend to Ozorne. She brought him out of his shell after his father's death, but they both drew away from the school at the time. They turned inward, associating largely with one another. Now they have taken a liking to you, and it has made them more sociable. Introducing you to the university has got them to be part of it again.'

Arram remembered that upon his new placement, the three of them had usually sat alone. Then slowly others decided to become part of their small group. Now new students joined them for meals, study sessions, and explorations in town. Ozorne, who used to talk largely to Varice and Arram, did so now with the others, if not as much.

'But why?' Arram enquired. He couldn't decide if he meant 'Why me?' or 'Why are you telling me?'

'Some special thread among you three,' Cosmas said quietly. 'It is not only that you are the most rapidly advancing students in the Lower Academy, either. A thread that has brought you together, perhaps. Here is your class.' He left Arram standing in front of the room. 'Good luck.'

For the first week of the term Arram tried to observe his two friends, looking for that special connection, but if it was there, he didn't see it. He watched them so intensely that others noticed. One day at lunch a schoolmate joked, 'What, are you in love with Ozorne? You goggle at him enough!'

Arram gaped at him. Then he snapped, 'Who invited you to sit here?'

Ozorne led the laughter from the others and slung his arm around Arram's shoulder. Varice did the same from the other side and told Arram's tormentor, 'If you can't be witty, you may seat yourself somewhere else.'

His cheeks flaming red, the boy gathered up his things and left the table. One of the others left with him. Varice and Ozorne released Arram's shoulders, each with a firm squeeze. Arram lowered his head, smiling and teary-eyed at the same time. They were such good friends!

'That was unkind,' Ozorne said. 'I didn't know you had it in you!'

Arram glanced up; Ozorne winked at him. 'I'm sorry – I didn't mean to be rude,' Arram explained.

Varice patted his arm. 'Nonsense. You are far too polite. Since we can't hit bullies without getting into trouble, we learn to say cutting things.'

'To start with,' Ozorne added.

'You're always joking,' Varice said, crinkling her nose. 'May we *please* finish our meal?'

Cosmas was right: Arram could handle the combined sigils and writing classes, which Arram considered to be a blessing. Fish and shellfish anatomy was as difficult as birds and reptiles, though his ability to sketch improved week by week. He even found himself making idle sketches of people and plants when he was daydreaming. He was so busy that it was a month before he noticed that Ozorne was escaping their lunch group several times a week to eat by himself. All of them did it now and then – the pace of schoolwork was so intense that sometimes it was necessary to find a corner to oneself. Ozorne had done it before, but this was more frequent.

He also talked less once he put his bedtime lamp out as February wore on into March. At study times they all talked only when they needed help with a problem. Arram noticed no difference there, but he felt snubbed when Ozorne replied briefly to anything he said and turned away.

One Friday night Arram asked, 'Do we have plans for tomorrow?'

'No, I do not have plans, and I do not want to join *in* plans,' the boy on the other side of the wall snapped. 'How many times can you look at the same stupid vendors and the same stupid animals? Just leave me be!'

Arram trembled at the sharpness of the reply to a perfectly ordinary question. He hugged his pillow to his face and tried to think of a proper retort. All those he considered were too extreme, too rude, or too childish.

He was still considering mighty retorts when he heard a deep sigh and bare feet on stone. Ozorne pulled out Arram's chair. 'Are you trying to smother yourself?' he asked.

'Go away,' Arram said, his voice muffled. He lifted the pillow to admit air and to emit his voice. 'I said, go away.'

'Arram, I'm sorry. I shouldn't have snapped. I don't have so many friends that I can afford to insult them – please forgive me.' Ozorne nudged the bed with his foot. 'Please? I must be coming down with something. My head aches. I just want to stay in and sleep, understand?'

Arram wanted to ask if he'd been getting ill for three weeks, but let it go. 'Anything I can do?' he asked.

'No. Look, I just get a little . . . cranky this time of year. Don't mind me, will you? Whatever I say?'

'Have you any idea why you turn . . . cranky?' Arram asked cautiously.

Ozorne gave an unprincely snort. 'Why does anybody get cross when the weather's like this, day after everlasting day? Even you . . . I've noticed you're forever sneaking down to the river. You come back with sand on your shoes. How are you getting out of the grounds, anyway? All the gates are closed and locked at sunset, and there's guards on duty.'

Arram sat up and shrugged. 'There's a tree with branches that hang over the wall in the citrus garden.'

Ozorne smiled. 'I'm surprised old Hulak hasn't caught you yet. Stop going there, will you? It's too dangerous in the dark, especially during the winter floods. They say Enzi, the crocodile god, roams the banks, looking for fresh meat.' He boosted himself from Arram's chair. 'I'll tell you what. I will try to be sociable, and you will stay away from the river, all right? It's been known to rise four feet in a day.' He didn't wait for an answer, but returned to his cubicle. He could be like that sometimes, thinking his requests – the ones that sounded like orders – would be obeyed instantly.

Arram stared absently into the darkness. Ozorne had it wrong. Arram didn't visit the river to escape the school. He went for the roar of swiftly moving water. He loved the waves that rose there only during the floods. The bellows of hippopotamus herds and masses of crocodiles thrilled him. The river was a god, taking trees, reeds, boats, and anything else it found. And he didn't believe the crocodile god, Enzi, actually roamed the river's banks. Gods didn't just appear in the Mortal Realms!

Someday he would take a boat along the river's length. He would discover all its wonders, and learn to use its every magic.

'Don't tell me Ozorne's not coming,' Varice demanded at breakfast.

'He said he must be getting ill. He wants to stay in,' Arram explained uncomfortably. He didn't think Ozorne was telling the truth, and he hated lying to Varice, even if it was just a lie he passed along.

Varice led them to an empty table. She set her tray down with a crisp clack. 'Well, that does it,' she said quietly. 'I've been concerned for this last week.' She patted Arram's hand. 'Don't worry. There are things we can do, after I attend services.' Varice was more religious than Arram and Ozorne put together, at least when it came to the temples of the university and town. Arram made the Sign on his chest for luck, before they both ate a hearty breakfast. It was a habit they'd brought from Northern homes: when Ozorne took breakfast, he had a Southern meal of yogurt, wheat or barley flatbread, a little fruit, and juice. He often teased Arram and Varice that by the time they were masters they would have to be rolled wherever they wished. It was a joke neither of his friends liked, but he seemed not to notice.

Breakfast done, Varice went off to her worship. Arram wandered out the nearest side gate and to the river cliffs once again. He had to give up the road to the wharf, since it was half underwater. The shaggy grass on the high ground was soaked. So were his breeches by the time he reached the heights that overlooked the Zekoi.

The view was better than it was at night. At night he mostly listened, half entranced by the sound of nature out of control. On his rare daylight trips he observed the waves that rose in normally flat waters, waves that tossed up spume like those at sea. He counted the whole trees and dead animals that passed, bracing himself against the grief of the animals' loss by telling himself they were sacrifices to the river god. He knew the farmers sacrificed to Zekoi, since the god provided the water that flooded their fields, bringing rich mud that sired bountiful crops. It made sense that the plants and creatures of the lands would do the same for their water and food.

Dwelling on these and other ideas, he lost track of time. When he came around, he was caught in the middle of a cloudburst. The gate guard laughed as the dripping boy passed through. Arram pretended not to notice as he trotted back to his dormitory. It was a relief to shed his soaked tunic and sandals next to his door.

It was much less of a relief to walk inside his room clad only in his loincloth – also soaked – and hear Varice talking quietly to Ozorne.

'Arram?' she called.

'Don't come around!' he yelped, ducking into his cubicle. He scrabbled in his chest for dry clothes. His face burned despite the cold water pouring down from his hair. First the tunic for cover, he ordered himself, then a towel for my head, and a dry loincloth . . .

He looked down. He had donned an old blue-and-orange tunic that was now far too short for his legs and arms, even for a Northern student.

'Stay there!' he commanded, more panicked than ever.

'Whatever you're doing, do it anywhere else,' Ozorne commanded, his voice weary and vexed. 'I *said* I wanted to be left alone. Are you two hard of hearing?'

Arram produced long breeches and yanked them on. Decently covered, if not attractively – the breeches were tan – he looked into Ozorne's cubicle. Varice sat on the floor near the opening, a book open in her lap. When she turned her head to gaze up at Arram, she began to giggle.

'Ozorne, look, he's wearing a turban,' she joked. 'I didn't know you were visiting the Ergwae tribes this morning!'

'I wish he'd taken you with him and stayed there,' Ozorne snapped. 'Don't you know the meaning of "go"?'

'Not when you say it,' she replied pertly. 'And Arram just lost his ability to hear it, didn't you?' She gazed up at Arram, patted the floor beside her, and mouthed, 'Sit down.'

Arram looked from her to the mound of pillows and blankets that was Ozorne. He'd never had to choose between them, nor had he got commands from both of them. He picked the middle road. Yanking the towel from his sodden curls, he scrubbed his hair.

'Great Mother, what happened?' Varice demanded. 'Did you take a nap out there? And what happened to your *feet*?'

Arram glanced down. Mud oozed between his toes and down his shins. 'The river heights are a little soggy,' he explained. He went out to the gallery, where the servants kept a rinsing bucket. He cleaned off the mud, then returned to mop his floor. Varice waited for him to finish, a wicked-looking comb in her hand.

Arram balked. 'That's going to hurt.'

'There's a little of Ozorne's scented oil in it.'

'Will you two *go*?' A sandal flew over the barrier between the beds and struck Arram's chair.

Arram backed up against the door. 'I don't want smelly substances in my hair, particularly not Ozorne's smelly things!'

Varice walked by and recovered the sandal. She whispered, 'Keep it up. He's getting livelier.' In a louder tone she added, 'Don't be silly. Oil makes hair easier to untangle.'

Arram drew breath for another protest, never taking his eyes from the menace of the comb. Without warning, the door swung open and knocked him forward to his knees. He virtually tackled Varice; she fell onto her rump with a shriek.

'What in the Divine Realms is going on here?' demanded Master Chioké. Although he sounded shocked, he still calmly shook water from his hands and satchel onto the two young people. His long black hair, pinned back in twists of braided gold chain, was perfectly dry, as were his feet. Disgruntled, Arram guessed that the master must have left waterproof boots and a cloak hung in the gallery outside.

'Student Varice, you are not supposed to be here,' Chioké informed her sternly. He stepped past her and Arram.

Varice struggled to rise. Arram reached out and helped to pull her arms so she could stand. Carefully he fought his own way upright without falling onto her again.

Varice curtsied. 'I have permission from the housekeeper, Master Chioké,' she said demurely, gazing at the floor. Arram knew that tone and downward look: she was furious that the master had knocked them down without helping them to rise. 'I told her that Prince Ozorne had missed the morning meal, so I brought him juice and food. I was reading to him from one of our lessons when Arram came in. Wasn't I, Arram?'

Arram nodded. 'Ozorne was telling us to go away. I'm sure he'll tell you to go away, too, Master,' he said, all innocence. Ozorne had told him once that Chioké said he thought Arram was talented, but perhaps a little simple. 'Ozorne tells everyone to go away,' he added in the face of Chioké's suspicious glare.

Ozorne sprang up from his heap of blankets. 'I *do* want you to go away, all of you! That's the thing about this poxy, deep-fouled place – a fellow can't get any quiet!' He raised a hand that held his other slipper. 'And don't look daggers at me! You don't know what—'

Chioké stepped around Arram and Varice, removing his satchel from his shoulder. Ozorne abruptly fell silent. 'I am surprised by you, Prince Ozorne,' the mage said quietly. 'Your royal mother would be most distressed to hear you speak to friends in such a manner, particularly when they act only from concern.'

'I hate clinging,' Ozorne muttered. He glanced at Varice and Arram. 'But I'm sorry. I've just been . . . itchy, of late. Itchy and cross and sleepy.' He glared at Chioké, who took a flask from his satchel and removed the top. It was a small cup. 'And what's the use?' Ozorne continued to rant while Varice clung to Arram's arm. 'I'll get sucked into palace business anyway . . . I'll never get to be a mage. They'll put me in the army . . . I'll be cut down, just like Father—' His voice was rising.

Chioké deftly pulled the cork that plugged the flask and poured a small measure of liquid into the cup. Arram could see the liquid shining brightly in the journey from bottle to cup and in the cup itself. Chioké offered the shimmering vessel to Ozorne. 'Drink, Your Highness,' he told Ozorne. 'All will be well.'

'You aren't bespelling him, are you?' Arram asked, despite his own caution around masters. 'We aren't supposed to take any cantrip unless given by the healers.'

'You *dare.*' There was danger in Chioké's voice. 'Just because you have dazzled a handful of soppish mages does not mean I will permit you to question me!'

Varice covered Arram's mouth with her hand. 'No, Master, please, he doesn't understand! Please don't be angry!' she pleaded.

'Then get him away from here and explain, before I teach him the respect he owes a master who will not coddle him!' Chioké ordered.

Arram protested, but Varice dug both hands into his arm. That was when he discovered that her beautiful fingernails were not only for decoration. Wincing, he let her tow him out into the corridor. 'But my clothes,' he protested. 'Proper clothes . . . And he isn't supposed to . . . mmph!'

She had clapped a hand over his mouth. 'Will you be silent and let me *explain*?' she demanded. 'My goodness, Arram, but you do clack on sometimes! Master Chioké is Ozorne's *personal* master.'

Arram peeled her hand away from his face. 'But it's only the ones that show great promise who get a personal master,' he reminded her. 'And that only in their last years at the Upper Academy.'

Varice sighed and leaned against the wall. 'Ozorne is different.

His mother and the emperor weren't going to let him return here at all after his father . . .'

Arram nodded. She meant after his father had died.

'Master Chioké stepped in and said he would be Ozorne's personal master, even though he's too young. He's doing it for Ozorne's family.'

Arram scratched his head. 'But he's a fire mage, not a healer.'

Varice shrugged. 'I suppose he got the medicine from healers, or Ozorne's mother. Take my word, those two treat Ozorne like gold.'

Arram looked at his door. 'So now what do I do?'

'You take these clean clothes.' The housekeeper, Irafa, stood in her open doorway. She offered a set of his clothing to him. How long had she been there, listening? Arram thought, horrified.

'Silly, she *has* to know about Ozorne, with him in her care,' Varice said, guessing what Arram thought. She asked Irafa, 'May he change in your room? I don't believe Master Chioké wants to be interrupted.'

Irafa waved Arram into her quarters and closed the door behind him. When he returned, he found her talking with Varice. As soon as Arram handed his dreadful clothes to the beckoning Irafa, Varice said, 'There's a glassblower down the way who makes all kinds of things you wouldn't expect. Do you want to go see? He's under the arcade outside the gates, so we won't get wet if we wear hats and cloaks.'

They returned from a fine afternoon of shop visiting and talk to take an early supper. Then, carefully, they looked in on Ozorne. Chioké was still present, reading in Ozorne's chair, when they entered the room.

'Very good,' Chioké said, getting to his feet. 'Irafa told me you were out. I want you both to know that he will sleep another day, maybe two. He has a cup and water beside his bed, as well as fruit and bread should he get hungry.' He turned back and blew out the candle he'd been using. 'However, I doubt he will wake. Send a messenger for me if you are here when he does. I am in good hopes that the medicine will do the trick in restoring his normal state of mind.' He nodded at them, gathered his things, and left without bothering to close the door.

They both looked in at Ozorne, who was once again a lump of blankets and pillows. Varice tiptoed over and rearranged the pile so her friend's nose poked into the open air. Then she turned to Arram and shrugged. 'He's the master,' she said with resignation. 'I suppose it's just you and me for breakfast for a while, then.' She waved and left Arram, closing the door behind her.

Two days later they were surprised at supper by a cheery Ozorne. 'It's still raining,' he announced as if he hadn't been dark and gloomy for weeks. 'Anyone want to race paper boats down the corridors?'

Arram and Varice both sighed in relief. Arram never remembered to ask Varice if she had seen the glow in Chioké's medicine.

THE IMPERIAL UNIVERSITY OF CARTHAK

The School for Mages

The Lower Academy for Youthful Mages
Schedule of Study, Summer Term, 436 H.E.

Student: Arram Draper
Learning Level: Semi-Independent

Breakfast – Third Morning Bell
Morning Classes

Gems and Stones
Four-Legged Animals: Anatomy
Language: Ergwae

Lunch – Noon Bell
Afternoon Classes

Protective Circles – Cosmas – Ozorne & Varice
Illusions: Objects – Dagani – Ozorne & Varice
Basic Spellcraft
Monkey, Orangutan, and Gorilla: Anatomy

Supper – Seventh Afternoon Bell
Extra Study at Need

CHAPTER 5

June 1-4, 436

Students were rejoicing in the lazy week between the spring and summer sessions when Arram was summoned to Master Cosmas's office. He went nervously, wondering what he might have done.

Cosmas was smiling when his assistant ushered the boy into the master's large office. He waved Arram to a seat and surprised the boy by taking a chair next to him.

'Well,' the master said cheerfully, 'you lived to the summer term. That wasn't so bad, was it?'

Arram turned possible replies over in his head. He rejected complaints about long hours of study and having to give up expeditions into town. Finally he said, 'I like the more complicated magics, sir.'

Cosmas nodded. 'It's a very good thing we are pursuing this course of study with you, then,' he said gravely. 'I know it's a great deal of work. It leads to more difficult courses in the Upper Academy, too. Still, they will keep that busy mind of yours happy, as they will those of Ozorne and Varice. You three won't be bored. Exhausted, but never bored.' He smiled cheerfully at Arram, who found that he was smiling back.

'Now,' Cosmas went on, reaching for a document and an

apparently heavy pouch that were on the corner of his desk, 'I have had correspondence with your mother and grandfather over the winter, through the Council of Mages in Tyra. We have come to a different arrangement with them as regards your education.'

'Sir?' Arram was puzzled.

'You see, it is impossible for us to educate you properly, as your talents demand, while asking for varying amounts of fees from your family to cover materials and books, depending on what you must study in the coming terms,' Cosmas explained. 'Even if they approved each course of instruction – and there are some that have refused to allow their youngsters to take certain classes—'

Arram grimaced. Last autumn Varice's father had ordered that she was to have no more classes in cooking magic, calling it 'nonsense'. Princess Mahira had forbidden Ozorne to study the part of a history class that covered the end of slavery in the Northern Lands. She said it was 'seditious poison' and threatened to complain to the emperor. Arram had always worried that his own family might not be able to afford his education in a bad year, but he knew they would never forbid a particular class.

'We will not allow your schooling to be vulnerable. Thus . . .' Cosmas offered the parchment to Arram. 'This states that your education from this point onward – supplies, housing, and class fees – is assumed by the university. On the first day of the interval between terms, you come to me. I will give you a clothing and spending allowance. Here.' He gave the pouch to Arram. 'Your books and supplies will be delivered to your room, just as Ozorne's are, the day before term begins.' He leaned back and folded his hands on his small round belly. 'A paper inside that pouch explains everything, including your classes for summer term.' He smiled. 'You appear dazed.'

Arram drew a shuddery breath. He *was* a little dazed. 'My parents . . .' he murmured.

'They have agreed to everything,' the headmaster reassured him.

Arram peeked into the pouch. It was heavy with silver thaki coins.

'New summer garments first,' Cosmas advised. 'But buy yourself something – several somethings, in fact. You've worked hard. Perhaps let Varice do the bargaining when it comes to clothes.'

Arram looked at Cosmas. 'I don't understand!' he said, baffled. 'Why me? What did I do that day in water magic that makes me worth so much attention?'

Cosmas sat back in his chair. 'Actually, we do this for others, students with talent who don't have wealthy families. But . . . Great Mithros, did no one tell you?'

Arram shook his head. 'Not really, sir.'

Cosmas rubbed his forehead. 'Lad, however you did it, you reached through the floor, through the foundation of the building, and deep into the earth, breaking through the protective shield under the university. Then you gathered water from the lake beneath us, miles below. If Sebo and I had not stopped you, you might have flooded the entire building! What occurred is called a flare. It happens with young mages who will manifest great strength once they mature. You may have other such flares as time goes on. We are watching for them now, and your masters are stronger than most. Youngsters with your potential – and your intellect – are worth extra trouble.'

Arram felt his cheeks go hot with embarrassment. Cosmas had to be mistaken – though certainly Girisunika had not drawn the water into the dish. She had not forgiven him after all this time, but glared at him whenever they passed each other in the halls.

'I hope I live up to your plans for me,' he finally said shyly.

'Don't worry about it,' Cosmas said, rising to his feet. Arram understood that this uncomfortable meeting was over and scrambled up, only to trip on the leg of his chair. Cosmas caught him as he pitched forward and set him upright, chuckling. 'There you go,' he said as Arram got both feet under him. 'You've grown enough that it must be difficult to keep track of your legs, eh? Now study hard.

'Oh.' Cosmas tapped the purse. 'And I would leave most of that with the bursar. Draw out what you need when you wish to shop. Run along – don't waste your week off!'

Arram went, with an assortment of thank-yous. His first stop was in fact the office of the academy's bursar: the purse felt conspicuous on his belt. He was glad to hand all but fifteen thakis over to the clerk, accepting a receipt for the rest from her.

He was wandering back to his room, considering what to do next, when Ozorne found him. 'I've been looking for you every-where!' the older boy exclaimed, clapping Arram on the shoulder. 'My lady mother has sent my allowance for the month. Let's find Varice and go into town. What do you say?'

'Master Cosmas said I need to buy clothes,' Arram mumbled, looking down at his knee-length breeches.

Ozorne tugged on his own tunic hem. It was supposed to come to the tops of his calves and only covered his knees. 'It seems you aren't the only one who needs a new wardrobe, and quickly. I wager we'll find Varice with her kitchen friends – come along.'

The afternoon was fun once they finished the dull work of choosing cloth, being measured, and bespeaking new clothes at Varice's favourite tailor. They prowled the booksellers, finding more than a few volumes they could not do without, ogled the jewellery sellers' booths, watched jugglers, and attended the latest play.

After a wonderful supper they were on their way out of the market when Arram saw a pastry seller's cart and halted. 'I have to do it,' he said, digging a coin from his depleted purse. 'He has tassen pastries, those three-cornered ones? Do you want tassen to take back with you? He has poppy, and it looks like apricot—'

Ozorne's hand clamped on his arm. 'Don't,' he said fiercely. 'Look at that seller – the blue headcloth, and the star pendant. He's a filthy Sirajit. He probably put dung in them, or piss. We don't buy from Sirajit pigs.'

Arram didn't protest. By now he had learned that Ozorne could not be shaken from his suspicion of anyone he thought was Sirajit. Arram only gave the pastry cart a yearning look as Ozorne pulled him away. Passing, he could see the vendor stood straight, holding on to his pride in the face of the students' snub.

Once they reached the university, Ozorne stalked off, leaving Arram to escort Varice to her room. At her door she told him, 'Don't do that again, not if you can help it. You can see how it upsets him.'

'I didn't even know those cakes are Sirajit things,' Arram protested. 'Mother bought them all the time. This was the first I've seen them since I came here. Of course I won't upset Ozorne, but the poppy seed ones are *so* good.'

Varice grinned. 'I love the apricot ones. I tell you what – I'll ask one of the cooks to get some, and we'll just hide them from Ozorne.'

Arram gave her a coin large enough to buy a number of pastries. 'You are wonderful, Varice!' he told her gratefully.

'I know,' she replied, twirling before she entered her dormitory.

Arram began the walk to his room, thinking about what a good friend Varice was. It wasn't long before, to his dismay, his member added its opinion, if not of his pretty friend, then of girls in general. Fortunately, his shopping satchel covered the bulge in his breeches, and the inconvenience shrank by the time he reached his room.

Two days later he and Ozorne went star watching with permission from the housekeeper. They lay head to head on the stretch of green behind the menagerie buildings, where most torchlight didn't reach.

'I saw the strangest thing the other day,' Arram began. 'This fellow was at his desk, and his – his . . .' This was his best friend, and he couldn't even say the word. 'Below his belt. His, um, manhood, got . . . large. He didn't even have his hands there.'

Ozorne moaned. 'Oh, that,' he said with amusement and despair. 'But – just a moment. Didn't you have the talk, the one they give to the twelve-year-olds . . . ? No, wait, that won't be until the autumn term.'

He fell silent for a short while until Arram said impatiently, 'Ozorne, *what* talk?'

His friend shook his head. 'I suppose . . . Well. They teach this to the twelve-year-olds when autumn term begins. You'll love it; everyone makes noise and they won't sit still . . . Really, you'd think our clever instructors would know that if you were so far ahead on everything else you might be far ahead on this! Sometimes these mages aren't practical, have you noticed?'

'Why? I'm not very practical,' Arram reminded his friend.

'Very true. Listen, then. This fellow – the thing with his member happens to most of us eventually. We could be looking at *dirt* and it will happen, or test questions, or things that have *nothing* to do with canoodling. Mother had our healer talk to me about' – he made his voice deeper – 'Becoming a Man the last time I was home. We start to get wet spots on our sheets or loincloths, too.'

'Wet spots?' Arram asked, horrified. He hadn't wet the bed since he was a baby!

'Because we have sex dreams,' Ozorne explained. 'Our members practise for the real thing. *That* has to be a gift from the gods, because bedding someone is all adults who aren't mages talk about. The liquid, that's what makes babies when it's put in a woman.'

'Why is life so complicated?' Arram whispered.

'Oh, don't fuss. We'll get to try it with a lover eventually – Look! A shooting star!'

Arram watched the stars fall, awed, wondering which god was

sending a fiery love letter to another god, or even to a mortal. It happened sometimes: he'd read enough stories about it. A burst of stars passed over, drawing sighs of wonder from both lads.

They were sharing a bottle of grape juice when a group of students Ozorne's age walked by. One of them looked towards the two boys and said something that made the others laugh, before they wandered on.

Arram glanced up and noticed his friend's closed look and clenched fists. Hearing the ugly thing the older boy had said, Arram murmured, 'The highest mark *that* one will get is his certificate in tree worm magic.'

Ozorne snorted. 'Is that meant to console me?'

Arram assumed his most innocent tone. 'Don't you *like* tree worms?'

The prince looked at him. 'One day they'll pay for that.' He took a drink from a flask he'd kept tucked away and offered it to Arram. 'It's only elderberry wine. My aunt married in Galla, and she sends casks of the stuff to my mother for ailments.'

Not wanting to seem rude, Arram tried a sip and grimaced. He handed the bottle back. 'You know they advise us not to drink or use drugs that affect our thinking. Our Gifts.'

'Elderberry isn't strong! I just like the taste – Look, are you going to turn into a dull dog?' Ozorne shifted onto his side to glare at Arram, who swiftly denied any possibility that he would get boring. Finally Ozorne waved him silent and asked, 'So did you want to ask something?'

Arram took a breath and hoped his friend wouldn't get angry again. 'Why do some people call you the leftover prince? I don't mean to upset you, but I'd like to know.'

Ozorne sat up, sighing. 'Oh, that stupid thing. When I was small, apparently I told strangers I would be emperor someday. First my father heard. He said there were plenty of princes ahead of me. Then the *emperor* found out.' Ozorne smiled grimly. 'He sat me on his lap before all the court and pointed out every prince ahead of me in the line of succession.'

Arram frowned. 'That wasn't very kind.'

Ozorne shrugged. 'It was honest. He said with so many heirs available, I was just a leftover.'

Arram remembered something from history class. 'But there aren't seven heirs, are there? One dead of a heart attack, one of the Sweating Sickness, your father . . .'

Ozorne took another drink of the wine. 'My father. Someday I will build a statue to his name and place it in the Square of Heroes, at the palace. You'll see.'

'I believe you,' Arram told him firmly. He believed Ozorne could do anything. His friend had spirit. His eyes had fire when he spoke.

Ozorne gripped Arram's shoulder. 'We'll show them all, won't we? Oh, look! Here comes a whole storm of stars! It's the gods. They're telling us we'll succeed!'

After lunch the first day of the summer term, Arram found that he was keeping pace with Ozorne as he hurried to class. Varice, too, was trying to keep up.

'Where are you off to?' he asked his friends. They were close to the end of one of the open-sided galleries, next to a garden full of pungent herbs that practically threw their scent into the students' faces.

'Here,' Ozorne said, opening the door to the last room. Arram checked the door's number against his schedule; it was the same.

'Mine too,' Varice told him, and shoved him inside ahead of her.

'Good afternoon, you three,' a cheerful, familiar voice greeted them as Arram blinked away the light spots summoned as they passed from the bright outside to the shady room. 'I hope you aren't too sleepy from your meals to concentrate on your work.'

It was Master Cosmas. Arram grinned. He was going to share the master with his friends.

'Be seated,' he directed, pointing to a long table and various stools placed around it. There were three slates on the table, with three small boxes. As Arram, Ozorne, and Varice took their seats, Cosmas pushed a slate towards each of them, followed by a box. Since he was closest to Varice, he opened the box before her. It revealed sticks of chalk.

'Are you settled?' he asked. All three of them nodded. 'Draw the most perfect circle you can manage.'

He clasped his hands behind his back and walked around the table, observing them. Arram broke two pieces of chalk before he realized he could just use a short piece instead of breaking more long ones. Then he and Ozorne spent time drawing curves and rubbing them out because they weren't smooth or circular enough.

At last Cosmas raised a hand. 'As you lads can see, Varice has done better by far – why is that, young lady?'

She looked at her circle and frowned. 'When I help in the kitchens, they often put me to tracing the circles for the pastry cooks.' When she noticed the boys' baffled looks, she explained, 'All those cakes and pastries that are perfectly round, and the circles of spice on top of dishes – someone has to draw them in heavy paper and cut them out.'

'Why not use round plates as patterns?' Arram asked.

Varice made a face at him. 'Because the edges aren't even.'

'And magic depends on perfection,' Cosmas interrupted. 'A mage must be able to create a perfect circle on the ground, in the air, on paper or chalkboard – anywhere. Arram, your hand wiggles.'

Arram hung his head.

'Ozorne, your lines are too short, and when you begin again, you don't quite match,' Cosmas said. 'When you go to work the spell, you will either have it break free of your control, or you will have to put extra Gift into evening the lines, just as Arram's spell will go everywhere. Varice, you must learn to do your circles more quickly.'

She nodded. 'Yes, Master Cosmas.'

The old mage stood. 'Now, I would like to see nine circles of the same diameter on those slates. I fully understand you may not have all nine by tomorrow, or by the day after, but each of you must have nine circles, all perfect, before we move onwards. You may not use your Gift, nor a round object.' He went to the desk in the corner and sat on the comfortable chair behind it, lacing his fingers over his belly. 'Wake me when the bells sound for end of class.' He closed his eyes.

The three students looked at one another, dumbfounded at a teacher who napped during class. Finally they returned to work. Cosmas began to snore softly.

When the bells started to ring, they made noise as they gathered their belongings. Cosmas yawned and waved goodbye. 'I will see you here tomorrow,' he told them as he struggled out of his chair.

They emerged into the open-sided corridor. The sun was baking the university. 'That was . . . instructive,' Ozorne remarked, trying to fit his slate into his bag without smearing the marks on it.

Varice watched, smiling. The inside of her bag was filled with a number of smaller bags secured together, each with a different purpose. She was the only one of the three who could find everything in her carrybag right away. 'I'll tell you two what,' she offered as Arram finally thrust his slate and chalk into his own carrier, wiping off most of the last hour's work. 'I'll get both of you the needed materials for a cloth container for your slates and chalks. I'll even help you start to sew the proper bags, but you do most of the work yourselves.' She walked into the next room, nose in the air.

'Do we have a choice?' Arram asked Ozorne woefully. He could see what remained of the marks on his slate rubbing off onto the rough inside of his leather bag.

Ozorne sighed. 'Not really, no. Unless you want to pay a seamstress to do it if she has time.' He walked into the room after Varice.

When Arram stepped over the doorsill, he halted abruptly,

colliding with Ozorne's back. His friend was frankly gawping at their new instructor. Arram knew her as the radiantly beautiful Master Dagani, who had been so kind to him the day he'd flooded his classroom. After a long time of only glimpses of her in passing, he saw that her beauty was enough to knock a fellow breathless, as it had done to Ozorne. She wore her wavy black hair pinned up in the heat. Her thin white silk tunic clung to her scarlet master's robe. A gold-embroidered silk belt was wrapped several times around her waist, displaying a number of small vials decorated with vivid paints and gems.

Arram gently kicked Ozorne and bowed. 'Master Dagani, greetings,' he said, trying to ignore Varice's soft giggles.

'Welcome to my class in illusions.' Dagani came forward and cupped Arram's cheek in her hand. 'You look far better than you did the day we first met,' she said in her musical voice. 'But you should take a breath and concentrate on your Gift. It is escaping your control again.'

Arram apologized and closed his eyes. Slowly he drew breath, in and out, ignoring the conversation around him as he let the flying edges of his magic fall back into himself. He found a handful of strands had wandered out of the room entirely, an event so strange that he forgot he was in class and let his mind follow them.

What in Mithros's and Shakith's names draws my power so far from me? he wondered as he tried to call it back to him. As he followed the strands down the corridor, past the masters' classrooms, the gardens, and the student classrooms, he failed to notice that more of his power was escaping him. What he did notice was the interesting thing, the attractive thing, that was drawing his magic. It sang to his Gift far more sweetly than any temple or street musician. He couldn't resist finding out what it was. He would do that, and then he would retrieve his power. That was his plan.

Then he struck the university's magicked wall.

The power on the other side was moving. He had felt nothing

like it before. It reared up, towering over the wall. It plucked his Gift with claws of fiery gold. Arram fought to yank his power from it, promising himself he would meditate until strange magics would battle to get free of *him*. The power was amused: it released the strings of his magic one at a time, letting them whip Arram as they returned to him.

Another Gift, cool and silvery, wrapped itself around Arram and yanked. He flew backward, away from whatever had entangled him, past the classrooms and gardens. His last confused thought was that he was going to die. He struck something with a hard thump.

Cold water trickled over his face and into his shirt. 'I was flying,' he mumbled.

'Did you see it?' That soft, awed whisper belonged to Varice. 'His Gift – it just flowed out of him, like . . . like ink!'

'It looked like the night sky, with stars. I thought he was dreaming something odd again, but awake,' Ozorne murmured. 'Is he alive?'

'Of course he is alive.' That was Dagani. 'Do his dreams always force his Gift to manifest?'

'Sometimes,' Ozorne replied. 'I've never seen it during the day before.'

'Did you let him know that his Gift was doing things in his sleep?' Varice asked.

Arram could tell by her tone that she was displeased. He tried to wiggle his fingers to indicate that she should calm down, or make Ozorne be quiet. He wasn't certain which he wanted to tell her, but it didn't matter – his fingers wouldn't move.

'Why?' Ozorne asked. 'He wasn't harming anything. And it's entertaining when I can't rest.'

'Arram, my dear, your Gift has hold of you,' Dagani told him softly. 'Make it release you. *You* are the master. Make it accept your will. Otherwise I will be forced to use stern measures.' She paused and said, 'They may involve removing your shirt.'

The thought of the beautiful Dagani seeing his bony chest made Arram fling his power around the fugitive tendrils, then shove them down into his centre with a strength he didn't know he possessed. Once they were subdued, sinking into the pool of his Gift, he sat up, banging into Ozorne's shoulder.

Dagani drew over a chair and sat on it. '*You* need to work on your concentration. You must not lose your hold on your power in your sleep – a greater mage might draw it from you as a spinster draws thread from wool.'

'I would never!' Ozorne said with a grin. Dagani quelled him with a raised eyebrow. The prince ducked his head and busied himself in drawing up chairs for himself and Varice.

'What happened to you?' the mage asked. 'One moment you were with us, and then . . . your Gift broke away and your mind followed it. You collapsed.'

Arram remembered and moaned with disappointment. 'I missed it! You see, there was this *tremendous* power outside the wall, so huge I could feel it—'

'Oh, please,' Ozorne said, though he was smiling. 'The master didn't feel any tremendous power! You're mistaking your own loss of control—'

Dagani held up her hand. 'This power, did it move consistently in one direction, or did it shift here and there?'

Arram had been staring at Ozorne with hurt – how could his friend say such a thing? The master's question distracted him. There had been one strain of magic, immense, but farther away. It hadn't come near him. It was the other that had moved, approaching the gate. 'It moved,' he murmured. 'I think it was going to come through the gate, even with all the magic on it, but it stopped when you pulled me away.'

'Well.' Dagani tapped her full red mouth with a finger that was tipped with blue lace-like designs. 'You would have learned these things in the Upper Academy as you grew more attuned to . . . the natural world, and the Divine Realms.' The three students stared at one another, amazed. They hadn't heard of this aspect of magecraft. 'Magic attracts magic. Normally it is not a factor, unless you are working very powerful spells. As masters you would be taught how to ward off magics that would interfere. But there are other magics that might be drawn to you.'

She rose and walked to the open door, looking outside. 'The power you felt – and I know you felt it – the slow one that moves in one direction is the Zekoi River and its god. I've been feeling the itch all day. He doesn't always come this far north, but when he does, you know it.' She leaned on the doorway. 'And the other that nearly caught you must have been one of the lesser gods.'

'Can they pass through the spells on the wall?' Varice asked nervously. 'I'm not sure I want to deal with any gods, ever.'

'If they do, Master Cosmas will summon a group of us to deal with whichever god it is, be it hippopotamus, crocodile, hyena, snake.' Dagani smiled. 'You need not worry, my dear. This place has drawn magical beings for centuries, and we always manage to deal with them. Now, Arram will meditate for the rest of our time, to settle down, while you two will undertake our first lesson.'

At supper Arram was trying to create an image of the power he had seen for his friends when a runner tapped him on the shoulder. The image flew apart. Arram turned to glare at the older boy. 'I almost had it!' he snapped.

'Shouldn't use your power in the dining hall anyway,' the runner informed him. He was chewing on a straw. 'Cooks don't like it.' He shoved a folded note at Arram and wandered off. Fluttering her fan, Varice watched him leave.

'Don't tell me you *admire* that oaf,' Ozorne scolded Varice as Arram unfolded the note. 'I heard he goes into the city with his bully friends and picks fights with the gumat.' He'd used the word for the street toughs in the poorest parts of town.

'Looking doesn't mean swooning,' Varice retorted, rapping her royal friend lightly on the shoulder. 'Arram, what is it?'

'I have a new class with Master Yadeen,' he moaned in dismay. '*Before* breakfast!'

'Hag roll the dice,' Ozorne murmured. 'Studying what?'

Arram knew he must look as puzzled as his friends. 'Juggling!'

THE IMPERIAL UNIVERSITY OF CARTHAK

The School for Mages

The Lower Academy for Youthful Mages
REVISED Schedule of Study, Summer Term, 436 H.E.–
Spring Term, 437 H.E.

Student: Arram Draper
Learning Level: Semi-Independent

Second Morning Bell

Summer Term – Juggling – Yadeen
Autumn Term, Spring Term – Stones and Magic, Juggling – Yadeen

Breakfast – Third Morning Bell
Morning Classes

Gems and Stones – Summer Term – Third-year student
Religions – Autumn and Spring Terms – Third-year student
Four-Legged Animals: Anatomy – Summer, Autumn, Spring
 Terms – First-year animal healer
Language: Ergwae

Lunch – Noon Bell
Afternoon Classes

Protective Circles – Cosmas
Illusions: Objects – Dagani
Basic Spellcraft – Summer, Autumn, Spring Terms – Fourth-year
 student
Monkey, Orangutan, and Gorilla: Anatomy – Summer, Autumn,
 Spring Terms – First-year animal healer

Supper – Seventh Afternoon Bell
Extra Study at Need

CHAPTER 6

June 5, 436–March 18, 437

'Inhuman,' Arram moaned to himself as he lurched up the gently sloping path. 'Should have – have stayed home with the family business. No friend keeping me up all night asking how I *knew* 'bout power if it was outside a shielded wall . . .' He stopped for a yawn that made the hinges of his jaw crack. Then he turned down the roofed corridor that would lead him to the master's workroom. Of course it was at the end of the walkway, past three gardens. Each had spraying fountains set in patterns of coloured stones. Arram would have loved to stick his head in a fountain to cool off – the sun had already turned hot, in only an hour! – but he had a long day ahead, beginning with Yadeen.

The last workroom on the corridor was open. Arram found Yadeen leaning against the far wall. He always forgot how big the man was!

He bowed. 'Good morning, sir,' he said nervously.

Yadeen, wearing a loose pale linen shirt and breeches, nodded. He was turning something over in his large hands. Before Arram could guess what it was – it was small enough to be hidden in Yadeen's grip – the master said, 'Catch,' and tossed it to him.

The wooden ball hit Arram in the middle of the chest – not hard, but enough that Arram noticed it was there. 'I'm sorry,' he said as he fumbled and dropped the ball. He retrieved it. 'I wasn't—'

'Catch.' Yadeen calmly tossed another ball at him. Arram reached for it and dropped both that ball and the one he already held.

'The idea,' Yadeen said, 'is for you to catch the first ball one-handed so you will be able to catch the second ball with your other hand.' When he saw Arram glance around at the shadowy room, he said, 'Let's go outside, where we'll have more light.' He led the way to a patch of bare earth next to the building.

'I don't understand,' Arram said when they halted. 'What is this for?'

Yadeen collected the balls from Arram's hands and walked until he was fifteen feet away. 'It is for concentration and coordination,' he said, raising his deep, accented voice so Arram could hear. 'Until you can fix your attention on one thing while your hands do another, you will be a very dangerous young mage, and not for the proper reasons. Catch.'

Arram caught the first ball with both hands. This time he only missed the second ball, since he remembered to keep the first in one hand. 'I'm sorry,' he called.

'Don't apologize,' Yadeen ordered. *'Learn.'*

Through autumn, Midwinter, and into spring term, Arram, Ozorne, and Varice worked hard. Arram might have felt sorry for himself given the extra hour with the stern Yadeen in the mornings, but the same day that Arram began the study of juggling, Ozorne announced he was to apply himself to an hour of swordplay, on his mother's orders. Varice, who never slept past sunrise if she could help it, decided to volunteer in the kitchens, in defiance of her father's wishes. Unlike many of their fellows, the three never complained of trouble falling asleep.

At Midwinter, Arram had the pleasure of buying more than trinkets for his friends. He got a fine pocket dagger for Ozorne and a carving knife of good steel for Varice. Each of them had obtained books that he had coveted all season but refused to buy, since he'd been saving his coin for presents. And for his birthday he got more gifts, not just from his friends, but from Masters Cosmas, Dagani, and Yadeen.

'It is the custom for a master to do this for the student, but *not* the other way around,' Yadeen said when he handed a package to Arram. 'It is assumed the student needs every nit he can find, if not for now, when he has a stipend, then later, when he is on his own. Don't bother to be grateful,' he said when Arram opened his mouth. 'I do poorly with gratitude. Open it.'

Arram gently unfolded the beautiful blue-violet shoulder drape the master had used for wrapping – where he'd wear such an elegant garment he had no idea! – to find a polished red wood box, figured with dragons and griffins. He opened it to discover hand-sized balls, six of them, each different shades of reddish, brown, or black wood.

'Juggling balls,' he said blankly. He looked up at Yadeen and realized the master's eyes were dancing. It was the first time he'd seen the man look humorous. 'I don't know what to say,' he joked, keeping his tone flat.

Yadeen clapped him on the shoulder. 'I knew you would be pleased. Try them out before classes begin again.'

Gifts from Cosmas and Dagani were books. Dagani's was on great illusions, including one that was supposed to have lured all the world's griffins out of the Mortal Realms and back to the Realms of the Gods. Cosmas's book told of unusual mages: those who did not follow the normal path to a position as a teacher or a serving mage for a government or for a noble or royal house. Ozorne and Varice both leafed through it and shrugged, uninterested. They didn't offer to show Arram the books they had received from Cosmas and Dagani, and Arram didn't ask. He was too interested in his own books.

If asked later, Arram would have said he didn't remember the passing of the weeks. He did recall students from the Upper

Academy lingering around Varice in the late afternoons. Arram was taking evening strolls through the halls with dark-eyed Sheni in January and early February, before she tired of his 'headache-making big words.' She left him for a student who hoped to be a healer when he reached the Upper Academy. It was just as well: Ozorne was bleak again and needed attention and reminders to take his medicine, as he had the previous spring.

Varice ignored the older students. She made extra money giving new turns to spring garments for other girls, stitching on lace, taking in seams or letting them out, and sewing on embroideries. When Arram pointed out one evening that surely her stipend covered all her expenses, she looked down her nose at him.

'There's the future to think of,' she informed him, holding her work up so she could be certain the seam was even. 'I'm putting money by for that.'

They were in one of the empty cubicles in Arram's room. Although they tried to talk quietly, Ozorne heard. He was in bed; they thought he'd been sleeping off another shadowy spell. 'I *told* you, you're going to live with me,' he called. 'We'll have our own place, in the mountains or a forest . . .'

'And if we're sent journeying once we're working for a mastery?' Varice enquired. She picked up a handful of lace and began to roll it neatly. 'You know they do it to a lot of them. *I* for one don't intend to sleep on the ground on a ragged blanket, eating charred rabbit I cooked on a fire!'

Arram snorted. Ozorne began to chuckle. The idea of Varice – of any of them – living in such conditions was too amusing to consider seriously.

'You know they'll settle us with a master elsewhere in Carthak, or somewhere north,' Ozorne said as he sat up and threw off the blanket. 'They don't just cast people they've taught so much into the winds of chance!'

Varice sniffed. 'I hope so, but I'm not taking *those* chances if I can help it.'

'I wouldn't permit it,' Ozorne told her cheerfully. Arram believed him, and his heart sank a little. It would be fun to wander alone, learning whatever he pleased. Perhaps Ozorne would let him off the leash now and then, when the time came.

The afternoon of the following day, he was so fascinated reading a book Yadeen had loaned him that he lost track of time. It began to rain. Only the appearance of a wet spot on the page, and the boom of the sixth-hour bell, jarred him from his trance. He yelped. He had promised to work on illusions with Ozorne and Varice; he was an hour and a half late!

Hoping to gain time, he jumped the waist-high wall to a herb garden. His plan was to run crossways over the rows of bare mounds that waited for warmer weather, which would cut his distance in half. He had not expected there to be a line of large jars positioned on the other side of the wall.

Down he went with a crash, spilling forward onto a mound with several shattered jars. The ground beneath him was decidedly damp. When he struggled to his feet, he found he was muddy from chin to toe.

His first instinct was to run and let someone else take the blame. His second thought was that this would be truly stupid. A mage could track him by the print his body had left in the mud. This occurred to him just as a man who had been kneeling near the corner of the wall rose to his feet.

He was stocky, not much taller than Arram, with skin a ruddy golden-brown. His black hair was cut short and streaked with grey. Dark eyes with long, sloping lids that lengthened at the corners looked Arram over. He wore a sturdy wool shirt under a sleeveless vest equipped with a number of pockets. His breeches, also covered with pockets, were heavily burdened with the tools of a working gardener. When he stood, it was easy to see that his legs were widely bowed, like someone who had spent a large part of his life on horseback.

Arram knew him. Everyone did who paid attention to the

university gardens. He gulped. 'Master Hulak, I'm so sorry! I never would have jumped the wall—'

'If you knew I was here?' the school's head gardener, also a master in the study of plants, medicines, and poisons, asked gently.

Arram's knees wanted to give way. 'No, Master!' he protested. 'If I'd known there was work being done here! I thought it was too early for . . .' His voice locked in his throat.

Hulak studied him for painful moments before he said, 'So you think because you see no plants there is no work to be done? It is fine to gallop over my rows?' He raised a hand for silence when Arram would have defended himself. Clearly he was still thinking. At last he enquired, 'You are Arram Draper, Varice's friend?'

Arram nodded. 'Yes, Master.' *Everyone* knows Varice, he thought.

'Not Master, only Hulak. You are said to be clever.' The older man watched him, his eyes seeming not to blink.

'I'm trying to be,' Arram replied honestly.

'You have left me with' – in a form of exquisite torture, the gardener pointed to each shattered jar and counted its number aloud – 'seven broken vessels I had planned to use in the morning. These things are money out of my spring term budget.'

Arram saw coins – his coins – flying out of a drawer in the bursar's office. 'How mu—'

But there was that upraised palm commanding silence again. 'No. More important is a student silly enough to think a garden is dead because he sees nothing above the ground.'

To add to Arram's enjoyment, it began to truly pour. Hulak did not even seem to notice. Arram did, as mud ran down his chest, breeches, and feet. He said nothing, feeling that the worst was about to come.

'You repay me by coming each school day, at this time, for an hour.'

Arram heard himself whimper softly.

Hulak ignored him. 'Today I am in the third garden from the river. Tomorrow I will be in the fourth garden, and so on, until I reach the end of this long corridor. The next day I will move south, to the first garden on that corridor, and on. Understand?'

'Yes, sir,' Arram mumbled.

'I will bring you better clothes for gardening, and sandals.' Hulak looked him up and down. 'Mages should understand plants. Varice knows this. Now it is your turn. Tomorrow, after your monkey lesson.' He looked along the row. 'Pick up the jar pieces, take them to the shed over there. Put them in the basket with others.' He returned to the row where he had been working.

Arram heaped as many shards of pottery as he could carry in half of a broken jar and bore them to the shed, walking around the garden instead of through. As he worked, one question plagued him: How had Hulak known who he was?

'Of course he knows,' Varice said when he finally met her and Ozorne for supper. 'Master Hulak knows everything!' She patted Arram's arm. 'You'll learn.'

Ozorne nodded. 'The university paid a royal sum to woo him here from the Mohon tribes that live north of Jindazhen.'

Varice giggled. 'It wasn't the money,' she informed her friend. 'Master Lindhall – he was the one who brought Master Hulak here – told him about all of the plants and trees in the East that Hulak had never seen. You just have to know how to talk to him.'

'Not this afternoon I didn't,' Arram grumbled. 'Now I have even more work before I can do my classroom studies!'

Ozorne patted his shoulder. 'Just wait till we get to the Upper Academy, my dear fellow,' he said cheerfully. 'You will dream of these happy, lazy days in the Lower Academy with wistful sorrow.'

Exhausted after his trying day, Arram gratefully fell into bed and slept almost immediately. It seemed as if he'd barely started a decent dream of a blonde girl who beckoned him to her when thunder crashed overhead. She vanished and Arram prised his eyes open.

'That was going to be a *good* one,' he muttered to the gods of dreams.

The thunder – no, not thunder, but pounding on the door – resumed.

'Make it stop or I'll make it stop,' Ozorne growled from his cubicle. 'They teach me explosive spells now.'

Arram crawled out of his blankets and stumbled to the door. 'What the — ?' he demanded as he threw it open.

He stopped. The burly fist raised to pound again belonged to Yadeen. He looked no more awake than Arram. 'If I am up and about, someone will share my misery,' he informed the youth. 'The marble slabs that are the face of the imperial platform – at the great arena – fell during an earth tremor. Did you feel it?'

Arram shook his head.

'I would like you to help me put new stones in their place,' Yadeen explained. 'To do so I need you to let me use your power as well as my own. Normally no one would ask this before you had learned the spells to stop another mage from drawing on you, but this is an emergency. Will you help me? I swear by Mithros, Minoss, and any god you prefer that I will make you do no lawless thing, nor hold back any amount of Gift to keep you subject to my will in the future.'

Arram gawped at the older man. Finally he found the wit to say, 'Wouldn't you rather have one of your personal students? The older ones, I mean?'

Yadeen grimaced. 'For a task such as this, they lack . . .' He hesitated, then continued, 'Sufficient raw power of the right order. I would need two or three of them, and one of my three is about to leave to serve at a quarry for a year. Rather than deal with all that, I would prefer one student, if possible.'

Arram jumped. 'Yes, sir, of course, sir!' he said, and grabbed the clothes he had placed on his chair for the morning.

'Say nothing to anyone with regard to my evaluation of how

many of my older students could do this,' Yadeen said, accepting a cup of tea from Irafa, who had emerged from her own room. '*Both* of you.' He raised his voice and looked towards Ozorne's cubicle.

'Your secrets are safe,' the prince called back. 'Though I'd say you need new students if your senior ones are this useless.'

'Their skills are elsewhere,' Yadeen retorted after a sip of tea. 'Have you been asked to throw fire yet, or to work a simulacrum of yourself good enough to fool a master?'

'No, Master Yadeen,' came the grudging reply.

Yadeen took another gulp of tea. 'In any case, our task is better done with a younger student if that one is strong enough. Older students have trained their Gifts in complex mental webs. It gets harder to pull them into solid ropes for great tasks. Arram, are you ready – ah, good. Enjoy your sleep, Your Highness.' Yadeen closed the door once they were in the hall with Irafa. 'You brought your workbag? May I see?'

Arram handed the bag over.

Yadeen examined the items and returned the bag to Arram. 'With luck you won't need this, but there's no telling.' He looked at Arram. 'Coat and hat?'

Arram pointed to the door to the outside corridor and yawned.

Yadeen smiled. 'Make certain they are there.' As Arram went outside for his things, Yadeen returned his cup to Irafa and exchanged a few words with her. Arram was struggling with his coat when the master joined him in the outer corridor.

Yadeen gripped Arram's coat sleeves and drew them properly onto the youth's arms. Next he thrust Arram's broad hat onto his head. As they set off, rain blasting their faces as the wind blew, he explained.

'The emperor hosts the ambassador from the Copper Isles in three days. They wish to see our new wild beasts. The platform must be as good as new,' he said. 'Old Mesaraz gets cross if things aren't perfect when he's showing off, particularly since this Kyprish fellow is here to talk trade. The emperor would also like to find out how he took ship at this time of year and arrived safe and sound. Lucky for us, all we need to do is smooth and polish some tons of rock and put them in place.'

Arram trotted beside the master, bubbling over with questions. He chose the one that worried him the most: 'Is it true, what you said, that it'll be hard, later, to get a single pure line of my Gift? One that isn't already tangled with spells?'

Yadeen glanced at him, a wry look on his face. 'It depends on the mage. I was largely trying to plant the idea in your friend's head, to see if he believed it enough to hobble himself a bit. I would prefer that you didn't say as much.'

'No, sir.' Frankly Arram didn't believe any suggestion would have power over Ozorne, and he hadn't felt magic pass from Yadeen when he'd said that to his friend.

'You'll find, as you grow older, that the Tasikhe line can be erratic. There hasn't been a mage for a generation, but the stories about the family are all about unusual behaviour.' They had reached the end of the corridor. It opened onto the Fieldside Road, on the opposite side of the university from the river and its road to the city. Waiting for them were two hard-looking men in leather armour. Yadeen handed his pack to Arram and went to talk to them.

At last the master beckoned him forward. The youth tied the strap that fixed his wide hat on his head and plunged through the gate. A bubble of light bloomed from Yadeen's hand, casting illumination over four horses standing in a roadside shelter. Arram gulped. It had been a long time since he had ridden a horse, and it hadn't gone well.

'Can't we walk?' he asked Yadeen.

'If the coliseum master had wanted us to walk, he would not have sent horses,' Yadeen said, his voice tight. Arram raised the brim of his hat to get a better look at him and understood: Yadeen didn't want to ride, either. Feeling sorry for both of them, he said nothing more. He let an armoured man try to help him into the saddle three times before he made it all the way. At least Yadeen mounted his horse creditably. 'Hand me your reins,' he ordered.

'Shouldn't I have them?' Arram enquired, obeying. 'You know, to pull on?'

'That is what I fear. I shall lead your horse. *You* will hold the horn and try to remain seated.' Yadeen folded the extra reins in his hand.

Arram looked about. There were so many bits and pieces on the horse's head! 'What is the horn?'

'Mithros, Minoss, and Shakith!' cried Yadeen, calling on the ruler of the gods, the judge of the gods, and the goddess of seers. 'Have you *never* ridden a horse?'

Arram gulped. 'Once, Master. The second time it wouldn't go.'

Their guides bellowed their laughter. Yadeen wiped his rain-soaked face with a wet forearm. 'It's that thing that sticks up from the saddle's edge, like a man's part,' he said. 'Grip it before you do fall. And you two, up front!'

One of them had the courage to glance back; the other straightened in his saddle.

'My student can do more with a finger than you can on these huge beasts,' Yadeen said. 'If you cannot behave decently, I shall let him show you. Now pick up the snake-sliding pace!'

Arram gawped at the master. No one but Varice and Ozorne had ever defended him before. 'Master—'

'Hush,' Yadeen said as he urged his horse into a trot. Arram's horse followed along. 'They should know even the smallest viper is a killer.' Arram opened his mouth to ask the question, but Yadeen held up a hand. 'Ask Ramasu or Lindhall about vipers. They'll say *I* can't teach you about them, for all I cut one off Ramasu once.'

Arram knew vipers. Lindhall had a number of them in the menagerie, and Arram had dissected at least two, carefully, in his reptile class. Arram shuddered. Vipers made him nervous, though Ozorne liked them and had never been bitten.

Instead he asked the real question on his mind. 'Is your using my Gift going to hurt?' he called. 'Me, that is. Will it hurt me?'

'Not at all,' Yadeen called. 'You'll control the thread. If it gets to be too much, all you need do is ease down on the thread. You'll see.' He looked back at Arram. 'Are you saying you doubt my judgement?'

Arram shrank in the saddle. He knew that tone. 'No, sir. Not at all, sir.'

By the time he thought his member and balls had been pounded to paste, he saw a bulk even darker than the rainy night looming ahead. It grew larger, until he realized it was a wall, not a hill. Torches with magicked shields stood in brackets on either side of a broad gate. A guard emerged from a small shed beside the gate to open one of its broad leaves, and the riders passed through.

The moment they did so, Yadeen's power rose to cover himself and Arram with a glimmering shield. 'Have to,' he murmured when he drew Arram's horse up beside him. 'This is the gladiators' encampment. They should remain in their dormitory buildings, but it's always best to protect yourself. Just in case.'

'But the guards aren't warded,' Arram said as they followed their guides.

'The fighters know what happens if they assault a guard.' Yadeen pointed. The area was spotted with shielded torches, offering something of a view. 'This open ground is where they practise. Barracks are over there.'

Arram nodded. Ozorne was going to be so jealous – whenever the emperor insisted that the princes attend the games, Ozorne made sketches of the gladiators and wrote down all the information he could glean. He would give anything to see this, rain or no. 'What are those things? The big white rolls, the log stick figures, and the barrels?' he asked, pointing.

'The white rolls are practice dummies for wrestling and hand-to-hand combat,' Yadeen replied. 'The log figures are for weapons practice. The barrels hold weapons. They must have taken the weapons themselves indoors. I didn't know you were interested.'

Arram was saved from having to explain that the information was not for him, when more guards opened another gate in a massive wall before them and waved them through. 'The arena,' Yadeen told him. To the escort he said, 'We can manage.'

One of them shrugged. 'Suit yourself, Master.' He and his companion rode back to the training yard. The slam of the gate as the soldiers closed it made Arram flinch. They were alone in the vastness of the sleeping arena, under the many rows of seats.

The way before them was a tall, wide corridor lit by baskets full of burning coals. Arram's jaw dropped. An appalling stench reached his nose: at once he was reminded of what he always thought of as the Day of the Elephant, when he had met one in addition to gladiators. The day he had seen a woman die. He swallowed. Part of the smell was definitely blood, human and animal, darker than the scent of blood in his animal dissections. Another part was sweat, and still another was animal dung. It made him dizzy. He held his sleeve under his nose as he clamped his free hand around his saddle horn.

They were passing cells on both sides, large ones, barred with iron. Both smelled equally of dung and piss, but the straw gave away the knowledge that the right-hand cages were used for animals. Arram wondered why anyone would place humans who would fight the beasts in cells across from them.

The huge gate at the end of the temple was wide open. Near it he saw cells far larger than those secured with iron on both sides of the tunnel. These chambers were closed and barred with wood. 'What are those?' Arram enquired.

If the stink bothered Yadeen, the master showed no sign of it. 'The healing rooms,' he explained. 'The wounded go in those.' He pointed to the doors on the left. 'That's if they've used up the tables in the workrooms on the right. Sorry – surgeries. Don't be in such a rush to learn about them. You'll be chopping and sewing men and women soon enough if Cosmas has his way. Got your hat on?'

Arram touched his head. 'Yes, sir.'

'Out into it, then. I hope they have a dry place for us.'

Yadeen led the way out onto the wet sands as the horses protested. The rain had begun to ease, but winds swirled around the vast structure, pulling at Arram's hat. In the distance thunder boomed softly.

'Odd to hear that!' Yadeen remarked as he steered them towards the lanterns that gleamed ahead. 'Thunder, so late in the season. The storm gods are amusing themselves.'

They passed the part of the arena where Arram had once sat with his father and grandfather, the length of rail where a man had once shoved him and Musenda had caught him. Arram's heart pinched in his chest. Was the big man even still alive? And what of Ua the elephant and her rider? He had put offerings of bits of meat at the school's shrines to Mithros, when he remembered to, and pieces of fruit at the shrines for Hekaja, the Carthaki goddess of healing, just in case, but he had been too afraid to ask those followers of the best-known gladiators if they knew about Musenda or the elephant riders. He didn't want to know if they had been sent on to the Dark God's peaceful realms.

Ahead he could see the imperial seats. They stood in the blaze of mage fires over the wall. A shadowed space filled the corner of the stand where it jutted forwards into the sands. A roofed structure had been built over the entire corner to keep the rain off the area.

Nearby was the tunnel used by the imperials and the favoured nobility to reach their seats high above. Torches burned in brackets on the walls, casting their light over large white chunks of stone on sledges. Each stone had to be as tall as Arram.

Yadeen reined up and drew Arram close to him. 'Keep my kit beside you,' he said quietly, his eyes never leaving the stones or the half-naked men who stood between them. 'No one but you must handle either workbag, understand? You will be more aware of the outer world than me. Only touch my shoulder and I will return to it.'

A burly man in a leather vest and kilt trudged out of the tunnel. 'Are you coming to work or gossip?' he roared. He was short and squat, with long, knotted black hair wound into a fat roll at the back of his head. His skin was not quite as dark as Yadeen's, but his eyes were as dark as the night around him. Hammers and chisels hung from his sagging belt.

'We are settling upon our own approach, Najau! When we are ready, we will consult you!' Yadeen bellowed in reply.

'I don't see why you brought a toothpick, unless he's for the elephants!' Najau shouted. 'He don't look like he could lift a pebble!' He stomped back into the tunnel.

'Who *is* that rude man?' Arram asked. No one addressed a master of the university in such a way.

Yadeen smiled. 'That is Master Najau, head of the stonemasons' guild. We've known each other for years. For a man without the Gift, he can make any stone do as he wishes. Of course the emperor demands the best for a task any decent marble cutter could do.'

Arram blinked at his master. Then he enquired, 'Aren't *you* the best?'

Yadeen chuckled. 'I am a mage. I can do certain things with rock, such as put magic in it, and shift it in the air. I can carve it by hand only to an extent – enough to make a clumsy bowl, unless I use my Gift. If you ever visit the palace grounds, try to get a look at the temple of Minoss. Najau did all of it, from the rough cutting of the stone to the carvings.

'Now, here's how we shall work while you keep our bags with you. I will use my Gift to prepare the stones and begin. Watch closely, particularly with your power – I shall want you to write up what we do for a paper. After a short time you will feel my summons, and you will loose only so much Gift as I need. Are you certain you will do this? As I said, you have my oath. Hold out your hand.'

Arram wavered, then offered a hand. There was a dent in the palm from his clutch on the saddle horn. Yadeen dismounted and walked over to Arram's horse. Drawing a small dagger from his belt, he slashed his palm and pressed it against the dent in Arram's.

The youth jumped. 'Sir, you didn't have to do that! I trust you! I—'

Yadeen sighed. 'This part is necessary for the spell. I am perfectly fine, see?' He held up the palm he had pressed against Arram's hand. A number of little scars marked his skin, including the most recent one, rapidly healing before their eyes. Arram looked at his own palm. He, too, had a mark.

'Don't tell the other masters,' Yadeen said. 'Only a few of us still work with tribal magic here, and Sebo would scold me for using it on a student. But I began with tribal magic. It is how my Gift speaks for me with the bigger magics.'

Arram nodded. He felt like he was glowing even more brightly than the torches. Did the master feel it, too?

'Let's get started,' Yadeen said. He picked up the reins for the two horses and walked towards the tunnel.

A woman in a coarse linen tunic, her feet bare, met them at the opening to take charge of the mounts. The moment they saw her, the horses surged forward more willingly than they had for Yadeen and Arram. They thrust their heads against her chest, whickering anxiously.

'Don't be rude,' she chided them softly. 'I'd guess they wasn't no happier'n you, out so late in slop for footin'. Can you dismount?' she asked Arram. 'They's big babies and snobs to boot, knowin' when folk aren't easy. They'll act proper if you want to get down yerse'f.'

Arram froze. Yadeen rescued him, unwinding his hands from the horn and drawing him from the saddle. The youth looked away from the woman, knowing that he blushed.

Yadeen handed both workbags to him and stripped off his own coat as the woman led the horses away. Arram could hear her scolding them gently as they vied with each other for the chance to lip her hair and shift.

'She's very unusual,' he commented, taking the master's coat and trotting to keep up as he headed for the tunnel.

'She's like the Banjiku people from the Far South, bonded to a certain kind of animal,' Yadeen said. 'It is a kind of magic that is not taught at the university, because we are either born with it or no.'

'But shouldn't we study it anyway?' Arram enquired.

Yadeen glanced at him, his mouth forming a crooked line. 'Not everyone wants to learn everything, boy,' he said.

Arram sighed. 'That's what Ozorne always says.'

Najau walked over to them, gesturing to a six-foot-tall, six-foot-wide block of white stone with tiny marks of black and grey stone inside. 'Unicorn white marble,' he said, with as much pride as if he had given birth to it. 'Brought by sea around the tip of the Roof of the World. Anyone caught with it without an imperial writ of sale is sold himself. Beautiful, isn't it?'

Yadeen walked up to the stone and leaned his head against the rough side. Najau and Arram watched him for a long moment before the stonemason turned and saw the boy. He stared at Arram briefly, then said, 'Go on, you. Touch it.'

Arram hesitated. 'I . . . I couldn't . . . I . . .'

Najau snorted. 'I stammered, too, when I was a lad and got worked up. I don't any longer – some of us lose such things as we get older, more confident. If I say you can put your hands on it, you can.' He flapped his hand, ushering Arram over to the great stone.

Arram obeyed, carrying the workbags. Standing near Yadeen, he reached out and touched the marble slab. Nothing happened. He was wondering what he was expected to do when a voice very like Yadeen's, loaded with amusement, boomed through the stone, up his arms, and into his skull.

Open your Gift to the stone, boy!

Oh, Arram thought, of course! He closed his eyes and let his power flow into the unicorn white marble.

It was cooler than it looked from the outside.

He was caught up in threads of stone, black, white, clear crystal, all of different sizes. The white ones were dominant. They hummed to him, rattling his teeth agreeably. They sang of the embrace of the deepest earth as it pressed and turned each tiny bit of them to shaped edges and points. Then black chunks, small ones that had collected in different pockets, found them, and clear ones. All twining together to become immense, proud stone.

A massive hand gently thrust him backward. *Enough for now,* Yadeen said. *You don't want to spend forever holding up the emperors of Carthak, do you? Back to yourself.*

Arram awoke inside his normal body, gasping for air. He was flat on his back, staring up at the marble. 'That was wonderful!' he cried. 'When can I do it again?'

Najau crouched beside him and held a leather flask to his mouth. 'Drink,' he ordered. 'Slowly.'

Arram drank as cautiously as he was bid. It was not some strange beverage, but water so cold it made his teeth hurt, flavoured with mint and lemon. 'That's so good!' he exclaimed when he returned the bottle to Najau. The beverage was the opposite of the stone, moving where the stone had only exact places to go, water and leaves and fruit where the stone was only stone. He felt himself, human.

The stonemason was looking him over more carefully than he had before. 'I see why Yadeen brought you,' he remarked at last. 'You'll do all right – better than those jumping crickets he's fetched to my place before.'

'I told you he would be fine.' Yadeen stepped away from the marble, rubbing his hands together. 'This is a sound block. I won't have any trouble doing the work.'

'Did you think I would choose flawed stone?' demanded Najau, indignant. 'I, the finest stonemason on the Northern coast of the empire? Possibly even the Western coast?'

Yadeen took the bottle from Najau and tipped it up, drinking as he poured.

'I said nothing of the kind, you silly old hen,' he retorted. 'The boy needs a blanket. I'll let you know when I have pieces finished. How many slabs will you need?'

Najau tapped his teeth with his thumbnail, then said, 'Six for safety, I think. Once this noise over the ambassador is done, I'll be testing the others in the stand to see if more stones are ready to drop.'

Yadeen nodded. 'With Arram's help I'll craft six, if you have the raw stone.'

Najau pointed back into the tunnel, where more chunks of marble waited.

'Very good.' Yadeen looked at Arram. 'Are you ready?'

Arram nodded vigorously.

'Until I tell you otherwise, follow only,' the master commanded him. 'Do not try to use your Gift. You don't know the spells to make the cuts straight and smooth along the entire face of the stone. I will teach them to you one day, but it's too complex now.' They walked to the first stone. Yadeen drew his hand over the surface, bringing it away covered with marble dust. He rubbed his palms together and raised them to his face, smelling them. Arram, hesitant, did the same. The dust had its own dry scent, pleasing to his sensitive nostrils. It lingered as he sat cross-legged next to Yadeen.

'Relax and wait,' Yadeen told him. 'Meditate. I will come to you when I need you.' He closed his eyes and was gone, his power flowing into the stone. Arram watched with his Gift as the master's green-and-brown streaked fire rolled into the stone and spread, forming a thin sheet inside the marble face.

As Yadeen moved on and on, Arram withdrew. He knew he'd be seeing enough of the stone's insides in time. Instead he let his Gift spread over the sands, cringing from the touch of old blood and bits of bone. But there were also faded pieces of flowers and ribbons that the arena keepers hadn't cleaned up, bird droppings – he didn't want to think about why birds might come to the arena grounds – and bits of fur. He roamed up to the seats, wondering why people came to such a sad place. Among the rows he found reasons: greed, lust, fury, excitement, all the feelings of people who forgot everything but the combats, including their struggling daily lives.

Yadeen was calling. Relieved, Arram let himself fly back to the master. He was no sooner returned to his body than he felt the gentle tug on his power. He let it mingle with Yadeen's, until they formed a cord between them that was one magic. Then they returned to the marble. The stone travelled inner paths that showed as white-hot fire crystals. Turning, they fit themselves into walls that lined up as the magic demanded, perfectly.

Then Yadeen drew Arram out, away from the stone. In the sudden cold outside the marble, he released his student.

Arram cried out and covered his ears from an assault of *noise:* voices, things banging, the crunch of footwear on sand, wind in the tunnel, and . . . the mumble of elephants? He forced his eyes open against the torchlight. At the front of the tunnel, elephants peered in curiously. The closest one had its trunk extended. Many-petalled flowers were painted on its forehead. A very large black man, as dark as Yadeen, with scars and a shaved head, petted the elephant as he cooed to it. Arram squinted, blinking rapidly to rid himself of the water spilling from his eyes.

'Mu-Musenda?' he croaked.

Yadeen was getting up. Arram remembered his duty to his teacher and struggled to stand until Yadeen gripped his wrist and lifted him to his feet. 'You know Musenda?' he asked as he waited for Arram to get his balance.

The gladiator advanced, frowning. 'You look familiar . . .' he said, puzzled. 'We've met, haven't we?'

As if impatient with the slowness of human introductions, the orchid-blossomed elephant thrust her way into the tunnel, wrapped her trunk around Arram, and lifted him up so she could peruse him, first with one eye, then the other. He laughed and leaned against her forehead. 'Ua, I hoped I would see you!' he cried. 'How *are* you, you gorgeous thing?' He looked down at the staring workers and told Yadeen, 'Musenda and Ua saved my life when I was younger!'

'Now I remember!' Musenda boomed. 'The boy who fell into the arena! You've grown so much I didn't know you! What brings you here?'

He and Yadeen talked briefly while Arram plucked straw from Ua's stiff forehead hair and whispered how beautiful she was. Finally Najau shouted, 'This is sweet as spring flowers, but we have work, all of us! Get down here, boy!'

Arram coaxed Ua to release him; the elephant reluctantly obeyed. 'We're here to cart the marble slabs to the stand,' Musenda explained. Four more heavy-muscled gladiators of mixed colour and nationality came forward with large flatbeds of wood attached to wheels. As Arram watched – Yadeen waved him away from this part of the task – Yadeen produced his Gift in waves. It wrapped around the first slab they had finished and lifted it as smoothly into the air as if it were a feather. Arram was shocked to see the flat edges and sharp corners on the slab, as well as the brightly polished front and rear faces. He barely remembered anything that might have been working the marble in that shape.

'*We* did all that?' he asked Yadeen when the master had settled the piece onto the wagon. Musenda was leading Ua and another elephant to the front, where workers fashioned their harnesses to the flatbed. Someone cried out, the elephants groaned, and the wagon began to move forward.

'We did all that,' Yadeen said, his eyes on the marble. 'We drew it in to be flat and smoothed it sharp, all from the inside. It's tricky work – you did better than I thought. You'll have to tell me how you met Musenda and Ua, but later. We must do three more, and then there's putting the slabs in place.'

'I thought we had to do . . . six,' Arram said, his voice faltering. Two more perfect slabs lay where the first boulder of marble had been. Yadeen was already using his Gift to raise one of them onto the newest wagon.

'It's easy to get caught up,' Yadeen said. 'And one plane inside the stone – one area we smooth out – looks much the same as the next after a while. We made three slabs from the first stone.'

When the last of the finished slabs from the first block were gone, they moved to the next stone. They got only two finished pieces from it. Yadeen decided they could do two more out of the next, using all the boulders in the tunnel.

'There's a relief!' Musenda commented. He had just come in for the slabs from the second boulder. 'Otherwise we'd have had to cart them away after all the trouble it took to bring them in. It makes a fellow cross.'

Arram frowned. 'It's not right, you having to fight and push boulders around, too.'

Musenda touched a forefinger to his mouth. 'We're at the emperor's service,' he told Arram. 'Us second- and third-rankers do whatever is required when we aren't fighting. It builds us up.' Lowering his voice, he said, 'And the master of gladiators reaps a pretty thaki or three from jobs outside the games.'

'That's wrong!' Arram protested angrily.

'That's the world,' Musenda replied.

'Learn it now or learn it later,' Yadeen murmured. 'But a wise man *does* learn it.'

Musenda saluted Yadeen and went to see the finished pieces taken to the stand. Arram and Yadeen made themselves comfortable beside the last piece of unfinished stone and went to work, Yadeen leading Arram inside the many lines and tracks of stone. Twice he had to call Arram's attention back to work: Arram hadn't realized he was drifting away. When he finally returned to himself in the tunnel, it took him several tries to get to his feet. His head was spinning. When he did stand, he was greeted by a foggy shape in a gaudy orange overgarment, topped in black.

'Yadeen,' snapped the newcomer, 'why are you dawdling? I can't dry things and harden the setting material until you have put the pieces where they belong!'

Arram wished he were at home and in bed. It was Ozorne's master, Chioké. He squinted at the green-and-brown fire that was Yadeen. He didn't even really need to see the master's body at this point. Yadeen could have walked down the road outside while Arram was still inside the marble and Arram would have pinpointed his location. 'Master, why is he here?' he asked. 'I didn't invite him. Did you?'

Yadeen clapped a large hand over Arram's mouth and pulled him into the shelter of his arm. 'The boy has been assisting me, Chioké,' he said, his voice flat. 'Plainly I have overworked him. Najau!' he bellowed. To Chioké he said, 'I will join you at the stand as soon as I send the boy on his way.'

'I know him,' Chioké said. 'That's the Draper boy who tags along after His Highness.' He said the word 'draper' as if he emphasized poverty, as if Arram were a commoner who did no more than weave and spin. Arram stiffened. He was *proud* of his family's craft. Chioké continued, 'Don't tell me he contributed much.'

'We have worked the stone together,' Yadeen said. 'I will see you shortly.' It was a plain dismissal.

Chioké whirled around, splattering both of them with the water from his wide coat, and walked rapidly out into the rain.

'Who stepped on his toes?' Arram asked. He rubbed the drops over his face: they were nice and cold.

'No doubt both of us. We aren't nearly wellborn enough for the likes of *him*.'

A short, broad, fuzzy shape joined them as Arram remembered what Yadeen had said. 'I don't want to go. You said I was helping.'

'You *were* helping. Now you're exhausted.'

'I am?'

'You're barely on your feet, lad,' Najau said. 'I'll get him back to school.' He rested a hand on Arram's shoulder. 'I've got a courier that's going to the city. He'll see to it you get home.'

Arram frowned, swaying on his feet. He'd let Yadeen down. 'I'm sorry I wasn't good enough.'

Yadeen squeezed his shoulder. 'You did far better than I had expected. Now go. Tell Irafa I said you were to sleep as much as you like.'

'Come along, boy,' Najau ordered.

As Najau led him down the tunnel to a waiting horse and rider, Arram asked, 'Can Musenda go with me?'

'You're drunk on marble. Musenda's a slave, boy,' Najau reminded him. 'He doesn't go anywhere outside without chains on. Now, next time you come to the arena, we'll make sure he gives you a special salute, to thank you for this night's work.'

Arram said nothing, even as the rider took him up behind him. He remained silent except to thank the man once they reached Arram's dormitory. He would much rather have had Musenda walking freely beside him, telling Arram about his life.

THE IMPERIAL UNIVERSITY OF CARTHAK

The School for Mages

The Upper Academy
SCHEDULE OF STUDY, SUMMER TERM, 437 H.E.

Student: Arram Draper
Learning Level: Semi-Independent

Second Morning Bell

Stones and Magic – Yadeen

Breakfast – Third Morning Bell
Morning Classes

Basic Medicines – Second-year student
Human Beings: Anatomy – Third-year healing student
Language: Yamani – Second-year student

Lunch – Noon Bell
Afternoon Classes

Fire Magic – Cosmas
Illusions: Small Animals – Dagani
Water Magic – Sebo
Plant Magic – Hulak

Supper – Seventh Afternoon Bell
Extra Study at Need

CHAPTER 7

May 23–August 24, 437

Without fuss, Ozorne, Varice, and Arram were moved from their former quarters in the Lower Academy to new ones in the Upper Academy. Arram and Ozorne were once more sharing a place, with the understanding that two more students would move in with them at the end of the summer term. Varice was placed with three other girls, all of whom treated her 'very decently', she told the boys. Then she added with a giggle, 'Of course, I did tell them that you and I have been friends for *years*, Ozorne.'

The boys gave Irafa gifts in thanks for her care when Varice nudged them. Arram would miss the housekeeper. Both boys would miss their ground-floor quarters, too. Their new residence was four floors above ground, and warm with the coming of summer, though they had little time to complain. All three had full schedules of classes.

Arram was most intrigued by his first lesson with the small, intimidating instructor in water magic, Master Sebo, whom he had first met the day he flooded a classroom. To his surprise, her classroom was outside the grounds by way of the Water Gate. His directions instructed that he was to take a left-hand trail away from the side road to the river landing. The sign for the trail was right under another announcing that the area was re-spelled against hippo and crocodile intrusion every year.

Arram prayed that was true. Once on the path, he would not see anything that came for him. It was hidden by reeds that grew higher than his head. A hippo would be on me before I could run, he thought nervously.

Following the trail around a curve, he found a clearing. At its centre stood a large round hut built of the same reeds that grew nearby. Sebo stood at its open door. He noted her clothes because Varice had made him promise to tell her: the teacher wore a brightly coloured wrap patterned in blue and white. Her grey hair was twisted into a number of small knots tight against her head.

'We're going in the river for our first lesson,' she informed him. 'You will be perfectly safe. You'll be able to breathe. And you will do *exactly as I say*. I've never taught one as young as you, so it's important that you obey, understand?' Arram nodded, but she decided to clarify the order. 'No jumping, no trying to swim off, no frightening the animals. The university mages place spells for a certain distance in the river every year so people may swim – you have seen the warning posts?'

Arram nodded. The posts were painted a bright yellow, and even bold swimmers like Varice didn't venture beyond them.

'We shall go past them, among the wild creatures. You are my guest. Don't make me regret taking you on. If I get irritated, I might drown you a little bit.'

Arram gulped. 'Yes, Master Sebo. I know how to act in – in other people's houses.'

She snorted. 'We'll see. Now follow.' She led Arram down a thin trail behind her own home. It emerged onto a broad, sandy cove.

'Don't remove your sandals here,' Sebo instructed. 'You don't want to be barefoot on the river bottom. Now, until you learn to do it yourself, I will place my wards on you. They will help you to breathe as well as keep you safe.' She rubbed her hands together. 'The animals will come close. Panic and I will send you to shore so fast you will be sick for a week.'

'You don't have to threaten me,' Arram objected.

'Do you know how many idiots I've had to toss onto the bank because they couldn't control themselves? Not everyone is fit for these conditions. Quiet,' Sebo ordered. She touched her fingers to his chest and chuckled. 'Ah, you're growing a pelt!' she said with a wicked grin.

Arram blushed. He would hardly call his few straggling chest hairs a pelt.

Sebo's lips moved as power trickled from the top of his head. It fell in watery streams down his body, spreading to cover his every inch. Her Gift sparkled like sun on the water, until he looked away, his vision covered with light spots.

Do all mages become this powerful as they get old? he wondered, staring out over the river. Is a water mage stronger than a stone mage? What about a hedgewitch? How do they know a hedgewitch isn't as strong as a master mage if no one ever tests people like hedgewitches or shamans?

'Pay attention,' Sebo said, flicking his nose with her finger. 'Lift your left foot.' Arram obeyed. As the cold, exciting trickles of power enfolded his feet, Sebo explained, 'This working blends air magic – drawing proper air from within and above the water – and sun magic – to draw warmth from the river's surface. If you go swimming in the warded area, you know the Zekoi gets cold, even in summer.'

As she spoke, Arram recognized the water, air, and sun magic that he had touched upon in other lessons, but in a much stronger form. The air surrounded him like a stretched-out cocoon, enclosing a mild kind of heat like that he felt while sitting in the dawn sun. The water magic came as floating weight, enough to keep his feet down, but not so much that he couldn't move. It also made a glass-like shell that let him see. He grinned. This was the most wonderful magic he'd ever witnessed! He couldn't wait to learn how to create it for himself.

'Can you walk on the ocean's floor in this?' he asked, excited.

'Well! You understand what this does and its possibilities. I thought so. Not everyone can follow the way I work, but I felt you paying attention. We shall do well, I think. Come along.' She walked down into the river and called back over her shoulder, 'Yes, you can work a form of this for the ocean. It requires a few tugs and tucks, but it can be done. You must study hard, of course.'

'Of course,' Arram murmured, following her closely. The river surged around his feet, his shins, his thighs, his chest. Sebo's shield fit itself around his body, leaving him full use of his hands. He was breathing, hardly aware of the cool substance against his lower body. Still, for all his excitement, he hesitated when the river was under his chin. His mind rebelled. It wasn't natural, to walk into water up over his nose.

Put your head under or I will thrust it under; it is all one to me, Sebo's unmistakable voice sounded in his head.

She could mind-speak! Arram sprang up with excitement, forgetting his surroundings. Coming down, he slipped and went under.

He thrashed, opened his mouth to shout – and no water came in. A striped mullet swam over to peer curiously at him as he regained his footing. He was now a foot underwater.

There was a trick to staying upright. He had to move slowly and carefully. He could breathe. The water touched the clear barrier, the one that sparkled faintly around Arram, and flowed around. He inhaled clean air.

Sebo waited until he was steady on his feet. Then she beckoned him to follow.

The river isn't as clear and clean here as it is in the South. Her voice in his mind was dry and matter-of-fact. *Humans dump trash into it – not the university or the palace, but villagers and city folk. Dead animals are here, of course. And there's silt. It comes from each river and stream that touches the Zekoi, as well as its own banks. All that dirt comes right through here. It makes the waters murky.*

Even in the murk there was plenty to see. Fish swarmed around them, confused and curious. Butterfish, uaha lampeye, and bresbarb stared at Arram as he stared back. It was strange to find such interest from something he was used to seeing on his supper plate. Green and painted frogs kept a cautious distance, but they were happy to approach Sebo and nudge her. She nudged them gently in return.

After giving Arram time to look around, she led him down the riverbed. He was soon shocked by waste in the mud: old jars, oars, entire boats or parts of them thrusting out of the silt, tree trunks, and even animal or human skeletons. He was unnerved by the human dead, his mind filled with questions about their presence. The sight of those bones and skulls made his skin crawl.

Over their heads passed the ferries and boats that travelled the river every day. Twice they saw hippos, but the great animals ignored them. Just after a small herd swam from view, he saw motion past Sebo's shoulder. He reached out and seized her arm: the largest crocodile he had ever seen was swimming towards them through the murk. It had to be more than twice the size of the biggest bull among those that sunned themselves on the riverbank.

Sebo, he said, fear in his thoughts. *Master – Master Sebo.* The spells she had wrapped around him felt like no protection at all. *There's a monster!*

The old mage turned to face the oncoming crocodile. *This is no monster,* she snapped, raising a hand in salute. *He is Enzi, god of the river crocodiles. If you cannot pay him due respect, keep your distance.* She walked towards the giant animal, who sank in the water until they were face to face.

Despite his fear, that sense of something huge squeezing his heart, Arram took several steps closer to his master and the god. Something streamed between them, almost like a colder vein of magic. Though he reached out with his own Gift, he was unable to touch it, but he was certain that a powerful force flowed between Sebo and Enzi.

After a moment Sebo began to walk forward again, with Enzi swimming above her shoulder. Gingerly Arram followed at a courteous distance, eventually renewing his inspection of the river's bottom. He had just plucked a small Stormwing figure from the mud when the water above him turned darker and cooler. He straightened and stared into a huge crocodile eye.

The giant reptile slowly swam around Arram once. It seemed to take forever. At last he returned to Sebo. This time, when he spoke to her, Arram felt the god's voice shake his poor skull: *He is too scrawny to make so much as a snack. Return him when he is at least a meal.* With a flick of his massive tail that rocked Sebo and Arram, he swam off into the clouded water.

'You handled that well,' Sebo told him as they waded onto the riverbank. 'Enzi likes you. He can add much to what you learn of rivers and streams. Our studies will not be easy, you understand, but first it was important to learn if you would panic in the depths. Though I will confess, I didn't expect Enzi to be here.' As soon as they were on dry sand, she released the spell over them both. 'Come back to my home for a moment,' she said as they headed along the path. 'I have a book you must study. Read the first ten pages tonight, and try to grasp what they mean in terms of the place of water in magic.'

He waited outside while she went into the round house for the book. When she returned with it, she was frowning. 'You may want to keep word of seeing Enzi to yourself,' she told him slowly. 'Many of the masters don't believe in animal gods, or magic that is not wielded by gods or human mages.'

'Master Yadeen does,' Arram replied.

Sebo smiled. 'We are "tribals", Yadeen and me from the Thak heartland, and Hulak, from the grass country north of Jindazhen,' she told him. 'We use the magic taught by our tribes and academic magic. Book magic. The masters who sneer are too blind to realize the gods and the immortals use no books. They think tribal magic is on the same level as hedgewitchery. They will mock you and do their best to shut you out of their oh-so-learned circles if you admit to taking other magics seriously. Lindhall is all right, and your other teachers. But be careful around the likes of Chioké and Girisunika. If you want to move up in Carthak, you stay clean of the stain of tribal magic.' She waved her hand at him. 'Now shoo. I need a cup of tea and a nap, I think.'

Arram trudged down the path and back inside the university wall. He was exhausted, as if he'd spent an hour labouring in the gardens. Like Sebo, he wanted to take a nap.

As he passed through the gate, the clocks began to chime the hour. 'Oh, no,' he moaned when he realized the time. 'Master Hulak!' He had forgotten he still had another class.

Luckily for him, the plants master looked at him and began to laugh. 'I heard that Sebo took you as a student today,' he said. 'What did she do?'

'We went into the river,' Arram said wearily. He glanced around for a safe place to set his new book.

'The river is hard at first. Never mind now,' Hulak said. 'It's too hot. Take a nice bath. Loosen the body. Just don't expect me to release you all the time.'

Arram didn't wait for Hulak to think twice. Thanking the master, he clutched the book to his chest and stumbled to his room for a change of clothes.

Hulak was right: his muscles were much more relaxed after a hot bath. He changed his original plan to go to bed and went to supper. Ozorne and Varice were eager to hear about his first lesson.

Arram told them all that he could. He showed them the bronze figurine and watched as they examined it. 'It's a Stormwing,' Ozorne said. 'I always wanted one.'

'You wanted one!' Varice exclaimed. 'They were horrible! They defiled those who sacrificed their lives in battle! They deserved to be exiled to the Divine Realms!'

'They're exactly what I want for those Sirajit dogs who killed my father,' Ozorne replied. 'Stormwings would tear their warriors to bits and throw the pieces into Siraj's stinking villages.'

He was grim-faced as he handed the figurine back to Arram. 'I want to triumph over my enemies. *Human* enemies.'

'You don't have enemies,' Arram protested.

Ozorne replied, 'Those who killed my father are definitely my enemies, and some of the dogs are still alive. Mother's agents tell her their final plan is to wipe out the Tasikhe imperial line.'

'The emperor doesn't think there's a conspiracy. He accepted the Sirajit surrender,' Varice reminded him.

'The emperor is old; his mind is not what it was. He agreed the fighting was over when the Sirajit generals were executed, even though my father's murderers were never taken!' Ozorne's voice was tight and low so that no one could hear but his two friends. 'When I've grown into my power, they'll pay.' He took a breath. 'And I'll need my friends.' He straightened and put a hand on Arram's shoulder. 'You ought to think about classes that will bring you more power, you know. You won't earn any kind of a living walking on river bottoms.'

'Ugh!' said Varice, shaking her blonde curls. 'Enough serious talk! They're holding a dance on the Great Meadow, and you two are going with me!'

'But I'm stiff,' Arram complained. 'And I don't know how to dance.'

Ozorne grinned, his dark mood gone as quickly as it had begun. 'We'll teach you. You'll have to learn as a prince's mage.' He tapped his chest to indicate the prince he meant. They gathered up their trays and dishes. With Arram still protesting, they towed him off to dance.

A week before autumn term, Arram returned from his bath to discover baggage in the two empty cubicles. Their roommates had arrived, or at least their belongings had done so. On Arram's pillow was a note from Ozorne:

You will not believe this. My idiot cousin Qesan, the one who cannot leave the ladies alone? He has been killed by a jealous

*husband. Alas, this means I must attend the funeral with the rest
of the family and ten days of mourning at the palace. Please tell
Varice. And would you both take notes in our classes for me when
things start? Make my apologies to our new roommates, please?
At this rate I will be the only prince left, don't you think?*

— Ozorne

Arram looked over at his friend's bed. Ozorne's normal mess
was tidier than usual; his bed was actually made. Arram's heart
sank. Ten days, or eleven, or more – Ozorne hadn't mentioned
when the funeral would be, and the imperial days of mourning
would begin afterwards – he would be all that time without his
friend, dealing with two new older boys. He wasn't at all ready
for this!

He folded the paper and put it in his tunic pocket. Mithros,
don't let something happen to the others, he prayed silently.
Don't let Ozorne be the only prince left. All he wants is to study
magic and be a master one day. He'd *hate* being emperor.

Arram went to eat with Varice and give her Ozorne's news.
'Oh, no!' she cried, and fled immediately to the kitchens. She
returned, beaming. 'We have one more prince to go before we
have to fast like the imperials,' she whispered in Arram's ear.
'The regular fasting is bad enough. And poor Ozorne will be
stuck in the palace again. Do you want to play chess?'

They had settled down to play when he thought of something
as intimidating as his new roommates. 'Is Prince Qesan important enough for games?'

'No, he's just dead. Beyond imperial fasting and imperial
games. I always think it's silly to hold games for someone who
isn't alive to enjoy them. Ozorne would love games in his
honour,' Varice murmured. 'And you'll be past this game if you
don't concentrate.'

Varice sighed. 'Come on, play. Your queen's in danger.'

He lost, of course. His mind wasn't really on chess. It was on
the succession and new roommates.

'Have you met the new boys?' she asked as he walked her back to her room.

'Not yet. I was happy when it was just me and Ozorne,' he admitted.

'You'll be *fine*,' she said. It was as much an order as a reassurance. 'If they give you a hard time, ask your friend Enzi to visit you.'

Arram grimaced. 'He's not a friend!' Twice now he had seen the huge crocodile in river lessons with Sebo. It was two times too many, being so close to a god. Despite Sebo's caution, he had told Ozorne and Varice about the immense creature. He knew they wouldn't turn up their noses over his arm's-length acquaintance with a 'tribal' god.

Varice chuckled and nudged him with her shoulder. 'All right, then, Master Yadeen.'

Arram shivered. 'I think I'm more afraid of bothering Master Yadeen than even Enzi.'

They reached the girls' dormitory and halted. The hall proctor never let males pass her. 'Breakfast?' Arram asked.

'I will see you there,' Varice promised.

For a moment he looked into her eyes. The urge to kiss her swept over him. There was the tiniest of smiles on her mouth, as if she wouldn't mind, as if she even expected it . . .

Three girls came running up, breaking the moment. Arram mumbled a good night and left her to be carried along by the others. He walked off towards his dormitory, feeling more cheerful.

When he opened his door, he found his new roommates. They had made their beds and distributed their belongings into wardrobes, chests, and desk drawers. Now they turned as one to stare at Arram. The taller of the pair was black-skinned, his hair shaved close to his scalp. His brown eyes were intense. He wore a comfortable tunic and breeches of the same bleached white cotton. A broad sash belt of the blue commonly worn in Zallara Province lay coiled on his desk.

The other youth sat cross-legged on the centre of the floor, while the Zallaran had stretched out and propped himself up on pillows so he could read. This one wore his black hair combed back. His skin was light brown like Arram's, his eyes as black as his hair. He had a long, stubborn nose and an even more stubborn chin. His clothes were expensive: green silk shirt, brown linen breeches, and white silk stockings. The boots that stood limply beside his bed were also expensively made.

'You're in the wrong room, boy,' he informed Arram lazily. His accent was pure Sirajit. 'This is the Upper Academy. You won't rate a bed here for years.' He grinned at the other youth.

Arram was silently complaining to whichever god had inspired the house staff to place an arrogant Sirajit mage with Ozorne. 'Actually, there's my bed,' he replied, pointing to it. 'And I *am* a student in the Upper Academy.'

The black youth sat up. 'Not amusing, my lad. Find your mother and have her move you where you belong.'

Arram looked at them. They had to be at least sixteen. They had more muscle and greater height than he did, but he couldn't let them chase him from his own room.

'Ask the proctor,' he replied quietly.

'Just because you're better at twiddling charms than your local grannywife, it doesn't make you as good as us, youngster,' the Sirajit youth said. His Gift began to spread beyond his skin until he cupped it in his hands. 'Start packing.'

Arram could hardly believe his ears. Who did these newcomers think they were? As always when he was angry or scared, he spoke more formally. 'The rules were in the documents placed on your desks,' he told them both. 'Didn't the person who signed you in say to read them immediately?'

'Do it,' the black youth told the Sirajit boy.

Arram had called up a basic protection spell, seeing the sloppiness of the older boy's magic. Now the Sirajit thrust the ball straight at Arram. These two might be older, but like most Upper Academy newcomers, they had not taken the very thorough courses in protective magics in the Lower Academy. The Sirajit's spell sank into Arram's guard, strengthening it. Out of the corner of his eye Arram saw the black youth fling a tight, fiery whip-lash at him. It was better controlled than the Sirajit's spell, but Arram knew the right counter. He yanked the whip, pulling its wielder to the floor.

'I'll have whatever charms you're using, and then we'll try again,' the Sirajit boy snapped, advancing on Arram.

The door flew open to reveal the floor proctor. 'Mithros's shield, I am working on notes, and *someone* is using his Gift to fight in here. I know poxed well it's not Draper – stop using your protections, Draper.'

'Yes, Master Muriq,' Arram said, and obeyed. He was shaking with the addition of such unfamiliar magic. No wonder the books said that most mages directed other Gifts into the ground rather than keep them, if this was the result.

Muriq was saying, 'Thank you. Draper knows playing with magic in here is *forbidden,* so it must be you two. Did you not read the academy rules?' He pointed at the black youth, heat shimmering around his finger. He *was* angry. 'Name, infant?'

Arram winced. He had forgotten that nickname for beginners.

'*What* did you call me?' demanded the black youth, bunching his fists.

'Draper, do me a service. Explain things to these two infants before I lose my temper,' Muriq said.

'We're all called infants for our first terms in the university,' Arram told him. His own infant days were years ago. 'No matter how old someone is.'

'Now, answer my question, you. If I ask again you will scrub floors for a week. That's in the rules, too,' Muriq said, fixing the black youth with his eyes.

Arram gulped. He really didn't think it was a good idea for a war mage like Muriq to have a temper.

'Diop Beha,' the black youth replied. 'Who are *you*?'

'A mage learns to size up a situation *before* he opens his

mouth,' Muriq said tartly. 'I am house proctor Master Muriq, and *you*, my friend, will be scrubbing floors for the next week in this wing, after supper.'

'You can't make him do slave work!' cried the Sirajit youth.

'If you had read your directions as ordered, you would know that I can,' Muriq replied.

'Do you know who my family is?' the Sirajit demanded.

'Your family means nothing here. That bed' – Muriq pointed to Ozorne's quarter of the room – 'belongs to a Tasikhe prince. The only difference it makes is that he attends a palace funeral at present. You may join Diop at scrubbing, after you give me your name.'

Arram saw rippling fire rise from the Sirajit youth's skin, then sink. 'Laman Hamayd.'

Muriq pointed his index fingers at each youth's desk. Sheets of parchment shook themselves free of other items and rose into the air. 'Take those,' he ordered. Neither Diop nor Laman moved. Muriq sighed gustily. Arram wished he were anywhere but here. 'If I have to repeat myself, I will place you on report for term. Any section proctor with chores to do will place your names at the tops of their lists.' He eyed Laman's clothes. 'Those pretty things won't last very long.'

Slowly the older boys shuffled forward and took the papers from midair. 'Read them. I'll wait.' Muriq glanced at Arram. 'If you want to go to a library, tell the hall proctors I gave you permission. It may be a little while before these two and I understand one another.'

Arram nodded and made a grateful escape. Rather than go to a library, he fled to the aviary. A few hours spent helping the evening students settle their charges and feed the nocturnal birds helped to calm his nerves.

He returned to find his new roommates had gone. Rather than stay for their return, Arram decided to take advantage of the fine weather. He rolled up a blanket and pillow and went in search of the rooftop stairs. He wasn't the only one seeking cooler air outside. Other students were there as well, talking softly or making themselves comfortable. Arram found a spot to place his blanket and stretched out on it, resting his head on his pillow. A slight, cool breeze came in from the river. With all the torches below the roof's height, he enjoyed a fine view of the bright constellations. Once, to his delight, a shooting star flashed by.

He wished that he would do well in the coming year, and slept.

CHAPTER 8

August 25-28, 437

The new roommates were snoring loudly when Arram crept into the room the next morning. He grimaced. Would he have to put up with that noise all year? He hated wax earplugs.

He dressed quickly, not wanting to deal with the older students so early on a free day. Of course, it was free for him. They had to go on the first of several tours of the university, learning the layout of the schools, and then their way around the different parts of the School for Mages. They had forms to fill out and tests to take to give the instructors a better idea of where to place them.

Once dressed, Arram trotted off to the dining hall. He halted in the doorway, seeing no sign of Varice. 'She isn't here,' said one of her friends who was standing nearby. 'She asked me to tell you they're letting her work in the kitchen during breakfast and lunch this week.'

Arram smiled at the older girl, a plump brunette with dimples. To his surprise, she smiled back before she walked off to her table. Arram spent a moment admiring the sway of her hips before he decided there was no point in eating indoors and alone. He gathered a napkin, fruit, cheese, and bread, and then ate his meal in one of the lemon gardens, surrounded by the trees' scent. Once finished, he decided it was too fine a day to remain indoors.

In a shocking waste of hours, he spent his day wandering from the menagerie to the university's many small museums. Agreeably weary, he was on his way to supper when someone grabbed him by the arm. Instantly he brought up a hand, a spell for stinging nettles on his lips. Then he recognized his black-clad attacker: Ozorne.

Arram's spell evaporated as he grinned. 'What are you *doing* here? You're supposed to be at the palace. I almost got you with a stinging spell, you dolt!'

'You were quick with it, too,' Ozorne said with approval. He and Varice had plagued Arram to have small, hard-to-detect spells for self-protection ready at a moment's notice, rather than trust to his unreliable fisticuff skills. 'What has you on alert? Never mind that. My mother's here. She's invited you and Varice to supper.' He spotted Varice and waved her over to them.

Arram was confused. Ozorne wasn't due back for at least another week. He also wasn't kitted out in full mourning. Of course he wore black ribbons and beads braided into his hair, black pearl earrings, and onyx bracelets. Black embroideries were stitched over his cream-coloured linen tunic in the signs for family, loss, death, and the Black God, but he should have been wearing a solid black tunic and a black headcloth. Most important, he should still have been in the imperial private quarters of the palace, observing the family rituals.

Varice frowned when she reached them. 'Ozorne? I thought . . .'

'Everyone thought,' he said, grabbing her by the hand and thrusting Arram out the door ahead of them. Students got out of their way as Ozorne towed Varice a short distance down the hall. 'When my illustrious uncle meditated on the circumstances surrounding Qesan's murder and took counsel of the priests, he decided that elaborate mourning for a man killed in the act of adultery had, as he told us, "a stink to it". There will be no days

of seclusion, Qesan will be buried on his home estates with only
his father and some distant cousins to mourn him, and the rest
of us may return to our lives. Before Mother goes home, she
wants to see you two.'

Varice balked at that. 'I'm not properly dressed to meet Her
Highness!'

'You're dressed like a student, so's Arram, and that's all that
matters. I'm begging you, show her your best faces.' Ozorne
halted before the ebony-inlaid door of one of the private dining
rooms and tapped on it. The door swung open, releasing the
scents of mint, thyme, cinnamon, ginger, and fresh-baked breads.
Slaves in black tunics stood against one wall of the room, staring
directly ahead. Arram looked away from them. These wore metal
collars with the round emblem of House Tasikhe in front. Men
and women alike wore their hair cropped very short. All were
dark brown or nearly black in skin colour, as if they'd been
chosen to contrast with the ivory skin of Ozorne and the lady
who sat in one of the room's well-cushioned chairs.

She watched them with eyes that were the same striking
shade of hazel as Ozorne's, but far more weary and sad, framed
by shadows above and below. They shared the same mouth,
nose, and strong chin, but there was unhappiness at the corners
of her mouth. Her dark brown hair was coiled and pinned in a
gold net and covered with a light veil of black silk. Her black
floor-length gown was belted at her waist with a gold chain set
with grey and cream-coloured pearls. Unlike her son, she wore
no rings or bracelets other than a gold wedding band. Her sandals
were plain leather dyed black.

Arram took all this in quickly. Sebo, when she didn't walk
him in the river or set him to learning the creatures and plants
that lived there, insisted that he learn to describe things he saw
only at a glance. Master Cosmas was the same. 'You may be
called on to save lives from fires as well as start and stop them,'
he'd said when Arram and his friends began the spellcraft side
of their lessons. 'Your ability to do so may rest on what you see

inside a room when you only glance into it.' Arram would not put it past any of his private teachers to demand that he describe Ozorne's mother perfectly.

He bowed as Ozorne said, 'Varice, Arram, I present Princess Mahira Lymanis Tasikhe, my honoured mother. Mother, may I present my friends, Varice Kingsford and Arram Draper?'

Varice curtsied deeply. Neither of them straightened until the princess lifted her hand, indicating that they might do so. Once he was upright, Arram saw that Ozorne's mother was inspecting him very carefully.

'My son tells me that you are good friends to him. For this I am grateful,' she said with a soft, wistful smile. 'He needs such friends, so far from his sisters and me.'

Ozorne mentioned his younger sisters so rarely that Arram often forgot that he had any. It was his mother he talked about, when her letters arrived, and his father.

'He is a very good friend to us, Your Highness,' Varice replied. 'We're fortunate to have one another.'

There was a flinty glint in the woman's gaze as she looked at Varice. 'Are you still a kitchen witch, girl?'

Remembering that he and Varice were supposed to like one another, Arram stepped close to her and clumsily took her hand, trying to make it seem as if he did not want the princess to see him do it. Varice looked up at him and smiled, squeezed his hand, and let go.

'She is far more than that, Mother, as I have explained,' Ozorne was saying. His voice was tight with irritation, and there was flint in his own eyes as he told his mother, 'She is excellent with medicines, herbal magic, and purification magic, as well as hospitality magic.'

Varice laughed, though Arram noticed her cheeks were flushed with anger, or was it hurt? Her lips trembled slightly as she replied, 'No, Ozorne, it's fine. I *am* a kitchen witch, if you think about it. My own father believes so!' She smiled at the princess. 'It *is* true, Your Highness. But as I have told my honoured father, consider how much a well-placed, talented person might do with the meals for warring clans who join to cement a marriage. Or what if a kitchen witch purchases the cooking supplies for a ship or a merchant caravan? Even a middling kitchen witch could turn such things for good or ill, and I am *not* a middling kitchen witch.'

The princess regarded Varice for a long moment. Neither Ozorne nor Arram dared to move. Arram wondered if the princess understood that when Varice spoke in that pleasant, perky tone, she was actually angry. He wasn't even certain that Ozorne had figured that out about their friend, even though he'd known Varice longer than Arram had.

At last Princess Mahira gave Varice the thinnest of smiles. 'You know your worth, it seems,' she murmured.

Varice bobbed a slight curtsy. 'Your Highness, like your son I have entered the Upper Academy at the age of fifteen,' she said. 'The university has already informed me of my worth.'

Mahira nodded and turned her regard to Arram. A small frown creased her forehead. 'How old are you, boy?'

'Thirteen, Your Highness,' he replied. Heat crawled up the back of his neck.

Mahira sat back in her chair. '*Thirteen?* You are but a child!' She looked at Ozorne. 'You said he is equal to the two of you, starting advanced training as you will this term!'

Ozorne grinned at his mother. 'All three of us are advanced students,' he told her. 'Arram has five masters teaching him privately – we each have four. Only a quarter of the third- and fourth-year students can boast even one master as an instructor. Most here study in classes until they graduate only with the certificate that places them just above hedgewitches and goody-wives.'

Again the lady frowned the careful frown of a woman who did not want to incur too many wrinkles. 'But not you, my son. Surely *you* will do better.'

'Your Highness, all mage students hope to do better,' Varice explained. 'Success is very different. Ozorne has Master Chioké in battle magic. Master Chioké is *very* highly regarded.'

The princess looked past them, as if she saw things outside the private dining room. 'My lord husband also told me success is different than what one hopes, not long before he was so foully slain,' she murmured. She looked at her hands, neatly folded in her lap. Silence stretched among them. It had begun to grow uncomfortable when Ozorne rested a hand on his mother's shoulder.

'Did I tell you what Arram here did right before we met him, Mother?' he asked. 'It was the talk of the whole school. He was supposed to raise a little bit of water from a bowl—'

'Ozorne, please, no!' Arram cried. When the princess turned her regard on him, Arram bowed, his hands over his face. 'Your Highness, it's a stupid story.'

'Not to hear our masters tell it,' Varice teased.

'And what happened to interest the masters?' Mahira enquired.

Politely, because good manners were thoroughly taught in the Lower Academy, Arram told the princess what had taken place that day, in Girisunika's classroom. Ozorne interrupted occasionally to say what he had heard about it in the general university, but Varice kept silent, the picture of a well-behaved maiden.

Mahira raised her eyebrows when Arram finished. 'And you were rewarded for such misbehaviour, Arram Draper?' she enquired softly. She let Ozorne urge her gently from her chair and lead her to her place at the table. This was a dining room furnished in the Carthaki style, with very low cushioned couches and low tables. Once the princess was seated with Ozorne at her right hand, Arram and Varice were placed on her left.

'Your Highness,' Arram said, 'if extra classes and more lessons were a reward, then I was very well blessed.'

The princess smiled and nodded. Apparently the nod was a signal. The slaves began to serve beef cooked with mint, cold chicken with pomegranate juice, and side dishes of salads and vegetables, each with its own unique blend of herbs and spiced vinegars. Arram hid a smile. He could see that as Varice did her best to keep up with the talk, she also tried to work out how each dish was made. Normally the university kitchens were more than able to cater to any guest, but Ozorne had once mentioned that the princess had her own cooks, since her health could be fragile. These dishes were very different from the school's familiar ones. Arram ate heartily. Any weight he ever put on only went straight up to add to his height.

The lady's requirements for conversation rested largely on Arram's studies. He tried to explain that he often made mistakes and he wasn't even sure that he belonged in the Upper Academy. She chided him for that.

'Your masters know far better than you, young man,' she said gravely. 'They are great in learning and magecraft, respected throughout the Southern and Eastern Lands for their wisdom. You must accept their judgement. Work hard to prove worthy of it.' She had that distant look in her eyes again. 'My son, you choose your friends well. I approve. Strong mages will be a great asset when you avenge your father's murder by the Sirajit dogs.'

That struck Arram like a bucket of cold water. 'Your Highness, surely . . . the Sirajit rebels who fought His Late Highness were defeated. We've been taught that there is no armed rebellion left.'

'Mother, we talked about this,' Ozorne said. 'I am going to be a master mage, remember? I'm not the imperial sort.'

The princess didn't seem to listen. She turned the wedding ring on her finger, gazing into the distance. Ozorne glanced at a slave, who nodded to him. 'Mother, thank you so much for this meal.' The prince got to his feet. Varice and Arram did the same as Ozorne went to his mother, knelt, and kissed her cheek. She didn't look at him or at the other two as they said their proper farewells and left.

Ozorne sighed. 'She has good days and bad ones,' he explained as they walked down the hall. 'In the last year she's been having more good days than bad. She's just worn out from being at court, or she wouldn't have slipped away in front of you.'

Varice put an arm around his shoulders and squeezed. 'It's all right,' she said. 'She was lovely. We didn't think anything of it, did we, Arram?'

'No, of course not,' he said, doing his best to sound cheerful, but he was unsettled. From the look of Princess Mahira as she spoke of the Sirajit people, he thought she would have killed them herself, given weapons and soldiers. Her eyes had been frightening.

He needed to break the news now. 'Ozorne, one of our new roommates is Sirajit.'

Ozorne halted and turned to look up at Arram. For a moment the older boy said nothing. Finally he looked away. 'But how charming. I'm sure we shall all get on like lotuses in a pond. Perhaps complete peace with the province of Siraj will begin in our humble little room. Wouldn't that be nice?' He sighed. 'In any event, you must do without me for another two days. Mother leaves for our lands then. You know I like to stay with her until the last moment. It steadies her, you see.' They nodded, and Ozorne kissed Varice's cheek in farewell as they left her at her dormitory. 'Bear with our new roommates just a little longer,' he said as he and Arram walked on. 'We'll see. Maybe they'll find out the university is hard on newcomers who think they are already mages.'

He clapped Arram on the shoulder, leaving his friend with goosebumps.

Upon his return to the room, Arram found it crammed with older students, all of whom were laughing and talking loudly, eating and drinking and occupying every spare inch of space. They barely moved as Arram fought his way through to his cubicle. He thought of trying to order them out, then thought of the laughter and mocking he would get. Instead he retrieved his blanket and pillow once again and left. He walked halfway up the steps to the roof before he realized the noisy talk and laughter were also coming from up there.

Growling under his breath, he decided to try something new. When he was in the Lower Academy, he'd been forbidden to venture outside the walls after dark at any time. As a member of the Upper Academy, he was permitted to do so between terms. He stomped out through the gate with a nod to the guard, who knew him, and across the City Road towards the river.

There were people on the beach there. It was too hot for older students and masters to pass up the chance to catch the river breezes, even if they meant to return inside for the night. From his studies with Sebo, Arram knew a track around a bend in the riverbank that led to a small cove. No one else was there.

He put down his blanket and pillow. Next he carefully shaped a circle in the sand around his things, using salt from a pouch that he always wore on his belt. 'Let them take your clothes,' Cosmas had told the three friends. 'Let them take your rings, let them take your shoes, let them take your . . .' He had twinkled at Ozorne. 'Let them take the very beads from your hair, but *do not* let them take your salt! It is the most basic ingredient we have, and it can help you to get everything else back!'

Arram used it now because, while there were spells to prevent hippos and crocodiles from coming up on these beaches, there were always land animals to concern him. As he walked the circle, he murmured a protective spell. To his delight, the line of sparkling fire rose above his circle and faded. It worked!

He lay down and tucked his hands behind his head, watching the stars and listening to the river's sounds. Hippos talked back and forth as softly as those great creatures managed. Now and then crocodiles bellowed. Fish leaped to catch insects and splashed back down. Clouds passed. He counted the constellations, starting with the Basilisk and moving on to the others, also reciting the magical influences attached to each one. At some point in his whispered recitations, he slept.

He dreamed he lay on a heap of sleeping dragons. Their skins were as lumpy and uncomfortable as rocks, and they stank. When one of them sighed in his ear, he woke up enough to object.

He'd flung an arm and a leg onto the bronze back of the giant crocodile god, Enzi, in his sleep. The creature's immense forearm was Arram's pillow. The stench in his dream came from the animal's mouth, filled with sharp teeth.

The youth scrambled to his hands and knees, wheezing as he fought for breath. When he glanced at Enzi, he saw that one of the god's golden eyes was open. The moment he met that ancient gaze, he froze.

You woke me, the god said. *We both slept well, and you woke me.* He released the spell of paralysis that held Arram. *Why must you flail so?*

'I didn't expect company!' Arram squeaked. He cursed his voice, then wondered what he had done wrong on his protective circle. He looked and saw one problem immediately. The god lay on half of it.

Do you know how little rest I get from the endless complaints of my own people and the hippopotamus people? demanded the god. *Clatter, clatter, we are hungry, the humans hunt us, your people eat our young. I find a nice place to nap and you woke me! Go away if you can't lie still!* The great eye slid shut.

'It's not my fault,' Arram grumbled, yanking on his clothes. He would have to get another blanket. He was not waking the god for the one underneath him. He marched up the path to the university. 'I didn't invite him to sleep there. It was *my* protective circle he ruined! *He* has things to complain about! He doesn't have to remake his life every year or two, or every few weeks . . .' He stopped. He had spoken with a god. Admittedly, Enzi was an earth god, not one of the Great Gods, who had their own separate realm, but how many people spoke with gods at all?

Would Sebo be angry? It wasn't his fault that Enzi had crawled into his circle. And so much for thinking he could work a good circle – he needed to practise!

He had planned to see if Hulak wanted weeds pulled after he ate breakfast, but his meal was interrupted. He was about to dig into a very succulent piece of cantaloupe when something like a cool, tingling rope twined around his neck. His tablemates stared at him.

'Arram,' Varice said nervously.

He didn't have to be able to see the Gift to know the person who wielded it. 'Sebo,' he told her and the others, and tried to fit a bite into his mouth. The rope around his throat tightened gently and got cold. 'I'd better see her.'

Once he was on his feet and outside, the grip on his throat released. He could barely see the rope stretching through the air ahead of him, leading him through the Water Gate. It didn't show the way to Sebo's hut, but took him instead to the riverbank. Sebo waited for him there, cooling her feet in the water.

'You are a lucky boy,' she informed him when he was within earshot. 'Do you know what might have happened, had Enzi not been amused rather than angry? He is capricious! You trusted protective circles – the university's and your own – to keep you safe from the god of the crocodiles!'

Arram blinked at her. 'I thought it was a good circle,' he said mildly, ignoring his own vexation at his failure. The air was damp and chilly, which meant the old woman's bones were hurting her. 'Doesn't the water make your feet hurt?'

She sighed, her rage seeping into the sand. 'It's warmer than the air,' she explained. 'It isn't just we humans and the big animals who have their own gods. The great things of this world – rivers, mountains, lakes, forests – have their own gods as well. The very large ones have more than one god. Old Zekoi is one, because the rivers and streams that come to him have their own gods. If you deal with one god – as you now have – you will see others. Treat them with respect if they come to you. Most will not say as much, but they are often called to battle against Uusoae, the Queen of Chaos. Our tribute, prayers, and respect give them strength to keep fighting, somehow.'

Arram frowned. 'I thought Uusoae was just a tale to frighten children.'

Suddenly Enzi was there on the riverbank. The air shoved away from him, making Sebo and Arram stagger. Arram caught his master by the arm, but she shook him off.

Do not speak so of the Dread Queen. She would devour us all if she had the chance, Enzi said harshly. *The gods hold her at bay, but she never stops planning how she will eat the world.*

'We fight beside you, in our way,' Sebo told the giant crocodile. 'It is our world, too.'

He will be called to the fore of the battle one day, Enzi said, looking at Arram. *He had better be ready.*

'What do I need to be ready?' Arram asked, but the god had vanished. 'I can't battle any Chaos Queen,' he told Sebo. 'I can't even fight bullies.'

She took him by the arm. 'Study your lessons and practise your spells,' she said gently. 'That's all that can be asked of you right now. Come. Let's walk the river.'

After he left her, he was completely absorbed in thinking about gods that did not take on the faces of human beings. Once he had bathed, he spent the rest of the morning in a library that specialized in books about religion, gods, and nonhuman creatures. He had plenty to turn over in his mind when he left, three books in his hands.

THE IMPERIAL UNIVERSITY OF CARTHAK

The School for Mages

The Upper Academy
SCHEDULE OF STUDY, AUTUMN TERM, 437 H.E.

Student: Arram Draper
Learning Level: Semi-Independent

Second Morning Bell

Stone Magic – Yadeen

Third Morning Bell

Fire Magic – Cosmas, breakfast supplied

Morning Classes

Advanced Law with Regard to Magecraft – Third-year instructors
Tribal Magic – Various instructors
Medicines – Ramasu, instructors

Lunch – Noon Bell
Afternoon Classes

Advanced Charms – Fourth-year instructors
Illusions: Birds – Dagani
Water Magic – Sebo
Plants – Hulak

Supper – Seventh Afternoon Bell
Extra Study at Need

CHAPTER 9

August 31–December 2, 437

Ozorne returned the day before class began with a pair of slaves carrying a trunk of gifts and new clothes from his mother. Fortunately, Diop and Laman were out, receiving their final schedule for their first term of classes. Arram was reading peacefully on his bed. He was so grateful to see Ozorne that he hugged him.

'Easy, old man!' Ozorne said cheerfully. 'You'd think I was gone for an eternity!'

Arram let him go. 'It felt like one.'

'Oh?' Ozorne waved off the slaves and flopped onto his bed. 'Tell me.'

Arram waved a hand in dismissal. 'It's just boring without you.'

Ozorne pulled up a chair and slouched on it, crossing his legs. 'Here's some cheer. Since Mother was inclined to spend and we even went to a bookseller, I got this for you.' He reached over, opened the trunk, and tossed a book to Arram. It was about shapeshifters.

They were both looking at the many-coloured illustrations when the door swung open. Diop and Laman had returned.

'Mithros bless us, another one,' Laman said. 'Had I *known* this place was degenerating into a school for children, I might have tried for the City of the Gods.'

'They say the school in Jindazhen is incredible,' Diop drawled, leaning against the frame. 'Bamboo groves, teahouses with singing girls who are happy to keep a fellow company, food better than the slop they serve here . . .'

'You must be the leftover prince,' Laman taunted Ozorne.

Ozorne looked at Arram. 'Great Mithros,' he said. 'I thought at least they'd be *witty*.' Then he smiled at the older boys. 'I have a long memory,' he said. 'I don't know why I'm telling you, but there it is. You'd do well to keep it in mind.'

'Is that a *threat*?' Laman asked with delight. 'Are you *threatening* us, little man?'

'I am explaining,' Ozorne replied. 'Isn't that enough?'

The older boys burst into laughter. Arram burned silently. It was bad enough when they laughed at *him*. He was used to it. But they had no call to laugh at his friend. They didn't understand what Ozorne had to live with – a murdered father, a mother who didn't always live in the real world, and people like these newcomers who jeered because he wasn't the direct heir to the throne.

'Stop it!' Arram said, getting to his feet. Sweat rolled down his face. 'He's a prince of the realm – you owe him that much respect!'

They only laughed harder. 'What can you do, little boy?' Diop managed to say.

'He'll run and tell his mama!' Laman said, gasping.

Arram clenched his fists. 'Shut up!' he cried. 'Can't you ever shut up?' He didn't realize that bits of smoke were drifting up all around him.

Ozorne lunged to his feet, grabbed the water pitcher from Arram's desk, and – to the sound of their roommates' laughter – threw the contents over him. Drenched, his concentration broken, Arram gasped for air and found none. He began to cough.

Diop and Laman stopped laughing. 'This is pathetic,' Laman said. 'We have to get rid of you two. Mop up that mess when you're done.' They left, slamming the door behind them. Apparently they didn't notice that the 'mess' was evaporating from the floor in small clouds of steam.

'I almost lost my grip, didn't I?' Arram asked when he could breathe.

'*I* was impressed,' Ozorne told him. 'I thought you would set the room on fire.'

When Arram moved, they found he had left the outlines of his feet burned into the wood of the floor.

They waited until the supper bell chimed, but no one banged on the door, demanding to know who had practised magic without leave. It was the first time one of Arram's slips had gone unnoticed by authority. For some reason, Diop and Laman chose not to report it, which pleased Ozorne.

When they reached the Upper Academy dining hall, they saw that Varice had already found a table – and new friends to share it with her. Arram actually ground his teeth.

Ozorne sighed. 'She's kept our usual places for us. We may as well show them we knew her first.'

They approached with their meals, and Varice waved to them. 'Here are my friends,' she told her newest companions. 'Prince Ozorne, Arram, these are . . .'

Laman, Diop, and their other two friends introduced themselves reluctantly. Diop even said, 'We've met.'

'Laman and Diop are our roommates,' Ozorne explained as he took his seat. 'I just had the pleasure of meeting them today.'

Arram caught Varice's quick glance from Ozorne to the newcomers. 'Well, you might as well get acquainted now,' she told them as Arram sat and dug into his food. 'If this summer was any indication, the Upper Academy won't leave us much time to chat.'

'You two curmudgeons never mentioned you had such a

lovely friend,' Laman said, smiling at Varice. 'Otherwise we might have been more polite to you.'

Arram watched the meal in silent appreciation as Varice got the new students to talk about themselves and to ask Ozorne about the university. She charmed them, and guided that charm Ozorne's way as surely as if she wielded magic. Arram was grateful she didn't turn that his way. He wasn't certain he could endure the sparkling eyes, the flawless smile, and the attention that had to be for him only. She applied it as easily as Yadeen applied his Gift to the inside of a marble boulder, making each of the young men beam at her and at each other. Even Ozorne, who should have been immune after all this time, ended the meal graciously.

'There, you see?' Varice asked her two friends as they left the dining hall. 'A little pleasantry over food, and people see one another in a much better light. So I can invite them tomorrow?'

Ozorne sighed. 'You know we can't deny you anything,' he said, and kissed her cheek. 'But if they get nasty . . .'

'Then we're done,' she promised. 'But when you're a great prince with a house of your own, you'll see this is a good way to do things.'

Ozorne smiled. 'When I have a house and lands, I hope you two are there to guide me. Being without you both these last few days has shown me how much better I do around you. It seems as if I'm in control of things knowing you're at my side.'

'The three of us – we're invincible,' Varice announced, spinning around. 'The world had best watch out!'

When the boys returned to their room to study, they found Diop and Laman had invited a number of their new friends to do the same. The older boys took up every space but Arram's and Ozorne's beds and, despite the fact that they were supposed to be studying, made plenty of noise. Finally Ozorne looked at Arram, shrugged, and glanced towards the door. That became the pattern for their evenings: they would retreat to a library to work with Varice, then run to their rooms to be in bed before curfew rang out. Their closeness made it easier for Arram to bear the older boys' dismissal.

As the term continued, Varice and Ozorne invited other friends they made to join their group at meals and library sessions. Their numbers always came and went in the library: it seemed few older students appreciated asking for help from the three younger ones. Some remained.

One evening when Varice and Ozorne had gone in search among the shelves for illusions on roses, one of the other students slipped into Ozorne's empty seat beside Arram. He blinked at her, brought out of his intense concentration on the laws regarding magic use in Tyra. Prisca, he thought, dazed. Her name is Prisca.

'Arram, hello, do you mind?' she asked in her pretty voice. All of her was pretty, from the tumbles of black curls caught up in a red ribbon net at the back of her head to the slender Northern-style gown of the same colour that outlined her curves. Her black eyes twinkled at him in the friendliest way as she placed a hand on his arm. Her skin, he noticed, was a wonderfully warm shade of brown. 'This is so much nicer than trying to whisper around poor Varice or poor Ozorne, isn't it?'

Arram ducked his head. 'How – how could I mind?' he stammered. 'Only a – a churl would – would mind.' Dolt! he shouted silently at himself. Mumble-mouth! Clod!

'So good of you,' she said, stroking his sleeve with light fingers. She took a deep breath. It lifted the curves between her bodice and the gown's neckline. Arram clapped his legs together and bit the inside of his cheek to get his rebellious manhood in order. 'You smell nice today,' she said quietly, leaning towards him. 'Very . . . outdoors-ish.'

He gave her a wavering smile. 'The Northern trees are losing their – their leaves. Master Hulak keeps their own climate around them so they – they grow as they would . . . you know, at home, and we were raking leaves this afternoon.'

She took her hand away, blushing. 'I, um, wanted to ask you something,' she said, fumbling with her slate.

Arram, used to Varice's polished behaviour, startled. She's nervous, he thought. And she gets awkward, like me! The tight knot that had formed in his chest when she sat beside him loosened somewhat.

'As long – as long as it's not criminal,' he told her, daring to venture a joke.

She covered her giggle with a hand. 'Oh, silly! But . . . Varice told me that you know basic healing plants.'

'Well . . . some,' Arram replied. 'Master Hulak teaches me in the gardens.'

'Would you help me with it?' Prisca asked. 'I'm desperate. I keep confusing some, and the examinations are coming . . .'

Varice returned and leaned over Arram. 'You know you're always welcome among us, Prisca! And if Ozorne and I are distracting you two, there are private cubicles in back where you can work.'

Arram thought he might die of embarrassment at the obvious hint, but Prisca said eagerly, 'That sounds wonderful! So you'll help me?'

Suddenly the term looked brighter.

The first night of December, Arram was woken by a soft thud on his floor. He sat up, blinking. His cubicle glowed with a silver light, and a three-foot-long silver crocodile was on his small rug. A bird the size of a starling sat on its back.

Summoning up a blast of his Gift in case he had to fight, Arram braced his back against his headboard. How did the thing get in here? He was opening his mouth to yell for his roommates to wake up when his visitor said, *Do not be a clapperknob, boy.*

His Gift still ready for attack, he crept to the edge of his mattress. 'Enzi?' he whispered very softly. 'You're so . . . small.'

You may speak as you like. None of these others will wake. I have no interest in hearing their chatter. The crocodile god looked around the cubicle. Arram's boxes and books occupied much of its space. *You can hardly fit yourself in here.*

It was hard to be terrified when the god was this size. 'Enzi, did you know you have a bird on your back?'

The crocodile snapped his jaws in vexation. *Of course I know, idiot! Will you come down? It is hardly comfortable to bend my head at this angle!*

'Of course,' Arram said, drawing his Gift back into himself. About to slide off his mattress, he asked, 'Would you like me to hold the bird?'

Please. Her claws tickle.

Arram obeyed, gently cupping his hands around the small creature and scooping it into his hold. The little bird made no complaint. She looked at Arram with great, luminous eyes that shone in mixed colours of yellow and orange, touched with spots of blue. Arram could have looked into those eyes for the rest of the night, if the god had not scratched him lightly with one claw.

'Ow!' Arram cried, still keeping his voice down. Had Enzi spelled all three of his roommates? He looked at the bird again, trying to work out what made her gaze so fascinating. 'Who, or what, is she?' Arram asked. 'And why are you *here*?'

I need to ask a favour. A large one, Enzi said. If Arram did not know better, he would have said the god sounded embarrassed. *You see, I was in the Divine Realms, visiting some immortal friends of mine. They are birds, and several nests were breeding. I believe that is when this little nestling hopped onto my back. When I am my normal size, my scales are so thick that I can't feel anything so tiny. I came home and stopped by a colony of my mortal children. They told me there was a young bird on my back. Do you know how Mithros feels about those who steal his sunbirds?*

'There are stories,' Arram said hesitantly. He thought with horror, *Sunbirds!* They're *sacred* to Mithros! He looked at this sample of a sunbird, wondering how she could grow to be such a legendary creature. They spent their days rising from the treetops in the Divine Realms, spinning, flying as high as they could go. They spread their giant wings to reflect the sun in blazing colours, their tribute to the god. Mithros could show a human no greater sign of his favour than a sunbird feather, and his wrath would fall on the thief so reckless as to steal one. The thought of what the god might do to anyone caught holding one of the precious nestlings made him shake.

I must find a gift of suitable magnificence as an apology to the god before I can return his nestling. There is a way to handle these things. Perhaps you have heard the story of the Trickster Kyprioth in his guise as the Youth, and the time he borrowed the Smith God's favourite hammer? The Great Gods are touchy. The right gift solves everything. I will only need a short time.

There was a crafty note in the god's voice that Arram didn't like. 'What do you want of me?' he enquired, though he had a funny feeling he knew what the god was asking.

Look after her, until I find a way to placate the Master of Daylight, Enzi said. *In return, I will do you any favour you may ask of me. A word of advice: Tell as few people as possible what she really is. You do not want Mithros to hear.*

'I can't,' Arram retorted. 'I'm a student, and we aren't allowed pets. They'll take her from me.'

Your path will be made smooth. I will see to it, Enzi said majestically.

'I can't leave her alone,' Arram said, growing more frantic. 'Look at her! She's all down!' He had learned more from his visits to the menageries than he had expected. 'She's still a baby – she has to be fed every hour or so!'

She is recently fed, and the way to tend to her will be made clear. This place is part of the roots of my power, the great river and the gathering place of my people. Arram felt the words roll through the air, like one of his masters' spells in their power. *What I desire here takes place, even among the two-leggers.*

Arram drew a breath, wishing he'd thought of this before. 'Why don't you ask Master Sebo? You're friends.'

She will take the young one straight back to the nest. All manner of unhappy questions will be asked. The sunbirds will remember I was there recently.

It occurred to Arram that perhaps Enzi's tale of the nestling falling onto his unfeeling back was not entirely true.

Sebo will say it serves me right to be pecked by sunbirds. They won't kill me, but they will try. Would you wish such a fate on me?

Arram opened his mouth to reply and closed it. Sebo *would* say that. She took a very dim view of those who stole young from their nests, even accidentally. He would hate to see Enzi tortured by creatures nearly as godlike as he was.

How had he developed a liking for this ugly, ill-tempered creature?

Arram looked at his handful. She regarded him with those beautiful eyes and peeped. 'I still think the school will not let me keep her,' he replied. 'How long will this take?'

Excellent, the crocodile god said briskly. *A little time and all will be well. You will hardly know the bird is here.* With that, Enzi was gone.

'He didn't even tell me what you eat,' Arram complained.

The bird looked around the room. He realized she could see in the dark when she spotted the roll he'd brought from supper on his bedside table and started to cheep. He set her beside it, and she began to rip tiny bites from it. He wondered if he should offer her some grapes, but she halted her feast with a scrap left. She shook her fluff and looked Arram over. Finally she voiced a noise like 'Preet!'

Arram looked at her. 'Is that a good sound, or a bad one?'

She cocked her head at him.

'Can you fly?'

She fluffed up a second time and began to groom herself.

'Have you a name?'

One multicoloured eye peered out of the fluff and blinked.

'I can't think of any good names, and I have to call you something.' Arram yawned as the bird began to groom under her tail. 'Will Preet do?'

She looked at him and said, 'Preet!'

'I hope that means yes.'

'Will you be *quiet*?' demanded Diop sleepily. Arram jumped.
'Bad enough he snores,' Laman grumbled into his bedding.

A hand clasped his shoulder. Arram jumped. It was Ozorne, face, hair, and nightgown rumpled, his eyes alight with curiosity. 'Where'd you get it?' he whispered. 'It's far too cold for baby birds.'

Arram scooped Preet up and admitted, 'I don't know what to do. She's so little!'

Ozorne tweaked his ear. 'Get dressed. I have a plan.'

A short time later they slipped outside in winter shirts and breeches. Preet was enveloped in a ceramic bowl wrapped in several wool garments, with only a tiny hole at the top to admit air. Arram knew they were on their way to Master Lindhall, but he couldn't think of any way out of it. He didn't know how to properly care for a nestling. The god simply didn't understand university rules, or how closely the masters watched the students – or at least, how closely they seemed to watch *him*.

Once more they made the long climb up to Lindhall's fourth-storey quarters. Arram was surprised to notice it didn't seem like such a labour as it did before, until he remembered that he now made a similar climb to the library several times a day. He smiled to think there was some good to being in the room with two rude older boys.

Once they were on the fourth floor, Ozorne looked at the door to the room used by Lindhall's assistant. Then he shook his head. 'Why deal with pudding-heads?' he asked. He looked at Arram, who was opening his mouth to protest. 'Besides, Master Lindhall likes you. He always asks after you.'

There was nothing Arram could say to that. While he studied with Sebo, Ozorne studied with Master Lindhall. He watched his friend walk over to the master's door and knock on it. After a long moment of waiting, Ozorne knocked harder.

Lindhall opened the door. He did not look happy. 'I swear to Kyprioth, if those cursed ostriches have escaped their enclave again . . .' He blinked. 'Ozorne, it is not *nearly* time for your class, and I was up past midnight healing broken ribs on a giraffe.'

Ozorne gave a little bow. 'Yes, Master Lindhall, I know, but . . .' He pointed to Arram's burden.

Lindhall squinted.

Trying to unwrap the bowl as fast as he could, Arram came closer. The last scarf fell to the tiles, revealing the small fluffy bird in the bowl. She blinked up at Lindhall as he blinked down at her. Finally she said, 'Preet!'

From inside the master's quarters Arram heard a chorus of bird cries and songs of every degree.

Lindhall grabbed Arram's arm and pulled him into his quarters. Looking back, he ordered Ozorne, 'You too.'

Ozorne gathered up Preet's wrappings and followed, closing the door in his wake. The noise was much worse in the master's sitting room.

Lindhall covered his ears and shouted, 'Would you tell them to be quiet?'

Preet croaked, and the noise from the other birds stopped.

Lindhall lowered his arms. 'Well, let's have a look at you.' He held out cupped hands. Gently, Arram tilted the bowl until the small creature tumbled onto the master's palms.

For the first time in his life, Arram created a fast lie. 'Sir, I found her on a walk a little while ago, but I've never, um, seen her like before, not in the garden where I found her, or the menagerie, or anywhere. She can't fly, and I couldn't find a nest. And I didn't want to leave her free while I went to class, or wake anyone to ask for a cage—'

That did it. The nestling began to scream. Master Lindhall neither dropped Preet nor squeezed her when she announced her opinion of cages: Arram was wide-eyed with admiration.

'Stop it,' the master told her. She looked up at him, made a small growling noise, and stopped. To Arram he said, 'I will forgive you for a story that is almost entirely lies. I suspect you have been sworn to secrecy. Certainly you reek of contact with a god. I am not certain what your bird—'

'I named her Preet, Master,' Arram said.

'You named her Preet.'

'She doesn't seem to mind.'

The bird looked at Arram and said 'Preet' very firmly.

Lindhall smiled. 'I see. Arram, those of us who are your masters, or yours,' he said with a nod to Ozorne, 'will know the origins of this bird, though that is not true of those below our level of skill. Not even the younger masters will notice certain . . . anomalies. You cannot see them, can you?'

'She looks like a small dun-and-grey bird to me, Master Lindhall,' Arram admitted. 'Except for her eyes.'

'She's the same to me, Master,' Ozorne said. Grudgingly, he added, 'Her eyes only look black, as nearly as I can tell.'

'That will change.' Lindhall rubbed his chin, which rasped from lack of shaving. 'Leave her with me while you are at class, but I expect you to be here after supper and at night to feed her. She will require feeding quite often. I will send a message to your proctor and to the guards to ensure you are not stopped on your way to and from this building. You will need to leave early to bathe in the morning and change clothing.'

'Yes, sir,' Arram said gloomily, thinking, Splendid! More work!

Lindhall yawned. 'Let us see to her housing. Come with me.'

He led them back down the hallway that Arram remembered, through his sitting room and past closed doors, towards the animal care rooms. At the end of the hall was a single door labelled 'Work Only' in bold letters. Lindhall nodded for Ozorne to open it.

Within was a long room. Lindhall spoke the word that caused the light globes overhead to come to life, revealing a place like a cross between a carpenter's workshop and a tailor's room. Shelves above and below the tables were built into the walls to hold bolts of cloth and lengths of prepared wood in addition to spools of thread, small jars of needles and pins, larger jars of different lengths of nail, measuring strings, hammers, and other tools. Arram couldn't begin to imagine what it was all for.

At one end a hearth was set into the wall. Lindhall went to it and, balancing Preet on one hand, felt the side of the kettle hanging there. 'Excellent!' he said with satisfaction. 'Ozorne, if you will pour three cups of tea?' To Arram's shock, Ozorne produced cups from a cabinet beside the hearth and did just that without complaint.

Arram blinked, feeling helpless. Preet bobbed up and down on Lindhall's palm, babbling as she fixed her gaze on Arram.

'Very well, youngster,' Lindhall said, carrying her over to him. 'Put her in your shirt pocket, not on your shoulder,' he advised. 'She hasn't the strength yet to grip tightly enough.' Arram obeyed, gently tucking the little bird into his pocket. Lindhall accepted a cup of tea from Ozorne. 'Now – Arram, am I right?' Arram nodded. 'See if you can choose the proper cage for her.'

Arram turned and found shelves that supported stacks of wire half domes, one on top of another. They formed rows of different sizes, from tightly woven cricket cages to four that were big enough to house owls. Arram made his choice of dome and base, placing them on a bare counter.

Ozorne sipped his tea as he handed a cup to Arram. Preet craned towards it, but Arram was not letting her try it. Setting it aside, he looked around and saw a small fountain in another corner.

'Is that drinkable?' he asked, pointing. 'Sorry, Ozorne.' He'd interrupted his friend, who was asking the master a question.

Ozorne grinned at Arram. 'Sorry? I haven't had this much adventure in weeks!'

'It is fresh water,' Lindhall told Arram. 'Get some for her.' He looked at Ozorne, who was gathering small, flat dishes. 'You truly love it up here, don't you?'

'Yes, sir!' Ozorne said. 'It's as good as magic, with all the birds, and the smaller animals. Even the larger ones. You never know what will come in the night, either – it isn't always us bringing you something, is it?'

'No, it is not,' Lindhall said as Arram scooped up a handful of water and held it for Preet. She drank daintily, without spills. As he was thinking she was unreal, she flipped several drops into his face with her beak. When he yelped, she fluffed up her feathers and preened.

'You don't act like any baby bird *I've* seen,' he told her. Those were tiny, bald scraps, blind and squalling, or bald heaps in menagerie nests or in Hulak's trees.

'Nor should you expect her to,' Lindhall said.

Ozorne and Lindhall fitted the dome over the hooks in the metal base that kept it secure. Lindhall filled one dish with seed. He handed the other to Arram. 'Water, if you please,' he instructed.

Arram obeyed. Ozorne extracted a small handful of straw for bedding and placed it inside the cage. Arram set the water dish down next to the seed.

'Put her inside,' Lindhall instructed.

Fortunately, Arram was setting Preet on the straw when she realized he meant to leave her there. She waved her tiny wings and began to screech, a powerful noise from so tiny a creature. Lindhall bent and pulled a dark, folded cloth from under the table, then changed his mind and traded it for a white one. He quickly shook it out and covered the cage with it. Slowly Preet quieted. Her last, tiny whistles made Arram's mouth tremble. He felt like a monster for leaving her.

'She will be fine once she sleeps,' Lindhall assured the youths as he ushered them out of the workroom. With a wave of his hand he dismissed the light from the glowing lamps overhead. The room was left in darkness as he closed the door. Arram thought he heard a last, faint peep and bit his lip.

Something chimed delicately nearby.

Lindhall halted the conversation he was having with Ozorne, saying, 'Ah! It's an hour before dawn.'

'What made that sound, Master?' Ozorne asked.

'A wonderful device sent to me from Jindazhen. It can be spelled to chime any hour you wish – very convenient for heavy sleepers, which I am not, or for those who lose track of time, which I so often do,' Lindhall replied. 'If you two hurry off, Arram will have time to bathe before his lesson with Yadeen. Oh, and lads . . .'

The two were about to leave. They faced him.

'Keeping Preet here is a stopgap. I suggest it only because examinations are coming, and she will be distraction enough without Arram having to care for her all day as well as all night. Before the spring term begins I shall make more liberal arrangements for your housing, Arram.'

The youths looked at each other, panicked, but said nothing. Lindhall was a master; they were students. They knew they'd been lucky to room together for so long.

'Now run along,' Master Lindhall ordered as he began to clean up.

'Thank you, Master Lindhall,' Ozorne said. No matter how upset he might be, he never forgot his manners.

'Oh!' Arram exclaimed. 'Yes – yes, thank you, Master.'

Lindhall called after them, 'There is a door to the hall around the corner.'

They took it.

CHAPTER 10

December 3-31, 437

The time until the autumn examinations sped by, thanks to Preet. Ozorne and Varice tried to study with the little bird in the room, but they found her too distracting, and they soon abandoned Arram to her care. Arram didn't find Preet distracting in the least, even when she insisted on perching on his shoulder as he studied.

The only time she made a fuss was late on the fifth night he tried to return her to her cage. As he opened its door, she flapped her wings and squalled. When Arram clasped her to move her more easily, she dug her tiny claws into his sleeve and screeched louder. Master Lindhall arrived, clad in his nightgown, bleary-eyed and unhappy.

'Preet!' he snapped. She silenced. 'I spent my day with cases of hoof rot! I have earned my rest! Continue this and you will go to the birds' menagerie, do you understand me?'

He stormed out and slammed the door after him. Arram waited a few precious moments, thinking, He's just like Ozorne when Ozorne can't sleep.

When he was certain the master would not return, Arram looked at the bird. She had turned herself into a fuzzy ball. 'He didn't mean it, Preet. But I have to sleep, too.'

She raised her head and quietly squawked.

Arram looked at her. 'Is that it, then?' he asked, his voice croaking with weariness. 'What if I roll over and mash you?'

Preet simply regarded him with her wide, sparkling eyes.

Arram sighed. 'I have to put you back in the cage in the morning, understand? No yelling from you. No argument.'

She cackled.

Arram took the cloth that was supposed to cover the cage and made it into a nest beside his pillow. 'There.' He placed the bird on it and blew out his lamp; he was still unable to call small fires or extinguish them without disaster. 'Good night, trouble,' he murmured as he pulled the blanket over his shoulders.

She chuckled softly. He was asleep in an instant.

Lindhall's predawn waking device played its musical tune, forcing a moan from Arram. He didn't know which he hated more, that delightful sound or the fact that he was wide awake before he'd heard it. About to sit up, he halted. Something made him wary. Sensing weight against his neck, he gently placed a hand there and touched feathers. Preet twittered at him.

'How long have you been there?' he demanded as he put her into her cage.

Preet did her best to tuck her head under her stubby wing and pretend that she was slumbering. Arram smiled grimly. 'Very well – you may sleep with me, since you managed to stay unsquashed,' he told her. 'But if you misbehave during the day, or refuse to stay in the cage when I'm not here, I will put you back in the cage at night and wear wax earplugs, understand?'

She made a small chuckling noise, almost like a tiny stream bubbling over rocks.

'That had better mean yes,' he told her.

She made the sound again. Satisfied, Arram straightened his bed. Then he ran to bathe and change into daytime clothes.

The weeks progressed in the same fashion, for the most part. Ozorne and Varice always insisted on visiting Preet for a short time after supper before they adjourned to a library to study for examinations. Arram and Lindhall's students, the ones who worked inside his quarters and across the hall, devised a bargain in which they could visit when the clocks chimed the hour to meet and marvel over the new bird. They stayed only for the turn of a very brief timing glass so that Arram could return to his studies, and they never came after the next-to-last hour of the day, so he might get a good seven hours' sleep. Lindhall popped in now and then to see how Preet was doing.

It was a quiet time of year. Students were always well behaved as term wound down to examinations: even the mischief makers had their noses in their books or their pens glued to papers, trying to make good marks. Even the dining halls and dormitories were calm.

The Friday after he'd spent his last four nights at Lindhall's, Arram came by his own room after supper. He needed clean clothes and to put his dirty things in the basket for the laundresses. The older boys were already in their cubicles, studying, he assumed.

He was turning, having got what he required from the large chest by his bed, when a pair of hands slammed into his chest. He was knocked backwards into his chair. His clothes flew; the chair struck his spine and skull a painful blow.

Laman popped out of his cubicle. 'Hekaja and Hag, what's this?'

Arram ignored him. He glared instead at Diop. 'What is your failing?' he shouted. He struggled to his feet, trembling from the surprise, the pain, and the dirtying of his best shirt for tomorrow and an outing with Prisca.

Diop advanced, his fists raised. 'You've spent every night this week somewhere else, toad pox!' he snapped.

Arram put his own fists up. He'd have preferred to use his Gift, but the penalties for that were far worse than they were for physical brawls. Ozorne had been trying to teach him how to fight. It seemed it was time to put his friend's teachings to the test. He wasn't going to back down. 'What business is it of yours?' he demanded of Diop.

'Did you read Master Girisunika's new rule? If we don't report you, *we're* in trouble, too.' He swung. Arram ducked out of the way and punched back, hitting Diop in the chest. He'd been aiming for the older youth's belly. When he straightened, he met with a fist to the eye. He swung again wildly and missed. His third punch hit Diop's arm, while Diop managed to get him in the belly. He threw up on Diop's expensive crocodile shoes.

'You disgusting — !' Diop cried, grabbing Arram's hair. 'Do you know what these *cost*?'

'That's enough.' Laman grabbed Diop by the shoulders and pulled him back. 'You risk us getting kicked out or put to chores for a term or whatever tortures Girisunika devises.' He then murmured something in Diop's ear.

Arram had kept a hearing spell in his own ears since an instructor gave him a month of chopping faeces-smelling jackal plant for missing an instruction. Now he heard Laman's whisper clearly: 'Remember what she said the last time? It'll be an Empty Room for you.'

Arram shivered. Empty Rooms were supposed to be horrible: no one could work their magic in one, or feel its presence. Even sight and hearing were muted in Empty Rooms. Either Diop had done something truly bad, or Girisunika was overblown.

The two older boys looked at him. Arram opened his trunk and extracted fresh clothing. 'Don't come back!' Diop called as he walked towards the door. 'You'll think what you got was a love tap.'

Arram flinched, but he kept going. The only thing I could say that'd even worry this pig's pizzle is if I threatened to tell Ozorne, he thought. I'm cursed if I'll do that. I'll fight my own battles.

He was tying his shoes when he thought, Or I could tell Enzi that Diop wears boots made of crocodile leather.

Despite the pain, he grinned.

Twice on the way he stopped to put cold water from the

fountains on his eye, but it did little good. By the time he reached Lindhall's fourth floor, all he wanted to do was curl up on the pallet Lindhall had found for him and feel sorry for himself. Every time he dared to touch the bruise, the thing seemed fatter. He hadn't been able to see through it since he walked out of his room.

And I can't sleep or hide, he thought. I have to study. I should have kicked both of them in the gems, even if it isn't well bred.

Lindhall's study was empty, for which he was very grateful. Much to his dismay, the hall was not quiet. Preet was screaming at the top of someone's gigantic lungs, because such a tiny bird was not capable of so much noise.

Stop it! he thought at her as he tried to hurry down the corridor without being heard. Stop, stop, stop—

He thrust open the workroom door to find an irate Lindhall, a laughing Ozorne with his fingers in his ears, and a frantic Varice trying to soothe the small bird in her hands. The moment Preet saw him, she halted her dreadful noise and emitted an actual *growl*.

'Stop it,' he ordered, keeping his face down so the humans couldn't see his bruise. 'I couldn't help the delay.'

'I believe we had an understanding that you would be here after your supper as . . .' Lindhall gripped Arram's chin with a broad hand and gently forced his head up. 'What happened? Please don't lie to me, lad. I was properly cross a moment ago, and I can retrieve it quickly.'

Arram shook his head. Preet was scrabbling at Varice's sleeve with her beak and a claw; he took her from his friend and let the bird tuck herself by his ear. Clucking softly, Preet nibbled gently on his earlobe, as if making certain for herself that he was not badly wounded.

'I see no reason why you can't tell us,' Lindhall said.

'Perhaps it's pride,' Ozorne suggested. 'It would be for me.'

Arram tried to glare at his friend, and found how painful that was when one eye was well swollen. 'Can't I keep some things to myself?' He flinched and looked at Lindhall. 'Meaning no disrespect, sir. But I'm almost grown. If I'd stayed with my family, I'd be making a man's wages by now.' He glanced at Varice. 'I could even be married. Surely I can keep some things to myself if they aren't magical, or they don't interfere with my schooling. Sir.'

Lindhall said nothing at first, thinking about it. 'I understand. Do you still mean to study?'

'We had better,' Ozorne said. 'Examinations start on Sunday.'

'Very well. Arram, why don't you and Preet work in my study? It will be far more comfortable there. Ozorne, would you wait for a moment?' Lindhall asked. 'I'd like to write a pair of notes for you to give my runners.'

As Ozorne waited for Lindhall, Varice and Arram settled in Lindhall's study. Varice sat on the study chair Arram had chosen and ran a soft, cool hand down the side of his face. 'Shall I poison their breakfasts?' she asked. Her eyes were as hard as sapphires.

'Wh-who?' he stammered, but he could tell she had guessed the source of his bruises.

'I wouldn't poison them a *lot*,' she reassured him with a sparkling smile. 'Just enough to keep them vomiting all during examinations. Just so they'll have to spend Midwinter making them up. I can do it. And I needn't even use magic, so I won't get caught.' She shook her head, looking sad. 'So many kinds of sickness this time of year.'

He grabbed her hand. 'Don't,' he said urgently. 'What if you get the wrong—'

'Stop it,' she said fiercely. 'Don't even try. Ozorne and I know poxy well who they were—'

'Well, then, you don't, because one stopped the other,' Arram whispered hotly. 'And I can handle the other one myself! I'm grown now!'

'Varice,' Ozorne said as he walked back into the room. 'Leave be. What were you talking about?'

'Poisoning,' Varice said brightly.

'Oh? Let him do his own poisoning when he gets to it.'

'I don't see how you two can joke about such things,' Arram retorted, shaking. He thought he was going to be sick.

'That's because we're old enough to have developed senses of humour,' Ozorne replied. 'Maybe you'll get one for your birthday.' Gently he ruffled Arram's hair. 'In the meantime, relax. We won't poison anyone unless you ask us to, will we, sweetheart?'

Varice sighed. 'Very well, but it would have been a lovely diversion from examinations. One can only remain wound up over books for so long before one has to do something wild.'

'Ozorne!' Lindhall shouted.

'My master calls,' Ozorne complained, and ran.

Varice picked up Arram's hand and kissed it. 'Don't be angry with me,' she said. 'I was trying to take your mind off the pain.'

Whether it was her suggestion and his panic, or her lips and perfume, she had certainly done that.

Preet croaked for food. Varice laughed. 'Aren't you a jealous thing!' she chided, removing a scrap of bread from her pocket. She offered it to Preet, who gobbled it. 'You're an even more jealous mistress than Prisca!'

'Prisca isn't my mistress,' Arram said automatically – how absurd, to be thinking of mistresses at his age. Then he added, more woefully, 'And she never gets jealous.'

'Because she knows you're too honourable to cheat on her,' Varice reassured him. 'Though only because she doesn't understand you're devoted to a scrawny little tree mite.' She walked down the hall as Preet screeched at her. 'I said "tree mite" and I meant it!' she called back over her shoulder.

'She's the most amazing girl,' Arram murmured, picking Preet up on a finger so he could stroke her. The little bird preened.

Lindhall returned from his office. 'I've sent a runner for a healing mage,' he told Arram. 'I take it you don't want to rouse questions from your teachers with that eye.'

Nausea welled up from Arram's belly. He had to wait to swallow, and wait again, as Lindhall watched with concern. When he tried to speak, the master held up a hand and disappeared into the small kitchen down the hall.

When he returned, he bore a cup of tea. 'Ginger, cinnamon, lemon, spearmint,' he told Arram, handing the cup to him. 'It will soothe both your nausea and the aches from your eye and belly.'

Arram drank in tiny sips until the liquid was cooler, then in gulps. 'It's very good,' he said when he finished it.

Lindhall nodded. 'I think you'll find your head and belly to be far better in the morning. In the meantime, you may undertake the studies you can manage out here – with your friends, if they are willing. When you are ready to sleep, I'll have one of the students manage Preet.'

Arram felt he should protest all this trouble being taken on his behalf, but he was rather sleepy – too much so to protest. He nodded off in the chair, waking only briefly when Ozorne returned to gather Preet. A blanket was placed over him at some point. He remembered nothing until the musical sound told him that it was an hour before dawn.

All the next day, in the classes they shared and when they met between classes, Ozorne complained. It was always the same thing: he didn't understand how Arram survived each day without collapse if he woke frequently in the night to feed a tiny feathered tyrant. Ozorne informed them he could hardly stay awake. By the time they sat down for supper, his sorrow made Arram laugh so hard that tears came to his eyes.

It was there that Diop found them. Laman was nowhere in sight.

'What did you do, bribe someone?' he demanded hotly.

Varice looked up at him and frowned. 'Goddess bless me, who bit you today?'

'Never you mind,' he snapped at her.

That brought both Arram and Ozorne to their feet. Varice

exhaled. 'Boys, I am perfectly capable of taking care of myself. Diop, for all your bragging about your splendid family, you are a guttersnipe,' Varice said. 'My apologies to guttersnipes.'

Diop glared at her, then demanded of Ozorne, 'Well? How did you do it? Who did you bribe?'

Ozorne gently brushed off the front of Diop's robe until the older youth knocked his hand away. 'I have no idea what you're ranting about,' Ozorne murmured.

'No idea, he says,' Diop told everyone at the tables around them. The other students were doing a bad job of pretending not to eavesdrop. 'No idea of a clutch of oafs coming into our quarters without permission, packing up the leftover prince and his bum boy here, leaving things all over the floor – no idea! You're to be lodged with the masters, they said. You, no more than first-years in the Upper Academy, and not even legitimate first-years at that! Who did your sainted mother bribe, *Prince* Ozorne? Or did—'

Using a move Varice had taught him, Arram got Diop's hand in his and shoved it up against the older boy's wrist. Diop gasped: he seemed not to have known how painful a wrist could be when bent into a U.

'Walk,' Arram whispered to Diop. 'Let's walk to the door before the proctors get here.' Out of the corner of his eye he saw Varice and Ozorne rise to intercept the proctors. 'Don't call out,' Arram cautioned, 'or I might get excited and break something.'

With all of his digging and juggling, his hands had become broad and strong. He might not have been able to trade punches with Diop, but his grip kept the older youth's attention. Holding Diop's hand in both of his, he steered his former roommate towards the nearest exit from the dining hall. When Diop opened his mouth to speak or shout, Arram prised the captive little finger away from the others, bending it backwards. Diop gasped.

'You can choose which you'll have broken,' Arram suggested. 'Your wrist or your little finger. Right before examinations, too!

The little finger would heal faster, of course, but all broken bones hurt for a time after they're healed, did you know that?'

He deposited Diop outside the hall and waited to see what would happen next.

The older boy rubbed his freed hand, his mouth quivering. 'This isn't over!' he threatened like a villain in one of the old stories Arram loved to read.

Perhaps it was the knowledge that a god owed him a favour. Perhaps it was simply that he'd had enough. Arram didn't know what caused him to shrug and say, 'Do your best – if you think it's useful. If I were you, though, I'd concentrate on my marks. From what I've been hearing, you'll be lucky if you don't have to retake half of your courses.'

He turned and walked back into the dining hall.

That day, and throughout examinations and the Midwinter festivities, Ozorne lived with all of their belongings in a spare room of the suite shared by Lindhall's runners. He took it in good part, to Arram's relief. The truth was that the normally proud prince was so happy to be a part of Lindhall's large staff that he could have joined Arram on a pallet in the workroom and still have been happy. Arram was simply glad not to be forced to deal with the two older boys any more.

With examinations over, it was the best Midwinter Arram had celebrated yet. A large mahogany chest, ornamented all over in intricate carvings, was given to him by Master Cosmas the day before the holiday began. It had come all the way from the Yamani Islands by way of Arram's family in Tyra. It was a perfect mage's piece, filled with boxes of different sizes that fitted together perfectly inside. Arram quickly learned that such boxes could be switched around to use more room or less and leave space for other things. The chest was from his father, who now studied silk weaving in the Yamani Islands. The rest of his family had placed smaller gifts in each box, to let him know they remembered him.

There were gifts that made him happy from his masters and

from Varice and Ozorne. He had done the same for Varice and
Ozorne, he thought, but when he gave Prisca a book on the
great queens of the Eastern Realms, wonderfully illustrated, her
thank-yous were less than enthusiastic. Her own gift to him was
a set of five linen handkerchiefs. Admittedly, he was forever
using up handkerchiefs and ruining many, but the gift didn't
seem very . . . romantic. She hadn't even embroidered them.

'Perhaps she isn't good at embroidery?' Ozorne suggested.
They were in one of many galleys rowing to the imperial palace
for a Midwinter party hosted by his mother, and Arram had
mentioned his disappointment.

Varice sniffed. 'Arram can do better,' she said.

'Better embroidery?' Ozorne asked, startled. 'Sewing, I'll grant
you, but—'

Varice tapped him on the shoulder with the sweet-smelling
wooden fan Ozorne had given her. 'Don't be a dolt,' she told
him sternly. 'That shirt doesn't fit you.'

'I love Prisca!' Arram protested.

'Do you?' Varice asked as the wind blew a drift of rain under
their cover. 'Weren't you saying just the other day she hardly
seems to listen when you talk to her?'

'I try to discuss things she likes,' Arram said, defending his
ladylove.

'And she says you don't know what you're talking about. I
know *that* much,' Ozorne said as their boat docked. 'Forget about
her for tonight anyway. I know Mother will have invited a
number of people our age who will take our minds off of
everything. Not to mention the splendid food and music!'

He was right. It was a glorious party. Not only was Princess
Mahira smiling, but she also deigned to dance. Twice she accepted
Master Chioké's hand, and once she did a solemn weaver's dance
with Prince Stiloit, second in line for the throne. The prince
might have danced with the princess more, Ozorne confided to
Arram, but he chose instead to take three dances with Varice.

She was blushing heartily when she rejoined her friends after that third dance. 'Apparently it's right what they say, about how bawdy seafaring men are!' she told them as she fanned herself vigorously. 'The jokes that man told me!' She grinned.

Arram and Varice returned early, near midnight. Ozorne remained to join his mother and the emperor for other Midwinter celebrations. Varice collapsed against their boat's cushions with a sigh of relief and made no attempt to hold a conversation until they were halfway across the river. Instead they were bundled under a couple of blankets – the rainy night had become colder – and listened to the river and droplets on the canopy.

'I do love to go to parties with Ozorne,' she confided. 'But I love to return from them with you. Ozorne will talk *all* the way home. He doesn't understand that sometimes you want to think about the lights, and the arrangements, and the lace . . .'

Arram, who could feel the fishes coasting lazily under their boat, smiled.

'And those little bites of papery bread around pomegranates and seasoned ground lamb with turmeric – just a touch. I'd like to try making that. The bread was the trickiest.'

'Like filo,' Arram suggested. He had never been interested in cooking before meeting her. He loved to help her with ideas, but the few times she had allowed him to assist her with cooking had not gone well, with aftermaths that involved scrubbing, scraping, and – once – repainting the wall of the kitchen they had used.

'Filo, exactly, only far more fragile! I'll have to experiment.' The boat was drawing up to the dock when she said, 'Will I ever have such wonderful friends as you and Ozorne again?'

Alarmed, he handed her to the boatman reaching for her from the dock. 'Were you planning on getting rid of us?' he asked, scrambling up the ladder after her.

'No, no!' she protested as Arram cast protection from the rain over them both. 'But a girl needs more than two friends in a lifetime.'

The midnight bells began to chime, signalling the change from midnight to the first hour.

'The Winter's Crone is here,' Varice said, and shivered. Arram pulled the blanket up higher around her shoulders and tucked it in. She leaned against him and sighed. 'But she brings good fortune, if we have the courage and stamina to seek it, and she holds the secrets to magic in her hands.' She sat up, excited. 'And she must like us, because look at us! We rise and keep rising – all three of us with more masters handling our lessons than most who graduate with their certificates ever see. As long as we work hard and please the gods, we'll keep rising!' She settled back against Arram's shoulder. 'It's going to be a wonderful year. I can feel it in my bones.'

THE IMPERIAL UNIVERSITY OF CARTHAK

The School for Mages

The Upper Academy
SCHEDULE OF STUDY, SPRING TERM, 438 H.E.

Student: Arram Draper
Learning Level: Independent

Second Morning Bell

Stone Magic – Yadeen

Third Morning Bell

Fire Magic – Cosmas, breakfast supplied

Morning Classes

Reptiles – Lindhall Reed, instructors
Tribal Magic – Urukut Ahilep
Medicines – Ramasu, instructors

Lunch – Noon Bell
Afternoon Classes

Advanced Charms – Faziy aHadi
Illusions: Birds – Dagani
Plants – Hulak
Water Magic – Sebo

Supper – Seventh Afternoon Bell
Extra Study at Need

CHAPTER 11

January 1-9, 438

The day after the end of the Midwinter holiday, Ozorne treated his two friends to a boat ride from the university to the port city of Thak's Gate, at the end of the Zekoi. The season wasn't ideal for boat rides, but they bore the winter rains for the excitement of visiting the markets, which were open and booming, filled with people from all around the Inland Sea. They came back exhausted and happy, carrying their purchases under their waterproof cloaks.

When Ozorne and Arram reached Master Lindhall's lodgings, they discovered he had planned a surprise for them. One of the fourth-year helpers, a stocky young black woman whose expertise lay with reptiles, encountered them in the hall and snagged Ozorne's arm. 'Come and see,' she told him, dragging him into the rooms she shared with two other fourth-year helpers. 'You know there's only three of us in these rooms now, since Baaro went east to study herds.'

Confused, Ozorne nodded. Inside the main lounge, the other two occupants – one male, one female – lazed on broad couches and read. They waved as the woman, Nyoka, opened a door. She indicated the room beyond. 'We did our best, but doubtless you'll want to shift things around.'

Ozorne went inside; Arram followed. Someone had brought Ozorne's things from his cramped quarters to these far bigger ones. He now had shelves, a good-sized bed, a proper desk and chair, and a standing cupboard in addition to his chest. It lacked only a window. '*Much* better,' the prince said as he dumped his belongings on the bed.

'There's no window,' Arram pointed out.

Ozorne shrugged. 'Who needs a window when you have a scrying mirror?' he asked. 'I've become very good at finding the lake and the woods at Mother's home whenever I want.' He led the way into the sitting room the four shared. 'This is wonderful!' he told them.

Nyoka took Arram's arm. 'Now come. You're dripping.' She towed him across the hall to the room that belonged to Lindhall's personal assistant. He was not there. For that matter, his collection of gaudy drapes and brightly coloured bowls was gone as well. Instead the bed was covered with plain red blankets and pillows, the floor with a brown rug. A desk fitted with shelves above it stood beside a tall set of bookshelves already partly stocked. There was a chair and a padded stool big enough to sit on. A table stood by the window. Branches of candles stood on the desk and table.

And on a lesser table, tucked into the space between the bed and the door, was Preet's cage. The minute she saw Arram she began to twitter and sing.

Arram looked at Nyoka, trembling. He knew what he thought, but he wasn't on the level that Lindhall would require from his assistant. 'I don't understand,' he said.

The door next to the desk was already open. Now Lindhall entered. 'My assistant, like several others among my group of students, is off to . . .'

'Amar District,' Nyoka told him with a smile. 'He forgets details about human beings,' she explained to Arram. 'Master Lindhall has asked me to take his tasks, but he can't have a woman living in the assistant's quarters with him alone. People will talk. I'll be across the hall. If he shoves in here in the middle of the night, just come and get me.' She grinned cheekily at Lindhall. 'Though we did rig a summoning bell. Except he seems to have misplaced his end.'

Lindhall tried to frown at Nyoka. 'I'm sure it's in my study somewhere.'

Arram looked at them. 'Is it on wire?'

'No, cotton cord,' Nyoka said.

'Better still,' Arram told her. 'I could probably find wire, but cotton should be easier.'

Lindhall raised his eyebrows. 'There are hooks in the hall between our doors. Hang up your cape – silly things. Useful only for shedding water. Hang it up, and you can come and try.'

It took Arram only a few moments to apply Master Hulak's spell for finding a particular plant. The leading end of the cord had become trapped under two fat books on songbirds and a cold teapot in the master's study. With the problem solved and Nyoka chuckling to herself, Arram retreated to his new home.

Lindhall followed him. 'I promise not to be in and out,' he assured Arram, 'but I did want to draw your eyes to this. I had it made over the holiday.' He picked up a piece of cloth from the desk and offered it to Arram, who took it. It was a blue pouch with a long, thick cord attached. The bottom bulged flatly. When Arram put his hand inside, he found a wooden rod was attached to the sides near the bottom, while at the bottom itself was a wooden disc to hold the sides apart.

Arram smiled at the tall Northerner. 'For Preet?'

Lindhall smiled back. 'You know what she is like if you leave her at night. I now feel free to inform you that if she is left completely alone during the day, she raises a very similar amount of noise.'

Stricken with guilt, Arram said, 'Master, I'm sorry!'

'Which is why I did not tell you before,' Lindhall replied, waving off the apology. 'Apparently sunbirds are very sociable. From all I have learned, and you may read *that* book as a start

on what we know of immortals that fly in general' – he pointed
to one of Arram's new bookshelves – 'sunbirds do not strike out
on their own. They remain in their original flocks, or when a
flock is deemed too large, they separate into smaller ones. To
Preet, you are her flock. Other humans – Ozorne, Varice, one
or two of my students, myself – will do, but in fact she wants
to be with you. I have sent notices to your teachers and to the
cooks that Preet will be with you throughout the day. Unless,
of course, Master Sebo takes you underwater.'

Preet made an ugly croaking sound. Picking her up to tickle
her chest, Arram noticed that she had grown since their first
meeting. She now filled his palm and reached the middle
knuckles of his hand.

Lindhall was chuckling. 'She doesn't mind splashing in her
water dish, but apparently walking into it is not to her taste.'

Arram stroked Preet's head. 'Don't worry, I won't take you
into the river.' He looked up at his teacher. 'I can't thank you
. . . This is so wonderful . . .'

'You need not thank me. I have sick rabbits and lizards whose
cages must be cleaned,' the master replied. 'Whenever you are
free, you should check the sickrooms to clean out those areas
that need it, and refill such dishes as require it. During the day,
gather up old teacups and dishes and set them on a tray outside
my door for the floor's servants to take away. And occasionally
I will require help around here.'

Arram could hardly breathe. Work with the sick creatures?
Help Master Lindhall? He felt as if he had gone to the Divine
Realms.

'At least, now that you are here with Preet, you will have a
proper bed and you will be able to sleep until dawn,' Lindhall
said, clapping him on the shoulder. 'Welcome to the menagerie,
as my other helpers say. Now, off to supper with you.'

Arram hurried to meet his friends, Preet chuckling from inside
her new pouch. It was going to be a splendid term.

* * *

The three friends spent most of their free time during the remainder of the term in Lindhall's domain. Varice worked on medicines at the direction of the older students, who told Lindhall of her precision with the measurements. It may have looked like work, and for Arram and Ozorne it sometimes smelled like work, but they thoroughly enjoyed themselves.

Prisca sent Arram a couple of notes asking if he wished to accompany her into the city. Once she stopped by. He was always too busy to go with her. He offered to show her around when she visited, but one look into the room where they had a group of snakes and lizards sent her on her way. Arram would have gone after her, but he had a number of tasks to do. He'd also discovered that Preet didn't care for her.

Before the friends knew it, the free week was over. Their spring term schedules arrived the day before classes began. Reviewing his, Arram saw only one change. He was now taking advanced charms with a specific teacher, someone named Faziy aHadi. It was an old name from western Carthak – female, he was pretty sure.

Together with the schedule came marks, always a matter of slight discord between him and Ozorne. Arram was unhappy to find more sixes and sevens for the last term, but not surprised. Diop had worn on him, and the arrival of Preet had distracted him in December. He would just have to buckle down this term.

Over breakfast Ozorne noticed that he had a mark lower than Arram's, though he ranked higher – as usual – in illusions. His marks for war magic were also high. He joked about it being good that he knew Arram was cleverer than he was, but his eyes sent a different message. Arram shrugged. Ozorne would feel better in a week or so.

He left his friends early so he could perform his day's chores for Lindhall and get a good night's sleep. Unlike them, he still had Yadeen's class and the one with Cosmas before the school day began. He wished Ozorne studied with Cosmas as well, but Ozorne now took fire magic later in the day, with Chioké.

With the new term they had some new workrooms in which to meet with instructors. These were separate buildings on the western side of the School for Mages, beside the service road used by tradesmen to bring goods to the mages and kitchens. All three of the friends had been excited about this the day before: they had to be moving ahead if they were to be admitted to the rooms where the mages did their deepest spell-work.

Arram's first experience in one naturally was with Yadeen. He wasn't sure what he expected, but the long, bright place with windows set near the ceiling was not it. The tables and counters were polished light-coloured wood, as were the tall stools. Stones were arrayed in tidy square boxes on shelves six and seven layers high on both sides of the room. Cabinets supported the counters. Braziers stood in each corner, supplying warmth – the morning was cold. One also supported a teapot.

Arram produced Preet for Yadeen to look at, but if Preet intrigued him, he showed no sign of it. He simply ordered Arram to place her near a working brazier so he could juggle unencumbered.

Arram was all thumbs when Yadeen tossed him a piece of amethyst in place of a fourth ball, but it seemed that at least one irregular object in the circle was the rule for the first half hour. For the second half, Yadeen introduced him to the art of magically breaking a crystal the size of his fist into many tinier crystals – or at least, attempting to do so. Arram reached the end of the hour sweaty, without removing so much as a speck of crystal with his Gift. Even worse, he could have sworn he heard Preet make a rude noise when he stopped. He was wistfully dreaming of life as a pedlar or beekeeper. His wrists were so tired that they ached.

'I don't understand,' he complained to Yadeen when they ended. 'It seemed easy enough when we split the chunks of marble into straight-sided pieces.'

Yadeen raised a heavy brow. 'I believe I was the mage in charge,' he reminded Arram gently.

Blushing, Arram gathered up his belongings and Preet, then thanked Yadeen and left the workroom. At least Cosmas's workroom was next door.

The breakfast that waited there helped. While Varice and Arram used pancakes with pistachios to scoop up eggs, Cosmas fed Preet whatever she expressed a wish for in between sips of tea. When the two young people sighed with content, the master told Preet, 'Try the seeming of a blackbird fledgling from here on. It will match your size better.' To Arram he said, 'Even the young creatures of the Divine Realms are more intelligent than our adult animals. How did you come by her?'

Arram didn't want to lie to this man who had been so good to him. Miserably he replied, 'I really can't say, Master Cosmas.'

The master looked him over, and then patted his shoulder. 'Never mind. I hope you'll be able to tell me eventually.'

Preet voiced a soft musical note that spiralled into the air. Her blend of light and dark grey feathers shifted to speckled brown on her belly.

Arram and Varice gawped at her.

'I thought she might possess her own magic. Now she is palm-sized and matches her feathers.' Cosmas rubbed his hands. 'Where did we stop? Drawing heat from the air itself. Varice, let me see you try.' Cosmas lit a candle. 'Give it a go.'

Arram's next class was with Lindhall himself. Other students were also present, including Varice and Ozorne. The prince waved to Arram and yawned; morning was not his best time. Arram settled at a corner desk – this room was a regular classroom – and propped the bird's pouch on his lap.

Lindhall turned away and began to write on the immense slate board on one side of the room. 'We shall spend this term in the examination of how reptiles give birth and raise their young. Also, of how parts of reptiles – skins taken when they are shed, eggshells left behind, bones once they are deceased – may be put in magic. We will have no capture or killing of wild reptiles under my auspices, understand?'

Arram grinned with excitement. This was exciting! Varice opened her notebook and readied her quill, while Ozorne sat up. Preet perched on Arram's shoulder, tucked against his neck. Once there, she fluffed her feathers and did not move again for the length of the class. Since Arram was in a corner, no one noticed her until it came time to go.

'Arram minds her for me,' Lindhall called over the student's exclamations. 'She is not a pet. Do you really wish to be late to your next classes?'

Ozorne and Arram trotted towards their class on tribal magic. 'You should have something more exciting for her than that dull old bag,' he told Arram. 'Something with more padding if you're going to bump her around like that. Varice would sew something if you asked nicely. Or Prisca.'

Arram made a face. 'I don't know about Prisca. She was having supper with some fellow from the School of Law last night, didn't you see?'

'Perhaps she's trying to make you jealous,' Ozorne suggested. 'You pretty well ignored her over the break.'

'I told her I was working for Master Lindhall. She has to understand how things are. And I don't like it when people play games like making other people jealous.' Arram kicked at one of the rocks lining the path and hurt his toe. Preet ran her beak over his ear – was she consoling him?

Ozorne held up a hand, panting. 'Stop. I have to catch my breath – I can't walk in all sweaty and gasping. I still think Prisca is trying to give you a hint.'

Arram looked down. 'I think so, too. Just not the "I'm making you jealous so you'll pay more attention to me" sort of hint.'

Ozorne patted him on the shoulder unoccupied by a bird. 'Too bad, but cheer up. There are other girls. Let's go to class.'

Master Urukut, in tribal magic, only glanced at Preet. 'That would be the bird you are minding for Lindhall?' the Apalite mage enquired. 'I will not allow it to distract the class.'

He waved off Arram's explanation that Preet would do no

such thing and pointed for them to take their seats. Since Preet was napping, the master took no more interest in her, nor did anyone else. Arram sighed quietly with relief.

The last class of the morning was held in Master Ramasu's large workroom, where Arram was the only student. When the big, broad-shouldered man looked him over, Arram felt compelled to produce Preet. Seeing her, the university's chief healer raised an eyebrow.

'Sir, this is Preet?' Arram said, though it came out more as a question. 'I think Master Lindhall mentioned I was caring for her?' He knew he sounded like a very junior student, but he couldn't help it. Ramasu the Cloud-Handed was the greatest healer south of the Inland Sea. Arram knew how privileged he was to be learning from the man, and how amazing it was for him to be the only student in the room at the moment.

Ramasu inspected first the bird and then Arram with eyes that were a strange mix of grey and brown. At last he said, 'That little bird will get you into more trouble than you can handle, boy.'

Arram scuffed his foot on the floor. 'Everyone knows I'm just minding her for lessons, sir. And a friend. Master Lindhall thought that since she's in my care, I should do a study of her.' He was talking too much, so he clamped his teeth together, hard.

'Indeed.' The master did not sound convinced. 'Do you know how long she is to be in your care?'

Arram tucked Preet back into her pouch. 'The friend wasn't precise.'

Ramasu turned to the big slate hung on one of the narrow sides of the room and picked up the chalk. 'Do you know why he was not precise?'

'He said there might be difficulties,' Arram replied, looking over the mage's shoulder. Ramasu wrote in large, sharp letters, *Sunbird?*

Arram gulped. 'Yes, sir, I know.' He shrugged. 'What can I

do, when someone vastly important asks for so small a favour?'
Reaching into the pouch, he petted the bird's soft head with a
finger. 'She's no trouble, though I might catch some one day, if
I'm cornered by somebody who won't wait for an explanation.
Somebody *truly* great. Outside the university, so to speak.'

'Demand a hearing before Minoss,' Ramasu told him. 'Such
a request must be honoured by all gods. Once you are before
the Great Judge, tell the truth. Bad things happen to those who
lie to him. You will be fine once Minoss hears you.'

Arram eyed the master. 'You say that as if you didn't exactly
learn it from a book.'

Ramasu looked down with a smile. 'I have not always been
the sober fellow who teaches herbs and simples. Now, when
was your – blackbird – last fed?'

Preet was nibbling on Arram's finger. Hurriedly he dug into
an outer pouch of his workbag and brought out a wheat roll.
Preet clambered up the arm still in her pouch. As soon as she
had a grip on Arram's wrist, she strained towards the shelf that
lay along one long wall beneath windows of real glass. Among
the healer's tools placed there was a plate of figs and olives.

'She seems to have indicated a preference,' Ramasu said.
'Since she is not a true bird, whatever her camouflage signifies,
we must trust that she knows what is good for her. Set the food
and the bird on the floor in that corner, if you will.'

Arram obeyed.

'Now,' the master said, indicating one of two walls of shelves
full of jars and bottles, 'my assistants have worked with you,
but I have not. What I have heard is . . . interesting, so I have
arranged this examination. You see I have turned these containers
to conceal the labels. Use your Gift to identify common herbs
and healers' potions, and describe their uses. That short ladder
by the door will let you reach the top shelf. Begin where you
please.'

Arram looked at the shelves and at his shaking hands. After
all he had heard of this man, he did *not* want to make a fool of

himself. He took off his robe, folded it, and set it where he wouldn't trip over it, along with his workbag. Ramasu took a seat on a tall stool near Preet.

Arram placed the ladder at one end of the shelves and stepped to the top. Drawing a deep breath, he let it go, summoned a cord of his Gift into his fingers, and touched the first jar there. The moment his power began to flow through his hand, his brain cooled and his body settled.

'Aloe in balm form,' he said. 'For burns and scrapes. It can also be used raw for insect bites and burns.' He touched the next container. 'Anemone. Sedation, dysentery, and fevers. Users must be wary of getting it on the skin. It can blister.' Another jar. 'Angelica. For women if they have trouble with monthly bleeding, to strengthen a body recovering from disease, to steady an irregular heart.' On he went, skipping those he did not know. He finished more than a hundred jars before the bell rang for lunch.

'Very good,' Ramasu said as Arram shoved his hair back from his face. He'd become very excited about naming the jars' contents and what they did. 'I am impressed,' the healer admitted. 'You know more than most second-year healing students. Now, tomorrow I must go to one of the city infirmaries. You shall go with me. I am in and out, so my students will continue to teach some of your lessons. You and I shall muddle along, however. Anatomy next. Have you studied musculature? Veins?'

Arram shook his head to both. 'Only skeletons, sir.'

Ramasu picked up a book from a nearby shelf. 'Read two chapters for Tuesday, when you and I will be back here. We will begin with veins. As for your friend . . .' Somehow during the last two hours Preet had migrated to his lap. Ramasu handed her to Arram. 'You may have her back. Off with you both. A promising start, Arram.'

He didn't think he'd breathe again after a welcome like that, but somehow he made it to the dining hall. Ozorne waited for him at the door. 'I see from your face it went well and the great man didn't crush you,' he said, clapping Arram on the shoulder. 'Very good. We thought we'd eat outside, since it's not so bad and not so cold. Varice is holding a table, and I'm getting her lunch as well as mine. How is your friend?'

'On my other shoulder,' Arram said as they went in and grabbed trays and utensils. 'She charmed Master Ramasu.' He turned so Ozorne could see Preet.

'She's a charming girl,' Ozorne said cheerfully.

Once they had their meals, they went outside to join Varice. Swiftly she cleared her bag and Ozorne's from the table. 'Where were you?' she demanded. 'I had to fight off three parties of idiots, as if this was the only spot.'

'We came as fast as we could,' Arram said. He lifted Preet from his shoulder and offered her to Varice. 'Let Preet soothe you.'

Preet was talking softly to Varice when a stocky young man asked, 'May we sit here?'

He and a slightly taller young woman had approached them, trays in their hands. He was a Northerner with the remains of a gold tan, hazel eyes, and golden-brown hair. Under his white Upper Academy first-year robe he wore a green tunic and brown breeches. Varice dimpled when he smiled warmly at her. Arram and Ozorne, who had just begun eating, exchanged frowns. They were always a bit mistrustful of anyone who set out to charm Varice right away.

His companion was a dark-brown-skinned woman from one of the middle districts of the empire. She had black eyes, slightly pockmarked cheeks, and coarse black hair. She wore it braided and fixed in coils with enamelled pins. Under her own first-year robe she wore a maroon tunic and thin yellow leggings, both made of wool. She looked them over. 'He is Tristan Denane,' she said. 'I am Gissa Rachne.'

'Have pity,' Tristan said, still smiling at Varice. 'I think yours is the only table where everyone isn't complaining of how miserable they are to return to class. Those who aren't complaining? They still look decidedly unpleasant. Except your group. You seem pleasant.'

'They'll still look unpleasant if you sit with us,' Ozorne told Gissa. 'We're not the most popular students here.'

'We'll take our chances,' she said with a wry smile. 'These trays are heavy.'

Sensing that his friends meant to agree, Arram moved closer to Varice so Gissa could fit between him and Ozorne. Varice made room for Tristan as Preet hopped back to Arram.

'Does anyone else have a pet?' Tristan asked. 'I haven't seen any.'

'She's not a pet,' Arram said, holding Preet against his chest and running a finger down her back.

'Arram minds her for one of our masters. He isn't exactly an everyday student, so don't take him for an example,' Ozorne cautioned. 'He's got single teachers for nearly all of his courses.'

Tristan raised his eyebrows. 'My congratulations.'

'You wouldn't say that if you could see his schedule,' Varice said, spooning up mouthfuls of chickpea soup. Pausing, she asked, 'Tristan, you're from the North, yes?'

'Maren,' Tristan replied. 'Gissa is from the Amar District here. I've been one of her father's students for the last two years, until he said we'd both do better here.'

'Welcome,' Ozorne said. 'We've introduced Arram, and his blackbird fledgling is Preet. He's from Tyra originally – Arram, that is.' He offered Preet a piece of bean, which she ate. He went on. 'I'm Ozorne. I'm Carthaki. She's Varice, from Tusaine originally.'

Gissa nodded at Varice. 'What classes do you take?' she asked. 'Have you got that scary fellow Chioké for the introductions to the university and the city?'

'Oh, goodness, no,' Varice replied. 'We've been here for years. We know the university and the capital. Ozorne even knows the palace pretty well.'

'If you like, we can take you around,' Ozorne offered. 'Chioké isn't bad, but he doesn't know the useful places. We can show you ones that don't charge too much. The introductory tours are well enough, but they tend to rush things a bit.'

'Thank you – we appreciate that!' Tristan said.

'Ozorne, I don't know if I can help,' Arram reminded him quietly. 'I have all that extra work.'

'Why extra? Are they punishing you for something?' Gissa enquired. She smiled crookedly at Arram.

'Actually, they are – he's clever,' Ozorne said.

'That *is* an affliction,' Tristan remarked with a smile for Arram. 'But I think we'll take our chances with you, eh, Gissa?'

'Of course. You aren't as *loud* as those others.' Gissa nodded towards the main dining hall. 'I came from a small village.'

Arram understood *that*, with his love of libraries. 'There are quiet areas,' he said as his friends nodded.

'And it gets better as the term goes on,' Varice added. 'People will have work to do. They won't be lively enough to carry on like this.'

Preet chose that moment to give voice to a soft, enchanting trill of song that made even Gissa melt and Tristan grin. When the bell to prepare for class chimed, they all sighed and reluctantly gathered their things.

As Arram and Ozorne waited for the young women and Tristan to emerge from the washrooms after lunch, Ozorne nudged his friend. 'Tristan and Gissa seem all right, don't they?'

Arram looked at him. Ozorne missed having more than two friends, that was clear. 'They're all right for now. We'll have to see.'

'Our luck has to turn sometime,' Ozorne said. To the returning girls and Tristan he said, 'I have truth-reading now. So does Varice.'

'I have it,' Gissa said, reviewing the schedule on a parchment in her bag.

'As do I,' Tristan announced.

Arram shrugged. 'Charms. Faziy aHadi – I don't recognize her name.'

'Poor Arram.' Ozorne looked at Tristan's schedule. 'The rest of us are all in the same room! Well, there's luck!'

'So it is,' Tristan said. He offered an arm to each young woman. 'Let us go and immerse ourselves in the truth.'

Ozorne followed them, smiling. Arram looked down into the pouch. Preet had tucked her head under her wing and was snoozing.

'I suppose it's just us, then,' he murmured, and set off for class.

Faziy aHadi had a workroom near those used by Yadeen, Cosmas, and Ramasu. He had to run to get there. He was late even so, and drenched by the rain that had begun to fall while he used outdoor shortcuts.

The woman who greeted him at the door was just his height at five feet ten inches, strong-bodied, with bronze-brown skin. Her wide white smile over a full lower lip dazzled him. She had a short, broad nose, dimples, and sparkling black eyes with long lashes. Her splendid black hair was wrapped in coils and secured with braids and gold hairpins in the shapes of tiny monkeys. She wore a blue wool dress under a yellow adept's robe, which startled him – he expected her to be a red-robed master.

'You are surely Arram,' she said, urging him inside. 'Isn't the weather vile? I had lunch with Lindhall Reed – his description of you was very good. But I was told you have a bird in your care.'

'Oh, Preet!' Arram had kept her under his arm and robe, out of the weather. He fished the little bird out of the pouch as she grumbled. Carefully he showed Faziy his new friend.

'But how adorable!' she exclaimed, holding out a hand for Preet to examine. 'A blackbird fledgling?'

'We believe so, um – Master?' Arram wasn't sure what to call her.

The woman laughed as Preet walked onto her palm and up

her arm. 'Faziy will do. Technically I have taken all the charms classes to be granted a mastery, but I had to take leave of the university for a time before I could complete my credential. It was decided I can teach charms to the Upper and Lower Academies while I finish my mastery.' She saw Arram's eyes go to the items on the shelves and the walls. 'Go ahead – look around.'

He did so, listening to the sounds she exchanged with Preet. The teacher knew a number of birdcalls, trying them out when the youngster didn't respond to blackbird sounds. He thought briefly that they should have realized this might be a problem, but he forgot about that in his fascination with the things on the wall shelves. They ranged from small metal, stone, and straw charms to necklaces, bracelets, dolls, braided or knotted strings, hand-sized mirrors, and wax or clay figures.

There were also several pieces like branches or sticks thickly coated in sand. One of them formed the shape of an O. He stretched his hand out over a slender shape. His hand tingled, and the hairs on the back of his fingers and wrist stood on end.

'Mages of long ago called them fulgurite,' Faziy said over his shoulder. Arram flinched. He didn't even know the teacher had come up to him. 'They are what happens when lightning strikes sand – well, very strong lightning. Beneath the surface it goes solid. We only know this when the sand on top washes off or is blown away.' She rested a hand on his shoulder. 'Go on. Pick it up. It was fused a long time ago; it won't hurt you.'

Arram gently wrapped his hand around a branch of it. He feared it would crumble to pieces, but it was as hard as stone. The tiny prickles raced up his arm again. 'There's lightning still in it!' he exclaimed, letting go.

She chuckled, a lovely, low sound in his ear. 'That's your imagination, my lad. The lightning was gone from these pieces centuries ago. *Ages* ago. You've been to the museum?' Arram nodded. 'You've seen the skeletons of the giant lizards and birds, the huge elephants? It's all from that time.'

Arram opened his mouth to argue, and closed it. Whether she had finished her classes to be a master or no, she was close to being one. It was not his place to argue. He did ask, 'Why is that round one so different? The others just look like sticks.'

Faziy laughed. 'Oh, that! I made that one!'

Arram gawped at her; even Preet squeaked.

Faziy looked down her nose at the little bird. 'You're not even supposed to be able to make sounds like that.' She looked at Arram. 'I didn't say it was *easy*.'

'You said it requires lightning!' Now it was time for him to squeak.

She smiled. 'And it does. I am lucky enough that the lightning snakes find me amusing. When they're about, sometimes I can coax them to help me do things. But it took years of practice, and knowledge, and study. Half of the time it doesn't work, because they're wilful creatures.' She flicked the bird on the beak with a finger. 'Most of the mages who try it incinerate themselves.'

Arram only grasped one idea out of all that she said. 'L-l-lightning snakes?'

Faziy sighed and settled into one of the chairs at the room's big table. She motioned for Arram to sit in another.

'Among the tribes, it is known that there is magic in far more things than the school mages believe,' she told him. 'Well, lightning snakes ride with lightning in the season of storms. Some think they are the lords of lightning and give them names. Some think they are simply creatures like the immortals of old, the centaurs and Stormwings. I think they are more like gods. If there's a big storm when we have class, I'll try to show you some. Now, where did you end when you took charms the last time?'

Arram left the class dazed and filled with wonder. Never mind that he had made a botch of a twisted straw-and-wire charm for good crops. The thought of snakes made of lightning enchanted him. He couldn't wait to see one!

He arrived early to his next class, which gave him private time to introduce Dagani to the sleeping Preet. Dagani eyed the bird and indicated a place where Arram could place her pouch out of the way as he worked.

'Lindhall told Faziy and me about her over lunch,' the master said. 'I understand you just came from Faziy's class.'

Arram nodded. Abruptly he said, 'She told me about lightning snakes. Have you ever seen any?'

'No,' Dagani replied slowly, tracing an outline of something on a worktable. It rose, turning and twisting as Arram watched, fascinated. 'But the desert shamans create their seemings in the fire. They want the seemings to find the real snakes, and call them to help the warriors in battle.' The outline fattened, turned jagged, and grew golden in colour. Jagged wings sprouted in its sides, two pairs. The head formed, long and narrow, with red-orange hot coal eyes. It turned its head towards the door as Ozorne, Varice, and Tristan entered. They'd been chattering until they saw the lightning snake. As it rose to stand on the tip of its tail, flapping its wings, they froze.

The lightning snake hissed. Ozorne and Tristan immediately called up protective shields for themselves and Varice, creating a conflict – their Gifts did not mesh, and they had not thought to make allowance for another mage's work. Sparks flew along with vile-smelling smoke, making the lightning snake screech. Arram called a breeze that took both smell and sparks out the still-open door, while with a hand gesture Dagani erased her simulacrum.

'I would say we have several lessons for today,' she told her students as the last of the smoke dissolved. 'Lesson the first: learn if protection is even needed. Lesson the second: learn if the magics of your allies are compatible with yours. If they are not, work the charm that makes yours compatible with theirs. How many of you read the introduction in *The Upper Academy: General Magic*?'

Arram and Varice raised their hands. Ozorne and Tristan found somewhere else to look.

Dagani rubbed her head. 'The word to reveal if the magics of others are compatible with yours, as well as the sigils that make your Gift temporarily compatible with that of those nearby – both of these things are in the introduction. They are in the introduction because they are intended to *introduce* you to working magic with other mages. We shall practise these things, the four of you, while you decide which living creature you will create as your first simulacrum. Arram, do *not* choose a lightning snake,' she said when he opened his mouth.

Arram closed it. He'd been going to try just that.

'The larger the choice, the more power it consumes. The more magical the choice, the more power it consumes,' the master warned. 'The simulacrum of a lightning snake would kill a beginner before that beginner even completed it.' Dagani looked at them all. 'Choose a seat.' She pointed a scarlet-tinted fingertip at Tristan. 'Your name?'

'Tristan Denane, Master,' he said, meeting her gaze.

'Tristan, tell me the word which reveals whether another's Gift is compatible with your own. If you don't know it, look it up.'

By the end of their time all four agreed – once they were outside the classroom – that the lovely, gracious Dagani was one of the hardest teachers they'd ever had, though Arram was willing to wager on Yadeen against her. Dagani had yet to throw a wooden ball at him.

It was a relief to change into sandals and his rough woollen shirt and breeches and report to Hulak in one of his glass winter houses. If the master was impressed with Preet, he neglected to mention it. Instead he instructed her to eat no seeds unless he gave them to her himself. He then fed her so much seed Arram feared she might burst after her lunch.

Sebo's reaction was a little different from those of the other teachers. By then the bird was awake and happy to ride Arram's shoulder once more. When the old master emerged from her home, she stopped in front of Arram and eyed his passenger.

As she did so, a frown grew upon her face, blossoming into a scowl of fearsome proportions. She smashed the foot of her staff into the sandy dirt.

'*Enzi!*' she bellowed with more volume than one of her years should have been able to manage.

The crocodile god was there. *I was napping* was all he got to say before she gave him a frightful blow across the back with her stick.

Arram darted for what protection he and Preet could find in the hut. From its shelter, hiding behind the open door, he could only hear cracks and a few words – 'Student . . . danger . . . mischief . . . troublemaker' – when the great crocodile wasn't roaring. Finally there was a long silence. Arram peered through the gap below the top hinge, only to encounter a glittering, baleful black eye.

'And *you* were fool enough to say yes to him!' Sebo hissed. 'Come outside!'

Arram didn't think. 'I don't want to,' he replied. Pondering his reaction afterwards, he was still convinced only a fool would want to face Sebo in that mood.

She slid her fingers through the crack and grabbed him by the nose. '*Outside,*' she ordered. She released him.

Arram emerged, rubbing his poor, abused nose. Enzi was still present. The remains of the shattered staff lay on his broad back. He glared at Sebo. *I am not the worst thing that will happen to your precious boy,* he told her.

'Please don't say that,' Arram begged. 'If you won't tell me why—'

I will not. You have a destiny. You aren't allowed to know it.

'Take back the bird,' Sebo ordered.

I dare not, Enzi retorted, just as Arram cried, 'No!' and Preet shrieked. Swiftly Preet began to scold, but she was not looking at Enzi. She was looking at Sebo.

Finally the old woman pointed at her. 'Very well, very well, be silent, or I will *make* you be silent!'

Preet gave a last squawk. Arram tucked her into the corner of his elbow and murmured to her that everything would be fine.

To Enzi, Sebo said, 'If harm comes to him because of you, I will make you pay.'

Yes, you irascible mortal. And also, I owe you an ebony stick for the one I graciously *allowed you to break on my poor back.* Enzi vanished, leaving a hollow in the dirt and the remains of Sebo's staff.

'You didn't have to be so angry with him,' Arram protested. 'I don't mind looking after her. Neither do my masters.'

'Because you're a boy, and daft by nature,' Sebo grumbled. 'And they are air-dreaming fools! I was going to teach you how to dowse for water today, but I have a headache now. Come in. You can read about dowsing, and we'll try it tomorrow if it doesn't rain. And you . . .' Moving quickly, she scooped Preet out of Arram's elbow hold. 'You are not to distract him. You may sing me to sleep.'

To Arram's surprise, Preet did just that. She nearly did it for him as well. He was just starting to nod off when the bell for the end of classes rang out. Arram sighed with relief. He didn't know about Preet, but he was ready for a nap after his brief night and the day's excitement.

CHAPTER 12

February–March 438

One early February Saturday Arram came back from supper with his friends to find a note on his door from Master Cosmas.

> *Dear Arram,*
>
> *Family business calls me away for a week. I have arranged for Master Chioké to join your instruction with that of Ozorne's.*
>
> *Be sure to thank Chioké. It is unusual for one master to welcome another's students into his workroom, and Chioké is stricter concerning these matters than most. He must value Ozorne's opinion, or mine, or both, to permit this.*
>
> *– Cosmas*

'You know I love you, to agree to be up at such a disgusting hour,' Ozorne announced when Arram arrived for class the next morning. His friend was leaning against the workroom wall, observing his approach with bleary eyes. 'Do you even *know* how many of those things you have in the air?'

'Four,' Arram said. He'd been practising juggling as he walked from Yadeen's to Chioké's.

'Aren't you worried you'll hit Preet?' Ozorne yawned hugely. Preet, who sat on top of Arram's head, cheeped as if to say she was fearless. Tired as he was, Ozorne chuckled. 'I think she would take on armies if she could.'

Chioké bustled up the path, looking fresher and more alert than Arram. He halted before his door and bowed slightly to Ozorne. 'Your Highness, good morning.' He eyed Arram. 'Must you bring the blackbird?'

Arram blinked, startled: unlike his regular teachers, Chioké did not seem to realize Preet was no ordinary bird.

Ozorne glanced at him, then explained, 'Master Lindhall is conducting an experiment, Master Chioké, on how birds raised with humans act differently from those that are captured wild. All of Arram's masters, even Cosmas, gave him permission to keep Preet with him. And she isn't at all disruptive.'

Chioké sketched the sigil that opened the door. 'Other masters or no, if that bird makes a mess, it goes. I keep a serious work-room for magecraft, not a birdcage.'

Cross, Arram followed Ozorne and his teacher inside. If anyone should be picky about such things, it was Ramasu, who fashioned medicines in his workroom.

They had just begun to eat the cold fruit and cheese that Ozorne provided – nothing like the warm breakfast Cosmas always supplied – when Chioké said, 'What has the old man got you studying, Draper?'

Arram blinked and swallowed his mouthful of cheese. Old man? He means Master Cosmas! 'C-control, sir,' he stammered, shocked.

'Control over what?' the master asked.

'Kitchen fires. Forge fires if the smiths don't mind. Starting and stopping hearth and brush fires,' Arram explained.

Chioké and Ozorne traded looks; Chioké began to laugh. 'Mithros and Smith's God defend us, this is the work of children and old men!' he cried. Only those who had been initiated into the rites of the smiths had the right to address their god by name. Others who attempted to do so regretted it. 'We study war magic here – the kind of magic that changes empires! That's what your power is for, young fellow!'

Arram looked at Ozorne, who was grinning. Surely Ozorne knew that the sort of magic taught by Cosmas would stop the kinds of fires that plagued cities and farms. Cosmas even had hopes that Arram might one day guide the lava that spilled out of Southern volcanoes, though Arram thought the master was overreaching.

'So much for staying indoors, at least for now. Come along, you two – let's see what our young friend can do when he's let off his leash. Step lively. The foretellers call for rain later.' Chioké led the way outside again.

They crossed the Tradesmen's Road to a large grassless space in a field. Arram had been here often with friends to watch older fire magic students create displays for holidays. Large parties and games between the university's schools were held here, with stone risers on either side of the field to accommodate viewers.

Chioké pointed to a tall stack of wood placed to one side of the area. 'Draper, get one of those. Bring it over to where I'll be standing.'

Arram hesitated. Would it do any good to protest? He didn't think so. Instead he put his book bag on the riser Ozorne had chosen and handed Preet to his friend. She cheerfully ran up his arm and began to pick through the strings of beads in his hair.

'Should I give her one?' he called after Arram.

'Don't. She'll eat them,' Arram called back as he trotted to the stacks.

'Is he joking?' he heard Chioké ask Ozorne.

He chose a three-foot-high round chunk of wood – he iden-tified it as cork oak – evened off on the bottom. Chioké walked five hundred feet into the centre of the bare ground, where he scratched an X into the dirt before he returned to Ozorne. Arram got the message: he was to place the piece of wood there. Ozorne's master was starting to remind him of some of the older students who still plagued him.

'Do you know the spell to project fire, as you would throw a spear?' Chioké asked when Arram returned to the other two.

'I've done it at targets,' Arram replied quietly. He felt his fingers tingle. His Gift knew he was about to handle fire. He was never sure whether he liked the feeling. At least he's not asking me to light candles, he thought.

The mage pinched his nose. 'As a war mage you must force it, of course. Concentrate your will, call the flame from your Gift, work the spell without faltering. *Demand* that it appear within that wood!'

Arram thought he should mention the risks. 'Sir, it isn't that I can't do the spell—'

'No debate,' Chioké said, his heavy brows snapping together. 'Do it!'

Taking a breath, Arram closed his eyes and prayed, Mithros, please shine on me.

The sky was covered with thick clouds; in the distance he felt thunder roll. The older he was, whether he was indoors or out, he had begun to feel any thunder around him, not only over-head. He'd told no one, not even Ozorne and Varice. He feared they might think he was putting on airs, or running mad.

Do it and get it over with, he ordered himself. Before the lightning comes.

He drew the spell-parts together in his mind – for simpler spells, it was considered more mage-like not to say them aloud – and bound them with his Gift. There was a roaring in his ears. Power shot through his veins. It was gone.

So was the wood, burned to ashes instantly. Arram couldn't see his spell, but he felt it still rushing on. If he hadn't yanked his hands down, driving its power into the earth – where it burned a track in the dirt almost to the edge of the clearing – it would have shot into the brush on the far side.

For a moment there was silence. Then Chioké yelled, 'You call that *control*?'

'Master, look at his target,' Ozorne said. 'Or what's left of it.'

Chioké walked over to the ash mark where the chunk of wood had been, and kicked at it. Then he went to the woodpile, working a spell that lifted another piece of wood, a thicker and longer piece, into the air. He sent it to a point six hundred feet from where the two youths stood, and with a flick of the fingers, he drove it into the ground.

'Hold your position there!' he shouted. He walked quickly to the stone seats and climbed up three rows, then crossed his arms over his chest.

'Does he want me to do it again?' Arram asked Ozorne.

'I think he does,' his friend murmured. 'He loves to look . . . mage-like.'

'What do you wait for, the immortals' return?' Chioké bellowed. 'Once more.'

The third time he demanded that Arram speak the spell aloud so he could ensure he was adding nothing to it. Ozorne had to stuff Preet into Arram's book bag because she screeched in outrage at Chioké's tone towards Arram.

The fourth time Chioké held Arram's hands, earning himself a burn when they grew too hot. If he had not been a fire mage, it would have been much worse. As it was, he had to suffer the indignity of using Ozorne's burn salve.

The fifth time he raised a barrier of his own power in front of Arram to slow the spell down. It incinerated his barrier and finally scorched *only* the chunk of wood.

'Is that the *desired* outcome?' Ozorne queried. Chioké whirled as if to shout at him, but Ozorne gazed calmly at the mage.

Finally Chioké managed a hint of a smile. 'Your Highness is always ready with a joke.'

Arram looked at the sky. 'That's lightning,' he said nervously. 'We should go in.'

He could more than see it. The hairs on his arms stood. The storm was moving fast. The lightning did not disappear instantly. Some of the bolts lingered and moved, like . . . 'I *really* think we should go inside,' he repeated desperately. The wind rose; drops of water struck the ground hard enough to raise dust.

Ozorne and Chioké were talking quietly and very earnestly. ' – see what I mean,' Ozorne was telling the man. 'How wonderful it would be to have him in battle—'

'Without control he's—' Chioké interrupted.

A triple arm of lightning reached out from the tower over the Mithran Library and brushed three fingers over Arram's face. He closed his eyes, trembling, hearing Ozorne shout, *'Arram!'*

'Don't worry,' he called weakly. 'It's only lightning snakes.'

More of them came to hold his hands and explore his shoulders, chest, and legs. He was jittering now, their energy flooding his veins. He would have given anything to see this from the outside. Then the rain came pouring down with a vengeance. Laughing softly in voices that crackled, the snakes moved on with the leading edge of their storm. After a moment hands seized his arms and towed him along. He looked up and saw only black. The rain stopped.

'Your hair's in your face.' Ozorne swiped it away with one hand so Arram could see the shield of protection Chioké had placed over them. Ozorne, book bag over his shoulder, gripped Arram's arm. Chioké clutched Arram's other arm; he had Arram's book bag. Preet thrust her head out of its opening and chattered at him.

'I didn't do it on purpose,' he tried to say, but his tongue felt swollen and clumsy.

To his dazed shock, Ozorne's surprise, and Chioké's considerable irritation, Faziy came running up to them through the rain, her face alive with excitement. 'Which of you did it?' she cried. When she reached them, she grinned. 'Arram, you did it! They found you!'

'Woman, get out of our way!' Chioké shouted. 'If you haven't noticed, we are getting soaked!'

If Faziy was put off, it was impossible to tell. She was dancing as she walked backwards. 'Arram and I had talked about the lightning snakes, and they found him! Have you ever seen such a thing?'

'Nonsense!' Chioké barked as he nearly pushed Arram into his workroom. 'Sheer tribal superstition!' Ozorne followed, while Chioké remained in the doorway, arguing with Faziy.

She seemed not to notice the rain. Ozorne, frowning behind the master's back, cautiously threw a rain shelter charm out over Faziy. She didn't seem to notice that, either. *'Tribal?'* she cried. 'In Arpis Narbattum's *Of Elementals*, he writes not only of his own experience in sighting them, but of several of the masters in the academy where he worked. They saw them clear as I see you, dancing on the rim of a volcano! The book contains their testimonials, attested to and sealed by an advocate!'

'Seven hundred years ago,' Chioké snapped. A gust of wind blew rain into his face. Ozorne glanced at Arram, who tried to look innocent. Preet made a chuckling noise.

Chioké backed inside and beckoned to Faziy to follow. Ozorne let his protective spell drop when she entered the room. Chioké continued, 'Doubtless Narbattum and his companions were giddy on volcano fumes when they attested to it.'

'They were masters just like the masters here,' Faziy retorted. 'Would they make so foolish an error? Was Somava Gadav giddy on fumes when she wrote of it in *Children of Fire*? She saw them many times in her life, and created a glass to show them to those who looked into it!'

Chioké frowned. 'I have never heard of this glass or this book.'

'The book is in the library of the Unsettled Age. I've borrowed it,' retorted Faziy.

While the pair argued, Ozorne pushed Arram behind a tall screen. He motioned for Arram to remove Preet's bag. Once Arram did so, Ozorne stood silently for a moment, then lifted his hand, palm out. His Gift streamed over Arram, covering him with pure warmth. Arram sighed with contentment, then winced – it had turned a little *too* warm. He signalled Ozorne, who relaxed. Now the temperature was just right again. Ozorne let him enjoy drying out while he returned to witness the argument.

After listening to Chioké and Faziy squabble over which authorities and reports were more reliable, Arram could tell that the two masters were now friendlier. Just as good, his clothes were dry. He gathered up Preet's bag and came out from behind the screen. Ozorne was perched on a tall stool. Chioké and Faziy stood beside the fire, while the master brewed a pot of tea. Both adults fell silent and looked at Arram.

He cleared his throat and said, 'I would prefer no one else knew what happened out there. Whatever you want to call it.'

Chioké leaned against a counter lined with models of miniature war machines. 'I shall have to tell Cosmas. He is the master in charge of your learning.'

Arram looked at the floor. 'About the lightning snakes?'

Chioké sighed. 'Young man, until a group of masters in *this* century of the academy says otherwise, there is no such thing as "lightning snakes", except in old tales and those of tribal shamans.' He deliberately did not look at the scowling Faziy. 'There is a *perfectly good* reason that whatever we saw happened. I would speculate it was a mixture of your Gift and mine that created those conditions, though to be honest, I would not care to experiment. Next time neither of us might be so lucky.'

'So except for Cosmas you won't tell?' Arram asked. 'I don't want people looking at me strangely any more than they do.' He glanced at Faziy. She shook her head.

'I may explore the matter on my own, I trust?' Chioké raised his brows.

Arram goggled at him. He was a master. 'I can't stop you, sir. Ozorne?'

'I'm steadfast, Arram, you know that.' Ozorne gripped Arram's shoulder in reassurance.

The university bells began to ring. 'Very well. Time,' Chioké said. 'Tomorrow we shall continue to work on battle magic and control.' A bit awkwardly he added, 'Honoured Faziy, if you would care to continue our private discussion?'

Once outside, Ozorne cast a rain protection spell over both of them and said, 'Surely you didn't mean I wasn't to tell Varice!'

Arram stumbled a little as they trotted down the path. Ozorne steadied him.

'Won't it upset her? The snakes? You saw them, didn't you?' Arram asked, checking that Preet was fine.

'I saw something. Besides, I think your hair will upset her more,' his friend said, laughing. 'You look like one of the deep-jungle tribesmen who combs his hair out in a huge ball around his head for sacred occasions. Doesn't he, Preet? Wouldn't he make a fine nest right now?'

Preet, who remained in the shelter of Arram's book bag, only grumbled.

'Chioké improves as you get to know him, I swear. Apparently I didn't prepare him for how surprising you are,' Ozorne said as they ducked into the nearest building.

'Ozorne, please don't let him try to make me into a battle mage. I wish you'd told me that's what you wanted.' Arram stopped and grabbed his friend by the arms. 'I won't do it. I'm not a killer. I'll never be a killer.'

Ozorne eyed him curiously. 'Not even to defend Varice, or Preet, or me?'

Arram sighed. 'That's different, and you know it. I don't want to be a battle mage, not ever. I don't want to sweep away a troop of men with a sigil and a snap of my fingers – or a bolt of lightning.'

'You are the worrying-est fellow,' Ozorne said, and shoved him down the hall. 'Let's hurry, or Master Lindhall will mark us late.'

After that day, it didn't seem to stop raining. The jokes about turning into water plants or water birds were far less funny in March than they had been in February. Little fights broke out over nothing at all, even between Varice and Ozorne for a day. Everything smelled slightly of mildew, no matter how hard the students and workers cleaned and dried everything that got wet.

Preet's song was Arram's chief comfort. The little bird sang Lindhall's people and animals to sleep at night and to wakefulness in the morning. In return, Arram always found gifts of her favourite foods in baskets or napkins by the door: any fresh fruits and vegetables that could be had, multi-seeded breads, and pistachios. He never had to worry about Preet going hungry, though she didn't grow. He assumed that was part of her disguise.

In late March Ramasu was gone for five days. It was not unusual for a healer, not as it would have been for Yadeen, Cosmas, or Sebo, who rarely left the university. Arram had duties in Ramasu's workroom if the master was not present: peel, seed, or chop any plants left in baskets on the main table, tend the contents of the cook pots, and follow the lesson instructions on the slate, put there by Ramasu's chief assistant.

On the sixth day of Ramasu's absence there were no instructions. Baffled, Arram began to catch up on his reading.

He had not been at it for long when the master himself came in. He wore an oiled cloak and hat, both of which streamed with rain, and carried a heavy basket. This he set on the floor. Coat and hat he set on hooks in the covered walkway outside.

'Put those away,' he instructed Arram. 'We are going to change course slightly.' As soon as the worktable was clear of Arram's books and papers, the master set cloth parcels from the basket on its surface. 'Name these for me,' he ordered.

Arram touched the red bundle with his fingertips and his magic. 'Shepherd's purse, for diarrhoea and lesions in the intestines,' he said. Putting his fingers on the brown one, he said, 'Red raspberry leaves, to fight nausea, vomiting, and diarrhoea.' He did the same for the others, which included white willow, liquorice, and herbs that soothed pain or calmed stomach and intestinal spasms. Well before he finished he realized what Ramasu wanted to treat with these herbs.

'Typhoid?' he asked softly.

The healer rubbed his chin. 'There went my next box of candied cherries from Maren. I wagered Sebo you wouldn't know why I needed them. And she'll gloat, too, which is unbecoming in a woman of her age and humiliating for me. Yes, typhoid in the Riverfront District of the city, and in Sweet Hollow. I've been at Riverfront.'

'I'll go with you, Master,' Arram said impetuously. 'I can—'

Ramasu held up a hand. He settled into the chair beside his desk. 'Start with the shepherd's purse. Grind it for medicine, as fine as possible. Grind all of it that's in the cloth. Place it in a jar from those cupboards.' He pointed to show what he meant. 'The ones with cork stoppers. Do that with each bundle of herbs. Don't disturb me until you're done.' He began to examine papers on the desk. A fire sprouted in the braziers in the room, driving back the chilly dampness.

Arram gathered the materials he would need: a big mortar and pestle and a necessary jar. He settled Preet near enough to a brazier to be comfortable. She fluffed herself up and gave a soft cheep of contentment.

Arram surveyed the table, wondering if he had everything. There was a cone to transfer the ground herbs into the jar. He'd got a brush to clear the herbs from the mortar, and a cloth to wipe it out.

'You have forgotten nothing,' Ramasu said, looking up from his papers. 'Staring won't get the work done. If anyone knocks, you don't know where I am. This is my first sleep in three days.' He closed his eyes, then raised a hand. 'Onestu will bring us lunch. Wake me for that.' He arranged his booted feet on a hassock next to his desk and linked his fingers on his belly. Within moments he was snoring.

Carefully Arram lifted the cloth under the dried plants and poured them into the mortar until it was half full. Then he went to work turning and grinding, mixing and pushing, until he had a fine powder. Carefully, using the funnel, he poured it into the jar.

He'd worked his way through the shepherd's purse and started on the raspberry leaves when a man he didn't recognize knocked on the door. He was a big man, a Scanran, with muscular arms and legs, and corn-gold hair that he wore in braids. 'I'm Onestu,' he said quietly. 'His *ragze*. I brought him a proper lunch, since he's been eating nothing but infirmary fare.'

Arram stood aside. 'I didn't know he was married,' he whispered. 'Forgive my bad manners.'

The big man chuckled. 'I'd be surprised if he ever talked to you about anything but medicine.' He saw a clear spot on a counter and laid out dishes and utensils, a soup thick with beef, chickpeas, and dumplings, fried balls of lamb kibbeh, aubergine dip, pieces of chicken, and fresh flatbread. 'Help yourself to some of this. Let him sleep—'

'I need food as much as sleep,' Ramasu announced as he lurched out of his chair. 'You were good to come, Onestu.' He walked his husband outside and returned shortly, looking tired but cheerful. 'He's a glassmaker,' he told Arram. 'And he looks after our children when I'm called out like this. A fine man – I don't deserve him. Where's the soup?'

Arram dished up a bowl for the master, then fed Preet and gave her water. Once everyone had been cared for, he got back to work.

Some plants were dry, lacking the *greenness*, or vigour, that the others had. He talked to them silently, a trick he'd learned from Master Hulak. Stand up for yourselves! he told them, letting the words float on his Gift. You can be just as strong as the fresh plant – I know it's still in you!

Slowly he felt their swelling pride and growing strength. They would do well.

When he looked up from the last jar, Ramasu had finished his meal. Arram hadn't noticed his movements, any more than he had seen Preet fly to perch on the master's shoulder. Ramasu was watching him, an odd look in his eyes.

'Do you often talk to plants?' he enquired.

'Master Hulak does,' Arram said defensively. 'He says it helps them to grow.'

'I don't believe even Hulak talks to them after they're dead.'

'I just thought they might like it,' Arram replied, looking at the floor. 'They were older than some of these others, and they felt bad about it.'

Ramasu stroked Preet's chest feathers. 'It's very interesting, where you live, isn't it, Arram?' He tapped his forehead to show what he meant. 'Does Hulak know you can do this?'

'He lets me encourage living plants, if things go well,' Arram replied. 'He says it's a reward, but I'm not sure why. The plants do it for him when he's just there.'

'Perhaps it's meant to be a reward for *you*,' Ramasu suggested. He was staring at Arram as he rubbed his hand over his unshaven chin.

Arram tried not to fidget. He was not quite comfortable with Ramasu. The man was always aloof and dignified. His snoring and the introduction of Onestu had made him seem more human, but the look in those eyes was making Arram nervous all over again.

'Well, you aren't getting any younger,' Ramasu said at last. He reached for paper and a pen. 'Can someone take your bird for a time?'

'Well – well, yes, of course,' Arram stammered, not understanding the reason for the question. 'Ozorne, Varice – they're my friends – Master Lindhall, of course . . .'

'Lindhall! Perfect!' Ramasu picked up a small glass globe and passed his hand over it. It whirled with coloured fires as the blaze of Ramasu's power formed a circle around it. 'Lindhall, it's Ramasu.'

Arram jumped when he heard Lindhall's impatient reply as clearly as if Lindhall stood there. 'Great Mithros, surely you know I'm teaching a class!'

'Yes, but I am returning to the city. I want Draper to go, and I need you to keep his bird. There's no telling when I will return the boy,' Ramasu told the globe.

'Haven't you been in—' Lindhall began. Then his voice softened. 'Oh. Must you? Your other beginners are at least three or four years older.'

Arram didn't like the sound of that.

'He is splendid with herbs. He strengthens ones that are weak. We knew he'd have to go into a plague centre at some point, Lindhall. Let it be now, while we might yet keep the disease contained.'

'He's in your workroom? I'll send Ozorne; he's here.' The globe went dark.

'How did you do that? May I have one?' Arram asked, his fingers twitching with excitement. 'Water scrying isn't as solid.'

Ramasu looked at him as he tucked the globe into his pack. 'May you have one? If I gave a globe like this to a student, Cosmas would have my head. Leave your bird. She may not go with us.'

Preet began the most woeful trilling Arram had ever heard her make. Ramasu picked her up. 'The place is poor, dark, and wet,' he told her softly. 'Young and old die there while their refuse flows on the floor. The stench is unspeakable. If you were seen – if you were heard – you would be caged and sold in a minute. It is too sad for you, my dear.' He stroked her as she quieted, until Ozorne knocked on the door. Arram had gathered her things by then.

He accepted the bird from Ramasu and passed her to his friend. 'I'm helping the master in the city,' he explained.

Ozorne frowned. 'The city?'

'A plague centre,' Arram said quietly. 'She can't go with me.'

Ozorne looked at Ramasu. 'Surely you have more senior students to help you. Arram's no healer. He—'

'I am his master, and I determine what he is suited to,' Ramasu replied firmly. 'I know that he is your friend and that you are concerned, but you are a student of fire magic, are you not? You understand there are no safe roads in our studies, not in the long run. At least, I hope you understand this.'

Ozorne looked at the master for a moment, then bowed his head. 'Yes, sir. I apologize.' He put a hand on Arram's shoulder. 'May Hekaja watch over you' – he glanced at Ramasu – 'watch over you both, and bring you home safe.'

Arram hugged his friend. 'Tell Varice I'm sorry I couldn't say goodbye.' He gave Preet's carrybag to Ozorne.

'Stay with me, Preet,' Ozorne said cheerfully. 'I'll show you the new finches that came for the university birdhouse. And Varice will be with us. You like her.'

Preet muttered unhappily but accepted her transfer to Ozorne's care. With a wave, Ozorne walked off down the corridor.

Once Ozorne and Preet had gone, Ramasu looked at Arram. 'Report to the infirmary. Tell them you're working with me in the city. They'll give you something to ward you against typhoid. Drink it all – it's cursed expensive to make, which is why we can't give it to everyone. Then meet me at the Imperial Gate.'

'But shouldn't I pack clothes, soap, and the like?' Arram asked.

'We supply what you need,' Ramasu told him. 'You want to bring as little of your own belongings as possible. Everything is burned when we're done.'

Arram looked at his boots. They had cost a good piece of his allowance, and he was quite vain of the painted designs in the leather. They were waterproof, too, just the thing for a Carthaki winter.

Ramasu smiled. 'Leave your student robe and boots with the staff in the infirmary. They will give you straw sandals for the plague districts.'

Arram could have kissed the man. 'Thank you, Master!'

'Don't thank me – get to the infirmary. Have them send someone for the plants you ground. A very good job, by the way. Now, go!'

Arram raced through the servants' hallways rather than deal

with students who were changing classes. The potion they gave him to stave off typhoid was the worst thing he had ever forced down his throat. The student who supervised as he took it made him sit on a chair and put his head between his knees to keep from fainting.

'Does it affect everyone this way?' he asked, embarrassed to see a number of pairs of feet pass by.

'Even the masters who take it 'most every year,' the student assured him. 'There's no getting used to it. Hand over them boots.' Arram obeyed, exchanging his boots for straw sandals. Once he was on his feet, the student sent him behind a screen to trade his clothes for a rough wool tunic and a broad-brimmed straw hat to keep off the rain. She gave him a token on a string to hang around his neck so he could claim his belongings when he returned. 'The stone, too,' the student said, noticing the small opal Arram wore around his neck. 'We're sworn not to steal, never worry about that. The last medicine student that stole ended up chained to the pillar of a house when there was rat plague. He wasn't given no potion, either.'

Arram remembered to tell her about sending someone for his jars of powder. The student ordered a youngster on that errand and handed Arram a large chunk of cheese and several flats of bread to go with it. 'Stick 'em in your shirt and nibble while you can,' she advised. 'Master Ramasu hardly remembers to feed himself, let alone students. And good luck. Gods all bless, Arram.'

His heart thumping from combined excitement and terror, Arram returned the blessing and headed to the Imperial Gate at a trot. Ramasu wasn't there, and they would not leave without him. Arram looked over the two carts with waxed canvas roofs to shed the incessant rain. In addition to supplies, two other healing masters and three senior students waited inside them.

When Ramasu arrived, the masters took him aside to argue about Arram's inclusion in their group. Whatever Arram's master said, it silenced them, but they glanced curiously at Arram on the journey. The three senior students napped.

The first sign that they were approaching the slums, and the plague areas, was the smell. Arram had wandered this far into the city with Ozorne and Varice in past years, looking for cheap books. On hot days there was a smell, but it had never been this bad.

The older students had woken and noticed he was covering his nose. They told him the stink was a combination of human dung, vomit, the rotting bodies of the dead, and the burning dead. The mages did their best to encircle the corpse fires with spells to kill the odour, but there were rarely enough mages who could be spared from working on medicines and tending the sick.

'Not enough mages?' Arram asked as they turned off the river road and onto mostly deserted streets. Many doors were marked with a white chalk O, the sign for quarantine. Several that Arram noticed were slashed through – Ø – to indicate that everyone who lived there was dead. Arram bowed his head and prayed that the Black God of Death would give them gentle treatment in his kingdom. He had a feeling there was no one left in the living world to pray their way into the Realms of the Dead.

'All of us fourth-year students who study healing have to work the plague breakouts,' the most senior of the students replied to Arram's question. 'It's how we get experience. Mages with only a credential will do a lot of that. But any of us who want to make coin, real coin, we contend for our mastery—'

'And when we have *that*,' the only young woman of their number said, 'we can find work where we'll be paid what all this muck-grovelling qualified us for. Then you'll never see us tending the flea-bitten and stinking again!'

As the carts made their way deeper into the slums, through Sweet Hollow and into Riverfront, the odour thickened with the rain. So did the mud. Down here no one filled the deeper gaps with stones. Over and over students and masters had to get out

of the carts and lift them free of mudholes. The few people out
and about made the Sign against evil and hid as they passed.

'Why do they make the Sign?' Arram demanded, outraged.
'We came to help!'

'Peasants,' a master said, and sniffed. 'They think our work
carries the disease.'

Children watched them, too starved or despairing to move.
Occasionally one or several would rush the carts, only to get
their fingers stung by the protective spells on the goods inside.

'Can we give them food?' Arram asked. 'We have plenty.
They're skin and bone!'

'We would have nothing if we gave handouts to every street
urchin,' the master who'd sniffed replied. 'Criers go about telling
folk where to go for soup and bread each day. We have more
important things to do.'

Arram looked down. Had any of them tried to live on one
meal a day? He hoped that he would never be as hard and
cynical as these people, or as cruel.

Finally they stopped at the last of a series of warehouses. Over
its door someone had set a shelf with a figure of Hekaja, the
Carthaki goddess of healing. Arram kissed his fingertips and
touched them to his forehead in salute. Silently he prayed that
he would make his teacher proud. He looked for Ramasu for
instruction or farewells, but the master was already being hurried
inside by two acolytes of Hekaja.

Arram wondered what he should do. He tried to ignore the
stench that made his stomach roll. With the other students he
began to carry goods to the door, but realized almost instantly
he would not make it inside.

A man took the jars in his grip. 'Around the side is the midden.
Try to make it that far,' he said, not unkindly.

Arram ran, slipping in the mud. Several times he nearly
skidded into a line of scantily clad, muscled men and women
who carried bundles in their arms: they were going in the same
direction. Once he stumbled and would have fallen if a big arm

had not gripped his and hauled him to his feet. Arram didn't dare to speak his thanks. Waving to his rescuer, he continued his flight around the edge of the long building.

Even in the bad light and rain he saw too much of the midden for his unhappy nose and belly. Men in rags stood around it with rake-like devices, shoving the outside material towards the centre so it would burn. The strong folk were tossing their bundles directly onto the fire.

When Arram reached the edge of the piles of rotten food, blood- and pus-stained bandages, and other unspeakable things, he began to vomit and kept doing so until he thought the next thing to come from his mouth would be his belly. At last he stopped, clutching his aching ribs and breathing with his mouth open. Now he sent a prayer up to Hekaja on his own behalf, so he wouldn't stumble and fall.

Someone put a ladle of water up to his mouth. 'Don't worry, it's safe,' said a deep rumble of a male voice. ''Specially if you're already medicked against the plague.'

He nodded and gulped the water down. 'Thank you,' he gasped when the ladle was empty. When he looked ahead, he saw scarred black legs the size of tree trunks and gnarled feet in straw sandals.

'Thought your head might come off there, youngster. Hold this,' his saviour instructed, shoving the ladle into his grip. Arram obeyed. Brisk hands slapped a thin cloth scented with mint over his nose and mouth and tied it firmly behind his head.

'See if that don't make it easier.'

Arram straightened, taking tiny sniffs of air. It was still bad, but the mint kept it from overwhelming him. Suddenly a woman tripped. Her bundle fell, spilling its contents into the mud and trash. She had been carrying a child's body.

Cursing, she bent and covered her burden with the cloth, then picked it up again. Arram stared, gape-mouthed, noticing the differing sizes of the bundles. These people carried the dead to the fire. His stomach heaved again. Quickly he pushed the mask away from his mouth, not wanting to soil it. After a few moments while his belly writhed, he straightened and lowered his mask. He'd had nothing left to bring out.

'Arram, what are you doing here, boy?' boomed his new friend. 'You're young for this, seems to me.'

Startled, Arram looked up into a familiar scarred face.

'Musenda!' he cried. 'What are *you* doing here?'

The gladiator smiled and waved a muscled arm to indicate the midden and the people working there. 'This. Why aren't you at school?'

'I study medicines,' Arram said, and hiccupped. 'First time working in a plague.'

His friend gave him a fresh ladle of water. 'First mouthful, rinse an' spit,' he advised. 'Then little sips. All the students I seen are older.'

Arram drank the last of the water and returned the ladle. 'Master says I grind herbs well,' he explained. He eyed the gladiator. He wore only a loincloth, which left his scarred chest bare. On his right shoulder was a branding scar: the image of a circle around two crossed swords. The mark of the arena. 'Aren't you *cold*?'

Musenda chuckled. 'You learn to ignore it. Look at you. First you break up rocks; now you work with the healers. What next – will you fly?'

Arram smiled. 'Forgive me for asking – how are you here? I thought you weren't allowed to leave coliseum grounds without guards.'

'Oh, they're around, somewhere dry,' Musenda told him. 'We can leave the coliseum sometimes. Especially when we are *privileged* to offer service to the crown.'

Arram looked at the line of muscular people of all colours who came around the corner, each carrying a limp, sad bundle. 'You mean when there's a plague.'

'*Especially* when there's a plague.' The man shrugged.

'Aren't they afraid you'll escape?'

The man chuckled. 'Oh, no, boy. No, no.' He turned to show Arram his left shoulder. A twist of sigils written there in yellow ink shone in his magical vision. 'If I go more than one hundred paces from this building, my heart starts to slow down. The farther I go, the slower it gets. They clean the mark off once we're back in the arena, but the next plague . . .' He glanced at his companions. 'I need to work. Are you going to be all right?'

Arram nodded. 'I should work, too.' He offered his hand. 'I'm glad I saw you, Musenda, even here.'

The gladiator looked down, then said, 'Not many people offer a hand to a gladiator and a slave.' He took Arram's hand in his calloused grip. 'We keep meeting. I start to think it's fate. Stay well, Arram Draper.'

'Stay well. Thank you for the water and the mask.' Arram watched the big man join the slaves who were returning for more of the dead.

CHAPTER 13

March 438

Arram trotted into the hospital, where a healer grabbed his arm. 'Where are you supposed to be, youngster?' she demanded. 'You don't look sick.'

'Master Ramasu said I grind herbs and strengthen them well,' he said, unnerved by the fierceness in her eyes.

'Oh, Hekaja, I thank you!' the healer told the ceiling high above, though Arram thought she could also thank Master Ramasu. 'Here.' She led him into a large area partitioned off into many small canvas rooms. Looking him over, she pulled a folded length of canvas from one of many piles stacked against the wall. 'Go in there, close the flaps, take off all but your loin-cloth, and throw the old clothes in the barrel,' she said rapidly, as if she'd said it a thousand times before. 'That includes your mask. Keep sandals and loincloth, nothing else. If those who sent you didn't say you couldn't keep your clothes, take it up with them, not with me. *Move*, youngster. I have work to do!'

Once he was done, she led him at a fast walk through long rows of canvas-fronted rooms for the sick, some with the canvas lifted wide to reveal plain, empty cots and chamber pots, others with the canvas shielding those who moaned or wept inside. Some chambers were open to reveal stacks of basins, sheets, blankets, buckets, and small tables. Others held those who were clearly well, visiting family or children. Healers, priests, and priestesses moved along the aisles, looking weary and preoccupied.

They reached the far side of the warehouse. Arram's guide opened a door and thrust Arram through it. 'Here we are,' she said. 'Healers work on supplies in here. There are cots for naps and food down that way.' She pointed. 'And medicines are that way. Good luck.' She left before he could even thank her.

A wave of plant spells, most of them familiar, flowed from behind the section the healer had identified as 'medicines'. When he extended a feather of his Gift, he felt the plants he'd ground earlier that day.

'Who did that?' someone nearby asked sharply. 'Whose Gift do I feel?'

He wasn't sure who had spoken out of the identically gowned people, so he raised his hand. A tall, slender black woman swept down on him. 'Who are you? You're much too young to be here.'

'Master Ramasu sent me to grind and strengthen herbs,' Arram replied.

'Are you the one who did the batch that just came in from the university?' she asked, walking Arram into the workroom for medicines.

Arram saw his jars on the floor in their crate, unbroken, the seals still whole. 'This is mine,' he told the woman. People never introduce themselves here! he thought. 'This crate and the one next to it.'

The new mage produced her Gift, using it to inspect the jars. When she released her magic, she looked at Arram. 'Some of the herbs – the plants are dry, but their power is as great as if they were green.'

Arram rubbed the side of his head. Between the journey, the stinks, and the vomiting, it hurt. 'I told you, I don't just grind, I strengthen. That's why Master Ramasu sent me along. You could ask him, and I could do something about this headache.'

'I'll do better,' the senior mage said. 'Gieyat!' she called, looking over the large space. 'I want Gieyat!'

A short Southern man, with the heavy muscles of someone who had worked hard labour all his life, appeared immediately. 'To hear your enchanting call is to be wafted to your side, O wise woman,' he said, his eyes twinkling. His head was shaved bald. His sleeveless tunic revealed the scar of the gladiator on his right shoulder, a circle around crossed short swords. Beneath it was a fresher scar, a stylized bird flying up towards the swords: the mark of a freed gladiator.

'Can you and one of your lads carry these to the medicine cooks?' the mage asked. 'Just these two crates, special. Have that savage Viya prepare medicine from these, no one else.'

Gieyat picked up the top crate as if it weighed nothing and handed it to a young man. 'I will see to it, Nazaam,' Gieyat said. 'And *you* were supposed to go to supper the last time I saw you.'

'As soon as I settle this youngster, I will, Mother,' Nazaam replied. 'Get someone to bring the lad the stomach-soft headache tea. The odours do not suit him.' There was less snap in her voice, and a softening in her eyes. She turned to Arram and said, 'Let's get you settled, boy, and me eating supper, or Gieyat will never leave me alone.'

It was plain that Nazaam and Gieyat were lovers. I'd like that, Arram thought as he followed Nazaam. To be comfortable with my lover, and laugh together, even when things are terrible. Like I do with Ozorne and Varice.

'How did you know I'd been sick?' he asked.

Nazaam took him to a worktable, one of many lined up against the chilly rear wall. Workers – mages and older students – stood at each one, pummelling and mixing the contents of mortars. A slate leaned against the big, bowl-shaped mortar where his guide halted. On it someone had written 'Arram Draper'. No one was positioned at the table on his right; a much older mage laboured on his left. He didn't even look up.

Nazaam twitched a finger; a man ran up with a sack. He cut

it open with his belt knife and poured its contents into the mortar until it was half full. Arram flinched. The herbs were so stale as to be useless. 'They're old,' he said, forgetting his company.

'Really?' Nazaam asked with awful sarcasm. 'What a dreadful oversight on our part. You'd think we'd laboured for weeks and gone through the fresh stuff.' She leaned close to Arram, her masked face a thumb's width from his, her gloved forefinger poking his chest. 'Now see here, *student*. If Ramasu foisted you on me, I must hope you have something useful. If you give me extra trouble, I swear to the Black God, granter of peace, you'll be outside keeping order in the burning pile, understand?'

Arram gulped and nodded.

'And if you slack on work when people are dying . . .'

Arram straightened and replied stiffly, 'I never slack on work, mistress.'

'It's Master. Master Nazaam. *I* judge if you slack. When you've finished with one mortar's worth, pour the contents into one of these' – she produced a bowl from a shelf beneath the table – 'and start on your next mortar full. If you must stop, tell the next person who asks you if you need anything. Don't leave until you've told that person, understand? We'll let you know when it's time for meals, sleep, or a halt.'

'Yes, Master Nazaam,' Arram murmured. He knew who she was now: the director of magic at the university's School of Medicine. When the emperor panicked, he sent for her. One thing of which Arram was certain – *he* would not call for her, no matter how panicked he was. She was too frightening.

He worked and worked. Sometimes he would stop to stretch and find a cup of water, or a cup of tea, or a bowl of soup just out of his elbow's reach. He would consume them all, stretch again, and return to his mortar.

As he worked the stale plants, his power over them grew. His Gift passed through the withered stems, leaves, seeds, and flowers as he ground them to fine powder. He drew out their memories of when they were fresh, drinking water and singing their prayers to the gods of plants. There was Mother Sun and Father Rain, both kind and cruel; Soil, without which there was no life; and the Biting Hordes, savaging their flesh when they were not devout enough. Arram carried away their memories of insects devouring them and made them vigorous once more, filled with the substance in each type of plant that would help bring healing to the sick.

Dimly he felt something grip him by a branch and shake him. He didn't think he had any ripe fruit to drop.

A voice he remembered – Nazaam? – shouted somewhere, 'Pox take her, that idiot Hirusy should have pulled him out of the line at dawn. He's been here hours past . . . Boy! Boy! What's his name?'

'Arram.' That coarse voice, he knew it, too. Gieyat. But what was Gieyat grass, or a Nazaam tree?

'Arram. Arram, let go of the pestle. Hekaja Healer, Gieyat, his fingers are like old roots.'

'Let me, Nazaam. When they've been fighting awhile, they can't always tell when the battle's done. Here you go, youngster. It's after sunrise. You need to sleep. You've been at it all night.'

But sunrise was the time for waking, wasn't it?

What had he been at all night?

'I swear, I'll put Hirusy on chamber pot detail. I'll take his other side. Good thing his Gift is relaxing. Ramasu would never forgive me if I damaged his boy.' Nazaam put one warm hand on his shoulder, so warm, like Mother Sun. Then Nazaam – Master Nazaam – struggled with his hand until she opened his fingers. They hurt! Great Mother, his fingers hurt!

Once Nazaam got her very warm fingers worked between his, the cramps began to ease. She and Gieyat first helped him to straighten, then to walk a little, then found him a bed. He toppled onto it and slept.

His sore and swollen pestle hand woke him around noon. He did not want to leave his cot. Staff members dragged him and several other swollen-handed young men outside into a cloth-surrounded enclosure. Once the staff dumped large buckets of very cold water on them, he saw the force of their argument. They made it up to him and his companions, once the young men had pulled on fresh shifts and their sandals, by presenting them with bowls of tea and bread rolled around cubes of lamb or beef, eggs, hot peppers, and yogurt sauce. Arram felt nearly human as he approached his post. Even the sight of piled bags of herbs didn't daunt him.

The place on Arram's formerly empty side was filled by a young man who diligently worked his mortar full of herbs. Arram extended a touch of his Gift and sighed enviously. His neighbour had much fresher plants than he did. He risked another glance at the young man before he opened his first bag and poured dry, crackling leaves into his mortar. There was something familiar about him, in the light brown shade of his skin and the length of his nose. He should know who it was . . . His pestle slipped and struck the edge of his mortar. He *ought* to pay attention to his work.

He'd begun his third bowl when he heard a quiet – and most definitely familiar – voice enquire, 'What, no leftover prince at your side?'

He glanced around a moment before he realized the query had come from his mysterious neighbour. He glared at the young man, about to snap at him, when he recognized the face that was now turned towards him. 'Laman?'

'I know, you didn't recognize me without Diop.' Arram's former roommate smiled at him. 'I scarcely recognized you without your friend. And they told me my neighbour thought he turned into a tree during his first shift.'

Arram looked down. 'I forgot myself.'

'If I'd known *you* were here, I'd have worked it out. Aren't you young for this?'

Arram scowled. 'Aren't you?'

Laman smiled crookedly. 'Everyone who specializes in healing magic starts with chores, I'll have you know. It was this or peeling. I can mash with both hands, but I can't peel with both. Here I am. I don't wear out like single-handed crushers.'

Arram covered his mouth so no one passing would hear him chuckle.

Laman pointed at him. 'Ha. You *can* laugh.'

Arram scowled. 'I do it all the time. You're the one who's so serious.'

'If you came from my homeland, you would be serious, too.' Laman turned away from Arram, staring down the corridor.

Arram asked, 'You've always lived in Siraj?'

Sighing, Laman turned back to his mortar and pestle. 'Until I came here, yes.'

Arram got back to work. 'You see,' he began, letting power flow into his herbs, 'I was wondering what happened in the Sirajit highlands during the uprising.'

Laman glared at him.

'I'm not – I'm not trying to offend,' Arram told him. 'But all I know is from the history books and the very little Ozorne says.'

The older youth snorted. 'Oh, yes, the hero's son.'

Arram wanted to defend his friend, but he wanted knowledge even more. A tutor had once informed him that his curiosity would be his doom. 'Please – I would just like to know about Prince Apodan's last campaign.'

'Campaign!' Laman caught himself and looked around, as if he thought he might be punished. He inspected Arram, then said, 'Never say you heard a word from me. It could ruin my family if—'

'I would never tell,' Arram said quickly. 'I swear by Mithros, Minoss, and Shakith.'

Laman blinked. 'The gods punish oath breakers.'

'I know.' Arram's books always had reports of what happened to them.

They returned to their work. 'The army's conquest of Siraj

ruined my great-grandfather and grandfather. They owned and sailed ships until the empire commandeered them to pay the expenses of the conquest of Siraj.' His face was bitter. 'My father restored the family fortune when he became the imperial governor's personal healer, and the healer for his family. That was his Gift. My grandfather was so heartbroken he took to the mountains, to my grandmother's family farm. He herded sheep, and did well at it . . . or he used to.'

He poured himself a cup of water from his pitcher and drank. 'My mother took me to visit Grandfather for my birthday. His place was in a northern valley, just outside what was the town of Medyat. We were there when the army came, so we went to see Prince Apodan and the soldiers as they marched through town. They were going to put down a rebellion farther south. Rebellion! A couple of tribes were feuding, and they had pulled more tribes into it. The prince saw his chance for military glory.' Laman looked at Arram and frowned. 'Are you Carthaki?'

Arram shook his head. 'Tyran.'

'You're almost dark enough to be one of us.' Laman's chuckle was a weak one. 'Who knows? Maybe our family lines crossed somewhere.' He bowed his head. 'Forgive me. This is a hard tale, but I want to tell you. Maybe because you're such good friends with one of them. You ought to know what they're capable of. See, we heard from those that could run. It really was just a tribal feud, like they're always having, over grazing lands, I think. Ozorne's father, that brave and courageous prince, wiped them out. Even the babies. He said he didn't want to leave any seed that would grow. Then he came back to Medyat in triumph.' His fists were clenched. 'The heads of dead men and women were tied to his men's saddles. We'd been shopping in town when they came. I saw a girl run to him with a gold cup of wine, and he drank it. Mother and I thought nothing of it, but Grandfather dragged us back to the farm. He made us leave everything and ride. I didn't want to return to Father – I knew I'd have to resume studying for the university – but

Grandfather threw me onto a horse and ordered me to be silent. When I couldn't open my mouth I found my mother's father had the Gift, too.

'He took his entire household, down to the last shepherd. We were several miles up into the hills when he told us he knew the girl from his favourite drinking house. She belonged to one of the tribes that were slaughtered. She was only in town because she wanted to earn a good bride price. Grandfather was positive the cup she gave the prince had poison in it – that's the way of the tribes. Blood for blood. Even though there was no way she would escape the army's revenge, she'd given up her life to avenge her people. Mother called him an old fool because he'd dragged us away on a guess. He put the silence on her, too. We kept riding.'

Laman took a deep breath. 'We'd gone a mile further, maybe more, when Grandfather stopped on a rise and pointed towards town. Medyat was in flames. We met up a day later with some merchants who'd sold supplies to the army. They told us the prince was dead, poisoned. The girl was dead. She'd killed herself.' He wiped his hand over his eyes. 'By the time we got to my father's house, the imperial heralds were proclaiming the whole mess was a military victory. The official word was that Prince Apodan Doroi Tasikhe died tragically in battle. My grandfather told my mother and father this is what happens to people who fight the empire. That's surely the lesson I learned. Try it, and you get smashed like a bug. I dug into my studies, and now I'm here, a good little imperial. I may pull your friend's tail a bit for fun, but I won't go too far. I don't want my head hanging from anyone's saddle.' He set a full mortar aside and filled another, then asked, 'Is Tyra nice?'

Arram remained silent for a moment, unable to wipe those pictures from his imagination. Then he gulped until his teacup was empty and tried to remember his birthplace. He hadn't seen it in years. 'Lots of canals and trees,' he replied. 'Islands connected by bridges, mostly. Plenty of insects that bite. Crocodiles, too.'

'I think I will pass that one by, then,' Laman replied.

They spoke little after that, only worked. Laman had gone off for a nap and Arram had finished his third bag of herbs for the day when Gieyat tapped his shoulder. 'Go for a walk,' the older man said. 'Loosen up. Talk to people. Don't come back till you stop thinking like a plant. Ramasu's orders.'

Arram opened his mouth to say that he wasn't thinking like a plant, only to find that words did not come to his tongue.

'Aha,' Gieyat said. 'There you are. Shoo.'

Arram shooed. He didn't want to see the other workers. They would make him feel as if he were slack to be away from his post. He did walk briskly up and down the length of the building several times, his head clearing more as he walked. He was about to return to the workroom when he heard children's voices. The flap on a larger-than-usual area between the sick-rooms and the work area was pinned back a little. Curious, he stuck his head inside.

A band of children of assorted ages stared at him. They sat, stood, or knelt among a variety of blankets, mats, and toys, all very battered. Their clothes were in much the same condition.

'What're you lookin' at?' demanded a boy with tribal scars on his face.

'This ain't a Player's show,' added a girl.

'Have you news of someone's parents?' asked an older girl.

Arram understood. They were waiting for their parents to heal or to die. Thus the sombre faces on all but the infants, who could not be left behind if there was no one at home to care for them.

Something bumped his foot. A toddler grinned up at him. He'd rolled a wooden cart over to Arram in an invitation to play. It gave Arram an idea – a way, perhaps, to cheer these youngsters up. He bent to pick up the hand-sized cart and a nearby ball.

'No, I'm sorry,' he told the girl who had asked for news. 'I only work in the back, making medicine.' He flipped the ball in the air, catching it one-handed over and over. He had the youngest children's attention right away. 'It's not the easiest work, because I'm such a clumsy fellow . . . Oh, no!' In dropping the ball, he threw the cart in the air. The children gasped as he caught the ball while the cart was above his head, then traded it for the cart. He dropped the ball deliberately, making some of them giggle, and chased it across the floor, still juggling the wagon in one hand until he got both up and going once more. Next he invited one of the boys to throw him another ball, so that he had two spheres and the wagon to wield. He finally had to stop. His arms were sore, and he was certain he had to report back to his post. The children's glowing faces were all the reward he could want. So too were the smiles on the faces of the healers and the workers who filled the doorway to the room.

He was about to leave when a brown-skinned little girl of nearly ten tugged on his sleeve. 'Do you know our uncle?' she asked. 'He's a famous gladiator.'

'If he's famous, how come he hauls dead folk outside?' one of the boys jeered.

'Because he's *strong*,' cried the girl. 'They want the *strong* ones to take care of the deaders, that's why! So just you stuff it in your bum, Atim!'

As a worker came forwards to end the quarrel, Arram crouched before the little girl. 'I did meet a gladiator,' he said to calm her down. 'What's your uncle's name?'

'Musenda,' she replied. 'He's very big.'

Arram smiled, glad to be able to please her. 'I did meet him, and you're right, he is very big. He's also very kind.'

'He is! He is!' The girl jumped up and down, excited. Two smaller boys ran over. She told them, 'He knows Uncle!' They grinned up at him, urchins in rags, one clutching a wooden doll painted like a gladiator. Their sister told Arram, 'Uncle Musenda started to watch over us when Da died. He was going to buy us a new place to live, but then Ma got sick.'

'I will pray to the goddess to spare your mother, and that one day you will have your new house,' Arram said.

'Will you come back and do tricks some more?' asked the older of the two boys. The other children in the room echoed his request, begging so frantically that Arram promised. He shook hands with Musenda's nephews and hurried back to his tasks.

The next time he was ordered to take the morning off, he surrendered to the cold bath, ate a sitting-down meal, and took a walk through the building. Then, as promised, he returned to the children's waiting room. He was delighted to see Musenda, still wearing the spell-mark that kept him in the plague area, seated cross-legged on the floor. He had a nephew on each knee and a cluster of children before him. They were intent as he told them a story of those who trained tigers in the gladiators' camp.

The moment he finished the tale, his niece flew across the room to Arram. 'Uncle,' she cried, 'this is our friend Arram. He juggles.' She seized Arram's hand and pulled him over to the big gladiator, who was rising to his feet. 'He says he knows you!'

Musenda offered his hand in greeting. 'We do know each other, Binta. You surprise me, youngster. I did not think you would manage so long.'

Arram smiled weakly. 'Neither did I.'

'I owe you my gratitude for amusing my niece and nephews,' Musenda said. 'They have been telling me of the light you bring to this place.'

Arram busied himself by taking some of the toys the children were offering him. 'They're too kind,' he told Musenda. 'If I make them laugh, it's when I drop things. Hitting myself on the head is a big favourite.' He smiled at a little boy who offered his stuffed elephant, and accepted it. 'It's good practice.' He began to send the first couple of toys spinning through the air. Musenda's niece, Binta, stood by, offering up each new item for Arram to juggle as he let them rise and fall in the air.

'I must go,' Musenda said quietly, understanding a loud voice would startle Arram. 'Only remember, I feel a debt to you for my family.'

Moving gracefully, he made his way out of the crowded room.

Arram looked down at the girl and her brothers as he changed the pattern of the toys he sent into the air. 'He's a nice man, your uncle.'

Binta nodded. 'He says someday he'll live with us, but Ma says he can't. Gladiators aren't allowed to live with people.'

It's not right, Arram thought as he watched the children. Keeping a man from his family is not right. And why? So he can die in the arena for people to wager on? For people to applaud? That's no life for anyone!

His hands wobbled, and a rain of toys fell on his head. The children and the watching members of the staff applauded. Arram sighed and gathered the toys again. If Ozorne were emperor, he thought, he would do something about it. He shook his head and began to juggle again. There were too many princes ahead of Ozorne, and by all reports, they liked the gladiators and games just as they were.

He had been working at the infirmary for four days – or was it five? – when he heard an unusual stirring in the work area. Nazaam came bursting through the door, practically crackling with energy. A man in a naval uniform with a silver chain around his neck walked on her right; another who wore an expensive robe and drape walked on her left. Both shimmered from caps to boots with strong protective magic.

'It is not as if you have been granted a choice in the matter, Master Nazaam,' the man in the robe and drape told her. 'His Imperial Highness learned that a number of his sailors or their families are in these places, and he *will* see them.'

'I cannot promise his safety,' Nazaam snapped. 'Nor that of his minions.'

'But Master Tajakai can and does,' the naval officer retorted, naming the imperial court's official mage. 'Will you gainsay him?'

Outside Arram could hear the muffled blasts of trumpets.

The robed man drew a parchment from his drape and offered it to Nazaam. 'A writ, signed by the emperor and Tajakai, with the imperial seal, which absolves you of responsibility should His Imperial Highness or any in his train take harm.

'Now, stop whining, woman, and—' The naval officer stopped talking. His mouth moved, but no sound emerged. His face turned red; his eyes bulged; his body trembled. He was frozen in place. Arram walked over, not to help the man, but to back up Nazaam should she need it. Laman followed, and with him every worker in sight. Gieyat walked up behind the officer, his hands bunched into fists.

'Don't be a fool, Captain,' the other messenger said. 'She is the mage most trusted with the emperor's personal health.'

'I will not have disrespect in my own infirmary, understand?' Nazaam asked, leaning in and speaking softly. 'If you do not understand that, Davrid, perhaps you would prefer a few weeks at your beak head after every meal, surrendering what you eat.'

Arram remembered crossing the Inland Sea at seven. His father had been forced to clutch Arram's shirt to keep his son aboard as the boy walked out onto that rocking point of the ship, positioned his bare behind over a hole that revealed the sea, and tried to make his poor bowels work. He promised himself never to offend Nazaam. 'Why does she hate the captain?' he whispered to Laman.

'Former lover,' his fellow student murmured in reply.

Nazaam released the captain, who staggered and choked. 'Get this folly over with,' she told the two visitors. 'His Imperial Highness and his mage may enter the sickrooms. No one else. Gieyat will serve as your guide. I am not to be disturbed; my workers are to be allowed to perform their tasks. No bowing and scraping, no audiences in the halls.' She walked off, and those who had gathered to watch moved hastily out of her way.

'After you, my lords,' Gieyat told the strangers, bowing politely.

Arram turned back to his desk, shaking his head as he thought about romance and revenge. Falling in love with a mage plainly had its hazards if things did not go well. Still, he admired Nazaam's inventiveness when it came to thinking of suitable revenge.

'What a woman!' Laman said with admiration as he, too, went back to work.

Arram stared at him. 'You must like to live dangerously.'

Laman grinned. 'If the punishment was different, it might be a glorious way to die.'

Arram spent the next hour or more trying to make sense of this as he reduced mortar after mortar of herbs to fine powder. He had moved from the mysteries of romance to the steps necessary to create a simulacrum of a cat when someone nearby boomed, 'What goes on here?'

He turned his head. Gieyat was approaching at the side of someone Arram recognized from Princess Mahira's Midwinter party. Their guest was Prince Stiloit. To Arram's surprise – and respect – Ozorne's cousin wore the same tunic and sandals as everyone else in the infirmary. Without the silver-trimmed cap he'd worn at Midwinter, Stiloit revealed tightly curled black hair. His winter's moustache and short beard were gone, leaving him clean-shaven for the summer. He'd even lost weight.

Arram's eyes must have lingered on the prince a little too long. Stiloit halted and pointed, the sheer orange veil of his magical protection stretching to keep his finger covered. 'Here – I know you! You're Lady Varice's friend, Prince Ozorne's friend, aren't you?'

Arram, startled, began to kneel, but Gieyat rushed forward and raised him by one arm. 'D'you want Nazaam to skin us? Look official!' He winked at Arram and bowed to the prince. Arram fumbled, then bowed.

'It's Arram-something, do I remember it right?' Stiloit asked.

Arram nodded. He knew he should speak, but his tongue refused to work.

'Come with me, just for a short time,' Stiloit urged. 'You can tell me how the lovely Varice fares.' He glanced at Gieyat. 'If your mistress grows cross, tell her I placed one thousand thakas in the offering box when I entered. My men are guarding it if you want to collect it right now.'

Gieyat beckoned to Laman and whispered in his ear. Arram placed a cover over his mortar. Laman headed towards Nazaam's quarters as Arram joined the prince.

'The lady does well?' Stiloit asked. 'I was sad to find she had left early at Midwinter.'

'She was still weary from our examinations, Your Imperial Highness,' Arram replied, thinking fast. 'We were all three moved to the Upper Academy this year – perhaps Prince Ozorne told you – and we had a great deal of work to do to catch up.'

'Yet I am told that you did quite remarkably, all three,' the prince replied slyly.

Great Mithros, Arram thought. He's been keeping track of us.

'You look like a startled gazelle, my young friend,' Stiloit joked. 'Now, where does this passage lead?'

Gieyat pointed to the larger cubicles on the right. 'Here, Your Imperial Highness, and beyond this larger chamber on your left are rooms for families. They are for mothers or fathers who are mending. Their children may stay if there is no one at home to care for them. Such rooms are also for groups of orphaned children.'

'And this room?' the prince asked, pointing to the largest one.

Gieyat grinned. 'Healthy children stay here during the day with caretakers. Sometimes Master Arram juggles for them.'

Stiloit grinned at Arram. 'This I must see! Come, lad – show me what you do for them! Do you need special tools?'

Gieyat opened the curtain. 'He keeps them here,' he said as the adults inside got to their feet. Obviously they had been warned that the prince might visit. All had been supplied with clean robes; everyone's hair was neatly combed. The staff bowed instantly.

The young people saw Arram first and began to shout his name. Their caretakers swiftly took hold of them and pointed out Stiloit. It took persuasion to get the smallest to release Arram's hands and robe so they could pay their respects to their imperial guest. Arram helped by gathering up several of them and explaining what they all must do together. They bowed as well as three- and four-year-olds might and said 'Good day, Your Imperial Highness,' almost together with nearly all the right words.

'Excellent,' Stiloit cried, laughing and clapping at once. 'Very well done! My own nieces and nephews could not do better!' He bent down so he was more on the level of the smaller ones and asked, 'Now, shall we see if Arram will juggle for us?'

Arram was so nervous in the royal presence that it took him a number of tries and even more drops to get his usual collection of balls, small hoops – a new addition since his arrival – and children's toys moving flawlessly in the air. The mistakes delighted his young audience, who thought he did it to make them laugh. Finally he rediscovered his skill and convinced his audience that he truly did know how to juggle.

'Well?' Laman asked when Arram returned to his post.

'He likes children,' Arram mumbled. 'What was I doing?'

'Go to bed,' Nazaam ordered. Arram was surprised to find the master working with mortar and pestle three tables away. Now she came over to him. 'Dealing with the powerful wearies you as much, if not more, than spellcraft.' To Arram's shock, she put an arm around his shoulders and kissed his temple. 'Hekaja bless you, boy. When he walked out of here, His Imperial Highness put a diamond ring worth *another* thousand thakas in the donation box! Gods bless him and his voyages! Now go sleep, and we'll wake you for work tonight.'

The next morning Laman returned to the university, done with pounding herbs for the present. Arram worked for another three days. By then Binta's mother, Musenda's sister-in-law, was in a room for healing parents, her children with her. Arram visited for a last performance for her and her youngsters.

Ramasu found him giving his juggling toys to the orphans. When Arram finished, Ramasu called him away.

'You'll barely manage the journey home,' he said when Arram tried to protest. 'You've lost weight and need rest.' He rested a hand on Arram's shoulder. 'I've heard little but good about you. We'll speak more once I return.'

'You're not coming?' Arram blurted.

Ramasu's smile was wry. 'There's much more for a master to do. Go and restore your strength.' He gave Arram's shoulder a gentle push. 'You will see me soon enough.'

After a hideously scented medicine bath to ensure he carried no disease away from the hospital, Arram crawled into a cart for the journey home. He had only one companion, another student as worn out as he was. For once it was not raining, though neither youth was in a position to care. They wrapped themselves in blankets and went immediately to sleep.

He stirred a little when the other student left the cart, then slept again. He roused to rough shaking and the carter's amused voice, saying, 'Wake *up*, lad. Here's a friend waitin' for you.'

'I'll help,' Arram heard Ozorne's familiar voice say. 'Mithros, what did they do to him? He's skin and bone.'

Arram fought to sit, not wanting his friend to see him lying flat like one of the dead, still on his cot, his skin grey. Arram scrambled forward, horrified.

He grabbed the driver's hands and Ozorne's to get down, continuing to hold on as the ground swayed under him.

Preet leaped to his shoulder, chattering and running her beak in small touches around his ear and through his hair. 'Oh, Preet, I missed you,' Arram said. His legs started to buckle.

Ozorne pulled Arram's arm around his shoulder, steadying his friend. 'I see – I smell – that you too got the cleansing bath.'

'It makes us safe to come home,' Arram retorted. 'Preet, you're going to make me deaf.' The bird was telling Ozorne what she thought of his remarks.

'Oh, that's the way it is?' Ozorne said to the bird. 'I'm your best friend for days, but the moment *he* returns . . .' He looked at Arram. 'You're taller. I just noticed.'

Arram was sliding down again, but not before he realized Ozorne's eyes were level with the bridge of his nose. He gave the only reply he could think of: 'Oops.'

'Here, lad.' The carter had secured his reins and given his horses feed bags. 'I'd best help with yon sapling.'

'But your cart, and the animals,' Ozorne protested.

'Can't you see the spell?' the man asked.

'I can see *a* spell,' Ozorne said. 'Not the manner of it. It's very good.'

'I can't see anything,' Arram added, and yawned. He was struggling to stay on his feet. 'I'm all used up.'

The carter got under his free arm and draped it over his own brawny shoulders. Preet walked over on the arm until she had a closer look at the man's face. 'The bird won't peck me, will he?' the carter asked.

Preet began to trill, coaxing a smile from him. 'She likes you,' Ozorne said. 'You should be honoured. She doesn't like many folk. So what kind of spell is it, that we only see there is a spell, but we can't see what it's for?'

'They put it on us that work during the big sicknesses. Folk think the wagons and horses belong to Players,' the man explained as they walked Arram through the gate. 'Everyone knows there's a curse from them that steals from Players. The spell turns clear when we go where there's plague, and ordinary folk know we're bringing help.'

'Clever,' Ozorne said with admiration.

'The healers have been here ages,' the carter said as they halted before their dormitory. 'Long enough to work it out. Is this it?'

'In a way. Now there's four flights of stairs,' Ozorne said

cheerfully. 'Look, you don't have to do this. I can go and get some of the others if they're around.'

'It's no bother,' the carter replied as they walked Arram inside. 'This is my last trip. I'm off home to my old woman and the grandchildren.'

'How is the situation in the city?' Ozorne asked as they began to climb. Arram did his best to help, but his knees were so wobbly. It wasn't just his body that was tired, Gieyat had explained as they bundled him into the cart. It was the draining of his Gift.

He hadn't known his Gift was so entwined with his bones. He would have to do something about it later.

The carter in the meantime was telling Ozorne that the death rate wasn't anything like the typhoid of 435. He remembered the smoke from the burning of the dead in that epidemic. The university had been safe from typhoid, but the smoke had drifted in the air for weeks. It was said plagues were the toy of the Queen of Chaos, tossed into the Mortal Realms when she was bored. Arram wished that he might one day do the Queen of Chaos an ill turn to even the score.

They had reached his door. Ozorne opened it, and together he and the carter eased Arram through and lifted him onto his bed. Arram tried to raise his head to thank them, but Preet hopped onto his forehead. Somehow her weight was too much. He sank back against his pillow.

Ozorne fumbled in his belt pouch for coins, but the carter shook his head. 'Not a copper will I take, youngster,' he said with a smile. Arram realized that the man had no idea that Ozorne was a member of the imperial family. 'I'd've helped your friend for nothing. Whenever they gave him time away from his work, he'd go where they kept the youngsters what was waiting t'see family, and juggle.' The man chuckled. 'The young folk loved 'im. Even the workers. He'd juggle for the sick, if they were awake enough to watch. It's no wonder he's falling over on himself.'

Arram turned away. What good had any of it done? So many of the children had lost their fathers, or their mothers, or any family they had.

Preet settled in the hollow between his shoulder and the free ear and produced a soft, slow trill that lured him to a deep and dreamless sleep. He didn't see the carter shake hands with Ozorne, to that prince's bemusement, and tell him, 'Look after that long friend of yours. He's a good 'un,' or hear Ozorne murmur, 'He is indeed.'

The next morning, still half asleep, Arram and Preet joined Ozorne on his way to breakfast. 'Aren't you supposed to be in class or something?' the prince asked, looking at him suspiciously.

'I have until Sunday classes next week to come about,' Arram told him, and yawned. 'Master Lindhall left the note pinned to my door this morning. He said to enjoy it. I won't get so much time to recover as I grow older.'

'How noble of them,' Ozorne said drily. 'Listen, I wanted to warn you, Varice is unhappy that you disappeared the way you did. I tried to explain, but . . .' Ozorne shrugged. 'Girls.'

Arram winced. 'I wasn't given a choice, you know! One moment I was chopping herbs, and the next I was up to my elbows . . .' He swallowed, a ghost of the smell haunting his nostrils. 'I was not enjoying myself,' he said weakly. 'And if there was a mail courier, no one mentioned it.'

'What, you didn't make a simulacrum of one to carry a note to us?' Ozorne asked wickedly.

Arram elbowed him and Ozorne elbowed back, while Preet scolded them both. 'It's good to have you home, friend,' Ozorne said as they walked into the dining hall.

While Arram went straight to the arrays of food, Ozorne went to their table. Out of the corner of his eye he saw his friend bend to whisper in Varice's ear.

Varice squealed Arram's name. A moment later a number of pounds of agreeably shaped female pounced upon him. Ozorne rescued the indignant Preet before Varice wrapped her arms around Arram's neck.

'You horrible thing!' Varice cried. 'Not a word to say goodbye, and I missed you so much!' As her weight pulled him down so she could reach his face, she kissed him first on his left cheek, then his right cheek, then a third time, very firmly, on his mouth.

Arram stood stock-still until she released him and said, 'Let's have breakfast.'

He fumbled as he picked up a tray. He would spend the rest of the day touching his mouth from time to time when no one was looking, still feeling the pressure of her lips, or thinking he did.

'I was worried sick,' Varice said as she briskly placed an egg dish on Arram's tray. 'There was no word of when you were coming home . . . Goddess save us, you're a rail. What did they feed you?'

'Soups and porridges, mostly, like they fed the patients and their families,' Arram replied, smiling. It was so comfortable to see Varice picking out his meal for him again. 'Perfectly decent food, you know.'

'Then you weren't eating much of it.' She added plums and hothouse berries.

From their table, Preet squawked.

Varice finished picking out her own meal. 'We are summoned,' she said, smiling up at Arram. 'Oh, it's *so* good to have you back!'

Arram could feel his cheeks going warm. 'So what did everyone else do while I was grinding weeds?' he asked as he settled at the table. Preet hopped to his shoulder.

'Varice and Ozorne were at the hospitals, too,' Tristan said, his voice sharp. 'Only in no grand a capacity as a weed chopper.'

'Tristan,' Gissa murmured, resting her head on her hands. 'He hasn't been bragging.'

'That will be enough.' Varice slapped the back of Tristan's head lightly. 'I stewed plants for medicines, and Ozorne helped pack the medicine wagons and oversee their unloading. It was all boring and I want to forget it.'

'Not me, dearest,' Ozorne quipped. 'I want to do it every day.'

After chattering in Arram's ear, Preet hopped to the table to inspect his plate.

'We have to warn you, she's become incredibly spoiled,' Gissa said, obviously trying to change the subject. 'Everyone feeds her when they get the chance.'

'Except Master Chioké,' Tristan reminded her.

'But you only have one class with him,' Arram said, scratching Preet's head. She made a soft growling noise, her angry sound. Since she loved head scratches, Arram suspected it was the mention of Chioké that roused the little bird's wrath. 'It doesn't matter if she misses a class's worth of meals.'

'I have two classes with him, O Student Behind the Times,' Ozorne informed him smugly. 'Chioké convinced Master Cosmas that it would be suitable for me to study detection of poisons.'

Arram blinked at his friend. At the Tasikhe court a person's exposure to poisons – whether studying them or their cures – was always watched very carefully. Any student of that area had to be approved by the emperor's personal mage as well as by Master Cosmas.

'Your uncle must trust you,' he said at last, wondering why this was the first he'd heard of it.

Ozorne shrugged. 'He trusts my mother and Master Chioké,' he said. 'He thinks I'll be useful to Mikrom when he ascends to the throne. And I believe his eye is on Chioké as well. The present court mage is starting to dodder a bit.' He laughed. So did the others at the table, except Arram. He couldn't see anything funny about the ageing of a great man who had served the emperor for decades.

'Come, soursop.' Ozorne poked Arram's shoulder. 'You've been among the dirty and downtrodden too long. Chin up! You're home!'

Slowly Arram smiled. Ozorne's sense of humour could take a cruel turn, it was true, but he meant no harm. And it was good to be back, among pretty girls, eating warm meals, and bathing in hot water. Best of all, he had four days before he had to haul himself out of bed at dawn, ready for school. Who knew? He might even be able to produce some magic by then.

CHAPTER 14

April 438

The day Arram returned to classes, he requested permission from Master Cosmas to go back to the typhoid workrooms. Cosmas firmly refused to let him do so much as chop wood for the fires. Preet agreed loudly.

'Hush,' the master told the bird. She quieted slowly. 'There will be other plagues, as I told Varice and Ozorne,' he informed Arram.

Arram grimaced. 'If that is the way to improve my education, I'd as soon not have any more plagues.'

Cosmas chuckled. 'Our care effort at such times is large, and it was time to try the three of you out in the field,' he explained. 'Everyone is impressed with all of you. Cheer up. We will not allow you to burn yourselves out. You are to *rest* and *study*. Let your Gift rebuild.'

The next day Ozorne found Arram by the river. He was knee-deep in the water, feeding fishes near the landing for the palace. The hippos who had also come to visit scrambled into the water when they saw the prince and his escort or, more likely, smelled them.

Arram had been wondering about the imperial barge that

waited at the land's end. He climbed from the water and approached his friend. 'Where are you off to?'

'Mother is unwell,' Ozorne replied with a frown. 'Keep notes for the classes I'm in, will you?'

Arram would have agreed, but the imperial soldier in charge of Ozorne's entourage ushered the prince along to the waiting craft. Slaves hurried to send it speeding eastward as soon as Ozorne was seated.

Preet uttered a questioning trill.

'I agree,' Arram replied absently. 'If she keeps calling him away, he'll begin to fall behind.'

Ozorne rejoined his friends at the dining hall after a three-day absence. Preet was the first to see him. She screeched and flew to him at the food tables, where she perched on his shoulder.

When they reached the table, Preet was grooming his hair and dislodging his beaded braids. 'Preet, three whole days is not an eternity!' Ozorne cried, laughing. 'Yes, I missed you, too!' He glanced at Arram. 'Arram, save me from your bird – she's ruining my hair. You'd think I'd vanished from the earth!'

Tristan sighed impatiently. 'So is anything exciting going on at the palace, Your Highness?'

Ozorne sat while Varice poured tea for him.

'Next week the emperor holds games to honour my cousin Stiloit when he takes the fleet out to sea. Mother was to make the arrangements, but she hasn't been well. She asked me to help – and she had conditions. Arram and Varice – and Preet, His Imperial Majesty wants to meet her – are to be the family's guests on the imperial stand. I couldn't get seats there for more of my friends,' he said apologetically to Tristan and Gissa, 'or the great nobles who already fill up the seats will have fits. I *did* secure tickets for the two of you in the section for the second-ranking nobles.' With an artistic wave of his arm, he produced two gilded papers for Tristan and Gissa, setting them down before Tristan. For a moment the older student looked chagrined, but the expression vanished.

'He's learned it isn't wise to let royalty know you're disappointed,' Varice murmured into Arram's ear.

Ozorne swallowed a mouthful of greens. 'Mother is sending
a carriage to bring the four of you to the games. I have to go
to her at the palace again after Friday classes, but at least I know
my friends will be looked after.' He glanced at each of them.
'Now have I earned your company? And the rest of my dinner?
I'm starving.'

Tristan, Gissa, and Varice had arrived just before Ozorne. They
rose to give him their most joking bows, then went to get their
meals.

'Stop frowning,' Ozorne told Arram as they dove into their
beef tajine.

'Not games,' Arram whispered. 'I hate them.'

Ozorne sighed. 'You can't insult Mother, remember? Varice
and I will distract you. You'll hardly know what's going on. And
I left proper clothing in your room. You must dress well since
we're on the imperial stand.' Arram gulped. Ozorne gripped his
shoulder. 'It's a *compliment*, featherhead!'

'You should have told me weeks ago,' Arram grumbled.

'Don't worry,' Ozorne said. 'We found a spot where you won't
see too much blood.'

All week Arram slept badly, dreaming of the female gladiator
bleeding into the sands. Friday night the dream changed.
Musenda was surrounded by typhoid patients in gladiator gear.
All the big man had for defence was the long rake used to
shove bodies deeper into the fires. Musenda fought his attackers
off frantically, but there were hundreds of them. His rake shattered. He fell to his knees, still trying to hold them back with
the staff.

Arram sat up in bed, sweating. Preet was chattering softly in
his ear.

Ozorne and Varice would notice if he hid somewhere – like
the privies – to avoid the action on the sands. He would spell

a couple of books so no one would see them and he could read all he wished.

No, he couldn't. No one was allowed to use magic in the emperor's presence. 'I'll take small books,' he said, padding into the study to light a candle. He brought it into his room and used it to light the others. The sky was still dark. He scrubbed his face and combed his curls. 'And shift my seat so my view is blocked,' he murmured, thinking aloud. Preet twittered in approval.

Ozorne had brought an expensive cotton robe of a green shade that would make his skin look bruised. No doubt the colour was fashionable. Ozorne would never deliberately pick something because it made his friend look ugly or ill.

As he slid into it, Preet chirred a question.

'Yes, you're coming,' he told her softly. 'The emperor himself wants to meet you. If the killing upsets you, let me know. I'll put you in my carrybag.' He wished *he* could fit in the carrybag.

A soft knock sounded on his door. 'Arram Draper?'

It was a slave clad only in a waistcloth. He wore a collar with the symbol of House Tasikhe. The man bowed and said, 'We've your carriage and Mistress Varice waiting.'

Varice stood beside the carriage. She took his breath away, she was so lovely. Her Northern-style gown of bright yellow silk clung until it reached the chain belt at her hips, where the skirt flared; a white gossamer undergown showed above the low silk neckline. Her hair was braided and pinned with bronze beads that matched those in her pearl-and-bronze belt.

Varice stroked Preet's head. 'I see Tristan and Gissa.' She stood on her tiptoes and waved as the slave stowed Arram's bag tidily on top of the carriage. Preet chuckled to herself, including tiny hissing noises. Arram smiled. Preet always hissed when she saw Tristan. Arram thought the sound was her name for him.

Within a few moments they were all four comfortably disposed inside, Arram and Varice on either side of a good-sized covered basket, Gissa and Tristan riding on the backward-facing seat.

Varice produced four cups and a flat-bottomed teapot from her basket. As soon as the carriage rolled forwards, she began to pour. She did not spill a drop.

Tristan rubbed his hands, grinning with eagerness. 'I have to create a proper thank-you gift for Prince Ozorne,' he said. 'I've wanted to see the imperial arena since I was a pup! Varice, if you have ideas . . .' He nudged Arram with his foot. 'Come on, Stork Boy, aren't you excited?' He took the cup Varice offered him.

Arram glared at Tristan and accepted his own cup from Varice. He didn't like Tristan's nicknames for him. Lately he constantly made jokes at Arram's expense – 'all in fun,' he often said.

'I probably have a *friend* in the games today, if it's the same to you.' Arram gulped back the contents of his cup.

'Which gladiator, Arram?' Gissa asked. 'We can leave offerings to the gods for him.'

Arram smiled at her. Gissa was all right. 'Musenda,' he replied. 'He's a third-ranker. They'll probably just keep him for the mass fights.' He told them how the big man had saved him when he was ten.

'I know his name,' Varice said. 'He's ascending. The gamblers think he may even beat Valor one day.'

'Valor?' Arram asked.

'Big Scanran,' Tristan replied. 'Muscles like boulders. Truly frightening.'

'Stop it,' Varice ordered. 'Musenda's a third-order fighter. Valor only goes against first and second orders. He's the imperial champion, the hero of the arena.'

'Those people are animals,' Tristan said disdainfully. 'They live to fight and kill. It's all that they're good for, you'll see.'

Arram stroked Preet, who sang softly. Eventually the carriage shifted. Varice gasped and nearly spilled her tea. 'We're turning! Put back your curtain!'

They all did as ordered. They had reached the Avenue of Heroes. Ancient trees on both sides offered shade and rest to weary walkers. Between them towered statues of Carthak's greatest generals and warriors. Crowds on foot lined the roads: these people had left the city before dawn to reach the arena.

Arram had a foggy recollection of it all. Much of it was centred on his memory of the elephant, and the blood, and his vomiting, or the huge, torchlit walls and the insides of stone. Now he would be on top of the rocks he had helped to mend, and far above the elephants and the fighters.

Tristan nudged him with his boot. 'Why the glum face?' he demanded. 'We have a beautiful day, beautiful company—' He smiled at Gissa, but his eyes flicked to Varice. 'And excitement ahead! Look!' He pointed out the window on his side. There rose the white stone oval of the Great Arena.

Arram's belly clenched.

Soon enough the roar of those already inside the huge structure swamped them. Arram tucked Preet into a pouch in the drape that fit his arm.

As imperial guests, they drove through both outer gates without stopping, and into the tunnel that led to the imperial section. The clatter of hooves and wheels made all of them grimace. Despite the noise, Arram hung half out the window. He could feel the marble: the mixture of his magic and Yadeen's, too powerful to have faded completely. He could even feel Chioké's power near the tunnel's entrance to the arena.

Once they halted, their coachman and the slave who had carried their things opened the doors and helped them to step down. The two young women wished each other a wonderful time, while Tristan patted Arram's cheek.

'Try to uphold the honour of the university,' he said with his most engaging smile. He offered Gissa his arm and led her towards the nobles' seating, their tickets in his hand.

Imperial slaves in crimson waistcloths and gilded sandals took Varice's basket and Arram's bag. Arram would have tipped the cart's driver, but one of the slaves saw his motion and shook his head.

'It is the pleasure of Princess Mahira to see to the comfort of the slaves,' he murmured to Arram.

'Her Highness is so kind to mere students,' Varice said, linking her arm with Arram's.

On the left side of the tunnel wall, hanging over it as it sloped down towards the top of the arena itself, dozens of people sat or leaned, watching each new arrival and cheering the ones they knew. They threw flowers or shouted jests and jeers to everyone who passed under their review. Varice inspired a cacophony of appreciative whistles and pleas for a smile from the pretty lady. Arram was teased for his height and his silly bird, drawing returning insults from Preet. She produced gales of laughter when she gave them her unmistakable imitation of a series of farts.

Arram shielded his eyes, ashamed and smiling at the same time. Then he heard someone yell his name. He looked up and saw three familiar faces. Binta and her two brothers, Musenda's niece and nephews, waving frantically to him. He waved back and shouted a greeting.

Their guide was glaring at him. 'We must clear the way, sir. The emperor will arrive soon. We cannot block his advance.'

Arram looked up at the children, pointed to the servant and Varice, and shrugged. The children shouted farewells as their mother pulled them back. She and Arram traded waves before she walked out of view, and he half trotted to catch up with his guide and Varice.

'Who were those people?' Varice asked. She was already wielding a fan Ozorne had given her for Midwinter. The day was promising to be unusually warm for April.

'Musenda's family,' Arram explained. 'Remember I told you they were at the plague house? I juggled for the children.'

'I do remember. Too bad he wasn't there to greet you with them.' Varice sighed. 'From the times I've seen him, he's gorgeous – so powerful!'

'And kind,' Arram said, not liking that she knew his friend

only in terms of the arena sands. 'He didn't have to save my life when I was ten, or care for his brother's family.'

Varice looked at him as they emerged into the sunlight. 'Arram,' she said quietly, 'my dear, it's not good to care for a gladiator.'

'Why do you think I hate the games?' he asked, his voice soft.

Inside the stone oval of the main arena, seats were arranged in four great tiers, with the most expensive at the lowest level.

Arram and Varice followed their guide up a stair onto the imperial stand, three broad, shallow platforms isolated from the rest of the audience by a crimson silk cover high overhead. Many nobles and their servants had already arrived, including Ozorne.

He approached with outstretched hands and a broad smile. 'Mithros be thanked, you're here,' he greeted them. He kissed Varice, once for each cheek, and clasped one of Arram's shoulders, unusual signs of favour. Of the three of them Ozorne was the least given to displays of affection. He gave the slave who carried their things a hand signal, and tucked one of Varice's hands under his arm. 'Arram, will Preet go with the slave?' he asked. 'Just until you've greeted Mother? She is not interested in birds, not like His Imperial Majesty.' He indicated a female slave wearing the insignia of House Tasikhe.

'Behave and let this woman carry you to our place,' Arram told Preet softly. To the slave he said, 'She won't peck or bite.'

She reached out a strong arm. Gently Arram held his wrist so the bird could walk over. 'Her name is Preet,' he said.

The slave bowed and followed the other slave across the second platform. Ozorne gave an imperious tug to Arram's drape to straighten it. 'Come *along*,' he demanded. As they stepped down to the first platform, he said quietly, 'Mother is having a bad day. I want everything to go smoothly.'

'Why didn't she just stay home?' Varice asked.

Ozorne grimaced. 'Not when Cousin Stiloit is taking the

Western Navy out for the summer. It's a great honour for him, the emperor presenting games in his honour. It shows he approves of Stiloit as the official heir after Mikrom – Mikrom must have done something to make His Imperial Majesty angry. So it's a very touchy imperial thing, and Mother and I must attend.'

'You never *had* to go to games before,' Arram murmured. He could feel the hum of fresh magic: Yadeen's again, and more powerfully, that of Chioké. He glanced around and saw the two masters seated to one side of the imperial throne. Startled, he realized he felt the masters' personal Gifts, power that was as much part of them as their muscles and bones. They were not using it; the power was simply *there*. Can they sense me like this, or Varice? he wondered.

'I was never third in line for the festering throne before,' Ozorne was whispering, 'and Stiloit wasn't second in line. Apparently *he* said unprincely things when Uncle ordered him to attend these games. You see why he spends so much time at sea, don't you? He'd rather bathe in tar than live a day here.'

They had reached the princess's station, a short step down from the dais. Mahira sat at a table decked with flowers, food, and a gold pitcher glistening with drops of water. A woman Arram recognized as the princess's personal slave stood at her elbow.

Ozorne leaned down and kissed his mother's cheek. She had been staring out over the arena sands, her amber eyes distant. 'Mother, do you remember my friends? Varice Kingsford' – Varice curtsied – 'and Arram Draper.'

Arram bowed and clutched his drape as it slithered off his shoulder. Straightening, he met the princess's flat stare. It was plain that she did not exactly remember him.

'He has the touch of the Sirajit about him,' the princess murmured, her voice icy.

'Mother, that's not true!' Ozorne protested.

'I was born in Tyra, Your Highness,' Arram reminded her. 'My family has lived in Tyra for five generations.'

'A Tyran will lie down with anyone,' she replied. 'As will a Sirajit swine. Their breed wallows everywhere, and goes on breeding.'

Why are people always nasty about pigs? Arram wondered, ignoring her accusation, even distant, about his family's sexual habits. He had learned to ignore insults about his family. It was the first subject people chose when they wished to upset him. Since they could not know his family, it meant nothing.

Ozorne flicked his eyes to the body slave, who filled a cup from the pitcher. Arram saw magic swirl faintly in the liquid as the woman knelt beside the princess and wrapped her hand around the cup. He frowned. No one was allowed to use magic so close to anything connected to the emperor. Ozorne lowered a flattened hand, their private signal for 'later'.

'Arram is a mage of great talent, Mother,' he said gently as the princess sipped from the cup. 'If he doesn't set himself on fire trying to light a candle, he should do great things one day. He is not from conquered Siraj. Any ruler will be glad to have him or Varice at his court.'

The princess took a deep breath and let it out. Her thin body, so tense a moment before, relaxed. 'Yes. Varice. You do so well with food, elixirs, and poisons, my dear,' she said. Her smile was more lifelike, her eyes dreamier. 'I understand I have you to thank for this.' She waved her free hand towards the pitcher.

Arram stared at Varice. Neither she nor Ozorne had said she was working on an elixir for the princess, let alone one that would change the drinker's mood.

Varice was blushing. 'It was both of us, Ozorne and me,' she said.

'I *watched*,' Ozorne said. 'Mother never would have accepted the gift otherwise. Varice did the rest.'

'It may well be that one day I shall offer you a post in my house,' the princess said. 'If you cook as well as you fashion drinks to ease an old widow's heart . . .'

All three of them protested against her claim to being old,

which made her smile. 'And I shall need no elixir to make me peaceful when I know my lord husband is avenged, shall I, my son?'

Ozorne whispered in his mother's ear. Arram bent down to tell Varice softly, 'We aren't allowed to give medicines to people!'

Varice flicked her fan open and held it to shield her mouth as she replied, 'Chioké said I could if he supervised. Are you jealous because I got to do something special?'

'No!' Arram said a little too loudly, enough to draw the attention of some nearby guests. 'No,' he repeated softly. 'But you never told me.' That hurt. Varice had done a magical thing for Ozorne's mother, and neither she nor Ozorne had mentioned it, let alone invited him to the crafting of it.

Trumpets blared in the entry tunnel, announcing the approach of an heir to the imperial throne. The princess nodded to indicate Arram and Varice were dismissed. Ozorne's wry smile told them that he had to remain with his mother for the time being.

'You could have said something,' Arram went on as they returned to their table. Preet sat beside a plate of grapes, glaring balefully at both humans for leaving her.

'I was scared it wouldn't work,' Varice replied. 'It was just before examinations. None of us could think of anything else. It's only a little potion to relax her when she broods, that's all. I started with a tea that healers give new mothers when they're overwrought. It's women's magic. Nobody cares about women's magic. My heavens, isn't Stiloit *handsome*? I had forgotten!' She shook her head. 'He probably doesn't even remember dancing with me that time.' She glanced at Arram. 'I think you told me he did just to make me feel good.'

The admiral was dismounting from a spirited horse. Once in view of the crowds, he stood for a moment, arms raised, as they shouted approval. Today he wore a purple robe and an elegant deep blue drape, but Arram couldn't help but think he would be far more comfortable in a sailor's canvas breeches and hardy shirt. He could see that Stiloit wasn't as at ease here as he had been in the plague infirmary.

With a final slight bow to the people in the stands, the admiral turned and saw Princess Mahira. 'My very dearest aunt! And my mage-cousin!' His voice had a carrying quality that Arram thought must be audible across the arena. It would be a very useful thing at sea . . . or for an emperor. Stiloit walked over to Mahira to kiss her hands, then her cheeks. He kissed Ozorne on each cheek as well.

Varice leaned close to Arram. 'Doesn't he know Ozorne dislikes to be touched unless he invites it?'

Remembering the admiral's humorous eyes, Arram said, 'I doubt His Highness cares.'

As the princess spoke to him, the admiral let his eyes roam until they halted on Varice. They brightened.

'He *does* remember you,' Arram murmured. Varice elbowed him discreetly.

Ozorne, noticing the prince's inspection, waved Varice and Arram over.

'The young mistress Varice!' Stiloit said. He lifted Varice's hand and kissed it, his lips lingering. Varice blushed. Arram and Ozorne both did their best to hide bristles. 'My beautiful dancer! So delightful to see you again!'

'Lady Varice Kingsford, Arram Draper, and I are students at the Upper Academy of the School for Mages,' Ozorne told Stiloit smoothly. Varice curtsied. Arram bowed.

'But, cousin, I have met this young man, during the plague,' Stiloit said. He gave Arram a quick, strong embrace. 'It is good to see you alive and well,' he remarked quietly, letting Arram step back. 'Did they keep you much longer after we met?'

'Just three more days, Your Imperial Highness,' Arram replied, his cheeks hot. He wasn't sure that he liked being touched by relative strangers any more than Ozorne did. 'Actually, all three of us worked during the plague – Varice in medicines and Ozorne transporting them.'

'I saw my cousin Ozorne after I met you that day,' Stiloit replied. 'He was not his usual well-dressed self! And if I had known the young lady was at work nearby, I would have paid my respects.' He caught up Varice's hand and gave it a second kiss, then released it. 'Perhaps I should recruit three such crafty folk to my navy!'

Varice laughed. 'You would have to wait for Arram's help on naval matters, Your Highness.' She placed a comforting hand on Arram's arm. 'His gifts are more in the way of healing and spell-work. Though he does walk on the *bottoms* of rivers.'

Her touch gave Arram courage. 'Indeed, I am the worst possible mage for the exercise of war, Your Highness,' he said, trembling at his own boldness. 'If I try to light even a small blaze, it goes anywhere but the target.'

Stiloit chuckled. 'Rivers aren't for the likes of me. Give me the sea and a strong wind any day.' He raised an eyebrow at Ozorne. 'And you, Your Highness? Are you a student of disease and river bottoms?'

Arram bit the inside of his cheek to still his fury. The man might be a prince and an admiral, but he shouldn't insult a fellow heir.

Ozorne's answer to his cousin was drowned out by the thunder of drums that announced the emperor's arrival. Everyone took their places.

CHAPTER 15

April–May 15, 438

As the emperor stepped up onto the first platform, everyone, even Stiloit, knelt. A rumble echoed through the arena as all those beyond did the same, from the vendors to the watchers on the upper heights.

Arram had seen Mesaraz Avevin Tasikhe before, but always from a distance. This was his first chance to observe their ruler closely. He sneaked a look at the master of the vastness that was the empire of Carthak.

Riding an elephant, armoured and crowned in gold and – for those mage-born who could see it – glittering with spells for protection and for show, he was a creature out of myth. Afoot, he was a dumpy, pale-skinned Tasikhe of Ozorne's height, raised by gilded black pearl-studded sandals with soles three inches thick. His crown – a cap of gold trimmed with silver and assorted gems – sat on thin white hair that had been combed straight back and cropped to the length of his earlobes. A black silk robe stitched with rubies and a scarlet drape bordered in gold did not distract a close viewer from the emperor's chubby cheeks, his pudgy nose, and the pouches under his dull brown eyes. His mouth was petulant rather than masterful.

And yet, except for the great Sirajit War twenty-three years ago, he had kept the empire at peace for the years of his reign, or at least, Arram thought, peace as the empire defined it. After Ozorne's father had crushed the Sirajit uprising, the armies spent their time breaking up tribal wars and noble feuds, subduing robbers and pirates who hunted without imperial approval. This doughy-looking man had survived at least nine assassination attempts that Arram knew of, and restored the empire's treasuries and granaries to a state of health unknown in the history of the five rulers before him.

Which just goes to show that looks aren't everything, Arram decided. After all, Sebo, tiny and old as she was, was more respected than almost any other mage at the university, even Cosmas.

As drums pounded and trumpets blared in the arena, a slave selected different fruits and set them on plates, then added small cups of sauce. Varice giggled when she saw that Arram regarded the serving process with mistrust. 'You dunk a bite of fruit in a cup, silly. It makes the taste more sophisticated.' She speared a grape on a thin-bladed knife and looked at the three small cups. 'This is tamarind syrup, this one is cherry, and this, I am sure, is lime with . . .' She dipped her grape and tucked it into her mouth before the syrup could drip onto her dress. 'Mmm, cinnamon,' she said with approval.

Because Varice was watching, he dipped a piece of fig into the tamarind sauce and smiled as the tastes filled his mouth.

'You should get to know different flavours, alone and mixed,' Varice told him soberly. 'We can be brought low by a common poison if we don't know when something wrong is added to our food and drink. Our Gifts won't warn us unless, of course, you know your poisons.'

He listened to her as he watched the parade of gladiators walk the arena. He could hardly bear to see the elephants, horses, and big cats. He hated to think of the injuries that would come to them in the battles that would soon begin.

A sudden thought shocked him to the bone. I could leave

Carthak when I'm a master. I'd never have to think about the games again.

He fed Preet to hide his confusion from Varice. A young noble had come to speak to her, drawing her eyes away from Arram. More thoughts crowded in. Leave Varice? He looked over to see Ozorne fanning his mother. Leave Ozorne? After promising we would stay together? I can't! They're my real family!

Preet, as always, sensed his distress and began to babble softly. He smiled down at her, thinking how lucky he was to have her company. He was getting carried away. When we're all in one household, Ozorne won't press me to attend the games. And how can I abandon Lindhall, or Sebo, or Cosmas? Let alone Carthak, when I've hardly seen any of it.

He was letting his imagination run away with him. Carefully he reached for his bag, stowed under the table, and opened it. A book, that's what I need right now. And my . . .

He groped wildly, first in one pocket, then two more. Where were his earplugs? Did he forget them?

The first game was announced, a battle between wildcats and warriors on horseback. Varice said farewell to her guest and leaned over to Arram. She reached out one arm, her hand in a fist. 'Take these,' she said in Old Thak. 'Be discreet. It's considered rude.'

She lowered her hand so the table hid it. Arram slid his palm under her fist. She dropped two wax earplugs into his hand.

She had also brought a deck of cards. 'Here, play with me,' she directed. Arram left one ear unplugged so he could hear her as they played. When she lost the first game, she sighed and said, 'My luck has to improve, doesn't it? Will you wager?'

Arram smiled as Preet scolded Varice. He waited for the bird to fall silent before he said, 'You won't catch me that way. Ozorne tells me what a fine gambler you are.'

Varice pouted. 'Still, another game?'

Arram nodded and rose to stretch. Seeing that the first combat was over and slaves were out clearing the sands, he removed his other earplug and walked down to the rail. Directly opposite the emperor's place, on the far side of the arena, was a great statue of Mithros, covered in gold. In this guise the god wore only the kilt and belt of the gladiator. He brandished the short sword and round shield that were the first implements gladiators learned to use. Over the imperial seats, on top of the roof, was a statue of Carthak's patroness, the Graveyard Hag, with a dice cup in one bony hand. She wore a black robe and hood that hid her features. The Great Mother Goddess was nowhere to be seen in this temple of killing and death, Arram observed.

'I see you smuggled your bird in.' Master Chioké had joined him. 'Does Her Highness mind?'

'I left Preet at our table when we greeted Her Highness, Master,' Arram replied politely. 'But I'm not so disrespectful as to *smuggle* Preet. His Imperial Majesty asked to see her today.' The rumour that Chioké might be a good choice as head of the School for Mages, should Master Cosmas retire, was persistent these days. Arram hoped he would be gone by then. Not only did he love Cosmas, but Chioké seemed too interested in the world outside the university. Ever since he had become one of Chioké's students, Ozorne spent a great deal of time thinking about the world as well. More personally, Arram had not forgiven Chioké for the day he had pushed Arram to throw fire until the lightning snakes came. He had nothing against the lightning snakes, other than that they were as unnerving as Enzi, but he hated to be pressed.

The master looked at the gates opening across the arena. 'Ah. The next bout. We should return to our seats.' Yet he remained, looking at Arram. 'Ozorne and Varice are very lucky to have such a talented – and closemouthed – friend.'

'I'm shy,' Arram replied, thinking, If he oozes much more he will be able to skid back to his place.

'Yes. I know. But not invincible or infallible. Just a lad yet.'

Arram bowed before he glared at the man. 'Excuse me, Master Chioké. Varice is waving.' He waved at Varice, so she would do the same when the older mage looked. Quickly he trotted back to her and plopped into his chair. The slaves were setting out more substantial dishes that Varice had brought.

'What did Master Ambition want?' Varice asked after the slaves moved away.

Arram turned his chair so his back was to the arena and tore up bits of bread for Preet. 'I have no idea and I don't care. "Master Ambition" is the perfect name.' He saw her eyes brighten at the action on the ground and said, 'Go ahead and watch. I can read.'

She got to her feet. 'Arram, look – isn't that your friend Musenda? It looks like he has a single fight! He's moving up!' She picked up her skirts and ran down to the rail. The lords and ladies there made room for her without looking away from the men and women who had marched onto the sands.

Arram stood, feeling sick. An arena guard pointed a spear with a bright red flag at the tip at a gladiator in the front of the small group on the sands. It was indeed Musenda. He would fight – and perhaps die – in full view of his sister-in-law and the children.

The Grand Crier, who announced all the events through a horn from the imperial stand at the emperor's feet, shouted, 'Of the first single match, from the bold warriors of the third rank—'

He was interrupted by a trumpet blast. The gate at the gladiators' end of the arena opened, and a leather-armoured man rode out on a beautifully steel-armoured horse. He galloped up to the imperial pavilion.

'That's Valor.' Yadeen had come to stand next to Arram. 'The great killer – or should I say champion? – of the games.'

'Valor does not wait!' the big man shouted up to the crier. 'Valor chooses his foes! Valor does not sit like a girl who waits for a lover! Valor will battle *now*!'

The crier looked up at the imperial dais. There was a long, terrible pause: Arram couldn't see the emperor or Stiloit.

'"Does not wait", my rock hammer,' Yadeen remarked scornfully, causing Arram to choke on the water he was drinking. 'He chooses a younger, less experienced gladiator from the third rank. He'll draw out the fight, make it look good, and then afterwards, he will say he took some small injury that prevents his taking on anyone else. His hopeful opponents of the first and second ranks are the ones who must wait.' He looked at Arram, who was trembling. 'The third-ranker – Musenda Ogunsanwo. That's your friend, isn't it?'

Arram nodded. The Grand Crier bellowed, 'Valor has his wish! He will fight Musenda Ogunsanwo of the third rank!'

Yadeen placed a gentle hand on Arram's shoulder. 'Pray. If there are any particular gods with whom you have a bond, now would be a good time to call on them.'

That was Enzi, but Arram didn't think the crocodile god could have any influence on the games. He was about to silently address Mithros, until he remembered Preet. If the god was not here today, it would be disastrous to bring his attention to the sunbird fledgling napping on his shoulder.

He pleaded with Hekaja to keep his friend uninjured or mendably injured – gods asked horrible prices of those who prayed for the impossible. After he watched Valor dismount and trade his costly armour for the plain greaves and breastplate of a third-rank gladiator, Arram looked up.

He could have sworn the statue of the Graveyard Hag had been staring directly across the arena, at her sister goddess Hekaja. Now she was looking down at the imperial pavilion. No, she was turning her head to look directly at him.

She winked.

A noise of alarm struggled to escape his throat. He closed his eyes, hoping he dreamed. When he opened them again, the statue was in its normal position.

Arram tried to relax and reached for the glass he had placed on his table. Instead his hand landed on something far smaller, with angles. He picked it up and looked at it. It was a clear crystal dice cube with numbers picked out in tiny spots of garnet. He prayed it was garnet and not his first morbid guess, that it was blood.

Yadeen was speaking to him. 'If you wish to turn around, I can sit here so no one in the imperial seats will be able to see you.'

Arram smiled weakly at his teacher. 'I owe it to Musenda to watch.' He clutched the Hag's die in his hand. Preet hopped to his shoulder and hummed softly in his ear.

The fighters moved to the centre of the arena, and the Grand Crier bellowed, 'In the name of Mithros and the emperor, do battle!'

The distance made it easier for a short time. The two men looked like miniatures, not human beings. Valor was shorter than Musenda, but he was built like a bull, with arms, chest, and legs thicker even than his foes. They used small, round shields and short swords, meant – Arram assumed – to bring them closer and draw blood quickly.

Twice Musenda caught Valor's shield edge on the guard of his blade. He used the brief catch to knock Valor's sword from his hand and bash Valor's face before the older man threw himself backwards, freeing his shield, grabbing his weapon, and rolling to his feet at a slight distance from Musenda. The third time Musenda tried the shield catch, Valor threw arena dust he had seized when he fell into the younger gladiator's face. Blinded, Musenda raised his arms to clear his vision; Valor stabbed him in a long shallow cut along the ribs. Arram turned his head away, his lips trembling, then made himself look. His friend was out there. If he could give Musenda some of his power, he would. He wished he could give him some of his will.

On the fight went. Valor knocked Musenda's shield out of his grip and yards away. After an attempt or two to retrieve it, Musenda didn't try again. He lunged and dodged, moving fast and keeping Valor moving. It began to cost the champion after a time; even Arram could see it. Still, he made Musenda pay, a cut here and a cut there. Arram wished it would end and prayed it would not.

Musenda tumbled and fell on his back. Arram leaped to his feet, clutching his Gift to him tighter than he ever had in his life, fighting to keep it under control when all of him wanted to pick Valor up and dump him out of the arena. Preet hung on to his ear with her beak, but the pain did not register. Yadeen's grip on his arm helped a little as Valor charged Musenda, both hands gripping his sword's hilt, the weapon raised above his head, ready to stab down. It was done; Arram knew it was done.

At the very last moment Valor was almost on top of Musenda when the younger gladiator twisted, slashing backhand down and across Valor's bulging, powerful thigh. The champion shrieked in agony and went down, face-first. He rolled onto his back, still screaming, as Musenda took the sword from his grip and stood.

The crowd went mad. They had gone from shrieking their adoration of the champion to demanding that Musenda kill him.

Musenda shook his head and held the sword so that it pointed downwards.

Trembling, Arram looked at Yadeen. 'Does that mean something?' he croaked. He must have been shouting for his friend if his voice was so hoarse.

Yadeen was on his feet, too. 'It means he wants to let Valor live.'

Arram looked at Musenda's many cuts. 'Could you do that?'

The mage shrugged. 'It's different out there, on the sands.'

The emperor stepped down to the platform next to the Grand Crier, and the crowd went silent. He beckoned Stiloit forwards and held his hand out to his second heir.

'He gives the prince the honour of the choice,' Yadeen explained to Arram.

Stiloit held his own hand out palm up, then turned it palm down. The crowd roared so loudly that the stone under Arram's feet trembled. Musenda raised his own sword-bearing arm and drove the short blade into the ground of the arena.

The rear gate opened. Healers ran out with a long piece of canvas secured between two long poles. One of them bandaged the big slash in Valor's leg to stop the bleeding before they loaded the wounded man onto the carrier and took him from the field. Musenda followed them, limping, as the crowd screamed his name over and over.

Yadeen was grinning. 'Well done,' he said. 'Very well done. I see why you like him. I mean to leave an offering to Mithros, to keep him alive.' He grimaced. 'Chioké wants me. Will you be all right?'

Arram nodded as he sank into his chair. He was not going to be sick, despite the blood the two men had spilled, but he was snake-eaten if he would watch any more of these things. And his hand was aching fiercely. He unclenched it to reveal that the goddess's die had pressed its outline deep into his palm because he had clutched it hard. Had the Graveyard Hag blessed Musenda? And why?

He looked up at the goddess's statue. To his horror, she blew a kiss at him before she returned to her usual position.

Ozorne came for Arram as workers were cleaning the sands of bloodstains. 'Good, you haven't vomited,' he joked. 'Uncle and Stiloit would like to see Preet.'

The horrors of this day will never end, Arram thought, getting to his feet. Ozorne rearranged Arram's hair – 'Oh, wonderful, you're using that oil I gave you!' – while Arram checked his robe for spots and groomed Preet to put her in her sunniest mood. As they walked over to the imperial dais, Ozorne said, 'I'm impressed by your friend Musenda. Valor is a crafty old dog, and he's pulled that "I'll fight *now*" trick too many times. In fact, I'd say he pulled it one too many times!'

'How is he?' Arram enquired, trying not to trip. 'Does anyone know?'

'I'll find out, if you like,' his friend offered. Arram could only nod. They had reached the dais. 'Now remember,' Ozorne said quietly, 'bow to the emperor first, Stiloit second. Bow *very* low to the emperor. If he points the sceptre at the ground, kneel. Don't talk until he says you may.'

Arram barely remembered his audience, except for his shakes and Preet's success at charming the old man. Stiloit seemed to guess that the conversation was a test. He only mentioned that they had met at the plague infirmary, where Arram worked very hard. Ozorne told him later that the emperor had asked about his family, and his plans for the future. There at least Arram had done the correct thing, saying that he meant to study as much as he could at the university because there were so many things he needed to learn. Apparently the emperor was so pleased with his response that he gave Arram a purse of gold thakas 'with which to advance your studies'.

When Ozorne walked him back to his table, Arram promised himself that he would not leave it again, unless he absolutely had to use the privy.

The afternoon was well along when Varice collapsed into her chair and deposited a heap of coins onto her napkin. Interested, Arram removed one earplug. 'You were wagering?'

'I found some dolts,' she replied smugly. 'The woman with the tiger was obviously going to win, I don't care how mighty those big strong men who fought them looked to be.'

There were only two bouts remaining when Varice noticed that a slave wished to speak to them.

'Yes?' she asked, very much an imperious Carthaki lady. Arram wondered where she had learned the manner. She had always been a good mimic.

'It is the young master,' the slave replied with a bow. 'It is . . . irregular, but His Imperial Majesty has granted permission, if the young master is willing . . .'

Arram stared at the slave, confused. Preet pecked him out of his fog. 'Ow! Preet! If I am willing to do what?'

'If the young master is willing, the gladiator Musenda Ogunsanwo asks if he may have speech with you.'

Varice leaped up, clapping her hands together. 'Speech! Arram, he wants to talk with you! Where is he?'

Arram blinked. With all the heat, the smells, and the noise stuffing his head, it took him a moment to realize what was being asked of him. He said faintly, 'Yes, where is Musenda?'

The slave pointed. 'In the tunnel.' As if they needed to be reassured, the slave added hurriedly, 'He is chained and guarded. You will be safe.'

Arram glared at the man. 'He is a human being, not an animal. Furthermore, he is a friend of mine.'

The slave took a breath, then bowed and said nothing. It was Varice who said, 'No, Arram, I've heard some of them can be savage after a match. They work themselves up to such a state to fight. It's not safe to talk to them unless they're in their cages or chained.' She tugged his hand. 'Let's go see him!'

Arram tugged back. 'Cages?' he asked, outraged. 'They live in *cages*?'

Preet chattered in alarm. Arram realized that people were turning to look at them. He ground his teeth and followed Varice and the slave down to the tunnel. There loomed Musenda, covered in sweat and chained at his throat, hands, and feet. He wore bandages over several of his wounds. All of them glittered with magical treatments.

Three men in armour with the arena's insignia held his chains. They wore heavy leather gloves and carried batons.

'It's all right, lady,' one of them told Varice. 'He don't go mad after his combats like some.'

Musenda grinned at Arram and offered a chained hand. 'You look like you've been eating better than the last time I saw you.' His voice was rough – doubtless from shouting in the arena, Arram thought.

'It's good to see you,' Arram replied. 'You had me worried out there.' He reached for the man's hand.

'Here, none of that,' a guard said, shoving his baton between Arram and Musenda.

Arram trembled. He wasn't sure if it was from fear of the guards or fury at learning those who risked their lives in the games lived in cages. 'Don't be ridiculous,' he said, his voice shaking. 'We've met before. He won't harm me.' He took Musenda's hand. 'It's *very* good to see you.'

The audience in the stands was bellowing. The second-to-last match was about to begin. Musenda's captors shifted restlessly. 'When I saw you up there, I knew you'd be luck for me,' the big man said. He grinned. 'But I'm a rude monkey. I haven't greeted this beautiful lady.'

Varice laughed. 'I'm Varice Kingsford. I'm Arram's friend. And your admirer.' She offered Musenda a small purse. 'I won a bit of money on your match, and I feel I must share. For one thing, Arram told me you support your sister-in-law and her children.'

Musenda bowed, his chains clanking, and accepted the purse. 'You're very kind, great lady. My family can always use whatever I earn.'

Varice blushed. 'I'm no great lady – just a mage student, like Arram.'

'Mage students who sit with the imperial family,' Musenda remarked.

'Our friend and his mother invited us,' Arram said, trying to understand the wary look in the big man's eyes.

'Surely you mean Her Highness Mahira Lymanis Tasikhe and His Highness Ozorne Muhassin Tasikhe,' one of the guards said. 'Great ones of the empire.'

Now Arram understood the look in Musenda's eyes. He'd been trying to warn Arram about the way he spoke of members of the imperial family. 'You're right,' he said, looking at his feet. 'I wasn't thinking.'

'Musenda has to go back to camp,' said the guard who had reproved Arram.

'Yes, of course,' Varice replied. 'And we should rejoin our hosts.'

'Please tell your family I said hello again,' Arram said as Varice tugged his arm. 'I saw them this morning. They look much better out of the infirmary.'

'Arram!' Varice tugged harder.

'Young masters! Princess Mahira asks for you!' One of the princess's slaves was leaning over the iron rail between the platforms and the edge of the tunnel. 'You must return to your places at once!'

Musenda said, 'Gods go with you, Arram. Good to meet you, Lady Varice.' He nodded to the men who held his chains. They began the process of turning so the four could leave through the tunnel without getting entangled with one another.

As they walked off, Arram remembered his manners and called, 'Graveyard Hag bless your future games!'

Musenda raised a hand as far as he could but did not turn around.

Arram and Varice returned to bow to Princess Mahira and chat with her again when the next match, a grand brawl between gladiators from the third and fourth groups, was over.

It's just as Master Sebo says, Arram decided during their ride home. Each bit of stone tossed into the river creates ripples, which create still more, which intersect with other ripples, each making a new pattern in the water. There is no way to tell what might result, once you pick up a stone and throw it. We can only be ready for where the power takes us.

He turned the crystal die over and over in his fingers. He almost wished he'd given it to Musenda. A gladiator was far better off with a token from the Graveyard Hag than a student was.

Once he was home, Arram was careful to write perfect, unblotted thank-you notes to the emperor, Stiloit, Princess Mahira, Ozorne, and Varice. When it was dark and Preet was sound asleep, Arram

did a quick sneak to the nearest shrine for Mithros with a donation for permanently damaged gladiators in Musenda's name.
Also, with considerable nervousness, he offered one of his
favourite finished stones, a lovely piece of amber, to the
Graveyard Hag – just in case.

In class the next day, he showed the die to Yadeen. The mage
picked it up and instantly dropped it. Arram, in an unusual fit
of grace, caught the piece before it touched the ground.

'Sir?' he asked. Yadeen never dropped anything.

Yadeen plunged his hand into a bucket of water. 'Where did
you get that?'

'Well, the, um . . .' Arram stammered. Catching a fiery look
from the master, he said, 'At – at the games.'

'Who gave it to you?'

'Master, I don't know.'

'I have never met this Master I Don't Know. Whoever he is,
I doubt he wanders through battle games giving away diamond
dice studded with garnets. Who gave it to you?'

Not for the first time in their relationship, Arram thought that
Yadeen had a very intimidating glare. 'Master, truly, I don't
know.' He took a deep breath, summoning his courage while
Preet scolded Yadeen. 'Stop it, Preet. Sir, I was looking at the
Lady of the South's statue in the arena.' Those who did not
wish to offend or get the attention of the Hag used her far more
polite name, taken from the usual position of her statues. 'A-and
I th-thought she was moving, and th-that appeared o-on my
t-table.'

'It is most certainly from her,' Yadeen replied sourly. 'Take
very good care of it. Keep it with you. And hope that she
continues to like you.'

'Absolutely,' Arram replied, wiping the sweat from his forehead and remembering the way his spine had tried to crawl out
through his skull when she had winked at him.

Yadeen shook his head. 'I have never known such a student
for getting himself into strange situations. First a peculiar birdie,

and now a die from Carthak's own goddess. This one thing is true: your future is written in fire.'

Arram stared at the master, hurt. 'I don't *try* to get into bad situations, Master Yadeen!'

'Hmph,' the man snorted. 'We are making jewellery today, young mage. Protective jewellery with protective stones, for a nice, manly bracelet. We'll wrap your die in a gold wire cage and attach it to the bracelet, if you like.' Arram nodded eagerly. He was terrified that the thing would fall from a pocket or get stolen from his room. 'Start with the proper metal chain to string it and your beads.' Yadeen held up a bead. 'Here's the proper size of bead to use, so be sure to get the proper size of chain.'

Arram took the bead from the master's hand and went to the rolls of cord and metal chain at one end of the room: Yadeen was often called on to make magical jewellery using powerful stones. He was about to measure out a length of his favourite blackened metal when he realized that Yadeen had said it would be a protective bracelet. Doubtless it was safer to choose protective metal as well as stones. His hand wavered between gold and brass.

'Take gold,' Yadeen said. 'Consult your own taste.' Once Arram had chosen his chain and measured enough for his own wrist and more in the event of mistakes, Yadeen pointed to a section of drawers. 'Those stones are drilled to accommodate that width of chain one way or another. I will tell you if I believe another stone will serve you better, or if I believe you should add gold spacer beads or stones for a different influence. But first we begin with protection from magic – any and all magic. What would you choose?'

Arram began with onyx, red jasper, flint, and black agate. When he added crystal quartz and garnet, Yadeen snatched them from the table and replaced them with diamond and ruby. He placed seven small round gold beads on the table beside a long oval bead of mottled jasper. 'For visualization and divination?' Arram asked, touching the long stone.

'And to find what is hidden, uncover lies, and obtain freedom,' Yadeen told him. 'The gold?'

'Success, protection, good health – what if it doesn't work, sir?'

'You will only have yourself to blame as the customer,' Yadeen told him. 'So I would make it the best protective bracelet you can.'

Arram's head was still buzzing at the thought of the costly bracelet Yadeen wanted him to make – who would pay for the materials? – when he reached Cosmas's workroom. The master was seated at the worktable, papers strewn around him. Looking up, he smiled and waved Arram to the breakfast laid out by the window, then bent over his paperwork again. Arram knew the signs. He settled Preet to her own second breakfast and served himself, sketching the arrangement of his beads on their chain as he ate. When finished, he put the dishes where the master's runners would pick them up and refilled his own teacup as well as the older man's.

Their time was nearly done and Arram was reading when Cosmas sat back with a sigh. 'Finally! I have to say, my boy, working out a schedule for your summer and autumn terms was no small task! I have only one question, and I am certain you will not be happy with it. You must give up one of your present classes – tribal magic or advanced charms. You may have one but not both.'

'Sir? Why? I like both!' Arram protested.

'And your teachers like you, which is something I never thought to hear from Urukut. He is not the easiest of instructors.'

Arram smiled. No, the teacher of tribal magic was not particularly easy, but he knew a great deal and warmed up considerably to a student who was truly interested.

'No, our problem is that Master Ramasu wishes to take you for three classes in a row,' Cosmas explained. 'You are to begin work in the infirmary that serves city people outside the Lion Gate. Lindhall says that since you live in his quarters, he is certain that you will continue to learn there. That leaves you with a choice. Either you will continue with advanced charms, or take Urukut's class instead.'

Arram ground his teeth. He loved both classes, but only one of them had Faziy. 'I suppose I'll stay with Faziy and advanced charms, if that's all right, Master.'

Cosmas blinked for a moment, then said, 'But, Arram, that's not possible.'

Preet uttered a questioning whistle. Like Arram, she was confused.

'Why, I would have thought . . . Well, you have been busy. Faziy has been hired away from us, if you can believe that!' Master Cosmas explained. 'The Inlands Trading House has offered her far more than the university can pay to inspect and price charms for the market. It's a splendid opportunity for her,' he added gently. 'You know very few mages do well in terms of payment, particularly those who are so young. Chioké recommended her for the post. Promise you will congratulate her.'

Arram drank the last of his tea. 'Of course I will, Master. I've just been learning so much from her.'

Cosmas sighed. 'It's true. She is very learned, and we shall miss her.' He shook his head. 'Shall we say charms with a new instructor, or Urukut?'

'Master Urukut, please, sir,' Arram replied glumly.

When Arram walked into Faziy's class that afternoon, she immediately recognized the source of his sad look. 'No, no, no!' she cried. 'You must feel happy for me, Arram! You must! I'll be able to bring the rest of my family here, and you know I miss them!' Preet flew over to the instructor's shoulder and twittered in her ear. 'Preet is happy for me, aren't you, pretty bird?'

That made Arram smile. He loved Preet, but she was a drab little thing, nowhere near pretty.

Faziy lifted a small black velvet bag, a sign they were about to begin. 'Tell me you wouldn't jump at work that would pay you as much as the university pays a master like Lindhall or Yadeen,' she challenged Arram.

He gawped at her. 'That much?'

'University teachers accept use of university tools, libraries, and supplies as part payment,' she informed him. 'And housing, for the ones who don't mind students everywhere. The outside world is always profitable. I'd be a fool to turn away an opportunity like this! Now, tell me what manner of charm I hold, how strong it is, what it is made of, and how long it will last.'

Arram sighed and did as he was told. He would have to find excuses to visit her at her new place of work. She was so much more amusing than many of his teachers, love them though he did. Suddenly he sat up straight. 'Will the lightning snakes follow you into the city?'

She laughed. 'Of course they will! Once they take a liking to a person, they stay! Now, your practice, if you please.'

That evening Arram and his friends were discussing preparations for the spring term examinations over supper when Ozorne returned from the palace.

'Where have you been?' Varice asked as she and Gissa rose to kiss him on the cheeks. 'We thought you'd be back last night.'

Ozorne slumped into a chair between Varice and Arram. 'Stiloit sailed with the fleet at dawn this morning,' he said. 'His weather mage said they'd have the best sailing of the summer in the next month, and Stiloit told Uncle he was going. There was a group of pirates off the southwest coast he just missed last year, and he means to take them.' Ozorne yawned. 'I saw Mother back to the palace and had a long nap.' He undid a pouch from his waistband. Opening it, he drew out a fan decorated with gold lace. A gold tassel dangled from the end. 'Stiloit heard you love fans,' he told Varice with a grin.

'Oh, sweet goddess,' Varice whispered, opening it. The fan glittered in the lamplight.

He handed the pouch to Arram. 'He wanted you to have this.

He said there is no point in getting you juggling tools, since you seem to just pick up anything – toys, spoons, bowls. He thought this might be more useful.'

Arram drew out a good-sized mortar made of a hard, ripple-filled gold and golden brown wood. It was dense and heavy in his hands. Arram recognized it at once. 'Lifewood,' he said. 'Great Mithros, this is . . . it's an amazing gift!' And there was another object in the pouch: a lifewood pestle. Healers cherished lifewood tools. Even those with no magic could draw healing from lifewood, while those who worked spells with tools made from it increased their power several times over.

'I think my cousin likes you two,' Ozorne said, smiling. 'I will say this – he has good taste.'

Varice laughed and fanned Ozorne. Arram, speechless, could only turn his new tools over in his hands. They were perfect for someone about to start work for three hours a day in an infirmary for residents of Thak City.

THE IMPERIAL UNIVERSITY OF CARTHAK

The School for Mages

The Upper Academy
SCHEDULE OF STUDY, SUMMER–AUTUMN TERM, 438 H.E.

Student: Arram Draper
Learning Level: Independent

Second Morning Bell

Stone Magic – Yadeen

Third Morning Bell

Fire Magic – Cosmas, breakfast supplied

Morning Classes

Medicines; Thak Gate infirmary – Ramasu, instructors

Fourth Morning Bell to Lunch
Lunch – Noon Bell
Afternoon Classes

Tribal Magic – Urukut Ahilep
Illusions: Small Animals – Dagani
Water Magic – Sebo
Plants – Hulak

Supper – Seventh Afternoon Bell
Extra Study at Need

CHAPTER 16

June–September 2, 438

The main thing Arram remembered from the spring examinations was his goodbye to Faziy. He had paid Yadeen some of his carefully saved money for the silver materials – slender chain, double loop clasp, setting – and a beautiful piece of jade, both for calm and prosperity. Even Yadeen, who was difficult to please, praised the necklace when it was done. Faziy wept when he presented it to her on the last day of class, and allowed him to help her put it on. She laughed when he showed her the mark he had engraved on the clasp: a tiny lightning bolt.

'I won't worry about your prosperity,' she told him before he left for Dagani's class. 'I know that one day everyone will know who you are. You should start to think about a mage name.'

'She's right,' Tristan said when Arram told his friends about it at supper. 'Arram Draper isn't the sort of name to inspire awe. No one is ever going to learn what my name was before I changed it.'

Varice leaned her chin on her hand. 'Something dark and mysterious, like you're growing to be. Though I'll miss Arram.'

'I'd feel silly with a grand name,' Arram said, feeding Preet bits of fruit.

'And I have to keep mine,' Ozorne said. They gathered up

their dishes and left the dining hall to work on their studies. The discussion was over, but every now and then Arram would toy with the idea, trying out new names and laughing at his efforts.

When the marks were posted, Arram was pleased with his. He was even with Ozorne and Varice in the classes they shared, which was all that mattered. Tristan and Gissa did well enough in their own classes that they mustered a group of friends and headed into the city to celebrate. Arram, Ozorne, and Varice retreated to the menagerie, where new leopard cubs had just arrived.

The friends' week of relaxation was done before they knew it, and Arram was pitched into his new schedule. He dimly realized at some point that he had expected to be making more medicines for Ramasu at the infirmary. In truth, that was part of his work, as was mopping, scrubbing, fetching materials for older helpers, and guiding patients to the rooms where they would be cared for and given a bed if necessary.

He had been there a month when one of the older students grabbed him by the arm and hauled him into an examining room.

Ramasu stood by a weathered, skinny man who sat on the worktable. The man wore a plain old shirt, breeches, and sandals, as well as a thick, dirty rag wrapped around one arm.

'Water, clean cloths, cleansing liquid,' Ramasu ordered.

Arram turned to get those things, but Ramasu said, 'Not you, Arram. Gerb will do it.' The student who had brought Arram there left the room. 'This is Daka. He is a farmer from one of the villages to the south. Daka, my student, Arram.'

The man nodded shyly to Arram.

'Daka had an accident a week ago, and waited until now to come to us,' Ramasu said with reproach.

Daka glared at the master. 'It's plantin' time,' he retorted, as if Ramasu had forgotten a central aspect of life. 'My woman is near to poppin' with another babe, so *she's* no help. The older two is some use, but she needs them at the house and the home garden.' He smiled. 'Him and the girl is hard workers, and a help to their ma.'

'And how did you hurt your arm?' Ramasu asked. Arram was startled. Talking with the farmer, his reserved and aloof master was gentle, even kind.

'Agggh!' Daka growled. 'I tripped comin' in from the field and hit a sharp-edge rock. It wasn't too deep, so my woman washed it in vinegar for me and wrapped it up. I didn't think no more of it till the thing leaked through the wrap. I took it off, and the thing were all swole up. I put a clean cloth on it, but it hurts and hurts.'

'Were there herbs in the vinegar?' Ramasu asked. 'Bits of leaves or sticks?'

'She puts plants in it for flavour,' Daka snapped. 'Everyone does.'

The student Gerb returned with the requested supplies and laid them out on the table, ready for use. 'Shall I remove the bandage, Master?' he asked Ramasu.

The master shook his head. 'Arram will do it. You prepare a wet cloth. I will be ready to hold Daka's arm if it is needful.' Ramasu looked at the farmer. 'We're cautious only because this cloth may now be stuck to your arm. I'd like you to hold still, if you would be so good.'

Daka looked at Ramasu, then Arram, gulped, and nodded. He held out the arm.

'Wash your hands in the fountain,' Ramasu instructed Arram. 'Use the soap. Touch nothing once they're clean, until you hold Daka's arm. Where is the injury?'

Arram could see the swelling of the cloth on the underside of Daka's forearm, but the man pointed it out anyway. The rising flesh under the bandage reached from the farmer's wrist almost to his elbow. Arram hurried over to wash. When he finished, he shook the excess water from his hands as he had seen Ramasu do. Then he walked over to Daka and undid the knot on his

grubby bandage. Gently Ramasu raised the farmer's arm until
it bent in an L shape. Arram would be able to look directly at
the injury when he bared it.

'You should see Arram in class,' Ramasu told Daka as Arram
carefully unwound the bandage from the farmer and wrapped
it around one of his own hands. 'He has a bird – the size of a
small blackbird – that goes nearly everywhere with him.'

Arram lost track of what the master was saying. In the lean
flesh under the bandage he felt something wrong, just as he felt
something wrong when he worked with sick animals. If he went
by what he knew of animals, the man had an infection, a bad
one. Already he could see yellowish leakage on the bandage,
then brown old blood on the last few layers. These were not
inclined to come away from Daka's skin.

The man grunted.

'I'm sorry,' Arram said. 'I'll take one more small pull, and if
that doesn't give, we can soak it a little to—' He tugged gently
on the cloth.

'Here,' Ramasu told him. Arram reached out with his Gift to
feel what the master did with a touch of his own power and
the sigil for release.

The cloth yanked free of the wound, peeling away dried blood
and other matter. Pus and blood spurted, splattering Arram's
face and shirt.

Instinctively he kept his mouth and eyes closed until he felt
no more fresh liquid. Then he grabbed the cloth over his shoulder
and wrapped it tightly around Daka's wrist, stopping the flow of
blood and matter. For a moment none of them said or did anything
else. Then Gerb soaked a cloth in the warm water he had brought
and began to clean Daka's arm. Slowly Arram unwound the clean
cloth until he could see the wound. It oozed sluggishly, an abscess
that would have killed the man without treatment.

'That seems bad,' Daka remarked. He looked at Ramasu, his
eyes filled with terror. 'If I get my arm cut off, my fam'ly will
starve.'

'It's no cutting matter,' the master said kindly, resting his hand on Daka's good shoulder. 'Watch. Arram, I understand you know the basics for the sharing of power.'

'But that was marble!' Arram cried.

Ramasu nodded. 'The combining of our power is much the same – I discussed it with Yadeen a while ago. The difference is in the lines. Instead of fibres within stone, we will work in terms of nerves. And you will not lend power this time. You will work as part of me, learning this kind of mending spell as you go.'

Worried – marble was far less vulnerable to his sort of mistake than a human body would be – Arram glanced at Gerb.

The older student shrugged. 'It's how he dunked me into the river of healing,' he said. 'I didn't drown, and I hear you're clever.' He grinned.

'You just experienced a small sample and lived,' Ramasu pointed out.

Daka glared at Arram. 'If you might get on, boy?' he demanded. 'I have chores at home.' He looked at Ramasu. 'I'll be able to do me chores?'

That settled Arram. He knew as well as the farmer that the loss of a day's work might mean the loss of some part of his family's meals. Besides, there was a baby coming. 'What must I do?'

Ramasu glanced at Gerb. 'I will have a poultice, the empha-sized honey—'

Before he could finish, Gerb said, 'Turmeric, and olive leaf extract, boiled linen poultice, cotton bandage.' He looked at Arram and explained, 'He thinks I never remember anything. It's his favourite mixture for an open wound. In a month you'll be saying it in your sleep.'

As he walked out, Ramasu muttered, 'I do *not* get my proper portion of respect.'

'Me, I like a youngster with spice,' Daka told him. He was a little grey and beginning to sweat. Without instructions, Arram began to clear the table of the things they had placed there before. One of the shelves was stacked with blankets. Arram took two and placed the first on the table. To his awe, Ramasu picked Daka up in both arms and gently set him on the blanket, then took the other from Arram and covered the farmer with it. Arram kept the wounded arm clear of the cloth and placed it across Daka's chest when Ramasu was done.

'Now you let us work,' Ramasu told Daka. 'When you wake, your wound will be clean and bandaged, and in two days you may remove the bandage.'

Arram yawned and glanced at Daka. The farmer was asleep. 'Not you,' Ramasu ordered. 'Let us link together.'

It began that way. At the end of the morning Ramasu handed Arram a battered volume titled *Master and Student*. 'It is so slow, the other way,' Ramasu told Arram as the youth leafed through the volume. 'I have perhaps a handful of students a year who I can teach this way, and not all of them care for it. We re-inforce what we learn through magic with studies you will undertake using this volume and in the infirmaries. You can learn just as much from the nurses and the senior students.' Arram nodded, remembering the staff at the typhoid infirmary. 'And it may be that you will decide the medical arts are not for you. If that is the case, I must know right away. I do not have so much time that I can waste it on someone who dislikes the work.'

'Oh, no, Master!' Arram replied, shocked. 'This is so much better than things like battle magic, or studying what will earn me a place among the wealthy!'

Ramasu smiled. 'You are young. You may change your mind – and if you enter Ozorne's house, you will labour for him as much as for the sick, remember.' He urged Arram through the door closest to the university's main entrance. 'Have a good meal. You will need it after all you have done today. And read that material tonight!'

When Arram returned to the infirmary in the morning, it was

to the knowledge that Daka's wife had presented him with a new son.

The next month was something of a blur in his memory until he got used to his new schedule. The infirmary and Lindhall kept him moving, and Hulak was all too happy to step up his learning with regard to medicinal plants. Yadeen decided that he'd done so well in making spells that came from magical jewellery that he increased Arram's studies in that area at the same time that Cosmas began to teach him about the uses of fire in the university kitchens. Dagani brought their small class of three to the next step, that of simulacra of small animals, but Ozorne, Varice, and Arram expected that. There the difficulty lay in the creation of believable simulacra of living creatures. They had done well with birds, but small animals, particularly pets, were more difficult. And Urukut decided that Arram was ready to learn magic from tribes that had vanished centuries before, leaving only their statues and stone markers behind.

Worst of all from Arram's point of view, Varice was angry with him for three weeks. She told him it was because he had snubbed two girls she had introduced to him. Ozorne told him privately that he simply wasn't paying attention to her the way he had before that term.

'I think it's the falling asleep over supper, frankly,' his friend added with a grin.

Arram tried to scowl at him but couldn't. 'What do you suggest?'

Ozorne consulted with the gold bead at the end of one of his braids – that week's colour scheme was gold, dark blue, and black. 'She has been admiring the bracelet you wear, and the necklace you made for Faziy.'

Arram looked at the prince with admiration. 'Where would I be without you?'

Ozorne chuckled. 'Surely it goes the other way.'

A week later Arram gave Varice the most delicate silver necklace he could fashion. Three small gems hung from it. He presented it to her in a silk bag after Hulak's class one August day. 'For love, prosperity, and protection,' he told her as she drew it out. 'And there's no magic on it, because I know you don't like magic things on your skin.'

Varice untangled the chain and held the necklace up. 'You made this for me?' Her eyes were wide and filled with amazement.

He nodded, looking at the ground. 'I tried to find a blue stone with the properties I wanted, but this seemed better.'

'Would you fasten it?' she asked, nudging him. 'So I can wear it.'

He knew she must fasten her necklaces all the time, but he couldn't resist her request. He stepped behind her to do up the hook, breathing in her scent as he did so. She wore woods-lily scent today, just the lightest touch. It made him a little giddy.

'There,' he said, facing her once more.

She had taken a mirror from her bag and was examining herself in it. 'It's lovely!' she cried, flinging her arms around his neck. Before he knew what was happening, she had kissed him firmly on the mouth. Preet sang, flying around them, before Varice let Arram go. 'I can't wait until Gissa sees it!' Varice told him. 'She'll die of envy!'

'No, don't,' Arram said, his head still spinning from her kiss. 'She might want me to make her one, and . . . they're special, that's all. It takes strength to make them.'

Varice looked at him. 'You said there isn't magic in it. I don't feel magic in it.'

He shrugged. 'There isn't, but . . . I think about them, when I work on them. About the power that naturally goes with the stone, and the metal. Jade and silver for money and protection, silver for the moon—'

'*I* knew that,' Varice interrupted. 'Silver for the goddess, remember?'

He smiled at her. 'And jade for love.'

She blushed. 'Oh, who needs love? A mage only needs fun – love gets us in trouble.'

'Well, but you might want it someday, and then there's the love of friends.' Feeling bold, he put an arm around her neck and kissed her hair. 'But it's hard, somehow, thinking about those things as I work on a piece. So don't tell her it was me.'

Varice sighed. 'All right.' She brightened. 'I'll tell her I've had it in my things for years and just found it again.' She kissed his hand and unwound his arm. 'Ozorne will be wondering where we got to.'

'So he will,' Arram agreed. 'And we have papers to write for Master Cosmas.'

To Arram's pleasure, there were no examinations for infirmary work. Gerb, who oversaw him when Ramasu was away, pointed out sourly that every day in the infirmary was an examination. Arram didn't mind. That month he had been assigned to work in the infirmary on Friday nights, where he cleaned wounds and healed black eyes in addition to judging more serious injuries and referring these wounded to the healer best at their particular hurts. Friday night, he learned immediately, was the night many of the poor families celebrated being free of work, even if they were too exhausted to attend their temples on Saturday.

What Arram liked was not so much the hectic hours, but the quieter ones, near dawn. He had made a new friend at the infirmary. Okolo was a curvy, lively girl who knew what to do with a shy, lanky boy in a storage closet when the waiting area was empty and the other healers were napping or playing card games. She always knew how to make Arram feel better when a sick or wounded child came in, just as she knew to fetch Arram when a child would not calm down for one of the other healers. She was fascinated by his juggling, and even learned to keep two balls of linen bandages in the air at once.

At the end of the term, she told Arram she was to be re-
assigned to an infirmary just for children in Yamut, far to the
east. 'They have so much poverty there, with all the fighting
that goes on,' she explained. 'But they also have healers from
Jindazhen and the Kepula and Natu island countries who come
to study and work there. Their ways are different than ours.'
She kissed him. 'I'd ask you to come with me – we'd have so
much fun! – but I know you would never leave your friends.'

He would have protested, but he knew she was right.

The term ended. Arram was released from infirmary duty to
travel with Sebo. They took a rented fisherman's boat through
the harbour at Thak's Gate and westward on the coast. Here
they camped in a secluded cove. Over their campfire Sebo talked
about the sea and its temperament, the swift way weather could
turn, and the glories of the water below the surface.

'You'll see tomorrow,' she told Arram just before she retired
to the tent their crew had raised for her. 'Later next year I'll
take you for more extended journeys. It's good to know seas
and rivers. Then we'll visit lakes and the more vigorous rivers
inland. Unless you object?'

'Never!' Arram said eagerly. 'It sounds wonderful!'

Sebo eyed Preet. 'Stop pouting, bird,' she commanded. 'You
can't go underwater with him, and that's where we go tomorrow.'

Preet croaked at the old woman. To Arram's ear the sound
was very rude. 'Preet! Manners!' he scolded.

She glared at him and croaked again, but apparently she was
not too vexed. When he settled in his blankets, she cuddled into
her usual place under his hair, against his neck.

'I love you, little bird,' he whispered very quietly. He had put
his bedroll down a short distance from the others. If he talked
in his sleep, he didn't want anyone to know if he called out,
especially if he called out a particular name, like Varice's.

Walking into the sea with Sebo in the morning required all
the nerve he could muster. It was not so bad in the cove, but

when he was up to his chest, an incoming wave knocked him over. He fought his way up and a yard forward. It was harder to touch the bottom in salt water, as he found when the next wave knocked him down. He was not going to drown – he wore the mages' bubble that kept him dry and able to breathe – but he floundered like an infant on a table.

Sebo made a sign in the water, one that glowed with her Gift. Arram copied it and immediately went to the bottom, standing as if he were on land. Walking was more difficult. The sea pushed back at him until he copied Sebo's walk, turned slightly slantwise into the tide. Now they made progress, avoiding the creatures that lived among the rocks of the bottom and confronting the fish that came to eye them. Arram might have stayed there forever if Sebo had not pointed out that it was getting dark above.

He said little as they rinsed and ate supper. He did tell Preet about it when he couldn't sleep. 'I didn't appreciate it when I came here,' he told the bird. 'But I was ashore then. The gods are truly wondrous, to have created this world.'

'Good,' he heard a voice whisper. He looked around, but Sebo was nowhere near, and that was her voice. 'A little piety is a good thing for a boy, and sleep is a good thing for an old woman. Sleep.'

Sebo woke him well before dawn to show him to a great moon tide. It bared the seashell creatures, crabs, shrimp, and slugs that normally hid in water-covered crevices. Arram sketched as many as he could before they were summoned to their boat.

On their way home through Thak's Gate's harbour, they saw people screaming and pointing at the water. Curious, Arram went forwards. One glimpse at the problem, and he yelled for Sebo.

The immense brownish-green shape in the river rose, revealing its vast upper body. Preet zipped across the river and landed on the monster. Arram called on a spell that would make his voice louder. 'He is a god!' he shouted to the watchers on land. 'He is Enzi, the crocodile god of the Zekoi.'

Very flattering, the god replied. *Preet, if you will devour those insects behind my ears . . .* Enzi sighed as Preet pecked at the flesh where the insects were vexing him. *I thank you.*

'How sweet,' Sebo said tartly as she joined Arram. 'Have you a good reason for terrifying half the city?'

I could not find you on the river, Enzi retorted. *You were nowhere near the university, the capital, the palace, or this sewage hole. How was I to know you were jaunting about on all that salt poison?*

'Do you have something to say?' demanded Sebo. 'If not, I am weary to the bone. I've gone out to sea before and you never objected.'

This is different, Enzi told her. *Troublesome times are coming. Troublesome for us all, land and water. Danger and death come. You are needed here.* Preet rose from his head and returned to Arram. *Thank you, child,* Enzi said. He glared at Arram. *And no, I have yet to find a proper gift. You may continue to look after her. Don't feed her so much.*

'Enzi,' Sebo said, '*what* kind of trouble is coming?'

What other kind is there? asked the god. *Blood trouble.* He smacked the water with his tail and vanished.

Sebo sighed. 'I will tell those I think are serious and wary. You concentrate on your studies. And offerings to the gods might be a good idea.'

The students insisted that the great storm that broke before the start of school came because the gods were cruel. It lasted all the night before and the final day of vacation, as well as the first two days of school. Like Lindhall's students, Arram immediately went to help with the animals. They rushed to get the outdoor creatures indoors and calm the nervous ones, as well as check that no rain leaked through to the rooms where the indoor animals were kept. The master himself muttered as he and Arram did their last check of their charges, saying 'It's too early for this, much too early.'

Worried, and perhaps just a little because he wanted to, Arram left Preet indoors during a break on the first day and went to the arena-like circle where he practised fire magic. Thunder crashed over the university. He knew a circle of protection would do him no good. He simply raised his arms and called to the lightning snakes with his Gift.

He didn't know how long he stood there as the rain drenched him completely. It was a while, because his arms ached when he lowered them. This first edge of the storm had passed overhead, taking its thunder with it. Puzzled, he climbed up to his room. The animals sleeping there complained when he dripped on them. He apologized quickly and gathered up dry clothing. Dumping his wet clothes in the hall, he tried to remember if he had seen so much as a single bolt of lightning.

He had not.

The next day he asked a number of people, including his masters, if they had seen lightning the day or night before. Some were positive they had not. Others were unsure, but were positive that they must have seen it. And still others demanded to know why he asked such a silly question.

Several waves of the storm, all lightning-less as far as he could tell, passed through before it ended sometime during the third night. Lindhall's students returned the animals to their normal homes, opening weather shutters to the sun and warmer breezes. For the rest, the university was in session.

Yadeen scowled when a yawning Arram greeted him. 'This year we turn to crystals, the tricksters of stone magic,' he informed Arram. 'If you give them so much as a moment's lapse of attention, they will slip your Gift along their surfaces and tangle it into a knot you cannot undo, so wake up!'

Arram covered another yawn. Masters – all masters – did not care for excuses.

Yadeen snorted. 'You'd think Lindhall believes you're his only student. All right, we'll go slow, but only for today!'

Arram stared at the master.

'You think I was never a student?' Yadeen demanded, his large eyes flashing. 'Now.' He opened a small box to reveal an array of bright stones in pink, blue, green, red, violet, and yellow shades. 'No magic. Identify these and the magic associated with them, and we'll work on your juggling. Your cross juggling is still a little awkward.'

Three days later Arram was deciding on lunch when he noticed how whispery the dining room was. He looked around. Everyone seemed shocked. Some girls, and a few boys, were weeping.

He hurried to his table. All of his friends were present but Ozorne. Varice was crying into a handkerchief while Gissa hugged her about the shoulders.

'I barely knew the man,' Varice explained. 'But he was wonderful.'

'What happened?' Arram asked everyone at the table.

Varice laid her hand on his arm. 'It's Prince Stiloit, and his vessel, and two other ships of the Western Navy,' she said quietly. 'That storm caught the fleet out to sea. Three ships sank. His Highness drowned.'

Along with his crew and those other crews, Arram thought. Was this what Enzi meant by his warning? It must be.

He thought of the prince, so alive and charming. 'Black God ease his passing,' he murmured. 'And that of his people.' The others murmured their affirmation.

'The imperial escort came for Ozorne this morning,' Tristan said. 'Twelve days' mourning at the palace, poor fellow. He asked if we could lend him our notes.' He looked at Arram. 'Too bad he can't borrow your notes for anything but illusions.'

'Tristan, don't needle him,' Varice said. 'He has no control over where the masters put him. You know that by now. And why should you complain? You two share fire magic and war magic, not to mention weapons magic and spy magic. Don't tell me differently, because I saw your schedule.'

Tristan glared at her. 'You hold yourself very high since hobnobbing with the nobility at the games,' he retorted, his face grown hard and far less handsome. 'Getting too good for us peasants?'

'Tristan, enough,' Gissa told him. To Varice and Arram she said, 'We're all upset today. We have to go on mourning food and mourning meditations for – How many days is it, Varice?'

'Twelve, just like the imperial family mourns,' the younger girl replied glumly. 'Three for Mithros, three for the Goddess, three for the Black God, and three for the Graveyard Hag. An hour of meditation before supper, and flatbread and butter for meals. Unless you know someone inventive. The kitchens will be closed and locked.'

Tristan leaned on his elbow, flashing a bright smile at Varice. 'My dearest, dearest friend!' he said teasingly.

Varice propped her chin on her hand. 'Of course, towards the end of the twelve days one's invention and supplies run thin.'

'We have a Saturday in all that. We can get a meal in the city,' Gissa remarked.

Arram was not listening. He picked at his food, thinking about lightning. If there had been no lightning here at the school, what if it had been over the fleet?

He hadn't seen it over the university during all that thunder, when Faziy said the two always came together.

Faziy.

She had told Chioké about lightning snakes, and Chioké had found her a job in the city that she would be a fool to resist. Such a favour put her in his debt and took her away from her university friends.

Chioké liked power. He had his eye on Cosmas's place, but surely chief mage to an imperial heir was better, particularly when bad things happened to the other heirs.

There were only two people who would listen if Arram mentioned it to them.

* * *

Sebo scowled at him when he finished. 'You did not tell me –
or Yadeen – about the incident when Faziy told Chioké about
lightning snakes.'

Arram thought of several excuses, none of them good, and
shrugged instead.

'Young people and your shrugs!' she snapped. They were
sitting on a log that had washed up on the riverbank. Now
she picked up her walking stick and walked to the water's
edge. Arram wondered if he should follow and decided to wait
instead.

She returned, but she did not sit. Instead she leaned on her
staff and frowned down at him. 'You saw no lightning in the
storm? *Felt* none?'

Arram shook his head.

'But there was thunder.'

He nodded. 'Right on top of me for a bit. Even in little storms
I can see flickering in the clouds, but there was nothing this
time. And I suppose I do feel, uh, *prickling* as a storm advances.
But only in the ones with lightning. Not the mild ones.'

Sebo stared off into the distance. Finally she asked, 'Have you
told anyone else? About this storm?'

Arram snorted. 'They'd make fun of me and call me—' He
was about to say what they really called him, 'an ignorant
tribesman', until he remembered that Sebo was born to a tribe.
'A fool,' he amended.

She smiled grimly. 'You'll have to learn to catch yourself better
than that, if you mean to enter a prince's service.'

A prince, Arram thought, dismayed. Ozorne. Ozorne will have
to live close to court.

She patted him on the shoulder. 'Tell no one. Not any masters,
either – I'll decide who should know. It's not just students who
think only ignorant tribespeople believe in the lightning snakes.
You were right to tell me, though. I think you know that. Don't
worry about it any more.'

'But something was going on, wasn't it?' Arram asked.

'Someone else who knew about lightning snakes did something, or got Faziy or someone else—'

Sebo put her hand over his mouth. 'And you'll keep *that* to yourself, too,' she ordered harshly. 'Understand? Or do I have to put a silence on you?'

Arram shook his head.

She took her hand away. 'You are too cursed clever for your own good. Learn to hold your tongue. Now, bring up your protective spells. We're visiting the hippos.'

'Do we have to?' Arram complained, but he stood and did as she ordered. He would think about her warnings later.

In twelve days the locks on the kitchen were removed. The students descended on the dining hall as locusts might on a field of wheat. Ozorne returned that night and piled his plate before joining them. Preet hopped to his shoulder once he'd eaten for a little while and began to inspect him, running her beak through his hair and over his cheek, then wandering down his arm to inspect his hand. Finished, she peeped at him until he stroked her.

'Yes, I've lost weight,' he told her and his silent friends. 'The emperor is strict in his mourning observances. I was more concerned for my mother's health than my own. I was finally able to persuade her physician to give her yogurt drinks during the day.' His smile was long and sly. 'He discovered he was more afraid of me than he was of the emperor, at least in such close quarters.'

The others laughed. Arram patted his friend's shoulder, but something about that smile and the flicker in Ozorne's eyes disturbed him. He dismissed the feeling. Doubtless the healer was made nervous because Ozorne was now second in line for the throne and too powerful to offend.

'How fares His Imperial Majesty?' Gissa asked. 'The shock of losing another heir must be dreadful.'

'He does as well as any man who began the decade with

seven heirs and now has two,' Ozorne replied. 'Now, please, everyone, let me *eat.*'

The others laughed and obeyed, turning to talk of their classes. Ozorne listened, his eyes alert, even as he devoured the contents of his plate. Once he'd finished, he sat back with a sigh. 'You'll help me catch up, won't you?' he asked Arram.

Diop, their old roommate, was seated with friends at the next table. He looked over at them, a strange light in his eyes. 'There's a laugh,' he told his companions, his voice loud enough to be heard by everyone nearby. 'I'm surprised they don't arrange for him to take all of His Highness's examinations.'

Ozorne tapped the table with his finger as he half turned in his chair. 'I don't recall anyone asking you to join our conversation,' he said mildly, despite that tapping finger. 'I have yet to hear it said that I have not done very well on my own.'

Diop sniffed. His tablemates were trying to hush him, but his voice got louder. 'But now you need not bother. Only command your freak to manage your studies for you, Your Highness.'

'You are even more obnoxious than you were when you lived in our quarters,' Ozorne replied, his eyes not wavering from Diop's face. His finger still drummed the surface of the table. 'For your information, the three of us have shared classes – and work – for a number of terms. I have yet to see *you* in our classes.'

'Did you have to pay so the other two could share your . . . classes?' Diop asked, his voice full of rude suggestion.

Ozorne lifted the finger he had been drumming and pointed to the doors. 'Out,' he ordered quietly.

Diop stared at him for a long moment. None of the students who were listening seemed to breathe. Then he gathered his book bag. 'You're not emperor,' he said, his voice shaking. 'And the three of you are nothing special.' He spat on the table and walked out.

'Well!' Varice's voice shook. 'Somebody sat on a snake.'

'People are jealous,' Tristan murmured with a shrug. 'They

would like to get to know Prince Ozorne better, but Highness, you limit your circle to Arram, Varice, sometimes Gissa and me, and anyone we may be courting. People grow bitter.'

Ozorne's eyes glinted sharply. 'I won't have my friendships dictated by the likes of Diop Beha.'

'There is advantage to be had, Your Royal Highness,' Tristan replied simply. 'Perhaps not with Diop, but with others. You could use allies.'

Ozorne looked at Tristan but said nothing.

Arram said wistfully, '*I* should like to know what put the burr in Diop's anus.' As Ozorne and Gissa choked on their drinks, Arram explained, 'He never liked us, but he hasn't gone after us for months.'

'He was kept back this year,' Varice said, stacking her dishes and placing them tidily on her tray. 'At least half of our first-year Upper Academy class has been kept back. Maybe you only looked at your marks, with the fasting and the prince's memorials, but I look at all the marks. Every fall class is reduced by a good number. The students are held back, or some go home, or switch schools.'

When Arram stared at her, Tristan said drily, 'Here is where the winnowing starts. Each term more of us will be left behind to repeat the one before. Not all mages are equal. Surely you knew that.'

Arram had known it in a vague way. Since it never had anything to do with him or his friends, he hadn't spent time worrying about it. He barely knew what year he was in these days.

'Forget Diop,' Ozorne said, putting a hand on Arram's arm and on Varice's. 'I'm just delighted to be back where I belong. Tell me all the gossip.'

They talked school and palace gossip until Gissa reminded them of the night's studying yet to be done. When they scattered, Ozorne looked more vigorous than he had when he'd first sat down at the table.

Late that night Arram woke and found it hard to go back to sleep. Resolving to find the most boring volume on Lindhall's shelves to put him in the right frame of mind, he pulled on his robe, called up a ball of light, and wandered into the study.

He was shocked to find Ozorne curled up on the floor between Lindhall's great chair and the table covered with enamel pieces. He had his head on his knees, while with one hand he was scratching Lindhall's large land tortoise, Sunstone, on the head. The animal was leaning against Ozorne's side, making soft sounds of contentment. Ozorne, too, was making sounds, but to Arram it sounded as if his friend was weeping.

He reached in a pocket and found one of several handkerchiefs. Gently he poked it through an opening between Ozorne's free hand and his knees, then sat with the table between them. He didn't want Ozorne to feel crowded. If he wanted to talk, he would.

At last the prince raised his face and scrubbed his eyes with his handkerchief. 'Tell anyone you caught me crying, and I'll . . . I'll tell Varice you fart in bed.' He blew his nose.

'And I'll remind her that you will say anything if you're trying to get revenge. Which of us do you think she'll believe?' Arram reminded his friend.

Ozorne lowered his knees. Immediately Sunstone climbed into his lap. His host sighed and helped the great animal to get his hind feet up, then spread the handkerchief on the table neatly. Tugging the corners into shape, he murmured, 'Why did he have to die? I liked him. The others I don't care about. Mikrom? Well, the less said about him, the less vexation to the gods. He'll be emperor after all. But Stiloit was always decent when he was around. When I was little he'd take me out on his ships and name all the parts for me. If he caught Mikrom bullying me, or anyone else, he'd give them what he called Sailor's Brew.' He raised a hand and tapped it lightly against one of his eyes. 'And now we can't even bury him. He's—' The tears were coming again. Ozorne covered his eyes with his arm. 'He's at the bottom of the sea.'

'I liked him, too,' Arram said. 'Even if he kissed Varice's hand too many times. He was generous with the plague infirmaries, and the children.'

'And a valiant captain in battle,' Ozorne said mournfully. 'He would have been so good for the realm if he could have lived.'

'Sometimes the gods take our best,' Arram said. He wasn't certain that he believed the old saying, but it felt like the right thing to tell Ozorne.

'Don't blame the gods,' Ozorne told him. 'I asked Uncle to have the shipbuilders investigate. That fleet was pronounced fit to sail in the spring.' His eyes flashed in the dim light cast by Arram's Gift. 'If they betrayed Stiloit to an enemy – if they sold good materials and used cheap ones, then pocketed the rest of the money – they will pay for it in blood.'

'Ozorne,' Arram said, hesitating. For the first time he was a little afraid of his friend. 'It was a storm. A storm and lightning. You can't behead nature.'

Ozorne was silent. Arram wished Preet had woken. She could always cheer Ozorne when he got in one of his dark moods. Finally the prince shifted. 'Sunstone, my legs have gone numb.' With a grunt he lifted the animal and gently set him on the floor. Muttering, Sunstone set off down the hall. To Arram, Ozorne said, 'Where would I be without you to keep me in check? Gods will it, I shall never find out. Give me a hand up.'

Arram clambered to his feet and pulled his friend up one-handed. Ozorne hugged him impulsively. 'Don't ever abandon me, Arram,' he said. 'I don't know what I would do if you weren't at my side.'

Before Arram could reply, Preet flew in, cheeping imperiously. She circled Ozorne several times, then landed on his shoulder and tugged at his braids. The prince began to laugh. 'All right, all right, I'm sending him back to you! Whoever heard of so strict a bird!' He kissed her when he lifted her on his finger and placed her on Arram's shoulder. Then, with a wave, he left for his own bedroom across the hall.

CHAPTER 17

September 15-30, 438

Ozorne had been back for two weeks or so when Arram, on his way to class with Sebo, found Enzi blocking the path. He greeted the crocodile god with pleasure; Preet said hello by running her beak along the creases in his rock-solid hide. Enzi had been away since giving his mysterious warning to Sebo and Arram. Now he was back, looking plump.

'The hunting has been good?' Arram enquired politely once he'd greeted the god with the proper respect.

Well enough, Enzi replied. *But it's good to be among intelligent companions again. I hear you lost another prince. You humans had best be careful – you only have two left.*

Arram shrugged. 'The emperor has placed all manner of guards on Ozorne. And if he isn't safe in the university, where can he be safe?'

Enzi looked up at him. *Humans. So proud of your rocks and sticks and spells. You have yet to see gods at* real *work.*

Arram looked away so Enzi would not see him smile. 'And frankly I hope that I never do, begging your pardon.'

You are in a saucy mood today. Where is Sebo? the god demanded. *There is something she must take care of in the river. I suppose you will come along, since you are here.*

'I used my crystal to tell Hulak that Arram won't be able to attend their lesson.' Sebo came down the path, as gaudy as usual in a yellow and black head wrap and purple body wrap printed with green and yellow flowers. She carried a cloth workbag that blazed with protective spells. 'Now, what is so important?'

Not tell, the god retorted. *Show, downriver. You must ride before we are close enough to walk. Come.*

'Bring your mage's workbag,' Sebo commanded. Arram nodded and took it out of his larger book bag, slinging it over one shoulder.

Preet returned to Arram as Enzi led them to the water, where an empty rowboat lay on the beach. Two good-sized crocodiles basked in the sun next to it. The god waddled briskly past the sleepers and into the river. *You two, get those ropes I showed you,* he ordered the mortal crocodiles as they thrashed and darted into the water. *Sebo, Arram, into the boat.* When he saw Arram hesitate, the god roared, *They are my great-great-something-grand-sons, dolt! They will not harm you!*

More than a little, a voice remarked. Arram guessed that the speaker was the bigger of the two mortal crocodiles. His guess was confirmed when Enzi lashed 'More Than a Little' across the nose with his tail. *Ow! Grandfather!* 'More Than a Little' protested, paddling back and away from the god. *It was a joke!*

You are within my aura, young idiot, Enzi snapped. *They can hear you. That is why the tall one smells of fear.*

Do not worry, the smaller crocodile assured Arram. *Grandfather fed us well before you came. We are not hungry hardly at all.*

Ropes! Enzi bellowed. *Into the boat, Sebo! Boy!*

Preet flew to the boat's rail and made a sharp, scolding noise.

Arram, Enzi grumbled. Sebo snorted.

Gently Arram held the master by the arm as she hiked up her skirts and climbed into the boat, her workbag over her shoulder. She took a seat in the bow. He eased himself onto the seat in the stern and nervously grasped an oar.

'Don't be silly, lad,' Sebo told him. 'Enzi's grandsons will tow us.'

Arram hadn't noticed the ropes tied to a ring that dangled off the bow. Each mortal crocodile gripped a rope in his mouth and began to swim downstream, towing the boat in their wake.

'What's going on?' Arram asked Sebo as Preet hopped onto his knee. 'Enzi didn't tell me.'

Sebo shook her head. 'He said I'd understand when I got there. Apparently it offends him greatly.'

It should *offend you, old woman.* Enzi rose from the water. *It is a work of human magic, and it is poisoning the river. You must stop it.*

'You should have got someone else,' Sebo retorted. 'I'm too old to be galloping hither and yon this way.'

Who was I supposed to get? Him? He swung his snout towards Arram. *He is a good lad, but he is not ready for this. I do not know the others, save for Lindhall, enough to trust them. You know how Lindhall is underwater.*

'I know,' Sebo replied sourly. She glanced at Arram. 'He doesn't like it,' she explained.

Enzi continued, *I will be doubly grateful if you tell those mages in the city and the palace that the next one to make a poisonous disposal such as this will be eaten.*

The god said nothing more. Arram shifted his weight until he could trail the fingers of one hand in the river. He was reasonably certain that Enzi would discourage any predators from trying a taste. Preet fluttered to Sebo's lap as the older mage said, 'If there's poison, we wouldn't pick it up here, lad. The river flows downstream, in case you've forgotten.'

Arram smiled at her. 'I haven't forgotten. I'm just sensing things.'

'Suit yourself,' the master replied. She removed Preet from her knee and took a scrying mirror from the bag of tools she had brought with her. The fire of her Gift shimmered around it as the boat surged downriver.

Arram looked at the bird, who now perched on the rail. 'Enzi, are you taking Preet back to her family soon?' The thought was a hurtful one, but he had to ask.

Again, you ask! I will say when I find the proper gift, Enzi snapped. Preet chuckled. *You mortals always rush, wanting things done immediately. Can* you *think of a suitable gift for the chief of the gods, the god of law and the bane of thieves?*

Arram, speechless, shook his head.

Then do not pressure me, boy. That god is inventive when he feels a fellow god requires correction. A proper gift must be selected with great care.

After a moment Sebo remarked, 'I hear lightning snakes are fond of Arram. I wonder how they might act if they thought he was being . . . bullied.'

Enzi rose half out of the water to eye first Arram, then Sebo. *Lightning snakes?*

'Lightning snakes,' the mage replied serenely.

Enzi sank down into the water before he replied, *Interesting.*

'They're very friendly,' Arram called. 'I'm sure they'd like you if they got to know you.'

They drew past Point Kovanik, the northern end of one of the army's sprawling camps. Arram looked up. Atop the camp's high stone wall, guards walked back and forth. A few hundred yards around the point, the many-greats-grandsons halted and drew back towards the boat, bringing it to a stop.

Arram frowned. He knew this part of the river after his time with Sebo, but never before had it been like this. There was something bad in the water, something rank. When he stretched out his Gift, he felt plants and tiny fishes dying a foot or two beneath the surface. Larger fish moved sluggishly, trying to escape the source of the . . .

'It isn't rot,' he said, pulling his hand from the water. 'Or any poison I know.'

'Let us accept that you do not know every poison in existence.' Sebo was always quick to remind Arram that, while he was advanced compared to his friends, he still had much to learn. More kindly she added, 'Nor is it something I know, but it is rife with magic.' She had not needed to actually put her hand in the water.

This is why you are here, old woman, Enzi said, impatience in his voice. *Do you mean to study everything from the boat? Have you forgotten my teaching of you? The only way to learn the river—*

'Is to be *in* the river, yes! I am no longer a young thing who forgets her own name for new magic!' snapped Arram's master. 'Boy, if you are coming, you will need better protection than your robe!'

Arram had been openmouthed at the idea that Sebo might have once been young and, even more shocking, absentminded. She never forgets *anything*, he thought, struggling out of his outer robe. Wearing only a shirt and breeches, carrying his workbag on his shoulder, he cleared his mind and carefully wrapped himself in the spell that let him walk and see underwater. He strengthened it against magic and poison, then double-checked every element, wary of his own tendency towards absentmindedness.

'Preet, stay here and be good,' he ordered. Then he followed Sebo and her workbag over the side of the boat.

The spell pulled him down to the bottom, just as he had crafted it to do. Here the river was murky with the leavings of the military camp and what the tides brought upstream from the port of Thak's Gate. He hated the mess, but he had walked in it before. That was why he had added vision spells, allowing him to see in the murk.

His protections did not help with the feel of the river bottom as he walked along it. He envied Sebo the spell-work that allowed her to glide above it like a fish herself. She never touched the mud, garbage, and sewage that boiled up every time Arram put down a foot. He had tried to learn the working, but without luck.

Now he saw extra darkness against the murk. Something

bulky lay on the river's bottom. A heavy stone block secured it in the mud. Chains led from the block into an area of shadows half a head taller and a little wider than Arram. The shadows were unmoving, a dead spot in the current that flowed around them. Arram joined Sebo. 'Is this the source of the poisons?' he asked her, his voice travelling through their protections.

Her eyes were bleak. 'What does your Gift tell you?' she asked. She had removed a knot of fibre from her workbag and was undoing the strands.

Always teaching, Arram thought with an inner sigh. He let his Gift flow carefully towards the shadows. His magic told him nothing was there but polluted water, though it passed over and around the darkness just as the river's currents did. 'What?' he muttered. He straightened and tried again, harder. His Gift flowed up and around the floating thing, not through – but if the shadows were simply river water, why did everything pass around them? His Gift passed through everything except his masters' strongest wards. Again his power told him that nothing was there, though *something* kept his power from going through it.

Arram ground his teeth. Perhaps he was spoiled, as some of his fellow students claimed, but these days he was used to his power telling him what he wanted to know.

'Boy, I wouldn't do—' Sebo began to say.

It was too late. Arram released his strongest spell of revealing. Yadeen had taught it to him so he might find particular stones far underground, but it also worked for finding objects and people in all environments. This time the shadows blazed with light and went dark; a giant fist punched Arram halfway across the river.

Fortunately, Sebo's water-walking spell was proof against almost anything. Arram was only dazed, not drowned. He lay among the roots of reeds, wondering where he was and why he had chosen to take up fisticuffs.

Enzi descended and shoved him so hard that Arram fell

forwards onto his face in the opposite direction. *Stop playing, and help Sebo!* the crocodile ordered. *I did not bring you here for your amusement!*

'Odd,' Arram said, pushing himself upright with care. 'I don't *feel* amused.' Slowly, still dazed, he walked towards the source of that poisonous wrong.

This is taking forever, he heard the god say behind him. Immense jaws closed on his waist. Enzi swam forwards with Arram clasped in his mouth.

To Arram's wonder, the god's teeth only dented his protective spell, rather than tearing it. 'How do you do that?' he asked. Enzi did not reply. He dumped Arram next to Sebo.

The mage had her fibres loose in her hands. 'If a little power doesn't do what you want, think of something else before you try using a lot of it,' she told Arram. He nodded, struggling in the boggy silt as he tried to stand. 'Protections this complex often have traps to ward off mages.' She swiftly wrote three signs in the air with a couple of her fibres, then dropped them. They burst into flame and vanished. Light flooded the water all around. 'Now,' she said as Arram finally got to his feet, 'stay here and anchor my spell with these.' She reached through their spells and handed him more fibres.

'Did I know we could pass through our protections?' he asked, touching her spells. His fingers did not go through.

'*I* am able to do so. And I suppose it is time you learned, but not today. Someone wanted this thing hidden; I want to know why. Stay here and anchor my spell. Clear your mind and concentrate on your Gift, understand?'

'Yes, Master Sebo,' Arram said, feeling dejected. Why did every good new lesson have to come later?

'Stop pouting and concentrate, or I'll give you something to pout over,' she snapped.

She raised her remaining fibres and muttered. Her Gift spilled out and away from her. Sebo walked forwards and around the poisonous thing, passing behind Arram as she shaped two complete circles. He barely noticed her movement, busy as he was anchoring her spells. Within his Gift his power shifted and surged, moving as it often did when it struck greater magic. One day, he promised, I will stop meeting Gifts that are greater than mine.

Even as he thought it, he knew that promise was an empty one. If they learned nothing else at the university, they learned there was always someone with more power. Arram only had to look at his teachers to know that much.

The circles that enclosed him quivered. He braced himself: Sebo was working the spells and signs that closed her spell. Instantly her circles enclosed the object like a cocoon. The water and the shadows flowed out into the river, exposing the thing they had kept hidden.

Arram gasped. His protective globe was gone! Still, he could breathe. 'Sebo?'

'I combined our protections with the larger one,' she replied.

Arram inhaled and coughed. The stink that rose from the thing that had been hidden so well reminded him vividly of the corpse fires during the typhoid epidemic. The object fell backwards with no water to hold it upright, splattering Arram's clothes. He gulped down vomit that rose with the odour and walked around the thing Sebo had uncovered.

Without shadows to mask it, he saw a series of chains and knotted ropes bound tightly around a collection of burlap sacks. Sebo motioned for Arram to remove the topmost layer of burlap. Inspecting it, Arram realized he would have to cut: the rough cloth had been pulled over whatever was inside and secured by the bindings. He drew his belt knife and showed it to Sebo. She nodded and waited, her Gift sparkling around her hands in case anything went awry.

Arram always made certain his knife was razor sharp. He needed it as the wet strands fought his blade. He started at the upper end of the thing, where he would not fight chains and rope as well as sacking.

There was another layer of burlap under the first. His knife lost its edge there. He had to borrow Sebo's for the final layer, which was spell-written silk. He could feel something rounded under his hands. Finished at last, he pulled the silk away from human hair, black, sodden, and limp. Shoving the layers of material down past slender shoulders, he revealed a half-rotted face that still managed to look familiar. The chin, the nose . . .

Puzzled and frightened, he looked at Sebo. 'Master?' He was proud there was no wobble in his voice.

'It's hard, when the rot's been at her,' she murmured. 'The wraps kept the fish away. I'd say she's been here three weeks, perhaps? Around the time of the storm. Have you learned the spell for a true appearance?'

His brain was still stuck at three weeks. Now that the cloth was off the corpse's face, Arram was positive that the dead woman was a mage. He knew it in his bones and had been trying to think if anyone had gone missing around that time. But there had been the mourning, and living on scant meals, and new classes to start . . .

Sebo rapped his head. 'A spell for true appearances, boy!'

Arram winced. It wasn't right that the master's knuckles should be so *hard*.

He touched the corpse's chin squeamishly and turned her chin towards him. That was when he spotted silver at her neck. Without thinking he reached for it and drew the necklace up. It was thin silver, delicate, with a double-loop clasp and a scratched piece of jade.

Numb, he took the chain with both hands and slowly turned it, trying not to tear the rotten flesh of the woman's neck. On one loop of the clasp, broader than the other loop, the artisan had carved a lightning bolt.

Sebo looked at Faziy aHadi. 'Girl, girl,' Sebo whispered, her voice sad. 'Look at you now. What did you get yourself into? All that new money cost you more than you could afford . . .'

'You knew her, too?' Arram asked softly.

'Of course I did,' Sebo replied. 'I'd take her the odd trinket from the river's floor, and we'd work out what we had. And then all that good fortune just dropped into her lap.'

Arram showed Sebo the lightning bolt on the fastener. 'I made this for her. Master, she knew lightning snakes.' His mouth trembled, but he refused to cry.

'What did you do, Faziy, that they took such care to sink your corpse? If not for Enzi, you would have rotted beyond anyone's ability to know you. I never come down to this cesspit if I can help it.' The master sighed. 'Arram, what does her placement here tell you?'

He didn't realize she was talking to him until she poked him with her elbow. He flinched. He didn't want to remember Faziy the way Ramasu made him think about the infirmary dead. 'Um, as you said, they didn't want her to be found.' He added, 'And if she was found, they didn't want her known. So whatever she was doing with them or found out about them, it was important. They went to a great deal of trouble to keep her on the bottom of the river, and to make sure people wouldn't recognize her if they found her. These spells are hard – advanced work.'

Decide who did this later, after you take the thing away, cloths and all. Enzi's voice made the globe of power that Sebo had placed around them shudder. *The magic that killed it corrupts the river. Do not leave the meat. The vileness has spread into it.*

'Then you must help us,' Sebo retorted. 'We cannot tow it ourselves.'

'We can't tow it at all,' Arram reminded her, pointing to the boulder. He grabbed a chain, trying to pull it away from the rock, and cried out as stabbing heat shot into his palm. A chain-shaped burn was seared into his skin.

'Hag's pox, boy, when will you learn to wait before leaping in?' Sebo demanded. She removed a small jar from her workbag and gave it to Arram. 'Just a little on that burn. No need to be wasteful.' She took out a second vial and removed the wax, then the cork that kept its contents inside. Carefully, crouching so she saw exactly what she did, she poured the tiniest of drops on two sides of one heavy link. Arram watched, halting in the middle of rubbing her ointment into his palm, as frost formed where the liquid had fallen. It spread. Abruptly there was a loud crack; the link fell to pieces. When it did, a puff of magic flew to the top of their protections. Arram tried to seize it but missed.

'Idiot boy!' cried Sebo. 'Never do that again, or I truly *will* beat you! You have no protection since I remade ours to include poor Faziy here. That wickedness would have sunk into your pores, poisons and all!'

Arram looked at the puff of grey magic. It sparkled with the different colours of Gift that must have gone into the making of it, only a foot over his head. It didn't look dangerous, but he decided not to try Sebo's temper again. Puff after puff rose to join the first until Arram was half ducking, trying to keep away from them. With a jingle, the chains fell away from the wrappings and Faziy's body.

Sebo corked the liquid that had eaten through the chains and sealed it. 'Yes, I will teach you how to make this,' she told him as she tucked the vial into her workbag. 'You're at the point when a potion to eat through metal might be useful.'

Arram gulped. He could think of all kinds of situations in which such a potion would be useful, but he planned never to be in any of them.

'Enzi, if you please,' Sebo called.

What do you want?

As Sebo explained her plan to the crocodile, Arram knelt so he didn't have to worry about the magics at the top of their bubble. He stared at Faziy's face, both the magicked living one and the rotting one beneath. Whoever had left her in this place had risked discovery, by fishers, garbage pickers, or boats. Even at night they would have needed concealment and avoidance spells.

They'd also needed a good-sized, strong boat to get that big rock all the way out here. They couldn't take the chance that a stone heavy enough for their purposes would be on hand already. So there were a few of them who knew about this. Or just enough strong mages. It would have to be mages, to disable other mages who happened by.

Sebo patted his head. 'Sit, Arram. We're going up. I'll need you to help me.'

'Whatever you say,' Arram replied. He sat gingerly as he tried to avoid lumps on the river's bottom. Once he was settled, he crossed his legs. He wanted to be out of Sebo's way and to touch as little as possible.

The woman looked down at him. 'You shouldn't be so accommodating about lending your Gift to others.'

'But you're my teacher,' Arram replied. 'If you meant to do something harmful with my magic, wouldn't you have done it earlier, when I couldn't defend myself?'

Sebo rested her free hand on his shoulder. In her other hand grew a ball of their mixed Gifts. Arram hadn't even felt her draw the power from him. 'I hope your ability to protect yourself is as strong as you seem to think it is,' she murmured. 'The world is an unpleasant place. Only look at what we just found.'

Her ball floated to the top of their globe of protection. There it spread in a wide umbrella, trapping the poisoned magics against the globe's ceiling. When the combined Gifts stopped spreading, Sebo wrote five signs in the air and touched each one with her finger. They vanished. The globe of power that enclosed them together with the dead woman trembled, lurched – Arram caught his teacher and helped her to sit – and began to tug itself out of the river's muck. It shook free of the giant boulder and resealed itself with a mild *pop!* So quickly had it happened that only a palmful of water leaked in. Slowly the globe began to rise.

The bit of water rolled over to Sebo. 'Get away from me, you nasty stuff!' Arram heard her whisper. 'The Hag knows what kind of filth is in you!' She glanced at Arram, who pretended to stare at the unpleasant magics overhead. 'Well, go on!' he heard his master say to the trapped liquid. 'I'll return you to the river when we must leave it. Go over there. *Over . . . there.*'

She was silent. When Arram glanced at her, he saw the handful was pooled in her lap without soaking into the skirt. How had it got there? She had talked to it as if it were alive. He looked at the place where he had last seen the water, in case there was more of it. No, the floor of their globe was dry, and the river bottom was receding into the murk.

Sebo had seen his glance. 'When we return – when I have delivered our discovery – I will give you a book to read about a thing called wild magic,' she said drily. 'I wouldn't talk about it in the university. It's supposed to be an old wives' tale. Well, I am an old wife. You might be interested, that's all.'

'I've heard about it,' Arram said quietly. 'I don't seem to have it, though. Except when it comes to lightning snakes.'

'Few of those with the Gift do. If you get Hulak or Yadeen alone, talk to him. Or ask Lindhall, but privately. No one likes to be laughed to scorn by his peers.' Looking up, Sebo said, 'How long does it take to reach the surface? I don't believe I can keep the air-giving spell going forever!'

The force that drove the large globe towards the surface quickened. The river's power dragged at the bubble's sides. The dead woman's smell got thicker and thicker, until Sebo and Arram found handkerchiefs and held them over their noses.

'Whatever Enzi considers a proper favour in return, it had better be good,' Sebo complained, her voice muffled by the cloth. 'I'm too old for this.'

Their globe popped free of the water, next to the boat. The two mortal crocodiles slapped the river with their tails until their many-times-great-grandfather bellowed for them to calm down. They braced the boat at his command, while he braced the far side of the globe, jamming it against the boat so it would not drift away.

Arram climbed out first, then gently took the dead woman's bound feet. When he tugged, the body slid out of the globe.

Arram's gut clenched. He swallowed the sudden mouthful of saliva that warned he was about to vomit, and pulled again, lifting as he did. Hand over hand he drew in the corpse of his former teacher by fistfuls of burlap and chain, using all of his strength. As he worked, he prayed for the Black God to heal her wounds.

Once Faziy was aboard, Arram slid her onto the boat's floor. He would have to remember the feet of the corpse would be near his own feet. Quickly he glanced at the far rail. The crocodile grandsons were clinging to it with their jaws and forepaws, weighing down the rail with the top halves of their bodies.

'Thank you,' he said, and hurriedly reached for Sebo. She held both bony hands out through the globe. Carefully Arram took them and lifted her aboard. Close overhead, thunder boomed. He cursed.

'Can't be helped,' Sebo murmured.

Arram swore to himself. Rain meant that the master's arthritis had burdened her for hours – it always came on when the skies were still clear. She had said nothing, had made no sign that she was in pain. 'You should have told me you were hurting.'

'Quiet,' Sebo ordered. 'Pull in the globe like fishermen pull in their nets. Leave enough room at the last for the vile magics that hid Faziy.'

'I can't see them,' Arram said, puffing as he hauled on the globe. Handful by handful he forced the air out of it. What if he got a faceful of those ugly spells?

Light, bright and even, spread over everything. He looked back. Sebo held up a small crystal globe. Touching it with a whisper of his power, Arram felt Yadeen's Gift, as plain as if his master shared the boat with them. Looking at Sebo, he noticed something else. 'Where's your puddle?'

'My what?'

'Your puddle, the one that was in your lap.'

Sebo grinned. 'I let the puddle, as you call it, go free when I got into the boat.' She held the glowing ball up again. 'If you would finish? I'm glad I borrowed it, but it's heavy.'

At last Arram held a bag the size of his head. All of it that he'd already rolled into his fists had dissolved, its purpose done.

'Now pinch what you have closed, firmly. Give it a rune of sealing with as much of your Gift as you can.'

Arram wanted to tell her that if he reached far enough, he could replenish his stores of power completely, but he decided not to. She looked weary, and the first splashes of rain were speckling the water within the light of the globe. She would want to know how he could tell, and when he had learned this. While he could answer the first question, the answer to the second was nebulous. He only knew that as he got older, as he developed hair in spots previously hairless, his awareness of how far he could reach for power had grown. He had tested it, and found his awareness was correct. He wasn't sure what he could do with it, or what might happen to him if he did, so he used it only on special occasions, when no one was watching.

Instead of saying this to his loved and trusted master, he pinched the opening to the magical globe shut with one hand. With the other he made the sign requested, pouring enough of his Gift into it that the opening was secured. The shadowed magics within the globe whirled and pressed, but they could not get out.

As soon as it was closed, Preet flew up to his shoulder and began to scold. 'Hush,' he told her softly. He looked at Sebo. 'Are we still being quiet?' Rather than wait for her answer, he told Preet, 'Hush, hush. All's well and we are going back. Sebo, we're going home, aren't we? Preet is worried. So am I, a little. Only a little. I'm not questioning you, mind, only Preet wants to know. And me. I do, too. It's raining.' He rubbed his face for a moment to freshen himself, then reached into the earth, feeling for the sense of water running off of rock. Once he had it, he drew it into his Gift and spread it over the boat.

While he worked, Enzi's descendants gripped their ropes and took their places at the bow. As the rain rolled away the invisible shield over the boat, the young crocodiles towed and Enzi pushed it upstream. Their speed was far quicker than their journey downstream, even though they swam against the current. The waves parted at the bow, but they did not slop inside. Arram decided Sebo or Enzi must have done something about that – more likely Sebo, because what would a crocodile care about getting wet?

'Put those disgusting magics next to Faziy,' Sebo ordered.

Arram flinched slightly. 'Sorry, Master. I forgot I was holding them.' He gently placed the globe of magics next to the corpse. Sebo was rubbing her temples and watching the riverbanks as they passed. The hippos and crocodiles were beginning to stir. It was late afternoon, and the sun was setting. He and Sebo had been underwater far longer than he realized.

'Why would anyone go to such trouble to kill and bury a mage?' he asked her.

'Every mage has enemies,' she murmured.

'These must have been really angry ones, then.'

'For your own good, lad, you should forget this ever happened. Ask no questions. Never mention Faziy's name, understand?' Sebo was digging in her workbag. 'Whoever they were, whoever she offended, they wanted her *forgotten*. As forgotten as if she'd abandoned her obligations and run off beyond the reach of anyone who cared. Anyone who asks questions will doubtless get the same treatment she did. Mind me, Arram!'

'Yes, Master,' he replied softly.

Sebo bent her head and whispered to her mirror. Despite the boat's small size, Arram could not hear her over the drumming rain and splashing river. Finally he gave up and folded himself in a kind of human tent over Preet, his elbows on his knees. His hair came loose from its rawhide tie and streamed down his forehead and back.

'You're lucky you weren't down there,' he told the bird. She stared up at him, her eyes glowing in the darkness of the shelter made by his curled body.

Who would kill a lightning mage? he asked himself. He'd suggested they were angry, but what if they weren't? What if they wanted to hide something that Faziy had seen – or done?

Like summon the lightning snakes, he thought suddenly. Like calling all of them to her from a really large storm.

And we found her when they didn't want her found, he realized. They will know mages did it. And there are mages who will look into it, at the university and in Thak City. That's why Sebo wanted those ugly magics. As evidence . . .

He must have drowsed, because the next thing he noticed was the lurch as the boat ground onto sand and stone. He nearly toppled onto the corpse. Preet flew up, shrieking, as Arram grabbed the rim of the boat to keep from falling on the dead woman. The two young crocodiles dropped their ropes and plunged into the river, while Enzi thrust the small craft higher up onto the shore. Suddenly the rain stopped.

Arram looked up. It was not the rain. Six mages on the river-bank had created a protective shield overhead, which now covered the boat. Yadeen came forwards and gently lifted Sebo from the bow. Preet flew to him, chattering quietly. Four other mages stepped up with a litter; Chioké was one. Cosmas stood in the background.

One mage made signs to lift in a Gift that shone pale blue. Chioké called up his orange magic. Between them they raised the dead woman in the air and settled her onto the litter, along with the ball of magics.

I will thank you humans to keep your murders out of my river in the future, Enzi said. He turned and slapped the water hard with his tail. It drenched Arram's back as he stumbled ashore. When he turned to shout at the god, there was no sign of him. The rain fell without letup.

'Come along, Arram,' instructed Master Cosmas. 'We may not

be as wet as you, but it is getting cold. I would like to shift this puzzle somewhere private before people come to snoop.'

'Master,' said one of the mages now holding the litter up. 'In front of the boy?'

'Arram can be trusted,' Cosmas replied mildly.

'But—' the same mage said.

'That will be all.' Cosmas's voice was still gentle, but the man closed his mouth. 'Sebo?' Cosmas asked.

'I will come now, if Yadeen will give me his arm,' the old woman said, obviously knowing what Cosmas wanted. 'Let the boy go to bed. He's done more than his share tonight, and without a word of complaint.'

'Sebo, Master, Masters, I'm fine,' Arram protested.

'Bed,' ordered Yadeen, and that was that.

CHAPTER 18

September 30–October, 438

After he took a searing hot bath, Arram joined Preet in his room and plunged into sleep. He regretted it. In his dreams he drifted in the river without protection, inhaling water, dropping to the bottom, and sinking into soft, lumpy mud. Several times he bumped into Faziy's unwrapped corpse, chained to its rock. The last time he *was* her body. He was still alive, screaming, and drowning as he fought the chains. Lightning snakes darted everywhere, trying to free him, but they only passed through his bonds.

This time, when he woke, he knew it was a couple of hours until dawn. Preet, normally a sound sleeper, was perched on his chest, cheeping anxiously.

'I'm sorry, Preet,' he murmured. He looked over the edge of the bed. Sunstone was there as well. Arram had yet to figure out how the tortoise got into the room when his door was firmly shut. 'I'm sorry, Sunstone. Bad dreams, that's all.' The tortoise wandered out, grumbling to himself.

Rather than risk more dreams, Arram gathered up his things. 'I'm going to take another bath,' he told Preet. 'You can come with me and sleep there, or you can meet me at Master Yadeen's.'

Preet hopped onto his book bag, choosing to come along.

* * *

Yadeen frowned when the wet-haired Arram arrived for his lesson. 'I would have thought you'd bathed last night.'

'I did,' Arram said, heading for the teapot. Yadeen already had his large cup in his hands. 'And again this morning.' The roll of distant thunder reminded him of lightning snakes, but he had more urgent questions. 'Sir, did you find out what killed Master Faziy?'

Yadeen, caught in the act of drinking tea, choked slightly and lowered his cup. 'I recall Sebo telling us you are never to mention this again.' He raised his free hand and wrote two signs in the air. Instantly Arram felt the tightening of his skin that meant Yadeen had enclosed his workshop in protections against eavesdroppers.

Reminded, Arram made a rueful face. 'You were there. I thought it would be all right if I spoke of it to you.'

'You are braver than me,' Yadeen said. 'I would not want the old woman angry with me.' He sighed. 'Drink your tea. You look about to fall over.' As Arram obeyed, Yadeen said, 'They will get nothing from Faziy's body. The mages who killed her melted her brain before they sank her. Sometimes it's possible to find the memories of the dead, but she was in the water for weeks. Any memories are a shot drawn at venture after so long. They made sure the shot would have nothing to strike.'

Arram couldn't tell what was more fascinating, that memories could be gathered after the spirit had gone on to the Black God's realm, or that the brain could be melted in its skull. 'And there's no way to untwine the magics in the wrappings, to see who belongs to what?' he asked, deciding to get all of his questions out of the way. 'They were all blended together, so I couldn't even tell what they were.'

'No,' Yadeen replied. 'It was a very well-constructed plot.'

Arram chewed his lip. Three weeks ago the lightning snakes had not visited him when the great storm rolled over the university and struck Prince Stiloit's fleet. If the storm had been a normal storm, nothing would have interfered with a visit from the snakes.

'Sir, do lightning snakes prefer storms when mages are mucking with them? Or are there mages who can trap lightning – including the snakes – and wield it deliberately? Make it go where they want it to go?'

'Why do you ask?' Yadeen leaned forwards, his eyes fixed on Arram.

He told him what he'd told Sebo: how he'd called the lightning snakes and they hadn't come.

Yadeen looked up as approaching thunder rolled. 'Outside. Preet, stay here.'

Arram began to shed his robe in resignation. He was going to get wet again.

'Good idea,' said Yadeen. He stripped off his shirt. Arram did the same, even though his next class was with Cosmas, who would dry off the rest of him. Or perhaps this time Cosmas would teach him how to do it for himself.

Yadeen led him out to the practice area where Arram had accidentally shown lightning snakes to Chioké and Ozorne. They waited in silence as the thunder boomed closer and closer. Finally Yadeen said, 'Call them,' and stepped away.

Arram reached up and silently called, imagining the long, jagged strokes against the sky, splitting into forks and lesser branches. His Gift flew out from his fingers, shaping the same kind of strokes in the air as it reached for the purple-black thunderheads. Light flashed behind the heaped clouds as they rolled forwards; noise made the ground beneath his feet shiver. The wind whipped his hair, the long grasses around the edges of the field, and the trees on the far side. Arram grinned in exultation. For a moment he forgot about the grim day before, enjoying the sound and sight of the storm.

He saw bolts of lightning strike out of the clouds and vanish, except for a few. These walked forwards through the air as if they felt their way. He called again. Thunder crashed. Solid whips of lightning joined the first, stretching and splitting as they reached out. When the first delicate fingertips touched Arram, his hair stood up. Then the hands surrounded him, the spirits that came with them giggling and asking him to admire their shapes, their thunder, and their clouds.

He assured them that he did. Then, taking a chance, he asked, 'Are there ways you can be trapped to do someone's bidding?'

They vanished, and the clouds opened up. Arram reached out, catching one laggardly streak. 'Please! I didn't mean *I* would do it, ever!' he explained as it flickered in the hold of his Gift. It stung fiercely; had it been larger it would have hurt him badly. 'Tell the others that. I need to know if someone *did* do it recently. I swear by the Hag I would never take advantage of you that way!' His mouth trembled. It was Faziy who had told him that the snakes answered to the local trickster god.

The whip of lightning hesitated, shimmering. Then it reached down and curled around his wrist. Silently it replied, *It was done. The moon was half full.*

Arram released it and looked for Yadeen.

When they were back inside, Arram repeated the lightning snake's words. Then he said, 'What if Faziy called lightning snakes three weeks ago?' He was about to ask, 'What if she turned the storm and the snakes on the fleet?' but Yadeen gestured. Arram closed his mouth.

'I know what you were about to say,' Yadeen murmured. He made a far deeper impression than if he'd shouted. 'Never speak of it, do you understand? If it is true, there is no way to prove such a thing. They still made certain Faziy would never speak. Stiloit had enemies, powerful ones. The kind of men and women who could pay a cabal of mages to drown any number of ships to kill one man. Do you think they would stop at one student?'

Arram gulped. 'No, sir.'

'I will see to this. But do not investigate further, understand?'

Arram nodded, though he couldn't help but think, What if these people go after Ozorne? What if Mikrom thinks Ozorne is trying to get rid of everyone between him and the throne? Or that his mother is the plotter?

It wouldn't be the first time a Carthaki heir chose to rid himself of those who were next in line. Emperor Mesaraz's grandfather had done just that, the truth coming out only after he was on the throne.

Had Stiloit faked his death by drowning, planning to hide until he had rid himself of Ozorne and Mikrom? That had happened at least twice in Carthaki imperial history. In fact, the entire history of the Carthaki throne tended to be a bloody one.

What if Ozorne was killed because he didn't know his danger?

Somehow Arram struggled through his afternoon classes and retreated to the baths for another soak. When he finally reached his room, hoping for a brief nap, he found Lindhall's area in an uproar.

Servants were carrying boxes out of the rooms across the hall. Three men in the uniform of the Imperial Guard, the elite soldiers who guarded the emperor and his heir, stood on either side of the door, eyeing the servants. Here in the university, where weapons were viewed as a source of trouble and, worse, an inspiration for mistakes, these forbidding individuals were armed. They carried short swords and at least three daggers, one in the belt and one in each black leather boot. Shimmering on their belts revealed magic: Arram sharpened his gaze and discovered protective spells keyed to spoken words, not the men's Gift, for they had none. These spells were the kind that would spread to cover people closest to the men who wore them.

He was so engrossed that he didn't pay attention to the third guard until the man crossed the hall and grabbed his arm. 'Here, you,' the soldier growled. 'What's your name and business here?'

Preet began to scream in alarm. A large dog who slept with one of Ozorne's roommates leaped through the door and began to bark. The three-legged hound and the tiny blind dog who also shared the suite followed and added their barks to his. The guards unsheathed their swords.

Arram, terrified they would kill the animals, snapped the first spell he could think of around them. It thrust the guards down the hall. When they began to run back towards Arram, he used the same spell to keep them where they were.

'Mithros rising, what is going *on*?' shouted Ozorne, walking out of his room. 'Sit, sit and be silent!' The dogs instantly obeyed. Ozorne rubbed his head. His hair was dishevelled and his tunic smudged. 'Arram, release my guards.'

'*Your* guards? Ozorne, what's this?' Arram asked, still angry. He kept his spell's grip on his captives. 'Those men drew steel on the dogs and Preet! Who are they, and what is this? Who's moving?'

'That would be me,' Ozorne said. 'The emperor insists. If I'm to stay, I need a ground-floor room with more exits, and I must have guards. I'm not happy, but I wasn't permitted to argue. Now, release the men, before they tell Uncle that you're a danger. He might not remember that he likes you.'

Arram released the men, who ran to their charge. Ozorne snapped, 'Sheathe those blades! Did you forget your orders? Only under real attack do they come out of their sheaths! And memorize this man's face.' He pointed at Arram. 'He is Arram Draper, my best friend, possibly the cleverest student at this university – except for me, of course.' He and Arram smiled at each other. The guards only bowed to Ozorne and turned their eyes on Arram. 'The bird is Preet. Harm one feather on her head and I will ask my uncle for yours.'

'Ozorne!' Arram protested. These men could not know Ozorne's sense of humour. They might believe he meant it.

Ozorne grimaced. 'Arram as well as Varice Kingsford and Master Chioké may be permitted to my presence at any hour, understand? No questions. I don't care if I'm sleeping.'

'Ozorne, does Lindhall know?' Arram asked as the soldiers bowed and separated to let the servants go by with their crates.

'Yes – he was there when the commander and Master Cosmas came with the happy news.' Ozorne slumped against the wall.

'Look at it this way – now I have room for all of us to gather when we're bored with the libraries.' He grabbed Arram's arm and dragged him into Lindhall's suite, shutting the door behind them. 'I *have* to find the good in this, understand?' Ozorne slumped against the frame of Arram's door. 'I didn't know it, but Chioké and Master Cosmas have been arguing with my uncle and my mother since we came out of isolated mourning for my cousin. They finally persuaded my family of how useful it would be to have an imperial heir who is also a mage. I had to swear all manner of oaths to let guards follow me everywhere.'

'Can you blame them?' Arram asked. He crouched to pet the three-legged dog. 'Your mother and the emperor, I mean. The other heirs haven't been particularly lucky.'

'No, only stupid or unhealthy,' his friend retorted.

'Ozorne!' Arram said, shocked.

'I'm not wrong, except where Stiloit is concerned. He was unlucky.'

Arram swallowed a lump in his throat. He wanted so badly to tell Ozorne that it was not at all a matter of luck for Stiloit.

The older boy scrubbed his face with his hands. 'Listen, I'm all over dust. Why don't I clean up? We can walk over to supper and then the library. At least I can get some studying done tonight.' He walked into the hall.

'But . . . your things,' Arram protested.

'I told these people where they go. They can arrange them better than I would anyway,' Ozorne said over his shoulder. His tone made Arram think that perhaps he was not as resigned to the presence of his guards as he claimed. 'Oh,' he called, and came back to the door. 'I have more news, the kind that delights you.'

'Better news than I won't have you snoring across the hall?' Arram asked.

Ozorne's grin was the essence of wickedness. 'So much better than that,' he said. 'Mother has moved her palace suite on a somewhat permanent basis. She means to entertain, and asked me to put you and Varice on notice. She wants you to attend the parties and dinners that she intends to stage for me.'

Arram whimpered. 'She wouldn't be happy with just one supper to say hello?' he managed to ask. Preet, on his shoulder, croaked her opinion. She knew she would never be allowed to attend such events, any more than Lindhall's students' dogs would be allowed. 'I have the infirmary, as well as my lessons . . .'

'Oh, no,' Ozorne murmured. 'She mentioned "bringing some life into the great barn". I don't know where she got the idea you might bring life, but . . .' He shrugged. 'Mothers.' He vanished into the suite of rooms again, the inside guard following. 'For the time being, you can teach me the pushing spell you used on the guards!' Arram heard him call.

Arram let his head fall back until it banged the wall. 'Mithros, Minoss, and Shakith,' he said, though what he prayed for he did not know. He shouted to Ozorne, 'It's only a mix of ordinary barrier spells and runes for movement, concentrated into one sigil that I wrote into my palm!'

'"Only," he says,' one soldier growled.

On Saturday Arram went downstairs for a trip to the city's biggest market. He and Preet joined Varice at the foot of the stairs. 'He's been shouting,' the young woman whispered behind her hand. Together they walked down to their friend's new home. There eight guardsmen and a furious Ozorne waited in the hall.

'Ozorne?' Varice asked, smiling at the guards. 'What's going on?'

'According to our *new* ruler, Sergeant Okot' – Ozorne waved a hand at the sergeant, whose face was diplomatically blank – 'according to *him,* this is how I am to go to the city, or I am not to go at all. Never mind that we've been perfectly safe without so much as a pocket picked for years!'

'Your Highness, you were not Prince Mikrom's heir in that

time, and your protection was not my responsibility,' the sergeant said. He spoke with the kind of patience that indicated this was not the first time he had made these arguments.

'My friends are as good as an army!' Ozorne snapped.

'If we aren't visiting the book stalls or the spicers.' Varice tucked Ozorne's arm in one of hers. 'Really, shall we spend the day here while you scream like a gull? This poor man is only following orders from your mother and your imperial uncle. Or do you want to see if we can match those jade beads you like so much?'

Ozorne looked down at her. 'How did you know I liked them?'

'Because you bought all the gem seller had in June, silly. He told you he'd have more in September. If he hasn't been holding them for you all month, I am a bonobo.' Varice smiled at the sergeant. 'He's ready to go now.'

Okot ushered them outside to a waiting carriage, while Arram murmured to Varice, 'Thank you.'

'I heard that,' Ozorne snapped. 'You two don't have to live with an extra clutch of people making your life their business.'

As Okot pointed Arram to the spot on Ozorne's free side, Varice said pleasantly, 'I know you'll feel differently the first time someone tries to kill you, Ozorne. Sergeant, do you have a mage to check—' She raised a glittering hand and smiled. 'Oh, *you're* the one trained in the detection of poisons and poisoning spells.'

Arram could tell the sergeant was a mage, but he hadn't tried to discover the man's speciality, if he had one. Ozorne saved Arram's pride by asking for himself: 'How did you know he's expert in poisons?'

Varice turned up her nose, looking very pleased with herself. 'How do you lads *think* a kitchen witch would know?' she teased.

More calmly Ozorne asked, 'Where did you study, Okot?'

The sergeant looked at Varice with respect. Bowing to Ozorne, he said, 'I began at the City of the Gods on Tortall's northern border. When they understood my Gift was best employed to protect and investigate, I was sent to Jindazhen and the countries of the West to learn what I could, and then to . . . other masters, closer to home. When I was judged fit to serve in a noble or royal house, I made my bow to the emperor.'

Varice sighed, the picture of a girl in love. 'I don't suppose – No, you must be far too busy.'

Okot raised his brows a touch. 'Once the lads and I are settled in here, and with His Highness's permission—'

Ozorne gave a bark of a laugh. 'Far be it from me to stop Varice from adding another string to her bow, particularly when I hope to benefit!'

'He's so good to me,' Varice told Okot.

'When I know my off-duty hours, I will let you know, mistress,' Okot said. 'In the meantime, if you have not read it already, you may wish to look at *Strange Things in My Stew* by Farmer Cooper of Tortall. It was written three hundred years ago and is out of fashion, but there are things in it you will not find in the modern texts.'

'Wonderful!' Varice said. 'Thank you *so* much, Sergeant!'

She is marvellous, Arram thought. This could have been a miserable outing, or no outing at all. Yet with a little flirtation, teasing, and honest curiosity, she made everyone feel better, even Ozorne. Even Okot.

Two men rode inside with them, the sergeant and another guard rode on top, and the other four rode around the carriage. It made for a quick ride down the broad city ways. City people, one of Arram's patients had told him, learned to spot house insignia on horse gear and carriage doors, and to get out of the way.

The market was crowded by the time they reached it, though their guards created an uncomfortably large space around them. The young people poked through carts and shops unhampered, but the vendors did not have their usual cheerful smiles for Ozorne and his friends. Other customers made themselves scarce at the sight of soldiers clearly on watch, which meant the stall owners were losing money. Ozorne was steaming and about to explode. Arram suspected he had wanted to sneak off to see a tavern girl he had been visiting when away from the music student he courted at the university. Arram thought the soldiers might understand, but judging by the look on Ozorne's face, the prince was in no mood to hear such advice.

They were crossing one of the broad fountain squares when Arram saw a ragged pedlar burdened with a heavy load of wood. A wealthy-looking merchant turned abruptly, banging into the pedlar. Furious, the man lashed the pedlar's arm with his walking stick. The poor man stumbled forwards, through Sergeant Okot's ring of guards.

The guard beside Arram drew his sword and used the hilt to shove the unfortunate man away. His voice friendly, he said, 'Here, you, be about your—'

Off balance, the man fell into Ozorne.

The honey pastry Ozorne had been trying to eat went onto his silk shirt. He shoved the pedlar just as the nearest guard seized the bundle of wood and yanked it off. Wailing, the pedlar fell. He raised his feet to hold off any attackers, only to plant his muddy sandals on Ozorne's new linen breeches.

Ozorne began kicking the pedlar. He screamed insults that started with 'Sirajit' until Arram threw a shield of his Gift between the prince and the man on the ground. The guard who had grabbed the bundle of wood dropped it and dragged the pedlar away from Ozorne. Another of the guards helped Varice to her feet – someone had knocked her down. Okot shouted orders: instantly the remaining soldiers encircled Ozorne, facing outwards. Okot bellowed for the gawking crowd to go about their business.

Ozorne rounded on Arram. His face, so often dreamy-eyed or amused, was red with fury. He clenched his hands into fists. 'You dare!' he shouted at Arram. 'You *dare* to use magic to thwart me!'

Arram let his shield vanish, though he feared Ozorne might

strike him. 'I was the only one who would,' he said mildly, his tone belying his shock at his friend's behaviour. 'Okot told us he knows poisons best, and I don't think Varice can manage that kind of shield spell.'

'Not that I can call up in a moment's thought,' Varice said tartly, brushing her skirts with both hands. They came away streaked in mud. 'Ozorne, *what* were you thinking? Now *everything* is ruined.'

Okot planted himself in front of their friend. His face was stone. 'In truth, Your Highness, this proves what I tried to tell you. We cannot guard you properly in the market. It is too crowded. That could as easily have been an assassin. While we rid ourselves of him, watched your friends, and held off bystanders, a confederate could have killed you.' The man paused, then bowed and said, 'With all respect due to you.'

Ozorne ground his teeth. Finally he said, 'I can protect myself, you know.'

'Obviously,' the sergeant replied. His tone was very dry.

'I *am* a mage,' the prince insisted.

Okot bowed.

At last Ozorne said, 'Well, I must return and change. Arram, Varice, there's no reason to ruin your day.'

'I have to change, too,' Varice said tartly. 'There's no point in coming back by the time that's done. Arram, if you'll buy some things for me, I'll cook us supper in Ozorne's new hearth.'

Ozorne's face brightened. He contributed money as Varice told Arram what she needed. Off they went, enclosed in a tight square of guards. Arram looked around and spotted the pedlar. The man had only gone as far as the nearest water fountain, where he sat on the rim and wept. He'd lost most of his wood, and the urchins who awaited opportunity in the square had stolen it.

Arram crouched beside the pedlar. 'I'm sorry.' The man stared at him, frightened. His face was marred with bruises, his clothes ripped. 'He's not usually like that,' Arram told him. 'But his cousin is dead, and the emperor has made him take guards wherever he goes. He's not used to the change.' The pedlar leaned away, obviously afraid Arram brought more bad news. 'Here,' Arram said, offering a handful of his own silver coins. Nervously, the pedlar held out his palm. Arram gave him the money. 'That should cover the wood, and a healer, and a few days to rest. We're really sorry.' The pedlar said nothing, only stared at the coins in his hand. 'Well, gods go with you.' Arram stood, dusting his hands off on his tunic. Seeing the pedlar's eyes widen in fear, he walked back so the man wouldn't feel so intimidated by his height before he turned and headed off to do his errands.

One of them did not involve supper. He searched through the market until he found the grand main shop of Inlands Trading House. The guard outside moved to stop him, but Arram took a tip from Varice's book. He knew he looked somewhat bedraggled, but the idea, she had once told him, was to act as if he were royalty, even in rags. He drew himself up, fingered the black opal necklace around his neck, and let his right sleeve slide back. At the beginning of the autumn term, Cosmas had presented him with a thin bracelet made of gold, threaded with sapphire, jet, and jade stones, just as Sebo had given him a bracelet of copper linking moonstone, celestite, and azurite. These were twined with the bracelet Arram had made with Yadeen and the Hag's die, and supported magic of all kinds. Between the black opal necklace and the twined bracelet, the guard would recognize a mage of talent and let him pass – as this one did. 'Never judge a mage by his clothes,' Hulak had told him once.

Arram looked around the shop until he saw a counter girl who reminded him of Faziy in her friendly, cheerful air. They talked a little over a shelf of opals before he asked her if she knew his friend and former teacher.

'I do, or I did,' the girl said, her eyes going dark with sadness. 'We started at the training class on the same day – learning where all the company's buildings are, and the docks, and who's in charge. We even rented rooms together.' She sniffed. Arram provided her with a handkerchief and walked her to a display of jewelled figurines so the senior staff would stop looking at them.

'I was seeing a servant from one of the big houses over in the Moon District,' she whispered. 'He bought us three nights in a nice inn, just the two of us. It was wonderful! I did tell her what we were going to do, just not where . . .' She sniffed again and wiped her nose. 'When I got home, our rooms were all torn up, and she was gone. She hasn't been back! I went to as many infirmaries as I could, and to the Imperial Guard . . .' She hung her head. 'And then they told me that if I lost any more time from my work, they would have to find someone else.' Tears ran freely down her cheeks. 'They said it must be robbers, or maybe they took her to sell her, and she'll never be found.'

Arram bought a trinket – he forgot what it was – and told his new friend how to find him if she ever got word of Faziy. He was halfway back to the university before he remembered why his friends believed he had remained behind. He was only just able to race back and buy what they wanted before the markets closed.

That night he went to bed early, but not before he wrote up what the shopgirl had told him. He gave the paper to Cosmas and stood cold-faced as the master spoke impatiently about involving himself in something he was supposed to avoid. Finally Cosmas gave up and ordered Arram to leave early for the infirmary.

After talking the brawl over with Varice on Monday afternoon, Arram visited Sergeant Okot. The university had moved a batch of students to give Ozorne's guards a headquarters across the hall from their charge. The area smelled of oil and leather. The common room was equipped with cushions, a few shelves of books, stands of sharpstones, leather, jars of oil, wooden practice swords, a slate with the guards' schedules, and the sergeant's desk and chair.

Arram tried not to be intimidated by the military atmosphere. Fidgeting, running his fingers through Preet's feathers, he explained to Okot why it was wise to keep Ozorne away from those who looked even a little Sirajit.

The man looked up from papers he was reviewing. 'Young sir, you think because you attend this overthought sprawl that you know more than a leatherfoot like me?' he asked, setting aside his feather pen. 'You believe I don't understand my work?'

Arram's voice squeaked when he first tried it. Preet scolded the sergeant for frightening her friend.

'They told us no pets,' the sergeant said, holding up a finger. Preet fluttered over to it and continued to scold.

Arram tried to speak again and coughed.

'Oh, Hag's droppings, drink this.' The man poured a cup full of water from his pitcher. 'Stop carrying on. I don't even have the right to flog you. And His Highness would have my sword if I laid a hand on you or the young lady.' He stroked Preet's chest feathers with a thick finger. 'Wouldn't he, birdie? Yes, he would!'

Arram gulped the water and cleared his throat. 'She isn't a pet,' he explained, feeling calmer. 'It's like the dogs upstairs; they're animals that were trusted to Lindhall for care, or animals he's studying. That's Preet. I report on her behaviour for Lindhall.'

'Talkative little thing,' the sergeant said.

Reassured by the man's gentleness with Preet, Arram explained, 'I'm not telling you about your work, sir. Varice felt, after the market, that you should know Ozorne's not normally that way. But if you could watch for anyone who looks to be . . . to save unpleasantness, just in case . . .'

The sergeant smiled up at him. 'That pretty little girl makes all you fellows dance, doesn't she? Don't worry, lad. My men are used to palace details. But the market isn't safe. You saw that. I made arrangements to get his favourite vendors to come here. All the royals do it.'

Arram stared at the man, shocked. 'But they'll have to haul their goods from the city in the weather, and lose business in the market!'

The sergeant shook his head. 'You don't know much about merchants, do you? They're *glad* to do it. Put the little plaque that says "Favoured by Prince Ozorne" over their doors? Get the chance to let drop to their friends at the temples – just casual, mind! – how they can't linger because they're taking a batch of books up for the prince to look at? Be able to say, "You know, His Highness may want just that sort of thing. I'll mention you to him"? They're happy to sell goods later than usual in the city if they can brag of His Highness's custom.'

Arram blinked. 'Oh. Human nature.'

The sergeant nodded. 'Human nature, lad. It's a wonderful thing.' Handing Preet back to Arram, he added, 'So's the anger of a boy for the people that killed his father, particularly when he sees he might get to strike back at them.'

'But the ones who killed his father are dead,' Arram protested weakly.

'Not all,' the soldier replied. 'Not their sons, or their nephews. My kin wiped out the last nest, and the emperor made peace. He knew they were ready to make peace. But that doesn't mean we got them all, and it did naught for the men who came home missing a limb or loose in their wits. There's plenty left if a prince wants his revenge.'

'Please don't tell him that,' Arram said. 'Those people have endured enough.'

'Not your worry, youngster. Leave it to the folk that sit on thrones and the ones that do their fighting for them.' Okot made a shooing motion with his hand. Arram was dismissed.

A month later Cosmas halted the fire magic class early and invited Arram and Varice to take a seat. He assumed his own desk chair and waited for Preet to settle herself in his lap. 'How is Ozorne managing with his guard detail? Not too intrusive, I hope?'

Arram and Varice traded looks. Arram shrugged.

'It's funny how such conspicuous men disappear in plain sight, Master,' Varice said for both of them. 'Pranksters try to distract them and get them to talk, but most leave them be.' She dimpled. 'Some of my friends were talking girl business before they realized Sergeant Okot was standing right behind them.'

Cosmas chuckled. 'We did ask that Ozorne's guards be discreet.'

'Have there been imperial heirs at the university before?' Arram enquired.

'Oh, yes, many times. Not recently, but Mesaraz was a student in the School of Law when his father was the heir. Sadly, Mesaraz was called to rule before he obtained his certificate, but his education is evident in the laws he has made, and the old ones he has rendered void. We are proud of him.' Cosmas looked into the distance, then shook off his thoughtful mood. 'Now, you are invited to supper with Her Highness and Prince Ozorne. It takes place at the palace Water Pavilion on Saturday evening. Yadeen understands that you will not be in class on Sunday morning, Arram, just as I am excusing you both from mine.' He tapped a pair of parchments on his desk. Each was ornately addressed in gold ink, one to Arram and one to Varice. 'I regret to say that Preet is *not* invited.'

The bird made a sound very much like a whine.

'Forgive me, lovely,' Cosmas told her, 'but the princess was firm on the subject about "pets at a royal occasion". You may take dinner with some of my fellow masters and me. If you are very good, we will allow you to have some of the mead you like.'

'Mead!' Arram cried, shocked. 'You've been giving her mead?!'

'It does her no harm,' Cosmas replied with dignity. 'Lindhall approved, and it stops her from crying for you when you work at night in the infirmary. None of us would do anything to harm our Preet, would we, my dear?'

Preet ran her beak under Cosmas's beard and chirred in content.

'Now, the instructions for how you are to travel are in your invitations,' Cosmas told them. 'I know you will do us credit. Don't forget the fifth chapter in your texts for tomorrow.'

As if the university clocks were set inside his head, the bells for the change of class began to ring. Once Preet had flown back to Arram's shoulder, Cosmas linked his hands over his round belly and closed his eyes for his morning nap.

Arram waited until they were outside before he cried, 'A party with the princess!'

Varice slung her arm around his waist. 'Please don't panic yet,' she begged. 'I'll let you know when to panic.'

When they arrived at the Water Pavilion, the princess greeted them with far more enthusiasm than they had ever seen her demonstrate. She even rose from her chair and walked over to them, smiling. 'No formalities!' she said as she raised Arram from his bow and Varice from her curtsy. 'My beloved son's guard told me how you rescued him from that Sirajit dog's insult!' She gripped Arram by the shoulders. 'You in particular, dear boy.' She kissed him on both cheeks. 'I know his household will be stronger with both of you there.' She took Varice's hand in one of hers as she kept one on Arram's shoulder. To Varice she said, 'Those restoring soups and perfumes you make have done wonders for my health, my dear. Where would he be without both of you?'

'Where would I be, indeed?' Ozorne murmured in Arram's ear as he came up beside him.

'But, Your Highness, truly the man wasn't—' Arram began.

Varice stepped lightly on his foot. Ozorne gripped his wrist, saying *'Don't'* in his ear. In any event, the princess had not heard Arram's attempt to say the pedlar had not meant any insult. She was asking Varice if she knew any perfumes to protect the wearer from poisons.

'Anything that gets her to believe we shouldn't be parted is a *good* thing,' Ozorne murmured when he was certain his mother wasn't listening. 'Otherwise she'll try to bind me to a pair of fashionable stiff-necks who will always report to her. And we're not sure that lout wasn't going for me. Now, you and Varice sit here, on my left, until we go to supper. You both look very fine.'

'*Varice* looks very fine,' Arram said. 'I look presentable.'

Their friend was lovely in a Northern-style pink silk gown embroidered down the front in silver Carthaki designs. A sheer pink silk veil was fixed to her hair with pins capped with tiny silver rosebuds, and she wore silver slippers. Compared to her, Arram was more sombre in a dark grey tunic, and a dark blue coat and hose. Only when he turned under the lamps did onlookers see glints of silver woven into the garments, reminding him, at least, of a late-night sky.

Ozorne outshone them both, of course, in a bronze tunic and silver hose. The beads in his dark hair were silver and gold; his nails were gold; his bracelets were jewelled gold and silver; and his toe rings were gold and silver. Since he had become the second heir, his allowance had increased, which meant his wardrobe had grown more outrageous. Only his eye make-up was not gold or silver: instead he had put blacking on both sets of lids, so the orbs shone out of darkness.

'You look . . . nice,' Arram ventured. He couldn't think of any better remark.

'Oh, it's fun to play,' Ozorne said, regarding the other guests. 'They've come to see if I'll make trouble for Mikrom, you know. None of these people understand how a fellow would rather be a mage than lounge on a throne and scheme.'

'Just tell them,' Arram suggested.

Ozorne chuckled. 'It doesn't work that way. Chioké taught me – if you say something, they're certain it's the opposite. They can take the most innocent event and turn it into conspiracy.' He glanced at his mother, who was introducing Varice to a young nobleman. 'She is in her element – Mother, not Varice,' he added hurriedly. 'Ah! There's Chioké. Excuse me for a moment?'

Arram watched Ozorne go to his mentor, nodding and smiling to guests who bowed or curtsied as he passed. Complain about court society as he might, Arram suspected that Ozorne had a wonderful time at events like these. He might be an outsider at the university, a peculiar student who took too many classes with masters, but here he *was* a master of sorts.

Arram was talking to Varice shortly afterwards when she glanced over his shoulder and said, 'Ah.' She gave her skirts a quick shake.

Arram looked to see what had attracted her interest. One of the household, a man in the long tunic of an imperial official, stood at the doorway. He took a deep breath and announced, 'His Imperial Majesty, Mesaraz Avevin Tasikhe, Bright Sun of the Carthaki Empire, God-King of Amar and Apal . . .'

Frantic, Arram looked for a place to fade away. Chioké, who had appeared suddenly, gripped his arm. 'Do not hide from the emperor, boy. Stay where you are and smile, understand?'

Arram nodded. His heart was pounding uncomfortably in his chest. Why did Ozorne and Varice have to like this sort of thing? Why couldn't they enjoy quiet evenings in the libraries or tending the animals?

Chioké talked to him about this and that, but Arram barely heard what the older man said. He watched the emperor walk through the room, stopping to talk to this noble or that mage, but always setting a course for the platform where the tall chairs waited for him, the princess, and Ozorne. Behind him came his mage, a tall white man with the colouring of a Scanran. He was said to be fearsome when it came to protective magics, with the ability to turn an attacker to ash with a flick of the hand. His pale grey eyes were expressionless as they took in the faces around the room. There were also several guards in imperial colours, and a handful of slaves.

Now the emperor was talking to Ozorne, who drew Varice forwards. Mesaraz smiled at her as she curtsied. When she straightened, he put his fingers under her chin and raised her

face as he asked her something. She gave him her sparkliest
smile and replied.

'There are advantages to being a pretty girl,' Chioké
murmured.

'Disadvantages, too,' Arram replied softly. 'People think she's
stupid because she's pretty.'

'And she is not stupid.' Something about the way Chioké said
it made Arram bristle.

'No one stupid could have made those potions for the princess,' he pointed out.

'It could be Her Highness's ills are of her own imagining, and
her imagining has now told her that the girl's kitchen witchery
has mended them,' Chioké replied coolly.

'Then why does she study on the same level as Ozorne and
me?' Arram was definitely starting to dislike this man.

'There you have a point. Stand straight. He is coming.'

The emperor was indeed coming towards them, Ozorne on
his left, his mage on his right. Arram and Chioké bowed low.

'Master Chioké, it is good to see you.' Mesaraz's voice was
deep and smooth in this kind of gathering, his eyes steady and
kind. 'Our nephew tells me that you keep him busy at his
studies. We hope you make sure he pursues law and diplomacy
as well as magic!'

'Be certain that I do, Your Imperial Majesty,' Chioké replied
with a smile. 'His Highness is up to the additional work.' He
winked at Ozorne, whose own smile was wry.

'And, young Arram, you have not brought your bird to us,'
Mesaraz remarked. 'I had hoped to see her again.'

'Um, Your Royal Majesty, it seems she has developed a – a
taste for mead,' Arram said hurriedly. 'I don't – don't dare bring
her to parties.' He bowed a second time, in case the first one
hadn't taken.

Those close enough to hear chuckled, including the emperor.
He said, 'Chioké tells us that you can throw fire three hundred
yards, young man.'

'B-by mistake, Your Imperial Highness,' Arram explained. He was confused when the older men laughed again.

'By Mithros, we should like to see how far you can throw it on purpose,' the emperor joked.

'Let us find a place large enough first,' the court mage said drily. 'The arena, perhaps.'

Arram shuddered.

'Once his control improves,' Chioké said. 'I should hate for anything to happen to the arena.'

'Indeed?' The emperor looked Arram over, his eyes sharp. 'We understand you are also able to walk on the bottom of the river.'

Arram gulped. 'My teacher, M-master Sebo, taught me how, Your Imperial Majesty. It's part of water magic training. She also t-taught me to be careful of the hippos and crocodiles.'

The older mages chuckled again. Arram felt his cheeks getting warm. He hadn't come here as entertainment, after all.

The emperor had not laughed. 'We believe there are many interesting things to be found on the river bottom.'

Was this a test? Did the emperor know about Faziy?

Whatever these people thought about his cursed stammer and his age, he was *not* a fool. He would not play jester for them, and he would not fall into any traps.

He shrugged and caught a glare from Chioké. Apparently it was forbidden to shrug in front of the emperor. 'I found a metal figure of a man with wings and claws for feet the first time I walked on the river bottom. It was a Stormwing, from the time before the banishment of the immortals.' He smiled. 'I prefer to study the living animals and fish I see there. The crocodiles and hippos don't seem to mind me any more.'

The emperor returned his smile. 'We hear you defended our nephew in the market.' He rested a hand on Ozorne's shoulder.

Arram decided another shrug might get him an actual beating instead of a scolding when he got home. 'It wasn't necessary, Your Imperial Majesty. Ozorne is very good at defending himself.'

'This is a good thing to know,' the emperor said. He glanced at the princess, who was still standing, still waiting to greet him. 'We must join our hostess. We look forward to seeing you again, Arram Draper. You are an interesting lad.'

The emperor and his attendants moved on, while Chioké turned on Arram. 'You do not talk to the emperor as if he were an instructor at the Lower Academy, and you do not *shrug* like a country lout!'

Ozorne put his hand on Chioké's arm. 'Master, it's fine. Uncle was amused as much as anything. Come, let's find your seat. The entertainment's about to begin.'

Chioké smiled at Ozorne. 'Don't worry, Your Highness – your mother wishes me to stay near her. I think you wish to sit with your friends, do you not?' He walked over to the seat that awaited him just behind the princess's elbow.

Ozorne and Arram wound through the crowd until they reached their own seats near the princess. Varice was already there. The moment she saw them she began to pour dark purple liquid into crystal glasses.

'Don't worry,' she told Arram when he regarded the glasses with alarm. 'I told the slave that wine made you a little odd. She brought us grape juice.'

'You're so *strict*,' he grumbled as he took his seat.

The crowd moved back from the centre of the floor, where a large ebony square was laid into the rich mahogany. The entertainment was a series of tumblers, dancers, and finally three pairs of gladiators who battled with padded weapons. Arram took an interest in the combats only when he saw the weapons were relatively harmless. Varice and Ozorne, of course, took more than an interest, wagering with their neighbours.

They did not do as well as they had hoped on the third match, when Musenda came out with a fellow gladiator who was nearly as big as he was. By now Musenda was becoming a favourite. Even Arram had noticed his image on posters in the city. No one would bet against him – no one near the imperial seats, at least.

The struggle was a harsh one, padded weapons or no. It soon became plain that Musenda's opponent – Arram hadn't caught his name – was determined to win. He had the bigger man bent backwards, his arm around Musenda's neck, and his free fingers going for Musenda's eyes. That was when Musenda grabbed the arm around his neck with both hands and snapped forwards with a roar of fury. Arram heard the distinctive crack of bone as his friend's opponent soared over his head, flipping, to land on his back. Since Musenda had not let go, the next sound Arram identified was the soft crunch of a shoulder dislocating. He had heard both noises when Ramasu assigned him to the butchers for a week, to help them dismember cattle and sheep.

Arram rose, about to help block the pain, but Ozorne pulled him back. Slaves came forwards to carry the wounded man away, while Musenda stood and accepted the cheers – as well as the thrown purses and flowers – of the crowd. Arram cringed. He had almost forgotten where he was and worked magic in the imperial presence.

'Sorry,' he mumbled to his friends.

'Why?' Ozorne asked. 'I *did* it once – just a little bird illusion, but Mother spanked me till I ate my meals standing up for a week. You stopped yourself!'

A large rose tumbled to the table. Arram looked up, startled, and saw Musenda was grinning wickedly at him. He grinned back and offered the rose to Varice. 'Pretend it's for you, or people will think there's something between me and him,' he whispered.

She picked up the rose and sniffed it. 'Well, it would explain why you can't hold on to a girl more than a month or two,' she teased. She blew Musenda a kiss, and the crowd roared its approval. He bowed to her and left the arena, waving to those who applauded him.

And they'd cheer just as loud if his opponent had won, Arram thought bitterly.

CHAPTER 19

October 438–June 439

The autumn term settled back into routine, with only the threat of examinations and the Midwinter celebrations to disturb Arram's peace of mind. His studies in healing expanded to include healing wounds, a process he wasn't certain he liked. He listed it as his second-to-last favourite, the worst task being lancing and cleaning boils. It always took some time for the stink to clear his nose. His favourite was diagnosing a patient's illness, something he had got very good at with the use of Ramasu's spells,

One Saturday morning after a night at the infirmary he went to the market where good secondhand shirts were reasonably priced. The term's classes were hard on his clothes: these days he could go through five clean shirts a day. He reminded himself to give the school laundry women good-luck stones for Midwinter, since they did so much work for him. He was deciding on which stones to give them when Preet crashed into his chest.

'Preet!' he cried. 'I almost killed you, silly bird! What were you thinking?'

Rising into the air, she gripped a lock of his hair in her claws and pulled him down an unfamiliar alley. Much to his surprise, they emerged at a side entrance of the cemetery dedicated to the Great Mother in her guise of the Crone. Devout women of the university were buried here.

A hundred yards in, a group of women gathered around a funeral pyre. Arram halted beside a tree, not wanting to disturb them, no matter how insistent Preet was. Then one of the women looked up and drew back her headscarf.

It was Sebo. She tapped her neighbour, who turned: it was Dagani. Arram also recognized the girl who had lived with Faziy. A couple of the other women were senior students and masters. One of them wore the black robe and torch insignia of a Daughter of the Temple. She carried a burning torch in her hand.

Sebo beckoned Arram forwards. He hesitated, not sure if he was supposed to intrude on a women's rite. Sebo beckoned again and scowled. In the distance, thunder rolled. The breeze twisted around, blowing full in Arram's face. The stink of rot filled his nose. Preet landed on his shoulder and bit his ear. Wincing, Arram forced himself to walk to the pyre.

As he left the trees, a group of men walked out of the temple: Cosmas, Yadeen, Ramasu, and Chioké. Each carried cypress boughs to cleanse the dead. At the pyre, they placed their branches on the linen-wrapped corpse, covering it from top to toe. Arram nearly panicked, having no offering, until he remembered the vial of meadowsweet essence in his healer's kit. He used it to calm people who were upset. Here it would bring his wishes for peace to this dead woman.

Placing the bottle on the corpse's chest, he saw why Preet had brought him here. Pinned on the linen where the body's neck would be was a familiar jade-and-silver necklace. This was Faziy's funeral.

The Daughter bowed to a short figure all in black who now joined them. A servant of the Black God of Death, the newcomer spoke the hopes of the faithful that Faziy would be remade in the Peaceful Realms, free of pain and sorrow. As she talked of the god's kindness, she was forced to raise her voice. The storm was rolling in fast, lightning flashing ahead of it. Quickly the

Daughter of the Temple lit the four corners of the funeral pyre. Once it was blazing, the witnesses retreated to the temple – all but Arram.

Arram shook his head as Cosmas and Yadeen tried to tow him inside. Instead he locked his eyes on the boiling clouds above.

The lightning snakes came. They twined themselves around the wood and the dead woman, weaving everything together into one blazing heap. It shrank into a hard, tight knot—

And was gone, wood, body, and bone.

The Daughter seemed to be angry with Yadeen. Arram caught some of her words: 'snakes', 'never, never', and 'never'. Arram let the master yell and looked for Preet. She had tucked herself under the temple's eaves, where she, too, seemed to screech 'never, never' and 'never'.

Finally Arram could hear properly. He looked at Cosmas. 'Who killed her?' he asked. 'We're a citadel of magecraft – surely we know who did this. Why didn't you bury her before? You thought you could work out who killed her. You know, don't you?'

'If he were my student,' Chioké said, 'I would lock him in a magic-less room on bread and water for a week.'

Arram turned to scowl at Chioké. He was about to tell Ozorne's master that no one had asked for his opinion, when three sets of invisible hands clapped over his mouth. 'I shall deal with my students – and my instructors – as I see fit,' Cosmas said mildly. 'Arram was very fond of Faziy.'

'He needs schooling in courtesy if he is to strut at court,' Chioké retorted. 'And so I shall tell *my* student. An ill-bred lout does his prince, *and* his masters, little good.'

Sebo stood next to Cosmas as Chioké gathered several of his friends and left the temple. 'He gets more troublesome every full moon, Cosmas,' she remarked. 'Perhaps you should send him on an exchange to the City of the Gods. He needs to cool down, and that's the perfect place.'

Cosmas patted Arram's shoulder. 'Avoid Chioké, Arram,' he

cautioned. 'He's every bit as likely to have sunk those ships as Faziy – and make it look like her work.'

Arram and his friends survived the Midwinter festivities and began the spring term. Arram, Varice, and Ozorne began to help Lindhall's people with minor healings at the university and imperial menageries, while Hulak began to teach them how to make the most-used medicines for animals. Arram's schedule changed not at all, except to grow harder.

When marks were posted, Tristan had his credential in war magic. He remained a fourth-year student in siege magic, fire magic, and air magic, and a third-year student in healing and other required classes.

'Just a matter of catching up,' he said carelessly, looking over his marks. 'If I bear down on those third-year courses, I should be able to move ahead into all fourth-year classes next year and start my schooling for my master's stone.' His friends, even Arram, clasped his hand in congratulation.

Gissa reached fourth year in most of her classes; Ozorne and Varice received top marks for the third-year courses. They were well beyond any students of their own age, studying with people who were in their late teens and early twenties on average.

Since Arram was taking mostly solo courses, he was amused by the titles his teachers had created for them. 'Gems in Combination with Other Substances' was Yadeen's contribution. Sebo's was less helpful: 'Manipulation of Water'. Arram supposed it was easier than explaining they had spent the winter shifting currents in the Zekoi to scour out silt that had built up in the main channel. Dagani's description of their lessons was one word: 'Creation'. Whatever his masters said they had taught him, they gave him top marks in all seven subjects.

He heard someone scoff, 'He'll end up in the libraries all his days, writing books no one will read!'

Except for one or two other complaints about 'the pet boy', the other students left Arram alone. By giving his classes odd names and keeping him out of the view of most students, his masters had made him too odd to torment. Arram, relieved, walked away from the boards of marks to join Varice and Ozorne for an afternoon's laze.

They were given a splendid treat in their free week. Princess Mahira obtained an imperial barge and invited Ozorne and his friends on a four-day journey up the Zekoi and back. They feasted on very good food, lounged in the sun or in shade cast by silk canopies, played chess or knowledge games, and visited temples and ruins on the river's banks.

At night there was music and dancing. Preet sang so beauti-fully that even Mahira was impressed. She gave the bird a thin gold ring that just fit over her claws to dangle around one thin leg. Preet was so thrilled with the gift that she soared in elegant loops around the masts, as if to prove it couldn't weigh her down. Then she perched on the arm of Mahira's chair and sang just for her.

'Strong little thing,' Ozorne murmured in Arram's ear.

Arram nodded.

The company also invited Arram to juggle. For this more jaded audience, and also because he hadn't brought his juggling equip-ment, Arram worked as he had in the typhoid infirmary and used anything at hand. Even Ozorne's imperious mother laughed and applauded.

On their way home, Arram leaned against the rail and studied the part of the river and its banks upstream from the imperial palace and the university. He saw the slip where the imperial barges docked. And on the university side he saw the dock used by the emperor when he wanted to attend the games. If Arram looked down the road that led from the dock, he could see the tall white mass of the arena itself. It filled him with dread.

Before his holiday began, Ramasu had taken him aside. 'A week after the start of the term, you will accompany me for two weeks at the gladiators' camp,' he told Arram. 'I spend time there with an assistant during every gladiatorial season. We treat people for injuries and ailments, and for wounds taken in the arena after the games. Make sure the kit you put together once classes begin is ready – I'll inspect it before we leave. The people in infirmary supplies know you'll be coming.'

Looking down that road, watching the sun bathe the area, Arram shuddered. He had done his best to avoid most of the games. Now he would be up to his elbows in it. Worse, he knew he could get out of it. All he had to do was tell Ramasu he couldn't bear to do it. Ramasu would understand.

But healing mages must learn wounds and surgery. What if he was confronted with someone who needed help one day, and he lacked the knowledge to save that person? He had to go. If he fainted, he was sure Ramasu would give him another try. He doubted the master would give him a second try if he said no now. Ramasu was a very yes-or-no sort of person.

He turned his back on the arena. He would see more than enough of it soon.

By the time the barge touched the university dock, Arram wanted to run to his room. He was weary of people. Soon classes would begin, and all of his masters had promised to work him like a field labourer. He believed them. He meant to sleep until then, in peaceful solitude – or as much solitude and peace as residence in Lindhall's quarters supplied.

He thanked Princess Mahira as elegantly as he could, told Ozorne he'd had a wonderful time, and hastened up the path, well ahead of the others. His bed called.

For the next three days Ozorne dragged him to meals. Lindhall requested his usual help with the animals who shared their quarters. Beyond that Arram kept to himself. He cleaned cages and boxes, restored stocks of seed, bandages, dishes, perches, and splints, and mended leashes, gloves, and hoods. The other students who had the duty over the holiday were happy to leave him to it.

Ozorne did insist that Arram join him on the flat rooftop of the building the night before the start of the term. Sergeant Okot himself took the guard position on the stairwell that led to the roof. He placed one of his most trusted soldiers on the stair, assuring Ozorne that neither of them was within sight or hearing of the two youths. Once he had taken his position, and Ozorne had checked both men himself in his scrying mirror, Ozorne produced cups and a bottle of his mother's wine. Arram spread the thick blanket he'd brought for protection from the gravelly roof. A loaf of bread and a bowl of buttermilk cheese followed. Ozorne set his prizes on the blanket, together with a knife for the cheese and a pair of napkins. Forewarned, Arram had filched grapes from supper.

'A feast!' Ozorne proclaimed it, and poured out the wine. 'The only thing missing is Varice, but the girls are having their own gathering.'

'Careful with that wine,' Arram warned. 'Don't start summer with a hangover.'

'Worrier,' Ozorne retorted.

They ate and drank, and at last Ozorne remarked idly, 'Mother wanted to talk future brides with me while the rest of you were visiting the temple of the Crocodile God upriver.'

Arram listened to a bat as it fluttered overhead before he asked, 'And?'

Ozorne sipped his wine. 'I convinced her that Uncle might take it ill if she was trying to find me a brood mare. Cousin Mesaraz is still very much alive and well and, I assume, capable of siring his own heirs. And Uncle himself isn't in need of his heir just yet.'

'Did that work?' Arram asked. He was trying to ignore the goosebumps that prickled over his arms and back at such casual, almost contemptuous talk of 'brood mares' and 'siring'.

'With a little persuasion.' Ozorne's voice was calm in the summer twilight. 'She doesn't think sometimes. She doesn't see how it might look to someone as jumpy as Uncle. I've heard gossip that Stiloit perhaps didn't drown – or if he did, it was before the ship actually sank. If Mother pushed for me to marry, Uncle might wonder if she was trying to advance me in the ranks of heirs. That Stiloit didn't die accidentally.'

'Do you believe that?' Arram asked, goosebumps of a different kind racing all over his body.

Ozorne chuckled. 'Are you joking? I was given a copy of what the men who survived told Uncle's examiners. The storm came up fast and hard, so hard they lost sight of the other ships. When it passed off, the mages identified what remained of the lost ships. The rain gods were irritable last winter, that's all.'

'We had the same storm,' Arram reminded him. 'I saw it. And it had no lightning, Ozorne. No lightning and no—'

Ozorne lunged and clapped his hand over his mouth. 'Don't say it,' he whispered. 'What if someone believed you? I saw them – didn't see them – too, remember? You, me, Chioké – and Faziy. And she's dead.' Arram stared at his friend. 'That was in Uncle's report, too,' Ozorne whispered. 'Chioké told them she was dead, weeks dead, when she was found. But others knew she was supposed to be able to get lightning to come when she called. He vouched for you and me – that's why *we* haven't been called before the examiners. Forget them, Arram. Forget *her.* Forget lightning snakes.'

Arram nodded. Ozorne was right. There were too many ways someone might think they had a part in that murderous storm. Stiloit was gone. Faziy was gone. What did he know of murder and emperors?

'I believe in ugly storms and the mortality of men. It was poor Stiloit's time, that's all. No one killed him.' Ozorne refilled his glass and swallowed deeply. 'May the Black God show him and those who died with him every mercy he can show.'

Including Faziy, Arram thought. Even if she used the lightning that sank those ships, or got the lightning snakes to do it, surely her own death paid for it. I only wish I knew *why.*

They watched the brightening stars and the rising moon in companionable silence. In the university below they could hear students laughing and shouting, enjoying their last free night for the next few months.

Finally, since they had skirted the possibility already, Arram asked softly, 'What would you do? If you were emperor?' He drank a little of his wine and made a face.

Ozorne sat up and looked in the direction of each of the guards. When he saw no sign of them, he sank back and whispered in return, 'I'd build a statue to my father in Imperial Square.'

Arram nodded, then remembered he was a shadow against other shadows. 'What else?'

His friend chuckled. 'I'd build Mother a palace at least two hours' ride away.'

Arram choked, then said in reproof, 'I'm *serious*.'

'So am I,' came the answer. Ozorne was quiet for a time. 'I'd build two more universities, one in Ekallatum Province and the other towards the eastern borders. Students will be able to study early before they need to come here. Or they can get their certificates at those schools. Our strength is in our mages, that's what Father always said. And two big schools for magecraft – ours and the one in the City of the Gods – isn't enough. Too many people with the Gift are forced to make do with bits and pieces, when they could learn greatness.'

'That sounds *wonderful*,' Arram said, awed. He hadn't even thought of that for the future. 'Have you thought . . . about the slaves?'

'What about them?'

'Freeing them. The North manages without slaves.'

'I don't know. I haven't thought it through, but . . . it's different with our people, surely,' Ozorne replied slowly. 'So many of them are uneducated – taken from the inland tribes. They can't care for themselves. Their masters do that.'

'They could be taught,' Arram said. 'The ones in the Eastern Lands managed.'

'But that area, those *Eastern Lands*, they don't have the open ground we use for crops,' Ozorne said, amused. 'They don't have the acreage along our northern coast, let alone what's in the south and the east. We have hundreds of thousands of slaves. They had nothing like that number! Besides, they freed them a few at a time.'

Arram exhaled with impatience. 'You could start with the children.'

'Maybe,' Ozorne drawled. 'I would really have to think and talk with others about it. Why don't you do the same? We need to avoid what happened in the Eastern Lands when they freed their slaves. People lost fortunes paying former slaves to do their old jobs – you read the same books I did. The great lords rebelled against their king—'

'Unsuccessfully,' Arram said impatiently.

'It would take time and careful planning. Years of it.' Ozorne filled Arram's glass. 'You are an idealist. Someone has to be practical. Not that we'll get a chance to try any of this.'

Arram sighed and sipped the wine. It tasted even nastier. Why did so many people like the stuff? 'You're right,' he told his friend. 'I don't wish your uncle or your cousin ill, after all.'

'Me neither,' Ozorne replied, putting down his own cup. 'If anything happens to them, I'll have to work. *There's* a dreadful fate!'

Preet descended through the dark and lit on Arram's hand.

'Come here,' Ozorne begged. 'Let me scratch that wayward little noggin of yours.' Preet complied. As she began to make her happy chirring noise, Ozorne asked, 'Do you know what I'd *really* like to do? Or were you just pulling my hair over slavery?'

'Of course I'd like to know,' Arram said.

Ozorne sighed dreamily. 'Southern Tortall or the Copper Isles. I'm not sure which I'd take first. I'd have to see what condition the navy is in. The lords of the Copper Isles have better ships than the Tortallans. It should be the Kyprish holdings, though. Once you have the Isles, Tortall is at your mercy, and the Yamani

Islands. Get Tortall, and the Yamanis and Scanra are nothing. And once you have those four, you can sweep the Eastern Lands.'

Arram sat up straight, staring at his friend's shadow. 'You've put a great deal of thought into this.'

'I have to do *something* with all those history and military history lessons, don't I?' Ozorne scrambled to his feet, making Preet flap over to Arram. He walked to the edge of the roof to stare towards the lights of Thak City. As he went, a wave of his Gift billowed out to form a dome over him and Arram: a privacy spell to keep Okot and his colleague from hearing. 'Think of it, Arram,' Ozorne said quietly. 'The emperor who did that would be known forever as the one who reunited the *original* empire, the Eternal Empire of the islands, the Eastern Lands, and the Southern Lands. One great empire – and one great emperor.'

Arram petted the bird for a moment, then forced a light note into his voice. 'So what comes after that? The moon?'

Ozorne laughed and returned, rolling up the privacy spell with him. 'Just dreaming, dolt. Let's pack up and head off, before we fall asleep here. It's not the most comfortable of beds.'

As he cast some light over them, Arram packed away their dishes. And you've given me an uncomfortable night, he thought. Whatever happened to the country villa, with Varice and me as your servants and counsellors? It seems you have a far bigger household in mind.

CHAPTER 20

Summer Term 439

On Tuesday after the start of the summer term, Ramasu halted Arram on his way out of the infirmary and handed him a document. 'For Thursday, pack for seventeen days – no robes, no good clothes, only plain stuff. Bring both your mage's workbag and your healer's kit. A hat, strong sandals. I suppose the bird will come, too. Double-check that everything in your kits is filled and up to strength, the knives and needles sharp, that sort of thing. Meet me at noon at the university's Arena Gate.'

Arram swallowed the lump in his throat. 'Yes, Master Ramasu.'

The man smiled and patted his shoulder. 'You are ready. I've already arranged matters with your teachers.'

Arram frowned. 'But – are they going to assign work for the time I'm away? I'll need my books. Usually—'

Ramasu said gently, 'They will not. They know you will be unable to do it. Now, off with you. I have packing of my own, and time to spend with my man.'

Arram bowed and left as ordered. Walking to the dining hall, he pondered the days to come with discomfort. He didn't want to let Ramasu down. He also didn't want to vomit on any of his patients-to-be. What if he made a serious mistake? He had yet to do so, but as Tristan was so very fond of saying, 'Everyone gets a first time.' Preet murmured softly and groomed Arram's hair with her beak, telling him that all would be well. Arram tried to cheer up, both for her sake and because he didn't want his friends plying him with all manner of questions over lunch.

It didn't work. The moment Varice and Ozorne joined him at the table, they knew something was on his mind. Tristan and Gissa had come to their own conclusions or, rather, Tristan had.

'He's not worth bothering today,' the young man told everyone. 'He's in one of his "I'm so talented and powerful, I must be doing something wrong" moods.'

Several of the others, including Gissa, laughed. Even Ozorne hid a smile behind his hand.

Preet said something insulting in sunbird.

Varice glared at the others. 'That shows what you know,' she said tartly, running her fingers down Preet's back. The girl looked at Arram, her blue eyes sympathetic. 'It's the arena, isn't it? Remember? You mentioned it when we were on the river.'

Ozorne clapped his palm to his head. 'Already? Arram, I'm sorry – I'd take your place, I swear, but I don't have medical training!'

'What about the arena?' Tristan demanded.

Arram ate his long bean and lamb tajine doggedly. He let Varice and Ozorne explain how he was to accompany Ramasu to the gladiators' camp for two weeks.

'You'll be there for the games, then!' one of their other companions exclaimed. 'What's to mope for?'

Arram glared at him. 'Yes, I'm there for the games,' he retorted. 'And while people are cheering as men and women are mutilated, I'll be behind the scenes, trying to keep what's left of them alive.'

Tristan rolled his eyes. 'They're slaves, Draper. *Criminals.* They've lived longer in the arena than they would in the mines or fields or galleys, trust me.'

'Not all of them,' another young man at the table argued. 'There were a few in that last new batch that didn't know right hand from left. They went down fast.' He smirked at Arram, who clenched his fists on the table. 'So you don't have to worry your pretty head about healing the likes of them. They were dead when they hit the—'

Arram's palms were tingling. He thought it was because he was clenching them too tightly. Then Varice squeaked. Preet pecked him sharply above one ear. The others, with the exception of Ozorne and Varice, were thrusting themselves away from the table. Ozorne pointed down. Arram looked: small bolts of lightning danced to and fro between his hands. His tajine was now a charred black lump.

The student who had smirked got to his feet, pointing at Arram. 'They shouldn't give you special work if you can't control yourself!' To Ozorne he said, 'Be careful, or your pet might just cook you!'

Ozorne looked up at him, a sweet smile on his lips. 'Be careful of what?' he asked. 'I saw nothing odd, did you, Varice?'

Varice carefully cut the fish on her plate. 'Not a thing,' she replied calmly.

Sergeant Okot, noting the fuss, came over. 'Is there a problem, Your Imperial Highness?' he asked.

'I believe some people don't care for my friends,' Ozorne replied, eyeing those who were still on their feet. Four were already resuming their seats. 'We will be fine once they have taken their leave.'

Okot inspected those who were standing. 'His Imperial Highness expressed a preference.' His voice was chilly. They gathered their things and left.

When the young man and one of his friends were gone, Okot picked up Arram's spoon and jabbed the blackened mass on his plate. It crumbled to ash. Putting the spoon down, Okot said, 'I'd complain to the cooks. It's overdone.'

Varice began to giggle. Soon everyone at the table did the same, even Arram.

Ozorne put a hand on Arram's shoulder as he was about to go for more food. 'You have a good heart, but be watchful,' he cautioned. 'Gladiators are beaten and starved till they're little better than animals. You *don't* want to turn your back on them.'

Arram nodded. Ozorne knew more about these things than he did. He would be careful. He wanted to come home again with every part of him still in its proper place.

Arram was waiting at the gate at noon on Thursday when he heard someone call his name. He looked up and down the road. All he saw was the distant shape of what he was sure was Ramasu and the cart.

'Arram!' He turned. Varice was running towards him down the broad path from the school. He hadn't seen her at breakfast, which had disappointed him more than he realized until this moment. His heart lifted. She was beautiful in the sun, her fast pace hugging her blue cotton gown against her curves. Her golden hair streamed out behind her. 'Arram, you great dolt, didn't you hear me call?'

Preet flew into the air before Arram caught Varice up in a strong hug. He thought for a moment that Varice fumbled with his backpack, but then she wrapped her arms around his neck. She even kissed him on the mouth, though he expected that was because she missed his cheek in her hurry.

'I wanted to say goodbye,' she said as he put her down. She straightened her gown and smoothed her hair. 'It's going to be so boring with you away. I know,' she said, holding up her hand when he would have argued. 'I have other friends. But Ozorne is forever talking politics with people, and . . .' She rested her palm on Arram's chest. 'I never know what you will say or do. You make me laugh. You *don't* make me feel silly or stupid.'

He put both of his hands over hers. 'You aren't either one. Varice, who has been telling you such things?'

She smiled up at him. 'They don't have to *tell* me. They laugh and they change the subject, or they say "*Nobody* cares about that, Varice," or . . . you know what I mean.' She looked around him and withdrew her hand. 'There's Master Ramasu. Will you bring me back a keepsake from Musenda? He's absolutely magnificent.'

Arram smiled. 'I shall manage something.' He turned and waved to the master, who was perched on the seat of a loaded cart near the gate. He could feel the tiny bit of her power shimmering there atop all the things that carried his own Gift. 'What did you put in my things?'

She looked down, blushing. 'A charm to keep you safe and bring you home,' she said. 'Goddess bless, Arram.' She returned to the university.

'Goddess bless, sweetheart,' he whispered. He bent to pick up the bag with his clothes. Preet cackled. 'I didn't ask you,' he told the bird, and went to join Ramasu.

To his surprise, the master said nothing about having to wait. He only instructed Arram to put his things in the wagon. Preet chose to sit on Ramasu's knee and talk to him while Arram disposed of his luggage. Quickly Arram felt under the opening in his extra pack until he found Varice's charm. He pulled it out and slipped it into his belt purse to inspect later. The rest of his belongings sank under the protective spell that Ramasu had placed on the wagon's contents.

'You're afraid someone will steal from you?' Arram asked as he climbed onto the seat next to the master. Preet hopped up to Arram's shoulder.

'You have not thought the matter through,' Ramasu replied as he clucked to the mules and set them forward. 'Ask instead how easy would it be to recover painkilling medicines and surgical knives from those with whom we shall be mingling.'

Arram did not have to think about it for very long. He shuddered.

'By the time we reach the camp, your belongings too will be imbued with my spell. If anyone but you or I touch them, you will feel a sharp blow to your hand. The would-be thief will feel something much worse.' Ramasu glanced at Arram. 'Never forget who we deal with here – men and women who have been brutalized for years. Even the soldiers who guard them are crude and vicious. Wariness must be our first principle.'

'Why do you do it, Master, if it's so dangerous?' Arram asked.

'Because they are not undeserving of care. No one is undeserving of care. It is not their fault that they have become what they are,' Ramasu said, his eyes on the road. 'They are slaves, chosen and groomed to become gladiators – which is to say, they are beaten, starved, and punished for their work. They grow old in combat and are slaughtered before their time. *You* are here because I can show you the wounds and injuries you would otherwise see only during a disaster or a war. You have a talent for healing. You may not care to specialize, but if you are to manage quick healing in an emergency, work at an arena is invaluable.'

Ramasu fell silent, guiding the mules past wagons coming into town. Arram had always thought Ramasu was distant and aloof. Now he saw that not only was the healer a kind man in his way, but he hated the games. Perhaps he even hated slavery. Arram knew Lindhall hated it, but that was to be expected. Lindhall came from the North.

Arram wasn't sure how he felt. Given a choice, he would have refused the visit to the gladiators' camp. Those muscled, scarred, roaring, violent people terrified him; he already knew he hated what they did. Perhaps Ramasu had guessed these things, which was why he hadn't given Arram a choice. Arram also wasn't certain he would have refused Ramasu, since the man was his teacher. If Ramasu – if any of them – thought he needed to learn something, he accepted their judgement.

He wished now that this time was over, and they were on their way back to the university.

'Has the crocodile god said when he means to return your charge to her family?' Ramasu asked as they turned from the road onto a well-travelled side track.

Arram flinched, then reminded himself that his teachers always knew things he didn't tell them. 'No, sir. He gets very grumpy when I bring it up, or when Sebo does. He says he has to find just the right gift, and he hasn't yet. Apparently he has to appease the god he offended when Preet hid on his back.'

Preet, who was grooming herself on Arram's lap, chuckled.

'*You* are a plotter,' Ramasu told her. 'You could have asked your crocodile to foist you on some hapless hero. But you decided to cause trouble for Enzi and poor Arram.'

'She's no trouble,' Arram murmured. Then it occurred to him that the master was speaking oddly. Ramasu was not in the habit of teasing.

Additionally, he did not usually sound like an elderly woman.

Arram looked at the master and received a shock. The mules' reins hung in midair, just as if Ramasu were still driving. The master himself had turned to look at the bird on Arram's lap, but his face was not quite right.

His eyes, normally grey-brown, were black and sparkling. His hair had turned to grey-and-white stubble. His face was creased with wrinkles.

'I'm keeping the teeth,' the goddess inside Ramasu said. 'It's not often I get a mouthful in such condition. He takes good care of himself, this teacher of yours.'

A whimper burbled out of Arram's throat. He was used to Enzi, who occasionally visited Sebo when Arram was there for his lessons. He had even learned to accept Enzi's company on their underwater walks. But he had also thought, many times, that he disliked meeting gods. There was just something so *overpowering* about them. And this god was even more important than Enzi. He knew her, because she had given him a diamond-and-ruby die the day Musenda had risen to become one of the top gladiators in the capital. He'd left the bracelet he wore it on at home.

He tried to bow and nearly squashed Preet, who scolded him fiercely.

'Stop that,' the Graveyard Hag ordered. 'You're frightening your poor birdie. Come here.' Arram felt himself slide closer to

Ramasu's body until they were practically touching. 'Much better,' the goddess said. 'Stop flinching. I like handsome young lads like you, particularly when I know they're going to afford me so much entertainment shortly.'

Arram stared into those black eyes. He had the dreadful notion that he could see constellations in them. 'E-e-entertainment?' he stammered.

'Oh, all you powerful ones are *wonderful* when it comes to kicking up a fuss. It's been deadly dull where I live, but you and your friend Ozorne will soon fix that!' The Graveyard Hag cocked her head to one side, eyeing Arram. It made him nervous to see her wrinkled features slide under Ramasu's smooth brown ones. 'Tell Ozorne for me, always trust those who are your true friends. If you do, you'll never go astray. He must think carefully about what people want from him.'

Arram bowed his head. 'I will, Goddess.'

'And you, birdie—' the goddess said.

Preet, who had settled on one of the reins, chattered at the Hag.

'What sort of name is Preet for one of your kind, and what are you doing here?' the Hag demanded.

Arram started to answer, but the Hag lifted Ramasu's finger, and Arram found he could not say a word. Instead Preet began to talk, whistling, chirping, and muttering until she came to a halt.

The Graveyard Hag began to laugh. Preet said something else, and the goddess shook her captive's head. 'No, I won't tell – this is far too amusing. Besides, I never let those snobs at home know anything interesting if I can help it. Your secret is safe with me.' She shifted on the seat and looked at Arram. 'Mules, do your job, and I'll make certain you have an extra good feed tonight,' she ordered. Then she cupped Arram's face with Ramasu's hand and lifted it so she could look into his eyes again. 'You poor boy,' she said, and grinned. It was a broad grin, the kind Ramasu never made. Seeing it on his calm features made

Arram queasy. 'You have *no* idea what my cousins hold in store, do you? No one can tell. Here's a bit of advice from a wicked old lady, for the sake of those beautiful brown eyes of yours. *Watch what you say.'*

As quickly as she had arrived, she was gone. Ramasu's hand fell to his lap; the reins dropped to his knee. Arram seized them before they fell to the road. Preet leaped into the air, shrieking, and the master thrashed.

'Arram, what are you *doing*?' cried Ramasu.

Arram had one rein but not the rest. He was about to fall onto the road with them. The mules halted and looked back, ears switching.

Arram's ears roared as Ramasu's familiar Gift wrapped around him and deposited him on the seat. The reins hovered before him, held by the master's power. Arram took them up.

Ramasu surrendered the one he still held while he cradled his brow in his hand. 'My poor head,' he complained. 'Do you have a water flask?'

Arram pointed at his belt. Ramasu took the flask and added something from his own belt pouch, then gulped the water down. 'Thank you,' he said. He propped his head on his hands. 'It will be a little while before the lozenge does its work. I'll take the reins back then . . . Which god was it?'

Arram started, jerking the reins. Both mules glanced back with evil intent in their eyes. 'Sir – how did you know?'

'I am not insensate, lad. There is a hole in my memory, you are holding the reins – badly, do not jerk on them like that—'

Arram loosened his pull on the leather straps.

'My head pounds, and everything I see shimmers with innate magic,' Ramasu said, rubbing his eyes. 'A god did that. It has happened to me before. Which god? Or are you not permitted to tell?'

Arram saw no reason to keep that information back. 'The Graveyard Hag, sir.'

Ramasu frowned. 'The Graveyard Hag? Now why . . . ?' Arram

glanced at the master, who had fallen silent. Then Ramasu said, 'Of course. Ozorne. The goddess wanted to speak with you about Ozorne.'

Arram nodded miserably. He wasn't sure that he should give the goddess's message to anyone but Ozorne, and it would be difficult to refuse one of his masters.

'Leave me out of it,' Ramasu said. 'Unless the god . . . ?'

'No, sir,' Arram said gratefully. 'It's only for Ozorne.'

'Excellent,' the man replied. 'Yes, I am very, *very* grateful she only used me as her conduit. She loves to make those who have her attention dance to her music.'

'That isn't very reassuring, Master Ramasu,' Arram said weakly.

The man reached over and took the reins. 'The truth so seldom is.' Setting the mules forwards at a crisper pace, he said, 'Sebo and I have been discussing a trip upriver in August and early September. She would like to visit some of the tributary rivers to the Zekoi, and I would like assistance in gathering medicinal herbs and insects I can find nowhere else. Would you be interested?'

Arram sat up eagerly, the touch of the goddess almost – but not quite – forgotten. 'I've only been a short way upriver with Her Highness,' he confessed.

They talked about the possibility as the wagon bumped over the narrow trail. Then Arram saw a stone wall rising above the tall reeds and, behind it, the even greater marble heights of the arena. He gulped. They had reached their destination.

When Ramasu had first mentioned the trip to the gladiators' camp, Arram had studied maps of the arena and of the training grounds until he knew them by heart. Their new workplace was part of a large, military-style camp built on the side of the arena. Behind a stone wall patrolled by hard-looking soldiers stood wooden barracks for men and for women, an infirmary, wide sand training grounds, an armoury with its own forge, and a stretch of garden for those who cared to tend one.

To the left of the gate, separated from the world, the training ground, and the barracks by another, shorter stone wall, were the beast pens. Arram could hear lions roar and elephants bellow as the cart approached the outer gate. He hated the practice of driving animals to battle as much as he hated the practice of forcing men and women to do so.

The guards' barracks were behind a wall on the opposite side of the wild animals' cages. The arena's horses were also there, since the sounds and smells of the larger, wild beasts frightened them. Ramasu had told Arram once that there were several gates to connect the guards' area to the gladiators' so there would not be a bottleneck of guards if trouble arose in the main compound.

Above it all loomed a big gate through the northern wall of the arena itself. The only openings that Arram could see were ventilation for the audience and were one hundred feet up or more. It was yet another reminder to the gladiators that there was no chance to escape. Only the gate to the arena remained to them, two leaves of locked metal a little over the height of the tallest giraffe.

The place was fairly quiet. This gate was one of iron bars. Four soldiers stood guard on the ground there, as well as on the wall over it. The man in charge greeted Ramasu cheerfully and led him inside the guardhouse to sign forms. Arram accepted the reins from the master and looked around, sweating. He could hear the thwacks of wood on wood and men's shouts from inside. He also glimpsed two women in leather shirts and very short breeches fighting with spears.

'I dunno, Blaedroy, he's awful scrawny for the ring.' A soldier walked over to lean against Ramasu's side of the seat. 'Might make a decent meal for one of the cheetahs, though. Put her and the cubs in with him, there's a good bit of fun.'

Arram tried to ignore the man, but Preet was having none of this. She roused from her nap on Arram's shoulder, fluffing out all of her feathers, and told the soldier what she thought of his idea of 'fun'.

'Hag's dice, what manner of bird is that, anyway?' the other guard shouted over her noise. He was white, blond, and blue-eyed, plainly a descendant of Scanrans. 'Tell it to quiet down or we'll feed it to the lions!'

'Preet, stop,' Arram said, trying to wrap a hand around her. She batted at him with her wings, telling him in Preet that a good peck or two would teach these buffoons manners.

'Lookit this,' Blaedroy said, grinning. 'He can't even make a wee bird mind 'im. He's arena bait for certain.'

Ramasu walked up behind the man. 'He is my assistant,' the mage said coldly. 'I require his services in the infirmary. Should you become injured while he is here, you may wish you had reconsidered your jokes.'

'You two, get to the gate,' growled their captain, who had followed Ramasu outside. The guardsmen hurried to undo the locks and shove the leaves of the gate open, inwards towards the training ground. 'Escort Master Ramasu and the cart to the infirmary and unpack it when he lifts the magic. Then stand guard there,' he added. He whistled sharply in two bursts. Another pair of guards trotted over. 'Escort the cart to the infirmary and guard it while these two pieces of gallows bait unload. You may then take the cart and horses to our camp. Master Ramasu, I hope you and your assistant will be so good as to take supper with me this evening?'

'I am pleased to do so,' the master said. 'Now tell us, what do we face?'

'We got two new loads of fighters yesterday,' the captain replied as he walked to the gate beside Ramasu. 'A third from other arenas, the rest New Meat.'

Arram urged the mules forwards. He kept his eyes on their shoulders as he heard the clank of chain and the scrape of metal on dirt as the gates were opened. A handful of gladiators were idling in the yard, moving slowly towards them, seemingly without plan.

A hard crack brought his head up. A guard on the gate had

produced a whip: four feet of rigid stick tipped by several tapering feet of braided leather. He raised and snapped it at the gladiators. They halted, their eyes going from the mages and their wagon to the guard and back. One of them had new red stripes on his arm. After a long pause the group broke up and returned to training.

'We are perfectly able to defend ourselves, guardsmen,' Ramasu said, his voice at its most gentle. 'There is no need for the hard whip.'

'The New Meat don't know that, Master,' the whip wielder said. 'They ain't been broke in. Once they learn the stick, we can teach them rules and they'll obey.'

'Yet if those stripes you just made get infected, you will have created more work for your healers, which means me,' Ramasu replied.

Goosebumps rippled along Arram's arms. There was a touch of iron in the master's voice.

'Should that happen, I shall feel it incumbent upon me to teach you the folly of using your hard whip when it is not absolutely necessary,' Ramasu continued. 'That would be unfortunate, but not for me.' He walked on, the captain at his elbow. Arram noticed that the captain glanced at the whip-bearing soldier but said nothing to him.

Arram followed the two men and the guards to a long, one-storey brick building with barred windows and shutters. It sported a wooden porch over the entry, which had a barred door. The regular healer waited there, a satchel by his feet.

'Ramasu, welcome, welcome!' he cried, embracing the mage.

Ramasu smiled and returned the embrace. Then he indicated Arram. 'Healer Daleric, may I present my student, Arram Draper? Arram, Daleric and his assistants will rejoin us in time for the games.'

'And we will be the better for that wonderful time away,' Daleric said, nodding to Arram. 'Before I go, let me offer you a taste of the best Maren red wine I've had in years. Your Arram can help the boys unload the cart. Captain, will you share a glass?'

The captain refused the offer of a drink and returned to his headquarters. 'Let me supervise,' Ramasu insisted. 'Arram is new. He has to learn to watch for nimble fingers. Then we can relax.'

'Very well,' Daleric said. 'I shall assist.' The healer drew Ramasu into the infirmary.

Once the cart was unpacked the two healers retreated into Daleric's small office, a box-like room set on one side of the infirmary. Inside the main room, Arram inspected the healer's stillroom and its tidy shelves of supplies, each spot neatly labelled. He stowed their own medicines, ointments, and bandages, appreciating that Daleric kept the place clean and orderly. Only the magical creations and poisons were left unshelved. He suspected they went behind a door that had a number of magical locks on it. Most, if not all, of them he could undo, but it seemed polite to wait for the healer or Master Ramasu to take care of that.

He heard voices in the main room. He emerged in time to hear Daleric tell Ramasu, 'And I am off.' He nodded to Arram. 'The goddess's good luck, youngster.' He bowed to the figure of Hekaja, whose small shrine occupied the western corner of the room. 'Don't let them trap you. They're beasts, when all's said and done.' He picked up a packed bag and walked out to the waiting wagon.

Ramasu closed the door behind the healer. 'Daleric will talk about them as human beings by the time he returns from his holiday,' he said. 'They wear him down over the course of a year, but he is dedicated to working with them, or he wouldn't stay.' He walked over to the shrine, bowed to the figure of the goddess, and lit some orris incense with a touch of his finger.

Arram did the same, though he lit his incense from the master's, not trusting his ability with a touch of fire. 'How long has he – Daleric? – been here?'

'Five years. Most last two years or less, but Daleric has family in Thak City. Some of them are healers, some guards. Let's see how you managed.' Ramasu only glanced over the shelves where Arram had placed supplies already. 'I expected you to do this well,' he explained. 'You could have entered the locked room yourself.'

'It didn't seem polite to do so without permission,' Arram said.

'You can never fail with good manners,' Ramasu commented, pleased. 'Go ahead. Without damage, open the room now.'

Arram touched a bit of the oil he carried in a vial in his belt purse to his eyelids. It allowed him to see magic without spending his own Gift. A couple of blinks showed him the spell letters on the locked door. They weren't the signs of complex spells, but he undid them carefully, in case anything nasty was hidden under a mild sign.

He and Ramasu had just finished stowing the magical and poisonous supplies when Preet came flying in, crying out in alarm. Arram followed her into the main room and heard the unmistakable sound of a man screaming. It was drawing close.

'Master!' he called as Preet flew up to a perch on a roof beam. Looking around, he spotted a cupboard on the wall with the word 'Linens' burned into the front. Beside it was a second cupboard labelled 'Bandages'. Arram threw open the linen cupboard and grabbed one of the bundles. He shook it out to get an idea of the size of the cloth, quickly folded it double, and placed it on a table. While he was in the front room, he opened the door.

He grabbed a tray from a stack of them and returned to the bandages cupboard, placing four on it. That would be enough until they learned what was coming. Ramasu stood in front of the closed door to the stillroom, cleansing himself with his Gift. His medical kit was open beside him on the floor, also awash in his power.

Four dirty, muscled men hurried in with a screaming man on

a rope stretcher. Arram had no problem guessing what was wrong: the heavier of the two main bones below the patient's knee had snapped and was thrusting out of his flesh.

'Ol' Daleric off to see the wife and kiddies?' a stretcher bearer shouted to Arram, panting. 'Miggin here's got the best of luck!'

Miggin, the screamer, took a breath and made several rude suggestions about what the man could do with his luck.

'Very inventive,' Ramasu said, waving the men forwards to the edge of the waiting table. 'Arram, I will do painlessness. You will raise our friend Miggin and set him down when these fellows move the stretcher. At a count of three?'

Arram fumbled for the right spell and chose the most basic. 'One,' he said, walking up to the stretcher. 'Two.' Arram cast the signs for an equal lift all around Miggin. 'Three.' Palms up, he raised his hands, and the patient, as Ramasu let a wave of his Gift flow over Miggin. With the experience born of practice, the bearers slid the stretcher out from under the injured man. Miggin was now breathing rather than shrieking. He hardly noticed what was going on. Arram gently used his own spell to push Miggin forwards until he was over the sheet-covered table, then carefully set him down.

'This one's good,' the man who'd asked about Daleric told Ramasu. 'We'll keep him if you don't want him.'

'That's very kind, but there are masters who wish to keep him,' Ramasu said. 'Tell me what happened to your friend.'

The men chuckled. 'He's not a friend,' replied one, a bearded Kyprish islander with a fearsome set of tattoos on his back and arms. 'He's fresh. Some funny man told New Meat here that if he went two falls with Anaconda he'd get respect. This is what happened in his first fall.'

'Now Anaconda's sad because we took his toy,' another gladiator said. 'You'll see more New Meat today, Master Ramasu.'

'Then you had best go out and collect it, lads,' Ramasu told them. 'Though I would appreciate it if you first told Anaconda that I am here. Any extra work he gives me will be paid for, by him, when I see him next.'

'Very good, Master Ramasu,' the tattooed gladiator replied. 'It would be nice to have some New Meat left alive for the arena.'

The man who had first spoken to Arram shoved past him towards the door. 'We're glad you're back, Master,' he told Ramasu. 'Daleric's all right, but he's not you.' All four of them bowed, then trotted outside with their stretcher.

'We see them at their best in here,' Ramasu told Arram. 'Now, tell me about Miggin's injury.'

Arram looked at the gladiator's leg. 'It's a compound break of the main bone of the lower leg,' he said, using a spell on his eyes that showed him the bones. 'We'll have a bad time reseating it without snagging flesh on the bone.'

Ramasu twitched his fingers, murmuring a short spell. One of several small tables tucked under the window counters skidded across the floor to his side. 'Here is where you learn about compound fractures, and about multiple fractures of bone that do not break through the skin,' he said quietly. 'We are likely to see a great many of them. If you will look . . .'

After several tries, Arram got the knack of drawing all the torn flesh out of the way. Ramasu was working a cleansing over both ends of the bone when Preet landed on the head of their worktable, fluttering her wings. 'Understood, Preet, but we cannot rush,' the master said absently.

Arram heard the approach of someone else howling in pain. His hands trembled for a moment before he forced himself to concentrate on his patient.

'Very good,' Ramasu told him. 'Now.' Both ends of the bone shifted together. 'Is the lower part of the bone seated against the upper part? Don't use your vision – it isn't accurate enough.'

Arram set a portion of his awareness in his Gift and wrapped it around the damaged bone. It was fitted back together as well as it could be. Ramasu had left no jags or tiny splinters to dig into muscle or flesh. 'It's very well seated, Master, except for what had to be removed.'

'Release the muscle first, then the skin to their former places,' Ramasu ordered. 'Gently.'

Arram released the two spells he had worked to keep both parts of the injured man's body clear of the damage. He could feel the veins, and the muscles, sigh in relief as they relaxed into their former beds. The skin was slower. 'I think the skin is hurt some,' he whispered. 'I'm sorry.'

'Either you forgot from your earlier work that the skin is the most easily damaged, or you haven't held it off its natural form for so long before,' Ramasu replied. 'This is normal. You've done well. I shall finish with this man. Prepare the next table and send our newest guest to sleep. The second level of his mind only, Arram. He must be unaware of his pain, not dead to it.'

Since he had eased pain before in Ramasu's infirmary, Arram only smiled at the master's mild joke. He had never put so much power into a painlessness spell that the patient could not feel anything for a day, though he knew a student who had. Carefully he drew his Gift away from the sleeping gladiator. He recovered it all just as three of the men from earlier and a fresh stretcher bearer came through the door. Arram rushed to seize a sheet and throw it over another waist-high table. By the time the gladiators reached it, he had the lifting spell ready to shift the injured man onto the table. This one had a dislocated shoulder.

'Worst pain in my life,' he whispered, his eyes bulging out. 'Worst pain' – he was trying to control himself, but his voice was rising in volume – 'in MY—'

Arram hurriedly sketched the symbols he needed to use in order to release a victim from pain, unlike Ramasu, who could do it with a softly whispered phrase. The man fell silent, though his lungs pumped his chest like a bellows. Arram drew a breath and descended into his Gift, where he could deepen the spell enough that his patient would not feel his pain for the time being. He glanced over his shoulder at Ramasu, who nodded.

Arram had dealt with two dislocations before, one hip and one shoulder. Using the man's own sweat, he wrote the necessary signs for painlessness in the shoulder joint first, before he wrote the sign of the closing lock, and poured his Gift into it. There was the dreadful sound of gristle and muscle returning to their proper place; the shoulder resumed its normal shape. Carefully Arram ran his fingers over it to ensure that the joint was whole once more before he looked at the gladiators. They were dipping drinks of water for themselves from the bucket by the door.

'Dare I ask – the Anaconda again?' he said quietly, wiping his hands clean of sweat and dirt with a damp towel.

'Oh, no, if that'd been the Anaconda, his whole backbone would've been all twisty,' said the Kyprish gladiator. 'No, this piece of offal thought one of the girls was there for double duty: fighting and' – he caught Ramasu's eye and obviously changed the word he'd been about to use – 'canoodling. Her never having made him an offer, nor any man, for that matter, she explained his error to him.'

'She shoulda knowed he'd never been in a camp where the lasses might be sisters of the game, too,' the new stretcher bearer said.

'He shoulda knowed to ask before layin' a hand on her,' replied the tattooed gladiator. 'He could ask any of us fellows.'

'Argue it outside,' Ramasu ordered. 'It's near to supper. I will send a messenger when this man is ready to return to camp.'

The men nodded and left.

'It wasn't so long ago that more than a scant handful of women could defend themselves like warriors,' Ramasu mused as he covered their newest patient with a sheet for warmth. Arram had already noticed, and been grateful for, the coolness spells placed on the infirmary by generations of healers. 'Only two hundred years it's been since all women could be soldiers, sailors, enforcers of the law. It wasn't only gladiators, Shang, and some of the Southern tribes as it is now.'

Arram smiled. He was always amused by the different view of time held by most of his masters. To them, two centuries was a short period, just a small part of the ages of history and magic that they knew. And he knew what Ramasu was thinking of. 'The rise of the aspect of the Gentle Mother.'

'The Gentle Mother.' In Ramasu's soft voice it sounded like a curse. 'They took a goddess with a scythe in her hand, striding the rows of grain, and turned her to present the self of a house-bound creature. I wonder when she will show her true face again.'

'Did they ever try to do that to the Graveyard Hag?' Arram asked. He couldn't imagine the old lady with any other face than the one she currently bore.

Ramasu chuckled. 'Oh, yes. It was amazing, the change of luck that struck *any* priest who attempted to make her into a kindly grandmother spinning by the fire. There is a book in the Faiths section of the library, *The Hag Speaks*. You may read it and write it up for me for the beginning of autumn term.'

Arram sighed. Why did a good conversation with a master always seem to end in more work for him? Still, he had to say, 'Perhaps the Great Goddess prefers the face of the Gentle Mother, or she would have done something like that.'

'I prefer to think that the Three-Fold Mother has not noticed, time being so different in the Divine Realms.' Ramasu was placing jars of ointment and bandages on a counter. 'I think that when she does discover what is being done in her name, she will let us know it.'

The doors flew open. Two men entered, one with a clumsy bandage on his chest, the other with one on his thigh. 'Worm-eaten, scum-lollin' country guard let one of his New Meats come in with a knife!' the man with the chest wound cried.

Ramasu pointed them each to a bench. He took the chest wound, a shallow diagonal slice, and Arram the thigh wound, which had just missed an important vein. 'And where is this New Meat with the blade?' Ramasu asked as he and Arram wet cloths and washed the injuries with a cleansing balm.

'He won't be coming here,' the gladiator with the chest wound said offhandedly. 'The lads settled his account.'

Arram's mouth suddenly went dry. He *thought* he knew what the man meant. He glanced at Ramasu, who gave a tiny shake of his head. Fingers trembling, Arram got back to the work of spelling the veins and arteries whole again, then turned to the muscles that had been sliced.

'Arm and torso work for you for two days,' Ramasu ordered Arram's patient when he was released. 'No full-strength blows, no running. Tell the cooks plenty of meat. And you, weapons repair for three days, then light sparring for the rest of the week,' he said, pointing to his patient. 'If your mentor has questions, he may see me. Off with you – I hear others on their way.'

The afternoon continued in this manner: a broken jaw, cuts, lesser broken bones, head blows that resulted in two more sleeping gladiators in the infirmary. Things slowed down at last: Arram realized he hadn't heard the *thwack* of wooden blade against wooden blade for a while. They released their last patient when he woke shortly before the evening meal. The other patients had returned to their quarters earlier.

Ramasu and Arram cleaned the infirmary, though Arram protested he could do so on his own.

'Things are less formal here,' Ramasu said gently. 'Today was actually fairly calm. There will be a few days while the gladiators torment the New Meat, particularly those who are here only because they look strong or were troublesome to their former masters. They will not be killed if it can be helped. They are meant to die in the arena.'

Arram made the Sign against evil on his chest.

Ramasu sighed. 'Even so. But some will live, if we make them whole enough when they face the arena. When the gladiators tire of the New Meat, they will turn to those who trained in lesser arenas, men and women who believe they are as good as the fighters of Thak City. I will need all of your strength then, so don't waste it in housekeeping. We share the labour here.'

The room was clean and the stillroom locked by the time a guard came to sit watch over the infirmary. Two army slaves took charge of Ramasu's and Arram's belongings, with the exception of their mage workbags. Those remained with their owners. Together they crossed to the military side of the camp.

Arram, to his shame, fell asleep at the table, to be woken and escorted to his room.

CHAPTER 21

Summer Term 439

THE ARENA TRAINING CAMP

Ramasu woke him before dawn to a good-sized breakfast. 'Eat,' the master said, digging into his own meal. 'Now that we are here, they will cease to go easy on the fresh arrivals to the fighting force.'

Arram tried to speak past the lump in his throat. 'Easy? They went *easy* on those men?'

'Yes. Today the new warriors, who believe they are practised, will learn that this arena is harder than they ever dreamed. As for the New Meat . . .' Ramasu shook his head. 'Let us hope they have enough native ability to survive their first four games. If they can do that, their chances are better than half that they will live past their first year.'

Ramasu was not joking about the sudden quickening of business. The gladiator with the compound fracture was even drafted to soak cloths. Arram quickly showed him to teach those who could walk how to wash their injuries in water that was treated to clean out dirt and infection.

Arram took charge of those with broken or cut arms and legs. Ramasu cared for those with more serious injuries. Preet, scolded away from the work down on the floor, perched in the rafters and sang, her voice soothing the wounded.

On their third day Arram was smearing salve into a new
man's sunburned back when a shadow fell over them. 'If you
don't mind?' he asked the shadow's owner politely. 'I can't tell
what I've got and what I'm missing.'

The shadow moved.

Arram finished the job and told the gladiator he had treated,
'You'll be fine when you go to bed. You shouldn't burn like that
again with the charm I gave you earlier. Now,' he said, looking
for the shadow's owner. 'What may I do for—' He recognized
the large black man leaning against the wall nearby. 'Musenda!'
he cried, grinning and holding out his hands. The big man
clasped them warmly. 'It's wonderful to see you!'

The gladiator smiled. 'Good to see you. You've grown, haven't
you?'

Arram was shocked: he was now just half a head shorter than
the gladiator. 'I must have done so, though it was not my inten-
tion,' he said as the patients close enough to hear chuckled.
'Now I see why the seamstresses keep complaining about length-
ening my clothes.'

'Arram, you know this man?' Having finished with his patient,
Ramasu came over to see who was talking to his student. 'Mithros
guard us all, Musenda! Or may I still call you Sarge?'

Musenda shook his head. 'You can always call me Sarge,
Master. It's the others I must remind I've never been a soldier.
Even the soldiers do it, once they hear me speak out.'

'You mean screech,' said a man with a sprained wrist.

'You mean *bellow*,' added a woman with a broken rib.

'*However* it is,' Musenda said, looking at the injured gladiators,
his right eyebrow raised, 'I can't make them stop, so I live with
it.'

'How is your sister-in-law? How are the children?' Arram
enquired. He motioned for the woman with the broken rib to
sit up straight. She did so, wincing, and he cast the painkilling
spell for her.

As Arram lay a wrapping of his power on her to see if she

had more hurts, Musenda said, 'My sister-in-law is well. She'll be pleased that you asked after her. I won't have the chance to see her much longer, though. They leave for Tortall next month.'

'Do you begrudge her?' asked the female gladiator as Arram gently placed his hands over the broken rib. Seeing her broken bone in his mind, he murmured the brief words of the spell to mend it, making sure that each splinter fit into its former place. Finished, he glanced at the woman and at Musenda.

'Of course I don't begrudge her,' Musenda replied. 'She is happy. Her new husband is a good man. I'll miss them, though, and the little ones.'

'Tortall?' Arram asked. 'Why?'

'Her man works for horse dealers. They want to open a new branch there. They asked him to go – he's one of the best trainers they have.' Musenda shrugged. 'They offered him a fine wage and a house of his own. *I* should have such luck.'

'Oh, remind me, I brought some toys for the children. Not much, just some little things,' Arram told the big man. To the woman he said, 'Meat, as much as you can eat, milk, and cheese.' She raised and lowered the arm on the side of the once-broken rib. 'Light work today and tomorrow. Nothing with that arm. You should do well after that.'

The woman smiled. 'If you were but a few years older, I'd give you a proper thank-you,' she said, getting to her feet. 'I'll wager those eyes are breaking the girl mages' hearts.' She kissed Arram on the cheek and left, cackling gleefully.

'Don't be looking for no kiss from me,' growled the man with the sprained ankle.

Arram blushed and tended to the gladiator's sprain. Later, when he returned from getting a drink of water, he found Ramasu speaking with Musenda. The infirmary was empty of patients, so he collapsed on a bench and relaxed among the cooling spells.

'I had no idea that you two knew one another, or I would

have sent word when we arrived,' the master was saying to the big gladiator.

'We met at the games, when he fell off the railing and nearly hit the sands,' Musenda explained. He grinned at Arram. 'I'll wager anything you like that Ua will remember you. Elephants remember everything. She took him in her trunk, stood on her hind legs, and handed him up to his family, as pretty as you please,' he explained to Ramasu. 'Arram, you were what?'

'Young,' Arram muttered, blushing.

'That's how Ua became the most popular elephant here,' Musenda told Ramasu. 'They won't even make her fight any more. She just marches in the parades and pats the children at the rail. And has little ones who become champions.'

Arram's stomach cramped. It was wonderful to know that the glorious creature didn't risk her life in the battles now, but how could she stand giving her children up to the arena? He had worked often with Lindhall's elephants, many of them too old or injured to fight, and the master had taught Arram everything he knew of the great creatures. They were more intelligent than most animals, and they had their own culture.

Musenda looked at Arram. 'Are you all right, lad?'

Arram shook his head. 'I never understand why people are so happy to see humans and animals chopped up in the arena. Isn't life brutal enough? The waste is indecent. So is the – the joy the audience takes in the killing of innocent people.' Thinking about the conversations he'd heard at school about the various gladiators, he added, 'Mostly innocent people, *and* innocent animals. It should be stopped.'

'Plenty of us would like that. Or we'd like it if contests were declared over before someone was killed,' Musenda said. 'Time was, a fight to the death was rare. Not any more. Our master emperor likes the sight of blood. So does his heir. That's to be expected, I suppose, being a general and all.' He shrugged. 'And who cares? We're only slaves, when all's said and done.'

'Valuable ones,' Ramasu said.

'Valuable? Not enough to let us live on a day nobles bet their gold on your *opponent* making a kill. Or when the crowd is crazed with blood lust and the ruler of the games knows he'd best sacrifice some gladiators or there'll be a riot, like there was in 402.' Musenda smiled crookedly. 'At least we got a new stadium out of that one.'

A gladiator poked his head in the door. 'Sarge? Shrike and Wild Dog are brawlin' again!'

Musenda sighed. 'If anyone dies in these games, I pick those two. Good to talk with you both. I'll come for the toys later, and my thanks.' He left at a fast trot.

As the days passed, Musenda – Sarge – became a regular visitor, whether he came with injured fighters or on his own. Arram often found Ramasu and the gladiator in conversation, walking around the exercise yard during quiet periods. Those came more frequently in the second week, when the newest gladiators had learned something and those from lesser arenas had been taught respect for their place in this one. As they learned, so did Arram. He also listened.

Most told him how they became gladiators. One woman, Quomat, broke Arram's heart. She'd been married at ten, a practice among many of the empire's tribes. After several miscarriages before she was fourteen, her village healer declared her barren. Her husband sold her to pay the bride price for his new wife.

'A merchant bought me. I was fine at his house at first,' she told Arram as he worked on a deep cut in her left thigh. Across her golden-brown stomach, left bare by the brief shirt that was part of her practice gear, was the tattoo 'Not for You'. 'They hardly beat anyone, and I could do any chore they gave me,' she said. 'The meals was good. Then I started to grow, up top and my bum. The men – not just slaves! – they fought over me. Mistress decided I was too much trouble and sold me. The master of fighters at the local arena saw me on the block, and here I am.'

Arram finished and gave his usual care instructions. 'Would you leave if you could, Quomat?' he asked, curious. She had a scar from her right temple across the bridge of her nose, and she had lost a breast to the gods of battle.

She slid off the table and stood, wincing as she put weight on the healed leg. 'Sonny, maybe you're trying to trick me or maybe you're just green, but what you asked can get a girl killed. I'm a slave. I don't have choices, only owners.' She patted his cheek with a brown hand knotted from years of wielding sword and spear. 'I'll give you credit and say you're green. There are worse ways to live than this. Like being pounded by an old man when you're only ten.'

She was barely out the door when two more patients came in. Arram turned away to scrub a tear from his eye before he settled them.

Not all tales were sad. Three men sold themselves to the arena 'for the glory', they said. Arram didn't understand. A six-year veteran of the games was a soldier who had killed a fellow soldier: he'd been given a choice of death or the arena. One female gladiator, Gueda, came from a tribe where women and men alike were fighters. She had been caught by enemies and sold to the arena, where she liked the life.

'I'm one of four women as'll take on a man,' she told Arram as he cleaned and mended claw marks in her side. She cackled gleefully, causing him to make a puzzled noise. She explained, 'A' course, I do me own fightin' with a trained tiger at me side, against three to five gladiators!'

'It seems to me working with a tiger is as dangerous as fighting against a man,' Arram murmured, touching the skin next to her longest wound. His Gift spilled into it.

'Tacuma was just testy this mornin',' Gueda explained, twisting to watch Arram work. 'I've told them and told them don't give 'im mutton, it makes 'im mean, but do they listen? *I'm* only the handler. Mayhap next time I'll feed a sheep t' Tacuma, aye. I'll turn 'im loose in the shed when they fix the cats' meals, see if the butchers like Tacuma when 'is belly aches, me poor big boy.'

'That seems ill-advised,' Arram said absently, using the spell to bind each layer of skin and muscle evenly. Her 'poor big boy' had cut all the way down to her ribs.

'I suppose you're right. Bad t' give 'em a taste for human. They're ruined if that happens.' She fell silent, only to stiffen a few moments later. 'What's that noise?'

During her silence Arram sealed her wounds. Now he placed a cream on the welts to fight infection. 'What noise?' he asked. A distant roar reached his ears.

'Lady of the Cats, that's Tacuma! Are you near done?' She rose to her knees. 'If they handle 'im when I'm not there, they'll get more than a scratch!'

'Give me a moment and *listen* to me,' Arram said, trying not to be impatient. Realizing that she was not listening, he wrote instructions on a sheet from his workbook and ordered her to wait. He rushed into the stillroom to put up a jar of infection-fighting ointment, since she was plainly the last person who would go easy on her wounds. When he returned he saw that she had taken a light tunic kept for those who wore shirts, and had it half over her head. The moment she was dressed she swiped the ointment from Arram's hand, glanced at the instructions, and kissed his cheek.

'Nice work, youngster,' Gueda said with a grin. 'If you ever visit with your girl, tell the guards I said you could come see me and Tacuma, no charge.'

The afternoon was filled with lighter injuries than Gueda's. Other visitors assured Arram that Tacuma quietened down once his human had come into view, before he could do serious damage to those who had fed him mutton. Gueda herself brought her cat around to meet Arram and Ramasu after the noon meal, before the animal settled for his afternoon nap. Both healers acknowledged the cat's splendour, Ramasu at a somewhat greater distance than Arram.

'But I thought you liked cats,' Arram teased his master gently after Gueda and her companion had left.

Ramasu lifted his eyebrow. 'If you like him, you may play with him. I will keep the kind of distance that shows so large a creature proper respect. Perhaps even a little more distance, so there are no misunderstandings.'

Arram grinned and turned to greet their next patient, a cook with a burned hand.

As things quietened near the supper hour, Ramasu left him in charge and went to take a nap. Preet chose the same time to fly outside.

Arram cleaned the infirmary, then sat out front, chin in hand. Gueda's mention of 'his girl' that morning had stayed with him. He missed Varice more than he had thought he would: her laugh, her teasing, her perfumes, her touch on his shoulder when she wanted to say something personal. He missed her, and Ozorne, and his masters. He missed the university gardens and the quiet libraries, the breezes that blew cool over the fountains, and the comfort of his room. He knew he would see his friends soon, but in the time between, the day of the games loomed like a thousand years.

He was occupying himself by rolling fresh bandages when a shadow fell over his work. He looked up. A burly gladiator stood in the open doorway. 'Where's the master?' he demanded.

'Out until after supper, but what is the problem? I am able to handle most injuries,' Arram replied.

The gladiator snorted. 'You? You're naught but a pup.'

Arram straightened. 'I was healer enough to look after Gueda's wounds,' he retorted.

The man snorted a second time and walked farther into the infirmary, drifting around as he surveyed the contents of the countertops. His eyes flicked too often towards the stillroom. 'What kind of injury do you have?' Arram asked. 'Or is a friend the injured one?' The stranger made him uneasy.

'What's in there?' the man asked, pointing his thumb at the stillroom.

'Nothing of interest to you,' Arram said, frowning. Was this fellow trying to find the more serious medicines? 'And the room is locked.'

'But you have a key.' The gladiator looked him over, sizing him up.

'I do not.' It was a lie; Arram knew the spells that would open the room. Now he really disliked this man. 'Unless you are hurt or seriously ill, I must ask you to leave.' He moved until he stood directly in front of the stillroom door. He fumbled for a protection spell that would be just enough to send this man on his way. He was terrified that he would use the wrong thing.

'I have a headache.' The man took a few steps towards Arram, a smile on his mouth. Arram recognized the expression in his eyes: it was contempt, something he knew all too well from school. 'Give me something for it,' the gladiator ordered.

'Your training chiefs have headache medications,' Arram replied. Ramasu had explained that on the first day.

'But I want healing from *you*, boy.' The man shook his arms out in front of him, as boxers and masters of unarmed combat did. He clenched his fists, making the joints crackle. His muscles bulged.

Arram called a ball of glittering black fire to his hand. 'Go to your training master, please,' he said calmly, glaring. 'Before I help you outside.'

'Kottrun, what are you doing here?' Musenda walked in. 'The practice chief is looking for you.'

'I have a headache,' the other gladiator snapped as Arram slowly absorbed his Gift. Kottrun added, 'And this piece of arena bait—'

Musenda cut him off. 'You'll have it worse when the practice chief gets his hands on you. Besides, you know the chiefs carry what's needful for the usual things.'

Kottrun glared at Arram. 'You'll regret this,' he said, his voice so quiet only Arram would hear. He walked out, passing too close to Musenda for politeness. Arram watched him go.

'What was he really after, youngster?' Musenda asked. 'You're standing by the room with the serious medicines.'

'We had only reached the headache area of our conversation,' Arram explained. He silently cursed the bone-deep school tradition of never reporting bad behaviour to instructors. Besides, the way days in the camp went, he might never have to deal with Kottrun again.

Musenda casually slapped the doorpost. 'Well, if he bothers you, let Ramasu or me know. Why don't you lock up and go to get something to eat?'

'I'll do that, as soon as I've finished my chores,' Arram assured the older man. 'Thank you. Oh, and wait!' He ran into the stillroom and retrieved the sack with the toys he had got for Musenda's family. 'They aren't much, but I thought the children would like them,' he explained as he gave the sack to the gladiator.

Musenda looked at the little doll, the lion, and the gorilla, all with moving wooden limbs. 'You're a good-hearted fellow,' he said gruffly. 'If I can ever do anything for you . . .'

Arram started to shake his head, then thought again. He grinned. 'As a matter of fact, a close friend of mine thinks you are the best gladiator who ever lived,' he said. 'She would love a favour of yours.'

Once Musenda was gone, Arram shut the door and locked it. Relieved, he sat on a bench and wiped his sweaty forehead on his sleeve. This thing with Kottrun was more like what he'd expected when he first arrived and hadn't seen until today.

That was wrong of me, he thought shakily. Treating him like trouble. What if he was truly ill? I will have failed him.

He didn't act ill, his common sense told him. He acted like a bully, or a thief. Arram answered him as he would have answered a bully. If I don't take it from the likes of Tristan or Diop, why would I take it from him?

Arram considered telling Ramasu but changed his mind. It wasn't necessary; Musenda had handled Kottrun. And Arram didn't want to confess that he'd been about to strike a non-mage with his Gift.

Still a little shaky, Arram left the infirmary, then checked and double-checked the locking spells on the windows and doors, in case Kottrun returned to break in. Only then did he go to supper. Soon enough he would be gone, never to return if he had his say. Let another bully clash with Kottrun, someone who was allowed to teach him a lesson.

'Don't waste time easing mild injuries,' Ramasu told Arram the afternoon before the games. The fighters had the day to themselves, so they had no patients. Instead they readied the supplies they would use the next day. 'You'll need your strength for the big ones. Treat them enough to keep them alive for a day, until we can tend their injuries properly. We will have many fighters with wounds that will kill them if we don't keep them alive. Pass the ones whose hurts you are unsure of to Daleric.'

The gladiators' usual healer had returned to his cottage on the Arena Road that afternoon. He had brought three more healers with him, two men and a woman, who would help on the day of the games and the days after.

Arram stopped packing a box full of jars of ointments and cloths. 'Unsure?'

'Unsure whether their injuries truly require healing or whether they are simply trying to get out of the next battle.' Ramasu put an armload of jars into another box and set them in order. 'Some new people will pretend they are worse off than they are, particularly since you are new. Don't let them do it. If they're caught by the commander of the arena, they'll be hanged off the side of the arena at tomorrow's sunrise.'

'Death by hanging has to be more merciful than the games,' Arram commented as he hammered a lid onto his box.

'They aren't hanged by the neck. They're hanged by the wrists and left to rot. The arena is kinder.' Ramasu rested a hand on Arram's shoulder. 'I'll have a nausea potion for you in the morning. And a sleeping potion tonight, for both of us. Understand, if you served on a battlefield, it would be far worse. There are so many more killed or wounded. This is the closest to a battlefield I can bring you at present.'

Arram began to place bandages in a fresh box. 'Why? Why is it needful?'

'Why was the typhoid hospital needful, or any other plague or surgery I've brought you to? A mage with healing skills must be ready for such things. This is how we repay the gods for our Gifts.'

Arram nodded, though the thought of working on a battlefield, particularly after the busier days here, made him dizzy. He was dreading the new day so much he had refused his noon meal.

'I knew nothing of desperate sickrooms with more than one person to tend when I was your age,' Ramasu said as they worked. 'I was to be a priest of Mithros and rise high in my duke's service. My marriage to a daughter of His Grace's house had been arranged since we were children. I was fifteen when my Gift blossomed. Within a year I had been disowned and driven from my city, my father's parting purse in my hand and my mother's curse in my ears. I had managed to destroy half of the god's temple.'

Arram stared at his master in awe. 'Mithros's temple?'

Ramasu began to chuckle. He poured a cup of tea for each of them. 'Great Mithros appeared in all his glory over the ruins, picked up his altar piece – which was untouched – and carried it to his preferred location for a new temple. So the god saved my life, but little else. To preserve their name and fortune, my family exiled me. I had only wanted to show the duke what I could do.'

He gave a cup to Arram, who cooled it with a sign he had devised to take the worst heat from food and hot drinks. 'Surely you had a teacher,' he said quietly.

'My teacher at home taught clever spells and charms to young nobles,' Ramasu replied. 'He was no more ready for me than I was for my Gift. I spent a few years wandering the empire, always working my way towards the university, but stopping to study with anyone who would teach me.' He smiled and looked at the palm of one hand. 'I chopped a great deal of wood and vegetables after my coin ran out. For the most part I learned from goodywives and hedgewitches. Proper mages had no interest in a scruffy fellow like me. Horse doctors, they would teach me, but not proper healers. Do me proud, when you go out in the world, Arram.'

'I will, Master Ramasu,' Arram said. His heart burned at the thought of his gentle, if aloof, master being treated like a beggar on the road.

They finished their tea and returned to packing.

When they were done, Ramasu stayed in the infirmary, making entries in his supply records. Arram ambled out into the practice grounds and, with the help of a couple of coins, persuaded the ever-watchful guards to let him go into the menagerie, where the fighting animals were kept. The head keeper warned him to stay away from the cages if he didn't want to lose a hand, then motioned for him to go ahead after Arram handed over more coins. Nearly everyone knew him by now, and assumed that however young he might be, a mage who could sew up a man's bum could be trusted not to tease a fighter elephant.

The people who worked with the animals either napped close by or had retreated to their rooms out of the sun. Arram was left to himself to admire – and feel sorry for – the great cats, including the famous Tacuma, rare wolves and hyenas, ostriches, elephants, giraffes, and zebras. The thought of them being ripped apart by gladiators and other animals broke his heart. He prayed for them to the Goddess as Maiden and to the Black God, asking that these torn and scarred veterans of the games be given rest in the Peaceful Realms.

He was taking a shortcut to an outer gate when he heard a familiar voice. 'You'll keep your word, then, and this will be but a taste.' The words were followed by the soft clink of coins.

'I know what I'm doin', Master.' Arram dimly knew that voice, too. He crept to the edge of the building that concealed him and peered around it, promising himself that he would start carrying a scrying mirror. The shorter man's back was to him, but Arram was very familiar with the heavily embroidered bronze wrap and the sandals heavy with topaz stones. He had seen Chioké wear both time and time again. The other man was the gladiator Kottrun, who had made him feel so uncomfortable. Now he grinned at Chioké. 'You'll get the victory you want.'

Arram stepped back, soundless. If they were setting up a crooked fight, he wanted nothing to do with it. Wasn't it bad enough when the fights were straightforward? He wondered what Ozorne would say if he knew his master was involved in cheating at the games.

Chioké was at supper that night, joking with the camp's captain and the healers. He even got Ramasu to smile slightly, claiming he had done his bit by bringing more supplies. 'I would do more . . .' he offered with a wicked grin.

'Gods save us, no!' exclaimed Daleric. 'The last time you tried to help with the wounded, we had to treat you for a broken arm!'

'I didn't know that fellow spoke Common,' Chioké protested.

'People really like him,' Arram told Ramasu as they headed to their rooms. 'Master Chioké.'

'He makes himself likeable,' Ramasu replied, yawning. Then he said quietly, 'Until he isn't. Remember that. And he doesn't like to share anything.'

Arram nodded. It was good to hear his own suspicions confirmed.

They woke and dressed at dawn, while their guardian brought around their cart. Six men escorted them through the gate into the gladiators' compound, while Preet grumbled drowsily to herself. He had tried to get her to stay behind, but no matter where he put her she had turned up on his shoulder or, more annoyingly, clinging to his hair, until he surrendered. He kept her in his lap as he looked around him at the gladiators' home. He had never been allowed beyond the infirmary. Now he was disappointed. All he could see looked the same as the guards' camp. There was plenty of open ground for practice, barracks for the gladiators, practice dummies and targets, and empty barrels.

'For the practice weapons,' Ramasu murmured. He had noticed the direction of Arram's gaze. 'The guards take them in at night. The gladiators can do a great deal of damage even with blunt wood.'

Arram nodded. He had spent days patching up samples of that damage.

He was denied even a glimpse of the stables or the cages where the wild beasts were held, because a fog had rolled in overnight. It masked all but the closest barracks and hung like a curtain of shadows over the looming arena. Two soldiers rode ahead to unlock the chains that held the gate closed. Then Ramasu raised a hand and murmured a few words. Slowly one half of the gate swung outwards. Ramasu drove the cart into the tunnel through the arena.

Although the broad road was packed dirt, their cart still sent up echoes. So did the slam of the gate as the soldiers closed it behind them. They were alone in the torchlit vastness of the sleeping arena, under the many rows of seats.

'The guards will return with Daleric and his people,' Ramasu said quietly. 'I like to be set up and have time to read and meditate before the noise gets bad. Which reminds me.' As the cart cast echoes from the tunnel's roof and sides, he reached into the pocket of the cheap, light robe he was wearing, a duplicate of the one he had given to Arram for the day. From it he drew a small packet. 'You'll want these. Don't worry about leaving them in. You'll be able to hear those close to you perfectly well. They'll be shouting as it is.'

Arram opened the packet to discover three pairs of wax earplugs. He smiled. 'Thank you. These will help, and I'd forgotten. Varice had some for me the last time I had to go to the games.'

'She's a clever lady,' Ramasu said. 'Devoted to you and Ozorne, I understand.'

'Well, to Ozorne,' Arram said, looking at Preet. He touched the warmth that was Varice's charm. It was the only thing he carried in his belt pouch today.

'No, I am fairly certain she is devoted to both of you, in different ways,' Ramasu commented. 'Of course, it would be a waste if any of the three of you were to marry at so early a stage in your careers.'

The word was like a hot poker in Arram's ear. 'Marry!' he yelped, his voice echoing through the tunnel. 'No, sir, no, none of us are thinking – Well, Ozorne's mother has brought it up, for *him*, but he doesn't want to yet, nor do Varice and I! We haven't even got certificates, and we all want to be masters of one sort or another!'

Ramasu glanced sideways at him. 'In the world outside the university, many people *are* married by now, remember, and starting families. There's no shame in it.'

Arram shook his head. 'But there's so much more to learn! I know I'm supposed to be advanced, but I look at what my masters can do and what is in the books, and I realize I've hardly begun to learn my craft!'

'I see. Forgive me – you're at an age when many students discover that love, or their families' marital alliances, are stronger than their studies.' Ramasu drew the wagon up. They had reached the gates on the other side of the tunnel. To their right were cells, large ones, barred with iron. To their left was a single great opening, closed by heavy wooden doors and locked.

Ramasu dismounted and touched a finger to the left-hand lock. It fell open. He pressed one hand to each half of the door. Both sides swung inwards, revealing a shadowed interior. Returning to the cart and picking up a box, he asked Arram, 'Would you do the lamps inside? Only those overhead, not the wall or ground ones.'

Arram gulped, then reached into the room with his power. To his great relief, the overhead lamps were huge metal braziers held in baskets of chains. Their contents were not charcoal but wax studded with a multitude of wicks. He didn't have to manage a tiny light, but a small wave of flame that swept along the braziers until all were lit.

'Very good,' Ramasu said with approval. 'A finely tuned use of your Gift. Now let's unpack.'

In stowing boxes on shelves along the far wall, Arram learned the room. There were twenty stone tables there, all with gutters in each side like a butcher's table. Arram gulped; these would carry away blood. There were new tall leather buckets at one end of each table, he assumed for trash.

'*Twenty?*' he asked, his voice cracking.

'Usually needed only when the emperor wants a great battle, or a blood feud has sprung up among the gladiators,' Ramasu said. 'Once we're done stocking the wall shelves, we will put surgical supplies and burn treatments on the shelves underneath the first ten tables from the door.'

Arram nodded. The healer would be able to reach what was needed easily, at least at first.

'Daleric is responsible for hiring and training runners,' Ramasu explained. 'They will restock when they see you are low on supplies. If you need something, hold up your hand and a runner will come for your orders. They will also fetch us water, or tea, or even something to eat during rests.'

Arram couldn't envision any time this day when he would want to eat.

'The bucket for discarded cloths, pieces of weapons, and so on is also useful for vomiting,' Ramasu said gently. 'I know this will be hard, Arram. Do not be heroic. I have often done this on my own with Daleric's people. Sometimes I work here with two mastery students. I—'

'*Two* mastery students!' Arram cried, as close to hysterics as he had ever been in his life. 'Then why not at least bring another instead of using only me?'

Ramasu raised his eyebrows until Arram caught his breath. Then he said, his voice kind and firm, 'Because I knew you would be enough.'

Later, as they listened to the clatter that heralded the approach of Daleric and his companions in the tunnel, Ramasu cast a shielding spell around them and murmured in Arram's ear, 'Mind what you say. There are listening spells here as well as the camp. And, son, if you have mercy for these people, once they've taken a sufficiently bad injury, don't heal them completely. They will have to go back into the arena today if you do. Unless, of course, they demand to return. The others can finish their healing tomorrow or the next day.'

'*Return* to the games?' Arram whispered, horrified.

'Some do. Hekaja only asks that we heal them, not that we tell them what to do with their bodies,' the master replied. He touched his fingers to his lips and to his forehead in salute to the goddess of healing; Arram did the same. He had noticed the goddess's image over the door to the tunnel. Someone had given her a fresh dressing of vivid paints, clearly an act of worship. Without thinking, his magic quick to his hand after days of constant use, Arram called up two small balls of light and sent them gliding to the figure. He silently asked the goddess to accept his gift. The balls hung in the air for a moment. Then each moved to one of the figure's outstretched hands and remained, as if she herself worked healing magic in the room.

'*Very* well done,' Ramasu said, resting a hand on Arram's shoulder with approval. 'I did my worship this morning. I have to say, I would not have thought of this, but I will from now on. It will give heart to all who see it. Now, let's try to get something to stay in your belly, if only for a little while.'

CHAPTER 22

Arram would remember that day as a giant stinking roar in hot darkness, one where hands clutched his arms and hands and, once, his throat. Despite the wax plugs, his ears filled with the screams of the wounded and the dying. They were carried into the room on stretchers by soldiers or gladiators, sometimes by the very gladiators who had been trying to kill them a moment before. They were slung onto a freshly cleaned table, where the next free healer looked at them and judged whether to take this one himself or herself or to refer the case to Daleric or Ramasu.

He vomited into the bucket more than once.

The wounded called on their gods, mothers, lovers. They cursed the emperor and no one hushed them, not there. They begged for death and screamed for life. He learned the truth of what he'd been told, that newcomers were hurt first.

And not only the newcomers. Quomat, who had been married at ten and fought for years, died just as she reached his table. Arram growled and reached deep into his Gift, thinking to go after her spirit and bring it back. He couldn't lose her to the Black God without so much as a fight!

Then Preet was on his head, pecking, having dropped from her perch on the candleholders above. Arram shook his head to dislodge her and put his hands on the woman's chest. Suddenly copper fire slid under his palms, coating her entire body to shield her from him. Arram glared up into Ramasu's face. Three of his patients had died so far. He would *not* surrender another!

'She has passed into the Peaceful Realms,' Ramasu told him, his eyes steady. 'Will you deny her that? Look at her scars. Look inside, at her muscles. How many are nicked and shortened by swords? This isn't life, Arram. Let her go.'

So he looked, and wept at the ragged mess that battles had made of a good, strong body. 'Black God bear you up and give you peace, Quomat,' he whispered.

'Gut wound here!' someone shouted. Ramasu left. Arram turned Quomat's remains over to the handlers and went to the next clear table. Someone told him there was time enough to catch their wind. The next event was a chariot race of twenty laps – twelve for the Goddess in her three aspects, four for Mithros, and four for the Graveyard Hag. Once the tables were cleared, they could eat if they wished.

Their wish was not granted. Three chariots crashed on the fifth lap, causing crashes in later laps as the drivers struggled to avoid the mess. One driver died on the spot, a helper told Arram. Two more came to the hall, one for Ramasu and one for Arram. His had a smashed collarbone and left arm, as well as a broken leg and hip.

'I'll take the leg and the arm, if you'll take the collarbone and hip.' Daleric had come to stand at the other end of the table. 'I don't have the power you do, to heal complicated bones that are smashed, but I can do these easy.'

Arram looked at the older mage with gratitude. 'Thank you, sir. That would be good.'

Daleric nodded. 'I'll do leg first, then arm? We'll switch places then.'

It was strange, feeling another's Gift run along veins and bones next to his, but it gave him confidence to pull the pieces of collarbone back into their original positions. He plunged into the painstaking work, shifting swollen muscle and veins into place, until he realized Daleric was pounding on *his* shoulder.

'What you have is good enough!' the man shouted over the racket. 'Splint it and finish the work tomorrow or the day after! Get the hip the same way – we have the rest of the race, the beast fights, and the prize matches yet. Save your strength!'

About to protest, Arram closed his mouth. Daleric was far more experienced at this. He nodded and moved down to his patient's broken hip, while Daleric summoned one of his people with a splint.

There were more casualties of the chariot race. Apparently that was the point of such things. The faces of the wounded blurred. Ramasu made him stop to rest when there was a lull, and Preet came to sing to him. Other healers and their assistants who were free gathered around to listen. It was a moment of quiet that ended too soon. The beast matches had begun, leading with the executions of criminals before the fighting. A few warriors came in, all cared for by other healers than Arram and Ramasu. They were restoring the supplies under the tables when another fighter was brought in.

'I want Arram!' she shouted in a fury. 'Arram, you rhino bums, you globs of elephant dung!'

'Here,' Arram called. He went to his position and waited, hands shaking. Should he have asked Ramasu to help him with someone obviously arena-crazed, as they called it?

Four workers carried over a woman on a stretcher and eased her onto Arram's table. She was covered in blood, with a large stab wound in her side, a smaller one across one forearm, and a large one in her thigh.

Arram had discovered there were no niceties here. A helper carefully poured a bucket of water over the gladiator, to wash away blood and sweat. It also washed sand into the wounds, but that was a problem for the healer to handle. Arram had changed a rock-moving spell he knew to cover tiny rocks: that cleared wounds out nicely. Only then did he look at the panting gladiator.

'*Gueda?*' he whispered, horrified. He had not wanted to see another familiar face on his table.

She seized his wrist with her good hand. Tears streamed from her eyes. 'They killed my beautiful Tacuma,' she croaked. 'My cat, my only friend, they killed him.' She turned towards Arram and sobbed.

For a moment he held her as if she were Varice. Then he whispered, 'I'm going to help you sleep, so I can do my work better. Is that all right?' She nodded. He said, 'I am so sorry. I know you were devoted to each other.' He eased her into slumber, to help her escape heartbreak as much as to ease her body's pain.

'Very kind.' Musenda, glorious in bronzed chest and leg armour, wearing a short sword and carrying a helmet, had come to the side of the table. 'I saw the match. They thought she'd be useless without Tacuma. Others have tried it, but these succeeded in killing the cat, at least. I know she talked to the keepers about Tacuma maybe not seeing so well in his left eye, and that's where they got him.'

'What happened to them?' Arram asked. He gently put Gueda flat on the table and let his Gift flow over her to see if he had noted all of her wounds.

Musenda smiled thinly. 'They're dead. She went berserk when they killed her cat.' He bent and kissed Gueda on the forehead. 'Heal, sword sister,' he whispered.

'Sarge?' someone bellowed.

'Time,' Musenda – Sarge – sighed as he straightened. 'We'll see if the emperor, or Prince Mikrom, feels merciful.'

Arram looked up. 'Prince Mikrom?'

'Oh, we're graced with the presence today,' Musenda replied. 'His Imperial Highness is here for a rest, if you can believe that. His Majesty wants to show him off.'

Arram knew better than to wish the big man luck. Gladiators

thought that wishing someone good luck before a fight was like
a curse. Instead he said, 'You look very threatening.'

It was good to hear Sarge laugh as he walked off.

There were fewer fights now as the popular individual warriors
engaged in battles on the sands. It gave Arram unwanted time
to think after he finished with Gueda.

Ozorne is there, I'll wager, and Varice, he thought. If Mikrom
is present in a ceremonial way, they'll be in attendance along
with the princess. And in the normal manner of things I'd be
up there with them.

He looked around. Helpers washed down the stone tables.
Ramasu talked with Daleric as they ate. All the wounded who
were bandaged and waiting for more healing the next day had
been carried into a room next to this one. They wouldn't hear
the screams of those freshly cut or dying.

'They think of everything here,' Arram said bitterly.

A nearby healer didn't appear to notice his sour tone. 'They've
had centuries to smooth away the wrinkles,' she replied. They
both heard the approach of someone screeching in agony.

'My turn,' the woman said. She touched Arram on the
shoulder. 'Get Ramasu to bring you back soon. Everyone appre-
ciates your work.' She reached a bare table just as men carried
in a huge gladiator. He was from the icy lands far to the north,
by his colouring. Someone had dislocated one of the man's
shoulders and broken both of his legs. Immediately another
healer joined the woman to assist her with the damage.

Arram had been talking for a little while with Ramasu, Daleric,
and some of Daleric's healers when a slow, rhythmic booming
filled the tunnel and the room. Many of the others ran to the
door to see what was going on.

Ramasu did not wait. 'Quickly,' he told Arram. 'Stuff your
table with supplies; be certain your waste bucket is empty and
your water bucket is full. If you need to relieve yourself, do so.'
He pointed to the privy door at the far end of the room.

'Why the rush?' Arram enquired.

'A grand combat is about to begin. They must have added it for the prince. Hag curse them, they could have warned us,' Ramasu said with unusual heat. 'Perhaps the prince brought captives he wanted to throw onto the sands. In any case, it's a crowd of fighters divided into two and ordered to fight. Butchery, sheer butchery. Get going.'

Later, after things had calmed down, Arram learned that Ramasu was right. Mikrom had brought the losers of his last battle home and sent them into the ring against those gladiators who were not used up. Sometimes Arram's nightmares were of this part of the day alone, a never-ending stream of screaming men and women, rushed to the tables as quickly as people could be found to carry them. Such pickups were dangerous work, as many who dashed between fighters in the arena discovered. Daleric set up a surgical table for them alone, to show his appreciation for their courage, or foolishness.

Soldiers strolled through the chamber as if they were on patrol. They made work harder. Arram heard later that they were regular army, not arena guards. Mikrom had sent them to ensure that no injured captive escaped a future in the arena by capturing a healer and threatening his way to freedom. It was plain to all that the heir did not understand how the gladiators were kept.

A soldier got in Arram's way for the third time. His concentration on his gladiator shattered. Arram turned on the intruder, his raised hand filled with sparkling black fire.

'Trip me up once more, and they'll send a *rock* for your family to bury!' he shouted. 'Or I'll trade your spirit for his and let *you* die!'

The soldier put his hand on the hilt of his sword but did not draw it. He could see the other helpers around the table were stepping back.

'Soldier, this man is going nowhere.' Ramasu stepped between Arram and the veteran. 'Arram has him under control.'

'He's half mad is what he is,' the soldier snapped.

Ramasu drew himself up to his full height. 'My word as a Master of the School for Mages. Your captive will not escape Arram. You are better employed elsewhere.' Ramasu wore dignity and power like a cloak, despite the blood on his robe and face.

Magic billowed away from him. It was the touch of something that made the soldier feel unwanted.

'Take it on yourself, then,' the soldier snapped as Arram turned back to his patient. 'If that rat on the table escapes and kills decent people, it'll be you to blame.'

'If Arram turns you to ash, it will be yourself to blame. Did no one teach you the folly of impeding a working mage?' Ramasu's voice was ice. 'Go, before I place a complaint before your captain.'

The man moved off, though he kept his hand on his sword's hilt.

'Thank you,' Arram murmured.

Despite the noise, Ramasu heard. 'You're lucky I was within earshot. Mikrom's men have been in combat for a very long time. It's not wise to tug their tails.' The man leaned closer. 'And you might find you don't have as much Gift for combat as you thought. It doesn't stretch like healing does, so watch yourself.'

Arram nodded and continued to do his best, praying softly to Hekaja to save the man before him. At last the moment came when he had done all he could do without draining himself completely.

'Graveyard Hag, roll the dice in his favour,' he prayed softly. 'Black God of Death, please turn him from your door.' Gingerly he touched his fingers to the man's throat. There was the tiniest trace of a pulse. 'He's alive. Leave him here for a while; see how he does,' he told one of the helpers. 'I'll move elsewhere.'

He bent to gather his bag of medical supplies. It was then his body decided that he should keep on bending, until his forehead struck the stone tiles. After that things went dark for a while. He roused briefly while someone carried him on a stretcher –

more than one someone, he corrected himself; it would take at least two people to carry him on a stretcher. Then he got the horrible idea that they thought he was dead.

'No, no!' he shouted, though the noise that came from his throat was more like a croak. 'I'm alive! I'm fine!' He tried to wave, but his arm proved too hard to lift.

'Is he tryin' to talk?' asked a voice down by his feet.

'Don't matter,' a hoarse voice near his head replied. 'The master gave us our orders.' A face – female, upside down – appeared in Arram's vision. 'Just you be quiet. Your master says you're done for now. You go back to sleep.'

'But I'm needed—'

'Boy, I've been arguing with gladiators and mages all day,' the woman told him. 'Hush. Sleep.'

He slept.

For the next two days, he and Ramasu, together with Daleric and his group of healers, rose at dawn to see to their wounded. For the most part they handled those whose hurts had not been deadly serious on the first day, and those who had been healed enough to keep them alive overnight. Preet sang to entertain the sick. Arram juggled after supper, when everyone was too weary to work magic or to endure having it worked upon them. Daleric produced a set of pipes, one of his friends a drum, and another a round form of harp.

On the third day, most gladiators and captive soldiers were healed and had been sent to the gladiators' housing. Those who were still abed could be handled by Daleric. It was time to go home. While the senior healers attended the captain's lunch in thanks for their work, Arram remained in the small cell he and Ramasu had shared under the arena, packing up the last of the medicines for Daleric's patients. He'd finished and was looking for Preet – she had flown off somewhere – when he thought he'd heard something.

'Psst!'

He *had* heard something. 'Who's there?' He raised his lamp and looked around the corridor.

Something tapped his shoulder.

He whirled and saw nothing. He was struggling to remember a spell of detection when he looked down. On the packed floor, clear in the lamplight and the torchlight from above, was someone's shadow.

His tormentor began to laugh. 'I forgot about the shadow – Master Chioké would mark me down for that!' The air in front of Arram rippled, and Ozorne appeared.

Arram gaped, then cried, 'What – ? Ozorne, how did you get here? Where are your guards? Where's Okot?' Preet dropped from the shadows, trilling happily, and lit on Ozorne's shoulder.

Ozorne smoothed her back. 'I love you, too, sweetheart.' Then he scowled at Arram. 'And *there's* a friendly greeting from you.'

Arram smiled and hugged his friend with a care for Preet. Ozorne hugged him fiercely in return. 'No, no, Ozorne, I missed you, of course I did. It's been miserable, but you shouldn't be here! It's too dangerous!'

'Dangerous monkeywash!' his friend replied scornfully. 'Even you didn't know I was here until you saw my shadow. I'll fix that next time, believe me! Okot doesn't know because my mother summoned him to report on my status *in person*. I think she wants to find out if Varice and I have gone to bed yet.'

'Ozorne!' Arram snapped as heat rushed into his cheeks. Preet gave a chuckling sound.

Ozorne clapped him on the shoulder. 'Oh, she isn't interested in me, nor I in her, not like that. Anyway, I gave the guards the slip, sneaked a horse, and came to see if I could find you. I didn't see you at the games.'

'I was back here,' Arram replied. 'Working.'

Ozorne studied him with sharp eyes. 'That bad, was it?'

Arram looked down the corridor towards the big room where so many had died.

Ozorne hugged him around the shoulders. 'All right, friend.'

His voice was gentler than before. 'You're going home. I'll make sure you don't get this kind of duty again.'

For a moment the thought of never hearing those screams, smelling those stinks, feeling blood and organs spill through his hands made Arram dizzy. Not to be afraid when a thick-muscled brute caught him alone in the infirmary . . . He shook it off and smiled at his friend. 'Don't do that. I'm needed here and places like it. Not enough of us can do healing spells. I have a knack for it. And some of these people are all right. Sarge – Musenda – for one. And there's this woman, Gueda—'

'Oh ho!' Ozorne said, laughing. 'A woman!'

He can always make me turn red, Arram thought unhappily as he protested, 'It's not like that. She's a gladiator, and a good one.'

'Wait, the one with the big cat that was killed?'

Arram nodded.

'She was *magnificent*,' Ozorne said with awe as Preet toyed with his braids. He wore no beads that would give him away with their noise. 'They killed her cat, and we thought she was done. Instead it was like she turned into a tiger herself – outnumbered five to one, and she killed them all. Varice made a fortune betting on her. Did she live?'

Arram smiled. 'Yes.' He didn't say he was the healer who treated her.

Ozorne looked at their gloomy surroundings. 'Would you . . . show me around? I may never get back here. You know they'll make me pay for this little excursion. I'll be lucky if Okot doesn't chain me to my seat whenever I attend games again.'

As little as he wanted to return to those blood-stinking rooms, Arram heard the touch of sadness in his friend's voice. It was true; the list of things that Ozorne was not allowed to do grew longer each year. He nodded and led his friend up through the underside of the arena. Without emphasizing it, he was careful to ensure that Ozorne saw the dark, stinking cells where the unhurt gladiators and animals were kept before and after combats, cramped lockups without fresh air, water, or privies.

'They deserve better,' Ozorne said grimly as they returned for Arram's bundles. 'They give their lives for us; they should have better places to wait.'

'They deserve to live,' Arram murmured.

'You cannot take the games from the people,' his friend said gently, helping him to collect the various packages of medicines. 'There would be rioting. There has *been* rioting, and murder, when past emperors have tried it. I have a book on the history of the games – you should read it.'

When Arram had everything he needed, Ozorne stood in the corridor and reworked his invisibility spell. 'I'll follow you,' Ozorne said when only his shadow remained. 'Where do you go when you've dropped these off?'

Arram had meant to attend the lunch, but he couldn't with his friend there. 'Back to my quarters to get my things, and then to the wagon to wait for Master Ramasu,' he said. 'We leave once he comes.'

'I'll ride on your wagon, then,' Ozorne said as they walked down the corridor. Preet flew ahead. 'I left my horse tied up outside camp. The trickiest part of this whole adventure has been waiting for someone to pass through a gate so I can go, too.' He fell silent as Arram let them out into the open. The guards waiting there nodded to him.

'I'm the last mage,' Arram told them. 'No one else is inside.' He walked on towards the temporary tent where the remaining injured gladiators were housed. He hoped that the sight of these fighters, battling the worst of wounds, their lives still in question, might convince Ozorne that changes should be made to the games. He knew the likelihood of Ozorne's becoming emperor was small, but as Mesaraz's heir he would have influence.

The yard was quiet. The wounded were resting. Two guards were dicing quietly in front of the tent: they nodded to Arram and returned to the game. They didn't notice that Arram held the flap open for a moment before he walked inside, making certain that Ozorne could walk in.

'Make the bird be quiet,' one of the gamblers said. 'She'll wake the lads.'

Preet was screeching from inside the tent. Arram stepped in and pointed at the flap he still held open. 'Preet, bad girl!' he scolded. 'Out!'

A pair of hands seized him and yanked him aside. A rough, callused hand clapped over his mouth; a muscled arm gripped him by the throat. Preet fled through the smoke hole in the canvas roof. Ozorne, shocked out of his grip on his spell, flickered into view. He was grabbed by a man who had been positioned behind the tent flap.

Arram clawed at the hand that blocked his mouth and nostrils. Suddenly remembering something Varice had told him, he stamped down hard on his captor's foot. The man behind him grunted; the hand over his mouth loosened. Arram grabbed the arm around his throat and pulled it back enough that he could catch his breath. Without air, he couldn't remember any spells. He shifted his hand and drove his thumbnail as deeply into the tender flesh next to the big wrist tendon as he could.

A dart of pain shot through his temple. A trickle of warmth rolled down his cheek – he knew it was blood.

'Next time I'll use more of my blade,' his captor said. 'And I recognize your friend. I can hurt him awful bad without killing him. You ease off or I'll tell *my* friend where to start.'

Arram looked at Ozorne. His captor had got him by the hair and yanked his head back. With his free hand he had a dagger point at Ozorne's ear. One movement and Ozorne would lose his hearing on that side, if he was lucky. Ozorne's eyes were wild with rage, but he dared not move.

Arram's captor said to Ozorne, 'I've no such qualms about this piece of dog mutton. I'll start with one of his eyes if you so much as say "ouch".'

Arram knew that voice. He'd heard it before the games, talking with Chioké. Arram glanced to his side. Kottrun, that was his name, held a short sword to his temple.

'Unless you want your face sliced away a bit at a time, put your hands behind your back,' Kottrun ordered. 'The slightest wrong move from either of you, and my friends will start killing the sick.'

Arram looked around. Three more gladiators stood inside the tent, the forbidden short swords in their hands. Each was within striking distance of one of the recovering gladiators on the cots, all five of whom had been gagged, then bound hand and foot with rope. Someone had put a sleep spell on them – they were taking no chances. Was it Daleric's attendant? There was no sign of him.

Kottrun swiftly bound Arram's hands behind him. 'Turn around, boy,' he ordered, slapping the back of Arram's head.

Arram did as he was told, eyeing the patients. 'I don't know what you're doing,' he said mildly, still trying to think of a spell that might work. 'We don't keep medicines here.' It was a lie, and a weak one. If this man had been after drugs before, he'd search for them now. And he could always use Ozorne to get some brought to him, though he'd never escape after-wards.

'Dolt, I was never after medicines,' Kottrun said, to Arram's disappointment. 'And now I can get anything I want. I don't even need you, not with the princess's only boy in my fist.' He pointed to the man who had finished binding and gagging Ozorne. 'Yemro, fetch the university mage. Tell him his student had an accident. Leave your sword.'

The man ran to do as he was bid.

'And as for you,' Kottrun told Arram, jabbing him in the chest with his sword, 'one word, one bit of pretty light, and I start trimming bits off each of you, understand?'

'You won't get Ramasu's cooperation if I'm dead,' Arram said.

Arram didn't see Kottrun strike. He only felt the blow against the side of his head that knocked him down. His ears rang. He lay still for a moment, battling a rush of fury as well as pain. Ozorne was bellowing behind his cloth gag.

'Quiet, prince,' Kottrun told Ozorne, 'or I'll give him something like this.' Kottrun kicked Arram in the belly. 'I don't *need* him now.' He pointed his weapon at Ozorne. 'Keep trying my patience and he'll get everything I've taken in the arena!'

Arram tried to curl up, yanking the ropes around his wrists. The pain in his stomach overshadowed the raw fibre digging into his skin. His Gift surged like wildfire, fighting the control he kept on it, threatening to flare and incinerate Kottrun. If he'd believed the gladiator would be the only victim, Arram wouldn't have struggled. He just couldn't be sure he wouldn't burn the entire tent and everyone in it. Slowly he breathed in through his nose and released the breath, fighting tears of pain and rage. Could he deal with this brute without speaking? Without allowing his Gift to show to non-mage eyes?

Kottrun walked over to Ozorne. The prince was trembling with fury, though no sounds came from behind the gag on his mouth.

'You'd be a splendid shield, but . . . no,' Kottrun murmured. 'Too gaudy. Too *visible*. They'd never stop hunting if I took you. But Ramasu will move the gods and the dead to save you, oh, yes.' He nodded and grinned.

He beckoned to one of the others. The man came over and helped Kottrun to haul Arram to his feet. He returned to his hostage when he was certain Arram would stay upright.

'Now we understand one another,' Kottrun said. The smile he gave Arram was tight and mean. 'Your master will get us a ship out of Carthak . . .'

Arram had stopped listening. There was a time when he worked magic without words but with gestures, standing in front of a class and a bowl of water. But he had *thought* about it, pulled on it, and had his concentration broken to flood his classroom. He was older and stronger now. If he tried to work the spells he could do silently and lost concentration, his classroom flood would be nothing in comparison.

'You are mistaken.' Ramasu walked into the tent with Preet on his shoulder and Daleric's assistant at his side. Apparently they had fetched the mage before Kottrun's messenger could reach him. 'I would never do something so criminal. The university forbids us from helping slaves in any fashion.'

'Cat turds,' snapped Kottrun. 'We have His Splendidness Prince Ozorne right here. You'll help us.'

Arram felt his ears tingling. He felt magic seep into the room – magic other than the stuff he was drawing on. He glanced at Ozorne, who nodded – he felt it, too. Mages outside were working sleep spells. He began to tremble. If Kottrun suspected, he would give the order to start killing the patients.

In fact, Kottrun was telling Ramasu his plans. 'The slightest *itch* of magic, and I will start cutting.' To Arram's horror, he pointed to Ozorne. 'I can do plenty of damage and still leave enough to be heir. I learned from experts.'

Ramasu shook his head. 'It will be as much as your lives are worth.'

'And the lives of you and your precious assistant and everyone here. *I'll* see to that, Master Mage. You don't come from here. The emperor sweeps wide when he thinks folk should have saved one of his darlings and didn't.' He looked at one of his yawning men. 'What's the matter with—' he demanded, and yawned. His eyes went wide with fury. He whirled and ran at Ozorne, his sword aimed at the prince's belly.

Arram could only see the blade aimed at his best friend. He opened his entire mind to the water summons that had changed his life. His Gift plummeted, far stronger than it had been in the Lower Academy, to plunge into the water table that lay for miles under and around university and arena. It rose, thundering up in the wake of his power, letting him guide it straight to Kottrun.

The hard ground quivered. The gladiator lurched.

The cold fountain smashed through the earth, knocking Arram, Ozorne, Ramasu, and the standing gladiators down. It drove Kottrun into the air until he struck the tent's ceiling. His sword dropped from his grip; he hit the ground with a thud. Preet immediately attacked his face with her claws, screeching. He lay there, unresisting.

Ramasu made a sign of undoing. Arram's and Ozorne's bonds fell away from their hands and mouths. Struggling to his feet, Arram dashed the water from his eyes and drew three fiery signs in the air with his Gift. The column of water halted as abruptly as it had risen and returned to the ground. Dizzy and trembling, Arram drew two more signs to knit the earth back together as Ozorne scrambled for Kottrun's sword. Rising to his knees, the prince levelled the blade at Kottrun's throat.

As the man's followers, glassy-eyed with sleep, blinked at their leader, Ramasu called out the most powerful sleep spell Arram had ever heard him use. The slowly rising spell cast by the mages outside leaped higher as Arram wrote the sigil on his palm that would keep him from falling victim to it. The attackers' eyes rolled up in their heads, and the swords fell from their hands. Their bodies followed. Ozorne, too, was caught by the spell. He collapsed onto the ground.

Soldiers rushed in and began to put manacles on the rebels. Ramasu glanced at the prince, then sighed. Reaching out, he sketched a sign of invisibility over Arram's friend. 'Make sure he doesn't get stepped on,' he told Arram quietly. 'It's better if we limit those who know he's here.' Arram nodded and shifted position to sit directly in front of his invisible friend.

Ramasu and Daleric's assistant checked the healing gladiators. The danger of the spell that had dropped their captors was that it was risky for men already in a healing sleep. When they were certain that all of their patients were unharmed, Ramasu turned to Arram to heal his still-bleeding cuts.

The captain of the camp's guard arrived as two of his men dragged the manacled Kottrun to his feet. 'Hag's dice, what happened here?' he demanded. 'Master Ramasu, Arram, are you hurt?'

'We are fine,' Ramasu said, helping Arram to stand. Arram swayed. Ramasu propped him up and told the captain, 'More important, our patients are fine.'

'But what happened?' the captain demanded.

'Arram thought the sleep was happening too slowly to put the rebels down,' Ramasu explained. 'So he opened a fountain in the ground and knocked the leader against the top of the tent.' He touched the ground with his foot. 'It's still a bit damp – we might want to put rugs down to keep the sick from getting chilled, and ask Daleric to put them in dry gowns.'

'Sorry, Master,' Arram mumbled.

'You were rushed,' Ramasu said kindly. 'Though you might trust the arts of your elders more next time.' He flicked his fingers at Kottrun, who woke. A guard dragged him to his feet. 'The captain – and I – would like to know what you were thinking,' Ramasu said mildly.

Kottrun replied with obscenities.

'They were going to force you to help them to escape, Master,' Arram said.

'Cackleheads,' the captain said with contempt. 'Everyone knows we search the healers' wagons when they go, in case someone tries to sneak out. A week of bread and water for this lot, and they get to play the Sirajit army in the next games.'

'Wait!' Kottrun yelled. 'I—'

The guard who had seized him cuffed him into silence. Arram glanced at Ramasu. For a moment he thought he'd felt a spell leave the master and attach itself to Kottrun and his men, but he hadn't seen it. He staggered in Ramasu's hold, dizzy again and barely able to stand.

Daleric rushed in and braced Arram's free side. 'Arram, what's this?' he asked with concern. 'You were fine when we left.'

'Apparently Kottrun and his pack took Arram and the wounded as hostages,' the captain explained. 'They must have run mad to think Master Ramasu could walk them out of here. Our mages put sleep on them, but before it took, the boy made a fountain that smacked Kottrun silly and then dropped him.'

'Kottrun hit me in the head, too,' Arram said cheerfully. His knees turned to water, and he sagged in the mages' grips. 'But I'm fine.'

Daleric raised his eyebrows. 'No wonder you're wrung out, then,' he told Arram. 'Three days of serious healing, a clout on the head, and whatever you just did on top of it. Don't tell *me* you're fine.'

'I am,' Arram protested.

'Mm-hmm,' Daleric said dubiously. He motioned for a soldier to take charge of Arram. 'Take him to the healers' quarters and let him lie down for a bit, will you?'

When Arram woke, it was full dark outside the window. He was on his cot, tucked snugly under a light blanket. The touch of soft feathers against his ear told him that Preet was sleeping there.

Movement in the room made him flinch. Preet grumbled and went back to sleep as Ramasu pushed a folding shade aside. He had been reading behind it, using a globe of magic for light. He set his book down and produced a bowl and spoon from a small table.

'Ozorne?' Arram asked, worried.

'Smuggled out while he was still unconscious,' Ramasu told him. 'You will have to convince him that he missed nothing spectacular.'

Arram sighed in relief. 'Good.'

'Now, I must ask, did you have any part in his surprise visit to this camp?'

Arram sat bolt upright. 'No, Master! I didn't know anything until he crept up on me in the coliseum!'

Ramasu smiled. 'Do you know, I believe you. It's that startled fawn aspect you wear when you have been taken by surprise . . . I think I shall have to speak to Chioké about giving Ozorne more challenging work, to keep him out of trouble in the future.'

'He didn't mean to get in trouble,' Arram protested.

'No, and it is the fault of his family for trying to restrict so high-spirited and clever a youth. It will be well, Arram. He is very lucky to have a friend like you.' Ramasu picked up a napkin and unfurled it. 'Are you hungry?'

Arram's stomach lurched, three-quarters with excitement and one-quarter with nausea. 'A little,' he admitted.

Ramasu passed the bowl and spoon to him, saying, 'Before you try that . . .' He shaped a glowing sign in the air. Arram's stomach settled immediately. 'Better?' Arram nodded. 'Eat, before it gets any colder.'

He said nothing as Arram wolfed the mild soup, but continued to read from his book. When Arram put the bowl aside, Ramasu asked, 'Have you any questions about this afternoon?'

Arram scratched his head. 'How did they get the weapons? I thought they were counted and locked up after the games.'

'Apparently they bribed an animal seller to bring them in last year. They buried them under their barracks until yesterday,' the master replied. 'And they arranged for an accident to happen to the seller the next time he came, with no one the wiser for why it happened.'

Arram yawned. 'I'll be glad to be home,' he admitted.

Ramasu gathered his bowl and spoon. 'As will I. It is useful work here, but it is hard on the body and the spirit. You have done very well. I am proud of you.'

Arram smiled. He was asleep as soon as he put his head down.

They loaded their things into the wagon first thing the next morning. Only Musenda and Gueda came to see them off. Arram's heart broke at the dark circles that surrounded Gueda's eyes, and the slump to her shoulders. He reached out a hand to touch her, then stopped. She might not care for that. 'How are you?' he asked instead, walking a little way aside with her.

She shrugged. 'They want to give me another cat, but I won't do it. I almost punched the captain of the arena when he asked me.'

Arram nodded. He'd feel the same if something happened to Preet and anyone offered him another bird the next day.

'But I mean to live,' Gueda said. Her eyes sparkled dangerously. 'You'll see. I'll have vengeance for Tacuma.'

'But . . . you killed the gladiators who killed him,' Arram said faintly. She looked deadly.

'Oh, aye, that, but there's those that scheduled us against them, and I mean to see if his feed was drugged. It's been done before,' she said in response to Arram's look of shock. 'When an animal's so good no one can beat 'im, no one bets against 'im. Gamblers don't like to lose money at the games, so they make their arrangements. If that's what happened, I'll sniff it out, you'll see. In the meantime . . .' She bumped her fist gently against Arram's cheekbone. 'Hekaja bless you for putting me back together – twice! I wish I could do better than thank you—'

'Your thanks is more than enough for me,' Arram said. He smiled at her. 'Gods go with you, Gueda.' He watched her as she trudged off.

Musenda turned away from Ramasu, who was already on the wagon's seat. They'd been talking quietly. Now the gladiator took Arram's hand. 'I told Master Ramasu it's fine with us if you return. Not once did you treat us like animals. That's rare. Take care of yourself, Arram.'

'If you will do the same, Sarge,' Arram replied.

The gladiator grinned. 'That's what I'm best at.' He followed Gueda back into the heart of the gladiators' compound.

'Arram,' Ramasu called.

Arram mounted the seat beside the master and nodded to the gate guards as they drove through. He turned to look back at the camp as the iron gates clanged shut. He shuddered. He had learned a great deal while he was there, it was true. In particular, he had found that he wasn't certain he could stay in a country where slavery was practised. He had always thought he would manage to avoid it somehow when he left the university, or that he would become used to it. Now he understood he could not avoid it. The university managed to live slave-free, but it was a lie. The shadow of slavery lay over it. The arena was only the very worst of this way of life. Lesser forms of brutality to men and women were everywhere. When people were bought and sold, it was just too easy for free people to treat them as things. He couldn't face that. Sooner or later he would have to leave his friends and his teachers. He could not stay here.

Lindhall greeted him with a warm hug. Preet announced her happiness over their return with a cheerful set of whistles as she fluttered all over Arram's stale room. The master opened the shutters to air the place out and went into the sitting room next door. He returned with wonderfully cold tea – Arram had struggled to learn the spell for a year without success – and a small bowl of cherries. 'With Hulak's compliments,' he said, placing the bowl on Arram's table.

As if by magic, the tortoise Sunstone appeared at Lindhall's side, making his begging groan.

'No, Sunstone. You know very well they aren't good for you,' Arram said with a smile. Little muscles all over his body were starting to relax. He hadn't even known how tense he had been until this moment. He glanced at Lindhall. 'How did Master Hulak know I was coming home?'

'Come – you know we masters talk all the time,' Lindhall replied, dusting Arram's table with his handkerchief. 'Ramasu kept us apprised on how you fared. We were concerned,' he said in answer to Arram's questioning look. 'We weren't certain that the camp was the proper place for you.'

Thinking of Kottrun's attack, Arram grimaced. 'It was . . . educational,' he replied.

'So we feared. Will you go again?' Lindhall asked. He sipped his tea.

'I learned a great deal of surgery quickly,' Arram told him slowly. 'I'd like to learn more, and make sure of what I've learned already. But perhaps I could do that in a city infirmary, and do the rest of my healing studies during plague seasons.' He looked away from Lindhall as his chin began to tremble. 'It's a horrible place.'

For a long moment the older man said nothing. Then he remarked, 'Certainly I will benefit from your knowledge, however acquired. The patients are smaller here, but perhaps their reason for coming to us is more . . . bearable. Speaking of patients, I have three meerkat pups left with me by a travelling show. The adults were stolen, but—'

Arram grinned. 'Meerkat pups?' He'd seen pictures and heard descriptions, but he'd never seen one in person. 'Where, the menagerie?'

Lindhall chuckled. 'No, these are *pups*. We've been fighting to keep them alive for three days. Are you sure you wouldn't rather rest?'

But Arram was already on his way through the sitting room to Lindhall's private nursery, stepping nimbly around Sunstone. Preet cheeped at Lindhall as if to say 'What can you do?' and perched on the older man's shoulder, ready to see these marvels for herself.

Arram went back to his room near suppertime with a small meerkat nestled in his shirtfront. He was trying to decide if it was worth the trouble of returning the youngster to the heated nursery before he went to the noisy dining hall, or simply looking for whatever Lindhall and the students had tucked away for snacks, when someone rapped on his door. He opened it, expecting to find a mastery student with Preet, who had gone wandering when the nursery proved too warm for her.

Instead he saw Varice, pretty in a pale blue cotton dress under her white robe. Her golden curls were pinned up, but some had tumbled forwards over her shoulders. He wanted to touch them more than he'd wanted anything in his life. He moved forwards to hug her – surely in a brotherly way – and remembered the meerkat in his shirt just in time. She was also holding a large basket with both hands.

She smiled at him. 'I asked Master Ramasu how you were, and he said flat with exhaustion. When I didn't see you at any other meal, I thought I'd bring you supper. There's plenty if Master Lindhall wants some.'

He took the basket. 'Oh, he's at some meeting at the masters' dining hall. Will you join me? We can eat in the study.' He led the way there, keeping his arms and the basket well away from his small charge. Once inside the study, he put the basket down with relief. It was *heavy*.

'Why are you walking so strangely?' she asked. 'Did someone hit you?'

Arram grinned at her. 'No. I'm being careful of my friend.' Unbuttoning his shirt, he showed her the meerkat pup. 'Master Lindhall has the other two,' he explained. 'He said he hopes they don't get lively during the meeting.'

'I've seen the adult ones in the menagerie,' she said, gently lifting the pup out.

'These were abandoned. Lindhall hopes the adults will accept them once we're certain they don't have any illnesses.' He watched her a little nervously as she set the pup on one of Lindhall's many cushions.

She stepped closer to him and said, 'I missed you so much. I can't *believe* how much.' Smiling, she stood on her tiptoes, twined her arms around his neck, pulled his head down, and planted her lips on his in a very no-nonsense way. She had kissed him on the mouth a few times before, just as a friendly salute. This was far more than friendly. Arram closed his eyes and sank into the kiss. Her lips were very soft. He held her comfortable body tightly, lifting her clean off the floor so their mouths were on the same level. She was running her hands over his shoulders and the side of his face. For once in his life he could barely think.

He was also barely breathing. Gently, regretfully, he drew back, setting her on the ground.

'Well!' she said, brushing her gown into order. There was a very pleased smile on her face. '*Finally!* I waited and waited for you to make the first move, like the gentleman is supposed to. If I'd realized you only needed *me* to do it, I would have proceeded *ages* ago!'

He smoothed her tumbled golden hair with trembling hands. 'Those were hints?' he asked plaintively. 'I thought those were . . . kisses like you'd give a brother.'

Varice laughed. 'You have very odd ideas about how I kiss my brothers, then!'

He wobbled. 'I'm sorry,' he said apologetically as they nearly tripped. 'I haven't eaten since – I think this morning, but it wasn't much.'

'That won't do. We'll get you fed and then—' She bumped him with her knee. 'We can discuss other things.'

Arram beamed down at her. 'I hope so.'

'I *know* so. I am tired of waiting for you to do something, Arram Draper,' Varice said as they turned towards the food.

He stopped. 'You remind me. I brought you something.' He hurried to his room for the favour he'd requested of Sarge. Ramasu had explained that the gladiators commonly burned their used-up gear, so foes in the arena or among the bettors could not steal it to use for spells to bring them down. Arram had persuaded Sarge and Ramasu to let him have a token, properly spelled to remove Sarge's essence, for Varice. He gave the silk-wrapped bundle to her. She gasped when she opened it. The glove was a nasty, dirty thing, worn out at the fingertips and the seams, but Sarge's name was inked on the back, and it had clearly been hard used.

Varice crumpled it in her hands. 'Is this — ?'

'One of his training gloves,' Arram told her.

She yelped and flung her arms around his neck for another kiss. Arram could have continued all night, if someone had not rapped on his door. Quickly they released each other and straightened their clothes before Arram gathered up the meerkat and went to see who had come to call.

It was Ozorne. Immediately he tried to embrace Arram, only to stop when he saw the meerkat pup. His face, already alight when he saw Arram, brightened even more. He reached a finger to the small creature. 'I heard Lindhall had pups,' he said softly. 'There are two more?'

'With Lindhall,' Arram said. 'This one was asleep until a moment ago.'

'Did Varice wake him? She wasn't at the dining hall—'

'I'm here,' Varice called from the study. 'I brought Arram supper.'

There was nothing else to do, and truly, Arram didn't begrudge his best friend for interrupting his time with Varice. 'Will you join us? Varice is staying – you know she brought enough for twelve.' He passed the meerkat into Ozorne's hands.

'Oh, oh, yes, of course,' Ozorne said absently, stroking the pup's head. He looked at the two guards behind him. 'I'll be dining here. You can wait.' He slid into Arram's room and closed the door. He lowered his voice. 'Listen, I wanted to say, about what happened . . .'

'There's nothing *to* say,' Arram said. 'We came out of it alive, that's the important thing. Sergeant Okot?' he thought to ask. He was surprised Ozorne's chief guard was letting him wander.

'Not back from Mother's yet,' Ozorne replied. 'I've been informed I'm in for it when he is, and I'm not to leave this building except for lessons.' He gripped Arram's arm with a many-ringed hand. He cradled the pup against his chest with the other. 'And there's *plenty* to say,' he said firmly, looking into Arram's eyes. 'We've been friends for a long time. I've always been glad of it, but . . . you saved my life in that tent. I panicked, Arram. I couldn't think of a single working—'

'You would have,' Arram assured his friend. 'When you'd caught your breath—'

'But I didn't,' Ozorne protested. 'You saw how the wind blew, and you did what had to be done before that madman gouged our eyes out. I will *never* forget that. I can't think of anyone who would do so much for me without wanting something – except you.' He frowned. 'Do you want something?'

'Supper,' Arram replied.

Ozorne laughed. 'I have never had friends like you and Varice. I don't know *anyone* who's ever had friends like you two!'

'And if you're lucky, you never will,' Varice called. 'Will you let him collapse of starvation, or will you come to the table?'

Arram had just settled the pup in a basket nest by his place when Varice asked, 'Why are you back so soon? You said your mother meant to keep you until late Saturday?'

'She did,' Ozorne replied, then grinned as they took their seats. 'But I'd had about enough of her chatter regarding the eligible girls I must try to meet this week, when she started over lunch. Lucky for her *and* me she'd invited Chioké to share the meal. Right away he started telling her how much trouble I was having in my classes with Cosmas and Dagani. How I was going to miss Cosmas's next examination and it will hurt my marks. Well, no *Tasikhe* will score badly in an examination! I tell you, my mother practically shoved me out the door!' Ozorne chuckled as he shook out his napkin. 'I wish I had Chioké's way with her.'

'You could try his technique,' Varice suggested, filling his cup with pomegranate juice.

Arram frowned. Gently, not wanting to upset his friends, he asked, 'Ozorne . . . you trust Chioké? *Truly* trust him?' He explained about the conversation between the mage and Kottrun.

Ozorne was silent for a moment before he said, 'It could have been that he was trying to rig fights. I know he does that.'

Arram was shocked. 'And you condone it?'

Ozorne chuckled. 'Arram, don't you know? It's good to have something on those who might try to gain power over you. Just in case. You gave me something to hold over Chioké, should he get artful with me.' He patted Arram on the cheek. 'I even have something on Mother.'

'And me?' Arram asked, trying to hide his outrage. 'Varice?'

Ozorne kissed his cheek. 'No. I believe in the two of you without reservation. A fellow never had better friends, Arram.'

'Ozorne!' Varice announced patiently. 'Arram! The food grows *cold*!'

'Your hearts are as true as gold,' Ozorne said, grinning as he slung an arm around Arram's shoulder. 'Let's eat.'

Arram sat cross-legged at the low table between his two best friends. Preet landed on his shoulder and squawked in his ear. Unseen, Varice rubbed one of her knees against his as she passed a dish of couscous. Ozorne was laughing as the meerkat tried to work free of his basket.

He listens to Varice and me, Arram told himself, offering Preet a piece of flatbread. I have years and years of studies before I'm a master. Something will work out so we can leave Carthak. Or perhaps Ozorne will convince the new emperor to put an end to slavery; then I can stay.

In the distance, he thought he could hear an old woman's cackling laughter. A Hag's laughter.

GLOSSARY

Apalite: citizen of the Carthaki district of Apal, formerly a nation-state to the far south and east of Carthak district (home of the capital), sister district/nation-state to Amar

beak head: hole in the point at the front of a ship used as a privy by sailors

belowstairs: palace slang for high-security cells under the oldest part of the palace, some particularly magicked to hold the strongest of mages

B.H.E. (Before Human Era): name given to the years before H.E., the Human Era. B.H.E. means the time when humans and immortals lived together, before increasing strife between them drove a group of mages to assemble in Carthak in order to create a working of magic that would exile the immortals to the Divine Realms (supposedly their original home). Common belief is that they succeeded in 852 H.E. and began in 836 B.H.E, though some are of the opinion that the spell covered only the Eastern Lands and the Southern Lands to the Roof of the World, the Yamani Islands, the Copper Isles, and perhaps the easternmost parts of the islands and countries west of there. It is even thought there are both very small and very large and powerful immortals tucked away in the lands supposed to be covered by the spell, which, in any case, has lasted a long time without renewal. It was destroyed when it was worked, and only partial copies remain

Black God (of Death): one of the Great Gods, those who reign over all the world under various names. The Black God is usually represented by a tall human shape in a black robe and cowl. He is seen as soft-spoken and kind, the reliever of pain and suffering. People come to his realms to rest, recover from, and forget their lives before they are reborn into new bodies. His priests and priestesses are robed in the same manner as he is. They prepare and bury or burn (depending on the family's choice) the dead and look after widows and orphans without family. They say prayers for the dead and look after graves. It is also their jobs to look after pigeons and doves, who supposedly carry the spirits of the dead to the Peaceful Realms, where the Black God reigns

broken seal: street slang for losing one's virginity, as in 'she broke her seal' or 'he broke his seal'; from breaking the seal on a document

cackleheads: slang for faeces-brained

canoodling: sexual experimentation or having sex

cantrip: academic word for a spell

commandeer: command, seize for use (usually military)

Common: Common Eastern, the language shared by Tortall, Tyra, Maren, Galla, and Sarain

Crone: aspect of the Great Goddess, goddess of the underworld, ageing women, wisdom, secrets, healing, the waning moon, and the natural fading of life

cross juggling: pattern in which the right hand throws the balls to the left hand and the left hand to the right hand, so they cross in the space between hands

detail: soldier's slang for duty or work

Divine Realms: home of the gods and the creatures known as immortals; also called the Realms of the Gods

Ergwae: people of Carthak's deep mountain valleys and western deserts, known for ornately woven and braided white turbans and embroidered scarves worn by men and women alike

Graveyard Hag: patron goddess of Carthak, a minor trickster and goddess of surprise changes in fate elsewhere in the Eastern Realms and Copper Isles; goddess of the crossroads and of gambling, represented by dice and a dicing cup, rats, and hyenas; also known as the Lady of the South (polite form of address), taken from the position of her statues in her temples and arenas

Great Mother Goddess: one of the Great Gods, those who reign over the world under various names. The Great Mother is usually represented by one of three aspects: the Maiden, goddess of girls and virgins, the hunt, the waxing moon, and spring; the Mother, goddess of women, childbirth, sex between women and men, summer, gardening, marriage, the full moon, and protection; and the Crone, goddess of the underworld, ageing women, wisdom, secrets, healing, the waning moon, and the natural fading of life; also called the Three-Fold Mother and the Gentle Mother (this last more popular in the past two hundred years than at present)

gumat: city street toughs, Carthak

Hag-curst: reference to the patron goddess of Carthak, the Graveyard Hag

Harvest: 1 August; the celebration before the hardest work of the harvest begins. The first fruits of the harvest are offered to the gods, and feasts are held

Hekaja: Carthaki goddess of healing

immortals: creatures exiled to the Divine Realms 795 N.E. (Northern Empire)/211 B.H.E. (before the Human Era), including winged horses of both kinds and all three sizes, merpeople, giants, ogres, centaurs of both types, Stormwings, unicorns of all three sizes, basilisks, Coldfangs, griffins, spidrens, tauroses, sunbirds, winged apes, and wyverns

insensate: without senses, unobservant

instructor: teachers in the Lower Academy who are juniors

and seniors in good standing in the Upper Academy and who
teach classes in exchange for wages, dormitory housing, and
library access

Jinda: person from the distant western realm of Jindazhen

kaygow: rude term among Hulak's people for a scavenger animal

Kyprish: adjective for the people of the Copper Isles; from the
name of their national god, Kyprioth

Lady of the South: alternative, more polite form of address
for the Graveyard Hag by those who don't want her attention;
taken from the traditional position of her statues in her temples
and in arenas

leatherfoot: soldier slang for a long-term soldier whose boots
and feet have reached the same level of hardness

Lower Academy: junior school for the Carthaki School for
Mages, usually for students ages ten to fifteen

lozenge: pill

Matasarab: Thak for festival of the spring equinox

mead: Northern-style honey wine

member: penis

Midwinter: holiday that occurs on and around the longest night
of the year; the morning after the longest night marks the
return of summer's sun. It is celebrated by a week of feasting
and gift-giving.

Minoss: god of justice, courts, and trials

Mithros: Great God of the sun, law, and war

Mortal Realms: part of the universe where those beings and
creatures who are born and will die exist

nit: copper Carthaki coin

Old Thak: original language for early Kingdom of Carthak; now
mage language taught throughout Eastern and Southern Lands
and Scanra

orris: another term for iris, a scent sacred to Hekaja and to
healers, as well as myrrh, myrtle, and poppy

pizzle: male animal's sexual organ

pounded, being: having sex

ragze: long-term homosexual partner in Carthak

ragzewi: homosexual in Carthak, any individual who is homosexual

Realms of the Gods: another term for the Divine Realms, the home of the gods and the creatures known as immortals

rue: hardy evergreen plant with a nasty odour and bitter, nauseating taste; for health and for clearing the mind and house

Saturday: day of the week set aside for religious observances

Shakith: blind goddess of seers

sigil: sign or figure

Sign (against evil): drawn on the chest as an X with a straight line through it; it is a star, a sign of protection against evil accidentally caused by oneself, as in thoughts that might be bad, or against harm that might come to one

soppish: soppy, sentimental, milksop, weak

spinster: woman who spins thread from fibre: wool, flax, or cotton; usually a young, unmarried woman of the lower or slave classes

stain(s): bum stain, scoundrel

stillroom: room in houses or small facilities in which herbs are dried and kept and medicines made and stored

sunbird: dull in colour; the size of a heron as adults; able to control their size in the Mortal Realms; in the Divine Realms they fly straight up during the day, spinning, wings outstretched, flashing brilliant colours in salute to Mithros

Sunday: Sun's day, best day of the week to start new ventures

sunwise: from right to left

Thak: contemporary common language of Carthaki Empire

thaka: gold Carthaki coin

thaki: silver Carthaki coin

Upper Academy: senior school for the Carthaki School for Mages, usually for students sixteen and up

walk out: form of dating; couples went walking

wandermage: mage who travels and does not answer to any one employer

ward: protect, particularly with magical spells

widdershins: counterclockwise, preferred direction for magic working

Winter's Crone: in the Eastern Lands, the ancient goddess who introduces the deepest cold of the season; she holds good fortune for those with the courage and stamina to seek it from her. She is a goddess of Northern magic: her chief temple is in the City of the Gods.

working: alternative term for spell-work

zoeg: Thak term for a homosexual relationship

ACKNOWLEDGEMENTS

First, I want to thank my home team, the people who help when I'm stuck, get my writing and make-up supplies (I'm just no good at judging make-up, or clothes, for that matter), gather to care for stray and feral cats, and ensure that I'm fed and that I don't duck my doctor appointments: my beloved spouse-creature (thirty-two years of marital something in 2017!), Timothy Liebe; my extraordinary assistant and fellow writer, Julie Holderman; and my writing partner and buddy, the djinn of middle-grade fiction, Bruce Coville. My gratitude to the new Tamora Pierce LLC staff for their work on the new webpage format, layout, and updates: Donna Burke, Jeremiah Tolbert, MJ Erickson, and Farrah Nakhaie. Thanks also to the Sunday Night Bollywood Team, writer Kathy Coville, Cynthia Bishop, and brother-in-law Craig, in addition to the Home Team.

As ever, I have the best professional support team a writer could ask for: Mallory Loehr and Chelsea Eberly at Random House Children's Books, with the powerful forces of the art department, the sales department, and the publicity department. For their meticulous work, my thanks to the copy editors. All of these people have introduced me to strange new magics. In concert with them are the excellent people at Harold Ober

Associates, my agent and friend of many years, Craig Tenney, and the president of Ober, my onetime boss, Phyllis Westberg – both of you have my love always.

I have my Manhattan buddies Raquel Starace and Denise Robert to thank for years of friendship, and my sisters Kimberly and Danielle: they are the real-life heroes who guard people's lives. To my stepmother, Mary Lou; my mother-in-law, Margaret; my brother-in-law Craig; and my nephew CJ, because family.

To my fans, who are passionate, funny, intelligent, creative, caring, and strong – you make me glad I took the path I did each and every day.

My nuclear family's deepest thanks, and the thanks of approximately fifteen to twenty stray or feral cats, go not only to the fine people who are named in the dedication, but to those listed here, and another number who will be listed on my website in the future. Thanks to them, those cats received housing, food, medical care, and in some cases new homes in 2014–2015: Cynthia Bishop; Isabelle Cseti-Wall; Nicola Drakeford; Wendy Elrick; Mary Evanov; Lacey Ewald; Christine Gregory; Marybeth Griffin; Ruth Heller; Rachel Ossmann; Beth Parker; Jesi Pershing; Amber Phillipps; Rhiannon Pretty; Danielle Putinja; Caroline Rivard; Brittany and Jared Rubio; Karrin Ryan; Siobhan Simpson; Karen, Liam, and Anastasia Smith & Becker; Dawn Thompson; and Adrienne Wiens. Those who took part in this fund-raiser that we did not reach in time for mention in this book we will include in the second book of this series. Again, our thanks!